**OFFICIALLY
DISCARDED**

the
snowman's
children

the
snowman's
children

glen hirshberg

CARROLL & GRAF PUBLISHERS

NEW YORK

THE SNOWMAN'S CHILDREN

Carroll & Graf Publishers
An Imprint of Avalon Publishing Group Inc.
161 William Street, 16th Floor
New York, NY 10038

ISBN: 0-7867-1082-9

Printed in the United States of America

Visit the author on the Web at glenhirshberg.com

For my parents and my brother
For Kim and Sid, with snow
And for M.S., J.R., K.M., and T.K.,
     whom I did not know and have never forgotten

the
snowman's
children

1994

In the dark, through the stinging sleet, the lightless buildings of downtown Detroit seem to tilt toward one another like sunken ships on the ocean floor. The streetlamp bulbs have all blown, so that everything wavers in the hissing shadows. Even the traffic lights float like buoys cut adrift to ride the Friday-night ghost current. I have the car window cracked open despite the cold. All I hear is the furtive slosh of tires and a faint industrial whistling. At first glance, this place looks exactly the way I left it seventeen years ago. Or maybe it's just the new snow, having its usual effect on me.

A long blue Buick coughs to life, pulling out from a row of apparently abandoned cars, its driver hunched forward in the cone of illumination from the dome light. She doesn't look my way as she slides past. On the corner, a decapitated lamppost sticks sideways in the cement, next to a tiny grocery with a hanging sign in Arabic, its electrified sliding door half open. I see figures moving up and down the aisles, carrying boxes. They could be looting or restocking or relocating or scavenging. Slowly, I turn for the Woodward Corridor.

The snow is already gray, and the smell of earthy air washes through the window. Disabled cars line the roadway, and I weave carefully between them as if I'm following an unseen lead vehicle out of the city toward Troy. I've got my own Trojan horse, too: a rented 1986 Olds with 78,000 miles on it and no defroster. I actually asked the guy at Rent-a-Wreck if he had any AMC Gremlins. Blue ones.

"Huh?" he said, and gave me a towel for the windshield.

I turn on the radio and find WJR, which is running the headlines: *Woman with Alzheimer's found locked in an East Detroit house with fourteen dogs; police currently searching for her son. . . . Execution-style shooting on Gratiot. . . . Wings win in San Jose. . . .*

Then it's out to another roving reporter who is holding his microphone into the night. *There*, he says. *Hear it?* And you really can hear it: the roads breaking apart like ice over a lake.

It's the thaw, says the reporter. *Yesterday's unexpected balmy weather, after two months of subzero temperatures, has affected the roads, and even though we're back to freezing tonight, the asphalt has already split, and cars are plunging into the potholes.*

Not until Nine Mile do the landmarks get familiar, and only a few even then. The Detroit Zoo water tower materializes dimly out of the dark over Ferndale. If I took a left, a right, drove five more blocks, I'd be at Spencer's house, where all three of us growled in our sleeping bags on the night the lions jumped over the zoo's retaining wall and escaped. That was early winter, 1976, before almost any of it.

I've driven past the corner where Mini-Mike's Slot Car Emporium used to be before I think to look up, but I already know it won't be there. In the only letter she ever sent us, maybe two years after we were gone—a greeting, five cryptic lines about finalizing her divorce and having trouble with her car heater in the frigid weather; nothing at all about her son except that he seemed "distant, still very angry and hurt, but okay, sometimes"—Spencer's mother enclosed an article about Mini Mike's heart attack and the Emporium's closing. Across the top, she had scrawled, "Just thought you'd want to see this." She also included a magazine photograph of Dr. Daughrety standing on a podium in front of a small crowd at Phil Hart Plaza downtown, accepting an Outstanding Motor City Citizen award. My mother showed the photograph to me, took it back, and murmured, "Son-of-a-bitch" over it as though praying or proclaiming a curse. Then she lit it on fire.

The girl at the Troy/Birmingham Moto-Court is pretty, ponytailed, not yet twenty. She's popping grocery-store sugar cookies into her mouth and listening to music that bubbles the pads of her headphones. She doesn't flinch when I sign at the register, after only a slight hesitation. My real name. Why should she flinch, and why should I care? She would have been maybe two years old then. And it's not as if I killed anybody.

Not quite.

1976

I t started during the week of my fifth Mind War. Jon Goblin had ruptured his appendix, almost died, and wound up in the hospital most of the winter, which is why I was the only boy at Theresa Daughrety's tenth birthday party.

All that snow, hip deep, as though the clouds had snagged themselves on the earth and unraveled. The ice crust on top of the drifts sliced into my calves as my feet sunk downward. I was staggering toward Theresa's, head down to protect my eyes from the wind, passing the birch trees the neighborhood kids had picked barkless.

From the bus stop at the end of our block, I could see her porthole window through the maples. Shapes moved behind the glass, not faces or even bodies, just shapes; and in the silence, in the snow, I felt like a fish swimming up to nuzzle the hull of a ship. A remora, perhaps (I'd read about them, over and over, in my *Strange True Fish Tales* book), mistaking this house for a whale.

Theresa opened the front door. Behind her, the first of her father's masks, black and horned, scowled from the wall. Healing masks, Dr. Daughrety called them. He'd accepted—often requested—them, he told us, as tokens of appreciation when he'd served as a self-described "idealistic young physician" on various Native American reservations and while traveling in Peru and Kenya. The masks were meant to scare the bacteria out of you. They hung all over the walls at peculiar angles because, according to Dr. Daughrety, "Sickness slinks and slouches. There's not a virus in the world that'll come at you upright."

Once you knew what they were, they should have been comforting. But every time I entered that house, I felt helpless, paralyzed. All those carved faces with no eyes and misshapen mouths made me freeze, then tremble. Not, I think, because of the masks themselves, but because of the terrifying things their existence suggested were loose in the air, things that could sneak inside you.

Jerking my attention from the walls, I looked at Theresa. She was wearing white—white *what* I don't recall—with a black ribbon through her short blond hair. I can't tell you much about her face. Even then, before any of it—except the death of her mother, years earlier—her eyes seemed to lurk under their lids and then flash at you, way too far into you. I didn't do much looking at people's faces back then, but I knew that Theresa's eyes, when they flashed at you, were brown and eerily opaque, the color of rain on the ground. She had a little extra cheek on both sides, and her mouth was always arched and poised like a bow.

Around the room, ten other girls, mostly from our class at school, sat clumped in their usual groups on the white leather couches or the shag carpet that rose to meet them like a luxuriant lawn. It was the first time I'd been there without Jon Goblin. They were family friends, the Goblins and Daughretys, and celebrated holidays together. The dawning awareness that he wasn't coming thrilled through me, freed me for a while from the glare of the masks.

"Happy Birthday," I found myself saying to Theresa, and smiled. Quite possibly, that was the first thing I'd said to her in a month. The year before, by unspoken agreement among all the members of our class, we'd begun to rearrange our desks by gender so we could nurse our newly awakened awkwardnesses from a comforting distance.

I might have gone on and said something else, because I felt almost sure, for once, that she was happy to see me, but as I held up the birthday present I'd brought her, Dr. Daughrety stepped smoothly between us.

"Mattie. Welcome. Way too long since we've seen you. Look, Thrr-girl, a gift from the arch-rival." He took my present, shook it, and slipped it into the pocket of his cardigan. When his hand reappeared, it had a popcorn ball in it. "Pre–Mind War eats?" he said, and tousled my hair and walked away.

I remembered his face so fiercely that I sat down and drew it one night in high school, several years later and thousands of miles away. The drawing got me into Parsons.

He was bald, and his skull shone like the hood of a car. He had the least liquid eyes I'd ever seen, metallic gray, and they looked screwed into their sockets. Nothing he tried—not what he called his "friendly guy" mustache, not his Mr. Rogers sweaters, not his relentless smil-ing—did anything to soften him.

"It's a decal," I told Theresa. My voice shrank into my turtleneck, away from Dr. Daughrety's masks.

"For the People Eater?" she asked quietly, glancing over her shoul-der but grinning.

"It says, FEAR in little rub-off letters. I designed it myself. It'll fit on the bumper or the grille."

Theresa's father had given her the People Eater, a custom slot car, for Christmas, which was a surprise, since he hadn't yet allowed her to come racing with Joe Whitney, Jon Goblin, and me. She'd named it for the Minnesota Vikings' front line and the pickle sandwich at Avri's Deli on Long Lake. It was faster than any of the cars the rest of us rented at Mini-Mike's Slot Car Emporium. But Theresa couldn't drive it very well.

"I made the popcorn balls," she said.

I tried mine. It cracked open like a frozen apple. Red watermelon-flavored juice trickled into my mouth.

"If you spit these, they'll stick," I announced.

Before she could dare me—the way she used to do in second grade when we sat together at the Brain Table—Dr. Daughrety materialized again in the dining room doorway.

"Will the co-favorites take their marks, please?" His smile made me shudder.

Over his shoulder, against the plate-glass window that ran the length of the living room, I could see the table that had been prepped for the Mind War: twelve chairs, five on each side for the birthday guests and one at either end for Theresa and me, so we could stare each other down. Pads of scratch paper had been placed before each chair, as well as a calculator, pocket dictionary, and two Ticonderoga pencils, the kind with the tips that splintered if you pushed too hard. The Honor Feather rested atop my pad of paper because I'd won last year, for the first time since I was six.

"Watch out for him," my mother had warned me at breakfast. She meant Theresa's father. "He'll do anything if it means helping her win. I don't trust him. I never have."

Still in their clumps, the rest of Theresa's guests slipped off the couches and drifted toward the table like debris being washed into a gutter. A few of them glanced at Theresa or me. Only a couple of them smiled. They looked the way I almost always felt: vaguely intimidated by something I couldn't quite name.

At age ten, Theresa already had a game face: bow mouth drawn taut, eyes narrowed. Jon Goblin's mother called it the Thousand-Yard Squint. Even her hair seemed curled into a fist. Theresa wore that face in the super-advanced math program we got excused from our fifth-grade class to go to every morning at ten-thirty. She wore it the whole week of the Young Poets of America Contest. She even wore it in art class during clay-project month, when she had no chance of beating me.

"Mattie-man?" Dr. Daughrety said. "Thrr-girl? Ready?"

The Squint had settled over her but hadn't hardened yet when I opened my mouth and said, "Tell him no. I dare you."

I don't know why I said that. I liked the Mind War. But I liked the thought of sabotaging it, with Theresa's help, even better. Of course, Dr. Daughrety could have dismissed my little coup attempt with a wave of his hand. But he didn't. He just folded his arms over his chest, leaned against the wall next to one of his masks, and waited, watching his daughter.

For a moment, something bloomed beneath the surface of the Squint, naked and colorless. I told my mother about it later. She shivered and shook her head.

"Don't worry, Mattie," Theresa finally said, her smile even chillier than her father's. "Runner-up gets all the popcorn balls he can eat."

Her father patted her arm, and I shrugged and nodded. At the time, I still considered myself a legitimate threat to what I'd once heard the Doctor call the "Daughrety Superiority." I knew I wasn't her equal anymore, but a threat, surely.

I took my spot at the table with the others, brushed the Honor Feather forward, and one of the girls next to me poked at it with her pencil, then looked across the table at a friend and snickered. If she'd looked at me, I might have snickered too. I liked the game but not the Feather, which was pink and puffy and meant mostly that I was a target for humiliation. But no one was looking at me except the Doctor and his daughter.

And the teeth mask.

Now I could be wrong about this. I don't think I am, but I could be. Back in second grade, when Theresa and I played together in each other's backyards almost every afternoon, I slipped on some leaves and fell on a rake in the Daughretys' neighbor's yard, and I ended up lying inside the Daughrety house with my eyes squeezed shut for almost an hour while the doctor tended to the gash on my forehead. As I remember, he sent Theresa out of the room so she wouldn't have to watch. Then he stroked my hair and said occasional reassuring things. The blood kept welling out of the rent in my skin and into my eyebrows before he wiped it away.

"Letting things cleanse," he said.

I didn't scream. I don't think I said a single word until I opened my eyes.

The teeth mask was white except for the teeth, which were black and long and looked less like teeth than needles jammed into the red-lined gums in the lipless mouth. There were no eyes in the white sockets, so the thing seemed to be gazing inward, rolling every piece of itself as far away from pain as it was possible to get and still, for a few more seconds, be alive. For the next three years, every time I turned out the light, I saw the teeth mask flash in the last split second of not-dark.

It is possible that the Doctor treated me on his dining room table or on the rug underneath it, and I'm just remembering wrong. But I think we were on his living room couch. And I think the mask was hanging over it. And I think he moved it, on Theresa's tenth birthday, to the one place where he knew I would see it. Despite what my mother may have thought and sometimes said, Dr. Daughrety would never, ever, have given Theresa hints about upcoming Mind War questions. He would have considered that insulting to his daughter. But he wasn't above employing the home-field advantage.

"Boy and girls," the Doctor said. "Ready?"

I just stared at the mask while the snow ticked against the window-pane and everyone else picked up their pencils to try at least. I wanted to look away; I kept telling myself to do so. But I couldn't shake my eyes free. Those empty sockets drew my gaze like black holes sucking in light. Distantly, I heard the Doctor take a long breath and begin.

"One-twelfth times negative 1/18th."

"Negative 1/216th," Theresa said, before anyone's pencil had touched paper. She hadn't even reached for her own.

The Doctor made a scratch on the score sheet and continued. The whole point of the speed round was to obliterate the non-competitive. I was still stunned to paralysis by that fanged and leering face, unprepared.

"Reporters for the *Washington Post* who—"

"Bernstein. Woodward," said Theresa.

Another scratch.

"Inaugurate. Define it. Spell it."

This was particularly cruel because nine months later, in the midst of the election, everyone in the room could have answered it. Now, everyone would remember that Theresa Daughrety knew it—and knew how to spell it—first.

By the time I shook out of my stupor and beat Theresa to a Michigan geography question about Mackinac Island, it was already too late. I snatched up my pencil and ignored the calculator—if you had to use it you were already doomed—and began burying the rest of my classmates as we raced into the word-problem round. I didn't get anywhere near catching up to Theresa. But I did look at her once, not far from the finish, and without thinking about it I grinned. She immediately grinned back. Then the next question flew, and we hurtled after it.

Later, in the last of the twilight, Dr. Daughrety took us all skating on Cider Lake. Theresa glided far ahead while I lagged behind. I was happy to be out of the gaggle of girls and stumbling along on my own until I fell and found myself face down on the ice with my eyes jammed shut. No matter what, I did not want to look into the lake. When I opened my eyes, I saw ice, gray and opaque as steel.

My father once told me this was a man-made lake, which I took to mean that swimmers somehow had left parts of themselves behind in it. After that, being in the water didn't scare me as much as being over it, on skates, did. I didn't want anything reaching through the surface to grab me. Even more than that, I didn't want to see anything under there that could. Shoving down with my mittens, I scrambled to my feet and slipped once more after the vanishing partygoers.

The Snowman had come, although no one was calling him that yet. No one had named a task force after him or held special assemblies about him at school. No psychologists had developed profiles. And no one had offered any speculation about what he was doing with his victims during the days, sometimes weeks, between the moments he took them and the moments he left them, lifeless but unmarked, in tidy bundles in the snow.

1994

Back in Louisville, Laura will be waiting, in the paint-spattered overall shorts she slips into every night after dinner. She'll have her banjo across her knees in bed — she only practices her banjo in bed — and a Rolling Rock on the nightstand, her dark hair pinned back under a black-and-red bandanna. I know she's expecting me to call. My own fault, really. I've become unexpectedly good at the mechanics of marriage: surprise dinners, hugs from behind while we're doing the dishes, bringing my wife another Rolling Rock before I go downstairs to draw.

My parents in Lexington will be waiting too, and they will not be pretending otherwise. My mother, especially, didn't want me to come back here. She told me I was being *that way* again. By *that way* she means fixated and daydreaming, under what she terms "the misapprehension that Detroit has any relevance whatsoever" to the mess she worries that I'm making of my life.

I dial my own number and wait. Three rings. Four. I'm almost hoping Laura's not home yet, that the bluegrass band she plays with at the Secretariat Club six nights a week had a hot show, and she's churning through an encore right now, stage-flirting through the smoke with that lingering laugh that comes from somewhere I can't reach, and later, she'll punch the answering machine and find my voice and know I called her right away. Because I did. I am calling right away.

Our answering machine has neither of our voices, just Laura playing her banjo, followed by a beep.

"It's me," I say, and before I can say *I miss you, I'm sorry, I'm cold, the roads have split open and the earth underneath is frozen and black,* Laura's voice fills the line.

"You forgot to pay the phone bill."

"I'm sorry."

"You're always sorry, Mattie."

The ensuing silence is long, familiar. I can hear her breathing. I can see her overall straps rise and fall, feel the snaps come open in my hands. I can smell her beer and banjo-resin smell.

A thousand miles away, in her bed in her room in her life, Laura starts to hum. "Blue Moon of Kentucky." She's humming the high harmony part, the one she sings onstage. It sounds eerie up there all by itself, like bat sonar closing in. I start to ask how her show was and stop. I start to explain again why I had to come here, why this weekend by myself in this place was the only thing I wanted for my birthday. But the explanations lack clarity, even to me, and none of them fill even a corner of the empty space we've cultivated between us for almost seven years.

"I've never told you the story behind the WANTED drawings, have I?" I say abruptly, and the humming doesn't stop but she's there, listening. Or she's gone and it's too late. Either way I have to tell her this. "Laura?"

Laura just hums, the verse about the guy who left, without any extra intended meaning. It's the nature of bluegrass; there's not a song in her repertoire that wouldn't dig at me tonight.

I close my eyes and watch as all those disembodied hands slip effortlessly from the places where I've buried them and crawl across the last two decades to claim me.

1985

By junior year, I had firmly established myself at the bottom of my class at Parsons School of Design, an illustrator at best with a whimsical streak and no genius whatsoever. In October, at the suggestion of a disinterested prof, I'd designed my first planned community: seven ordinary subdivision homes with swimming pools and high back fences, except that these back fences all had secret openings triggered by springboards that flew up or slid sideways on rollers or leapt out of line into the bushes. Owners were encouraged to decorate and disguise their entrances to suit their own tastes. The idea, I wrote when I presented the thing, was to reconstruct the community by unblocking its arteries, so that kids—the lifeblood of any subdivision—could flow freely through it.

I got my first **B** on that project. The grade was a gift, really, because the whole thing was pretty banal; even the fences were naive. But I think members of the distinguished faculty were relieved. They'd finally found a pursuit for me that they could, in good academic conscience, recommend, and they probably thought my movement in such a utilitarian—as opposed to fervently artistic—direction would weaken my friendship with Scuzzie Li.

Once, and once only, I went home with Scuzzie to his mother's place in Martinsville, New Jersey. The house had huge glass bird feeders suspended from each corner of the sloping, slatted roof, so the eaves were perpetually haunted with sparrows. Scuzzie's parents—his father was a geographer, his mother a painter—had come to this country from China in the early seventies as part of a cultural exchange program at Rutgers. Only his mother had stayed, keeping young Scuzzie with her. I have no idea whether she defected or emigrated, and when I asked, Scuzzie seemed confused about the difference. I also have no idea where her money came from, but she apparently had plenty of it. She wore paint frocks and black skirts and black tights and wouldn't look at me at all. She talked incessantly to Scuzzie, following him through rooms and up and down flights of stairs, chattering in Chinese. He rarely answered; instead, he conducted conversations in English with me right over her shoulder. But he'd look at her sometimes, in the middle of whatever we were doing, and she would stop talking for a moment or two. Sometimes, Scuzzie would laugh, but she never did.

Despite the way he dressed at school—seventies-vintage black leather jackets with big buttons and belts that hung off the back, spandex pants, dress shoes with enormous heels that tilted him forward so he always looked as if he were being forklifted—Scuzzie's nickname had nothing to do with his appearance. It had grown out of a verbal tic. Instead of saying because, he said bescuz in response to practically anything anyone ever asked him. Whether it was a childhood habit or a deliberate choice, I never knew. But I always thought it suited what he and I both recognized as his peculiarly art-school sort of brilliance.

Late at night, careening on coffee and ecstasy and spasms of brain energy, he'd erupt out of bed with a canvas under his arm, hurtle past the hall denizens stretched across the floor with their clove cigarettes dangling from their lips and blank sketch pads propped open on their laps, dart through the people clumped on couches in the TV lounge, and disappear into the laundry room and lock the door.

Hours later, he would emerge with pieces of abstract art that positively vibrated color: veins of obscene orange snaking through reds and tans that gave out two-thirds of the way across the canvas. My favorite, called "Crush," was a sort of collapsing iceberg of sea-greens swooning into blue, plunging toward black, and finally collapsing off the bottom of the frame. It used to hang over my bed in Louisville, but Laura couldn't sleep with all that color crashing down on her. Now it hangs in our hallway, safely shrouded in perpetual shadow.

Scuzzie and I became friends on the first day of school, freshman year. I gave him the top bunk so he wouldn't bang his head when he lunged awake in the middle of the night with his brushes in his fist. We stayed friends, I think, because Scuzzie's knowledge of his own inevitable failure as an artist pained him—physically—to the point of paralysis, whereas the ongoing confirmation of my more evident lack of vision came as a profound relief and was very possibly the reason I chose to pursue art in the first place. I'd managed to get as far from Mind Wars and Brain Tables as I could.

So we went on rooming together, eating together, and failing together, in our separate ways. Scuzzie painted, took drugs, accumulated accolades from the faculty. I curled up comfortably in his wake and stayed unnoticed. And whenever Scuzzie wasn't painting, we went to the track.

That winter, Manhattan stayed weirdly warm all through January while the rest of the country wrestled with snow. In the TV lounge, my fellow weather-channel junkies and I would watch the Accu-map in hypnotized fascination. State lines blurred and faded. Mountains sank to their shoulders in the relief landscape. It seemed as though every city but Manhattan had been erased.

I was the only one still in the lounge on the morning that Scuzzie emerged from the laundry room with his hands clenched into claws and his hair dyed the color of a bruise. He looked as if he'd been dipped into one of his paintings.

"Matt-tee," he said, with more pronounced oriental shading than usual. "Aqueduct."

Bleary-eyed, I squinted at his hair, then back at the TV. "Can't," I told him, and gestured at the Accu-map. "The snow ate it."

"You bet with me today," he said, limping down the hallway, first on one leg, then the other, heels tipping him all too soon into the future.

Outside Manhattan, the subway emptied quickly. Our only companions were college students bundled into city-stained ski jackets and scarves, an old guy in a fedora singing Eastern European folk songs, and one black mother whose kids whirled to the window every time the train rose aboveground. The snow lifted off the abandoned buildings and rubble-strewn lots and settled down again like furniture coverings in a deserted house. I watched the kids and shivered backward almost ten years into the drainage ditch at the bottom of our yard, where I had lain in the drifts, head-to-head-to-head with Spencer Franklin and Theresa Daughrety, playing dead-things-rising-from-the-grave. They'd found several of the Snowman's victims face down in ditches, their bodies warm enough that the paramedics had tried to revive them.

By the time we reached Aqueduct, I was already remembering the hands. I started to tell Scuzzie about them as we exited the train, which flew from the station in a sucking sort of rush, like air expiring into space.

"In Detroit," I said to Scuzzie's back, feeling a disconcerting pressure in my stomach, "when I walked home from school. . . ."

Suddenly, he stopped and leaned against the side of the stairway with his hands on his knees.

"Scuzzie, are you all right?" I asked.

"I reek." He was talking about his art, I knew, and by then had almost used up the venom he could inject into that word.

"I reek worse."

"Today you bet with me."

It was the second time he'd said it. He needed to win—or maybe lose—with someone today. Anyway, he was leaving me no choice. If I didn't bet with him, he wouldn't translate any of the conversations around us.

"Will they come today?" I asked him.

He shrugged, winced, and started up the stairs again. We paid our five bucks and passed through the turnstile into the clubhouse, which shared its smell of electrified urine with every other public building connected to the subway. I followed behind, shaking my tingling hands, looking for Chinese women.

To this day, I don't know if they go to Aqueduct all the time or only on specified dates. All I know is that every time he took me to the track that winter, we'd emerge from the stairwell into a bustle of black-haired Asian women clutching racing forms and munching chestnuts, all of them eyeing and chiding and seemingly threatening one another in Mandarin that trilled up the clubhouse walls like birdsong.

There were fewer of them this day, maybe ten out of the twenty-five or so people bent over newspapers and beer while waiting for the betting cages to open. One of the ten, in an open trench coat and house frock, nodded at Scuzzie.

"Oh, my God," I said. "Scuzzie, look outside."

"What?" he said, then turned toward the window and stared, the way he did when he circled the Rothkos at MOMA. "Wow."

You couldn't see the track or the starter's gate or the tower. A miasma—not snow, not fog, but gray-white vapor—had swamped the grounds. Occasionally, shapes or streaks of color would surface: a horse's haunch, a purple shirt, an unidentifiable bubble of blue. It was like looking through the moon at the rest of the earth. Quietly, relentlessly, disembodied hands climbed toward consciousness. I was seeing windows, my neighbors' houses in suburban Detroit, Theresa Daughrety sitting up out of the snow and making a mummy-moan.

"Hands," I said, and Scuzzie finally looked at me. I kept my eyes on the whiteness that was burying the world. "Kids had disappeared. A lot of kids. They gave these tests to parents, and if you passed you got a hand to paste in your window. At assemblies in school, they told us if anyone came near us on our way home, we should run to the nearest house with a hand in the window."

He was looking at me more intently than I'd ever seen him look at me before. "And?"

"We called him the Snowman," I murmured, knowing I wasn't making any sense. I could feel the sting of his name on my tongue.

"Let's bet," Scuzzie said. He sounded angry, almost, though I had no idea why and couldn't quite focus on him anyway. "You bet with me. Then we go home."

I stood still, seeing hands suspended in glass like palm prints from ghost kids.

Ninety minutes later, Scuzzie dragged me to the betting cage to cash in our exacta. I let him handle the transaction while I stood next to him, still drifting. He handed me eleven dollars. I watched the woman in the house frock behind us as she held out her racing form. All over the margins, and not just in the margins, Chinese characters scuttled on their little legs, carrying off bits of newsprint like raiding ants.

"You friend demon?" the woman said, when Scuzzie turned around.

The question scared me. I couldn't imagine what she meant. I didn't think she was referring to Scuzzie, or even to me, although I'd been staring at her.

"I'll get you home," Scuzzie said. He had seen what was happening to me as soon as it had started on the stairs leading to the clubhouse. And he'd seemed to understand it before I did.

On the subway, I tried to talk to him about our bets, his newest painting, anything that might have provided a distraction, but he just closed his eyes, folded his hands over his leather jacket, and ignored me. I finally gave in, sat back shuddering as the train wheels screeched over the rails, and stared into the snow that clung to the windows like gauze.

He left me alone in our room. Three hours later, I had finished all three drawings.

They were white sheets of plain typing paper, blank as the snow in the Aqueduct window. Across the top I had spattered word-shaped blotches of ink. At the bottom I wrote dates. Not current dates, not the Snowman's dates. I don't know where these dates came from: 10/12/57, 7/23/68, 12/31/91. On the first piece of paper, in the gaping white space between the splotches and the dates, I drew eyebrows above half an almond eye; on the second, a neck with a tie knotted around it but no body beneath; on the third, off-center and floating, I drew a little kid's hand, or more accurately, the outline of one. I stole a piece of Scuzzie's canvas and stapled the drawings to it, one beside the other, and across the top, in the blackest paint I could find, I painted the word WANTED.

Six weeks later, when they gave me the Spring Prize, Scuzzie moved out. He said he wanted to give me more room. He stopped eating with me too, though he continued to come by at least once a week and drag me out to the track to watch horses and listen to the chatter of Chinese women.

Once, when he'd drugged himself so deep into a stupor that not even light and color could rouse him, he showed me the letter he wrote nominating the WANTED drawings for the prize. He said they tore words loose from language. He said they burned body parts into fossils.

He said they were terrifying.

1976

aybe it started at Theresa Daughrety's birthday party, on the day I told her to say no to the Mind War, or later that spring when I began raising my hand for both hot lunch and from-home lunch at school, effectively sabotaging the meal count for the cafeteria. Certainly by Red-Gray Day, June 11, 1976, my semiconscious transformation into a less dependable sort of kid had begun in earnest, three months before I ever met Spencer Franklin.

Until then, I hadn't done anything too thrilling. I put strips of construction paper in Garrett Serpien's Koogle and banana sandwiches, but everyone put strips of construction paper in Garrett's sandwiches. I rubber-cemented Jamie Kerflack's math workbook shut, but he didn't even notice for over a month. When he did, he just snickered and punched his nearest crony in the arm.

It was Theresa Daughrety who got removed from the Brain Table for two weeks for talking, not me. She'd been talking to herself, mostly, but talking nonetheless. I still outscored her a good third of the time on tests and quizzes. Once, during the end-of-the-year tournament, I upset Jamie Kerflack in Four Square, and even Mr. Lang, who called me Mathilda because I couldn't do a pull-up, clapped me on the back. On my final report card, sent home the week before Red-Gray Day, Mrs. Van-Ellis said I'd had *a major growth year*, and I could *do anything*. She said one more thing too, which my mother read to my father and my brother Brent at the dinner table that night. She said I'd *started feeling safe at last*.

That comment served as documented proof of what I'd already begun to suspect: that smallness, and feeling alone, isn't necessarily something you grow out of, just something you learn to disguise.

On Red-Gray Day, I told my parents I needed the wheelbarrow for one of the races at school. Neither of them even looked up from their breakfast. In the garage, I packed the wheelbarrow with handcuffs from my little brother's cop set, the white painting smock my parents had given me with the easel for my birthday, and the posterboard signs I'd spent most of the night before preparing, and wheeled it into the Michigan summer.

The light that day was cement-colored, the heat and humidity so heavy that even the cicadas had stuttered to a stop. The only sound was the whirring of air-conditioner units. Cats crouched in the shadows of cars, slinking from space to space on the asphalt in an effort to escape their own body heat. As I wheeled over the drainage ditch at the end of my driveway, the first mosquito of the morning plunged into my arm. I grabbed the skin around it and squeezed until the mosquito ballooned and burst like a tiny soap bubble.

I don't remember mulling over my plan—the whole thing was pretty well concocted by then—but I must have been concentrating on it, because I walked right past Barbara Fox, who was standing on her lawn. When I realized she was there, I whirled around. She was smiling, arms open. I ran for them.

"Mattie, watch my—" she said, but I dove into her, and she crumpled into her astonishing tan like a paper bag. "It's all right," she sighed, sitting down hard, flinching. "It's all right, honey." She was holding her left knee. Her black hair, longer than I'd ever seen it, fanned over her face.

"Get down here," she said.

I knelt and she hugged me, and I felt her khaki shirt rustling.

"Feel this," she said, and put my hand on her kneecap. It rolled beneath my fingers like an air-hockey puck. "Dislocated."

"How?"

"Fell off a ladder—that was leaning against a hut."

I couldn't believe she was back. Eighteen months was such an incredibly long time to me. I'd half believed I'd never see her again.

She looked at me so long it felt like touching, and I fell back a little, afraid. Her face reflected light-and-leaf patterns like shade from some phantom jungle tree.

"You really do remember me, don't you?" she said.

"Don't be a dork," I said casually, as if I hadn't invented a substitute for sheep-counting that centered on her for all the nights I couldn't sleep. I would lie in my bed and imagine twenty-two-year-old Barbara Fox and me cradled inside a giant cocoon, hidden together forever.

She'd been in West Africa, Mali mostly, teaching and town-building with the Peace Corps, though my mother told my father it was all just an excuse to get far away from her parents.

She leaned back on her elbows in the grass and stretched her legs over mine. For several minutes, I sat there watching the knob of her ankle. Then I put my index finger on her kneecap again and felt the blood beating beneath it. I was going to be late for Red-Gray Day and my grand plan. I couldn't have cared less.

"You wouldn't believe the grass in Africa," she said, instead of Mattie-move-your-hand.

Closing my eyes, I concentrated all my energy in my fingertip, until it seemed as if I could feel the grass brushing against her.

"After the rains, Mattie. God, you wouldn't believe the rains. Get your finger off me, you little lech."

Blushing, I jerked back my hand.

"When are your parents going out next?"

Something began to fizz in my head until I realized she meant baby-sitting, and then I blushed again and shook my head.

"I don't need a baby-sitter anymore. I haven't for years."

"Not even me?"

"We just wanted to give you something to do on Saturday nights."

Barbara jabbed her fingers into the ticklish spot between my ribs and I collapsed onto the lawn. I tried rolling away, but she'd clamped her good leg over my chest and I couldn't get up or even breathe. She was about to let me go, I think, when I felt her stiffen, then push herself to a standing position, favoring her trick knee.

At the screen door, her father had appeared in his undershirt. He looked even hairier, now that his hair had gone all the way white all over his body. It puffed out of his shirt and hooded his red-rimmed eyes. He looked like a chicken.

"Well," he said, and I remembered when he came back from Vietnam. He'd been a reporter, not a soldier. Even so, my father sat me down and told me he didn't like me going over there. "Frankly, son," he'd said, "Phil Fox makes us nervous. He's not the same man. He needs real help." Mrs. Fox had still lived there then, and Barbara spent a number of her college weekends at home with them and baby-sitting me.

"Morning, Mr. Fox," I said, and stood up.

"Go to school, Mattie," Barbara said, her eyes locked on her father, and she moved toward the house without a wave or a backward glance.

I lifted the wheelbarrow and trundled off past the trees in the suffocating sunlight. The thought that if I wanted, I could stop at the Fox place on the way home, knock on the door, and find Barbara there made me smile.

As soon as I turned onto Cider Lake Road, I saw Theresa a half block ahead. I pushed the wheelbarrow off the sidewalk onto the gravel shoulder so the pebbles clamored around it. Finally, I made enough racket that she stopped and turned around. Her flower-print skirt swirled around her ankles. She stood and waited, lips moving. Such an incredibly strange girl.

"Hey," I said. "You're here."

"No kidding," said Theresa, as she fell in beside me. She didn't ask about the wheelbarrow. She looked at it, though.

"You're actually coming."

"He actually let me."

This was new information. I'd always thought Theresa chose to get sick on Red-Gray Day because she couldn't win anything.

"Sec that?" said Theresa, pointing at the living room window of the gray house in front of us. In the lower right-hand corner was a little hand, outlined in red tape.

"What is it?"

"If we're attacked, we're supposed to run for the nearest hand."

"Attacked by what?"

She didn't answer for a while. She walked, and I walked beside her, until she said, "Anything."

"Rabies?" I said, and she grinned.

"Radioactive ooze."

"Jamie Kerflack."

"Bessie Romano," she said, and both of us tooted mock clarinets in the air. A few months before, Bessie had decided she didn't like being fifth-chair clarinet in the band. So, one by one, she picked up all four chairs ahead of her, and all four people in them, and flipped them over the flutes into the percussion section.

"Do you think you have friends at school?" I asked.

She just walked, with her eyes forward. The path to school curled through the trees—like a skip rope, with all the tree trunks beside it poised for the leap—but when we reached it, Theresa went the other way, around the bend in the road that led to the lake.

Without a word, I followed. If we'd been luckier, no one would have seen us. We'd have spent the morning in the mud beside the storm-stripped pier, committing a double hooky so unlikely that even Dr. Daughrety probably would have laughed. Sometimes, I really think, if no one had seen us, we would have waded all day in that man-made lake, and by the time we got home it would have been plain old summer, which would have given way to an ordinary fall, and none of the rest of it would have happened.

I left the wheelbarrow and my shoes at the top of the knoll, and we stumbled together down the grassy berm through clouds of dragonflies that rose up ticking. Theresa shed her sandals at the water's edge and hiked up her skirt. Her skin looked sketch-paper white, as if she'd never been outside before. She stepped without cringing into the aluminum-colored lake, which closed around her ankles and locked her in place.

"My grandmother's here," she said, as I eased into the muck beside her, and for one horrible second I thought she meant in the water. I wasn't afraid of Cider Lake, not the way I was in winter when I looked into the ice. But I never liked the feel of the bottom, how it sucked at you.

Theresa had her hand on the pier, which seemed to have less metal left in it than the lake, a skeleton pier picked clean by raindrops. Across the water, the houses of two GM executives shimmered in the heat, swaying in it as though dancing cheek-to-cheek.

"Your grandmother?" I said.

"My mom's mom."

That was it: the only time, in all the years I knew her, that Theresa mentioned her mother.

Her mother died when we were in second grade. I didn't find out that she died in her car in the garage with the doors closed and the engine turned on until my mother told me fifteen years later, when she also told me that Theresa was the one who found her.

At that moment, in the lake, I wanted to ask Theresa about her mother. I could barely remember her. I don't know why I was so curious. But the morning had magic in it already, courtesy of Barbara, and Theresa's legs in the water, and the dragonflies all around.

Instead, I asked, "Is your grandmother why your dad let you come to Red-Gray Day?"

As usual, Theresa didn't answer right away. Then she said, "Last night, my grandmother said getting old is like becoming a lake."

"A lake," I said, and shuddered, thinking of my own icebound nightmares.

"Yeah. Everyone starts looking at you and not seeing you, and when you get all the way still and flat and just reflect, like a mirror, you're dead." She was holding her foot up in front of her, watching the bottom silt slide down her toes. I watched too, thinking abruptly about Barbara Fox's leg. I was having an interesting day as far as lower limbs were concerned.

"Looks like worms," I said.

"Blood," said Theresa.

"Your foot throwing up."

Both of us laughed. Her leg slipped back beneath the surface. Every few seconds, I heard the suck of her feet in the mud, as if something was exhuming itself. I kept my own feet where they were.

"Sometimes I think you're my friend," Theresa said, and as she adjusted the ribbon in her hair, the bow of her mouth unstrung for a second and went slack. And for a moment, I thought maybe I was.

"Like when?" I asked.

She smiled. "Like when you beat me at stuff." Her smile spread, not out but down, deeper inside her. She opened her mouth and said something else, but I didn't catch it because Jon Goblin's voice erupted behind us.

"Hoot-hoot," he crowed, in the falsetto that he and his friends used for taunting, although it never sounded like taunting when Jon did it. His hoot was too cheerful.

I caught a glimpse of Theresa's face as I whirled, saw her eyes aimed out over the lake but the smile still in place, and I realized, too late, that we could have stayed. I could have kept my back aligned with hers and ignored Jon Goblin and we could have stayed.

"Mattie and Theresa standing in the lake," said Jon Goblin, flashing his Goblin grin. "Are they going to shake-and-bake? Hoot-hoot."

"Look at his sneakers," Theresa said to me.

No matter how much wet grass, lake muck, and pine-forest scum Jon Goblin plowed through, his Pumas stayed white. His blond hair hung flat and combed on his head, except in one spot near his right ear where it ballooned like a bubble-gum bubble.

"What are you doing?" he asked.

"Becoming the lake," I said.

But Theresa didn't hear me. She was already out of the water, wiping her feet in the grass. Her smile had succumbed once more to the set of her mouth.

And so, despite everything, I really did wind up at school with my wheelbarrow. For two and a half hours, I bided my time, totaling scores for the tetherball tourney, the shoe kick, the two-soccer-field backward dash, which Jon Goblin won by a soccer field and a half. Then, just before lunch, I spotted Mrs. Van-Ellis with her back turned and her hands in their customary clasp behind her back. She didn't even notice me until the handcuffs snapped home around her wrists, and by then it was too late. I was charging forward behind the wheelbarrow with my white smock flying behind me. She must have seen me at the last second because she bent her legs to lessen the impact and let herself flop into the wheelbarrow as I jabbed it beneath her— not hard; I wasn't trying to hurt her—and then she was falling, yelling, "Mattie, ow!"

"Crazy woman comin' through," I howled, and shoved us onto the soccer field. The MEADOWBROOK LOONY BIN sign with the drooling faces I'd painted tumbled off the side with the first lurch. And Mrs. Van-Ellis proved heavier and harder to wheel than I thought. But I pushed her a good three steps through the throng before toppling both of us into the goalie box. When I looked up, she had somehow scrambled to her feet. She almost laughed, then stood there shaking her head and flexing her legs.

"Get these things off me," she said, gesturing with her chin at her manacled hands.

From somewhere in the crowd I heard someone say "Hoot-hoot" softly. I looked around for Jon but couldn't see him. Theresa had disappeared too. Guilt—and more than guilt, confusion—settled around me and yanked itself taut. The feeling, I think, was a protective thing, intended to freeze me, so I couldn't do anything else to the world. I'd never experienced it before.

Mrs. Jupp, our principal, pretty much waved the whole thing off, though she said it "showed an uncharacteristic lapse in judgment." In the midst of this brief lecture in her office, Mrs. Van-Ellis appeared at the door with an ice pack on the back of her thigh.

"I'm sorry," I said, interrupting Mrs. Jupp. I was sorry and something else too: electrified, somehow. Tingling.

"Also shows his goddamn creativity," said Mrs. Van-Ellis.

Mrs. Jupp clucked and said, "Nancy."

My mom picked me up forty-five minutes later. As usual, she'd managed to miss some of her hair dye, and a jagged trickle of it had dried on her temple like blood from a bullet wound. She did not smile at me.

I sat in the car in the heat and felt as if I were choking. I fantasized briefly about suffocating to death right there in the passenger seat. My mother wouldn't notice until I was already something other people looked into without seeing, just as Theresa's grandmother had said. But as we pulled into our driveway, my mother grabbed my arm and studied me with such a serious, unfamiliar expression that I stopped choking and started to cry.

"Sssh," she said, straightening my hair and leaving her arm outstretched, as though she thought I might fall. "Not so safe yet, huh?"

1976

Even before it had ended, the summer of '76 seemed like something the whole city dreamed. Downtown, the twin spires of the still-new Renaissance Center towered like lighthouses over the riverfront, so resplendent in glass and chrome, dominating the collapsing warehouses and wasted lots around them, that they actually seemed capable of luring new families back to those infamous neighborhoods.

At Tiger Stadium, on a miserable night in June when the heat haze rolled over the light stanchions and sank into the bleachers, I took turns with my father and eight-year-old brother Brent in the one seat we had that wasn't behind a post and got my first glimpse of Mark the Bird Fidrych. His curly hair erupted out of his cap like humidity-activated popcorn. His uniform pants were smeared with dirt from sudden dips to his knees to smooth out ripples in the mound and chat with the resin bag. His mouth chewed words instead of tobacco as he cheered his own pitches. Every time he struck somebody out (which wasn't often, even then), the stadium's antiquated sound system would crackle with drum and guitar, and the whole crowd—and there were crowds, that one stolen summer—would leap to its collective feet to stomp and sway to "Surfin' Bird."

On the first weekend after school was out, I set up my Strat-O-Matic tabletop baseball set on our screened-in porch, opened the pouch full of just-printed player cards from the season before, and played the first game of the 1976 Mattie-Ball season: Detroit vs. Cleveland at cavernous Municipal Stadium. Ben Oglivie homered off Jim Kern in the bottom of the eighth to win it for the Tigers. With no giveaway display of emotion, I packed up the two teams, checked the schedule, pulled out Baltimore and Milwaukee, and kept playing. That evening, after dinner, I went outside with my mitt and glove and whiffle ball and reenacted Oglivie's moment three times. Over and over, at the proper instant, I stepped up to the bare patch of grass I used for home plate and drove the whiffle ball over our red slat fence into Kevin Dent's yard. The last time, I looked up and spotted Kevin and his pal Grange creeping into the bushes to spy on me. With a grimace, I stoppered the flow of sportscaster-speak, stepped up to the bare spot, tossed the ball in the air, and parked Ben Oglivie's home run one more time anyway.

When my mother wasn't working in the yard, she was at the special ed school administering tests to autistic kids. My brother Brent would watch *Tattletales* and *The Price Is Right*, then head for Cider Lake with Dean, our freckle-faced neighbor, in the afternoon. My father would come home from his job at the GM research lab and play stickball with us and whomever Brent had brought home for dinner, then duck into the living room to tinker with his speaker cables. For as long as I could remember, he'd been trying to coax sound from that stereo. Finally, at the end of June, he ushered the whole family into the den and waved his hand over the black box he called an amplifier, once, twice, three times, his mouth moving like Mark the Bird's, and then hit the ON button. The system burped once, hummed a few seconds, and shut itself down with a shriek. My father beamed as though he'd just delivered a baby.

Sometimes I'd go to the lake, where Brent and his friends—every one of them taller than I was, even though I'd grown almost an inch that spring—would occasionally stop calling me weird-ass long enough to let me show them how to do the butterfly and backstroke. Thursday nights I went to Mini-Mike's with Joe Whitney and Jon Goblin; even Theresa came along when she wasn't studying for Compu-Kids. Bikers had begun frequenting Mini-Mike's, and though they never spoke to us, sometimes one or more of them would get up off the orange stools surrounding the track so we could view it properly. Theresa's People Eater was the fastest car in the place, but she still couldn't drive it very well. My father had helped me build my own machine, a gun-gray Mustang that tore past the miniature palm trees and roadside Harley shops and dinosaur pits lining Mini-Mike's slot tracks. Even against the bikers, I won a lot.

I remember July fourth on the banks of the Detroit River, the day the country turned two hundred years old. I lay on a blanket among the packs of suburban white people who'd streamed into downtown to see if it was still there. It was the biggest—and most integrated— crowd at the riverside since the riots. Right before the fireworks started, I twisted myself over on my back and began rolling down the bank between and over blankets, somehow hitting no one, all the way to the bottom of the hillside in a whirl of faces and skyscraper and sky. As the ground leveled beneath me, the bicentennial display boomed overhead, and lights erupted, and I watched the sky rain red, white, and blue ashes over the water, which still rolled, steely and savage under all the oil and sewage and industrial waste.

On July 28, Dr. Daughrety took me and Theresa to the all-new Pontiac Silverdome to watch Jon Goblin's soccer team win the state Under-14 Division Games. Jon scored three times. At halftime, we got hot dogs from the concession stand and stood dazed in the air-conditioning, trying to figure out what this filtered air and weird blue light reminded us of. The answer, I think, was nothing. The Silver-dome is the only place I've ever been that reminded me of nowhere. Returning to our seats, we spotted Barbara Fox with some friends a few rows away (I found out later that one of her friends had a little brother playing). All of us waved. I hadn't known, until that moment, that the Daughretys even knew her.

After the game, we all went to the Oakland Park Cider Mill, which had opened early that year. The cider tasted too sweet. Dr. Daughrety said it still had too much summer in it and wouldn't really be tart for another month. Theresa and I wandered into the wheel shed next to the main mill building and stood on the footbridge that ran the length of the room, among the usual cluster of kids watching the giant wheel crush apples. We listened to the water collecting overhead in the pad-dle at the top of the wheel as it pushed the wheel forward into the pile of cored apples at the bottom. We kept watching until the paddle with the hand-carved heart came around, where Richard and Grace, the only two teenagers ever to vandalize this place, had etched their names. None of us could ever figure out exactly how they did it.

Somewhere during those months, in all that heat, the Snowman drifted among us. He drove his blue AMC Gremlin through play-grounds and cul-de-sacs overflowing with children and did nothing. Drove on.

On the last weekend before that school year began, my parents got all spruced up and, on a whim, they packed Brent and me into the car and drove us to Greek Town in downtown Detroit as the sun smeared orangey-red over the rooftops. We parked five blocks away under the few working sodium lights and walked down the center of the deserted streets, past empty windowless hotels and rusted cars with shadows wriggling over the backseats like groping teenagers.

That's why Greek Town, when we got there, burst upon us like a massive firecracker. Thousands of people leapt into being in a blaze of light and food smells. There were blacks and whites, parents and children, management and labor, Mentally Gifted Minors (that's what they called us at school) and ordinary minors, everyone twisting and reshuffling, searching, it seemed, for the way they fit together through the smoke and shouts of "Opa!" Suddenly, the stories of downtown Detroit I'd heard all my life were just stories, nothing more, an elaborate scare tactic to keep out the timid and the weak, so that the last surviving explorers could party on forever in the wreckage of the Motor City.

1994

"So," Laura interrupts, having said nothing for almost two hours while I've rambled on over the phone about Scuzzie and the Bird and that long dry summer. I'm not sure her voice alone could have stopped me, but there are overtones in it I don't ever remember hearing, and they make me wince, close my eyes, stop.

"So, Mattie, does this mean you've found what you wanted for your birthday? Since you decided not to involve me in the celebration, I was just curious, you know? Happy birthday, by the way."

I glance at the clock-radio by my bed: 11:58. The time on Laura's clock in Louisville reads 12:28. I know, because she keeps it half an hour ahead so she'll panic when she wakes up in the morning and sees what time it is. That's the only way either of us has found to get her moving.

"Got your Rolling Rock?" I ask.

"Are you going to answer my question?" I hear fury and hurt and something else, something so fundamental that I don't recognize it for a while, and when I do I am stunned into silence.

"Are you?" snaps my wife.

Once before, on our wedding night, the moment the door to our hotel room closed and we were alone, Laura exploded into tears that continued well into the morning. The fury wasn't directed at me, that time. It was about her brother's death from cystic fibrosis at seventeen and the way her relationship with her parents had decayed in an all-new way after his death.

"They had no one to pound on and save at two in the morning. So the night after the funeral, they came to my door, stood outside it and listened, and when my breathing didn't make enough sound, they got scared and burst into the room and woke me up. Before my brother died, they'd barely acknowledged I was there. They sent me to banjo lessons or sleep-away camp or pretty much anywhere to keep me out of the house. I hardly even knew my brother. He liked beef jerky. That's what I knew. Seventeen fucking years, and that's all I knew about him."

Several times, I'd tried to hold her while she ranted. Once or twice, she relented, but mostly she just sat on the floor and slapped the carpet. She had the veil from her wedding dress in her lap, and she used it periodically to wipe her face. I had never felt closer to her.

Around me now, the motel walls seem to have tilted out of true like the sides of a collapsing shoe box. A little more pressure, I think, and this whole life-size diorama will bust apart and all the people populating both of our pasts will scurry out into the present.

I start to say my wife's name, although I have no idea what I'll say after that, and then I hear the hiss of her breath.

"Mattie, you bastard, come home."

The hand I'm not using to hold the phone burrows into my sweat-shirt, grabs at my skin. The calm I have always heard in her voice is exhaustion, I know that. She wasn't made for the hours she keeps. But only now do I realize that exhaustion has been part of her strategy for staying married to me, surviving on what I've been able to give her, because I haven't even begun to dig at the place where her loneliness lies. I've given her love, but not my love, somehow.

After a silence that seems long, even for us, Laura mutters, "At least I finally understand what that freak was doing at our wedding."

"He didn't used to be quite so much of a freak," I say, wincing at the memory of Scuzzie bursting into a tuneless song-and-screech straight out of Chinese opera in lieu of a best-man toast. Last I'd heard, he'd attempted to open some sort of post-race nightclub in Saratoga, featuring half-naked stable-girl burlesque reviews and free body piercing for the kiddies.

"He stuck his foot in our wedding cake," Laura reminded me.

"Kind of an in-joke," I murmured. "Not even a joke."

"Mattie, why don't you draw anymore?"

I can't tell whether it's the question itself, the bite in her voice, or something else entirely that makes it feel like an accusation. "I'm not an artist, and I don't want to be," I snap back. "It just happened. Once."

"I'd like to have known you then."

"I wasn't any less. . . ." I'm too tired to search for words. "Muddled."

"Mattie, I need to know if you're in trouble. Are you going to hurt yourself?"

The question yanks me off the bed to my feet. Seconds later, it's still buzzing in my ears. "How can you even—" I start, but she's talking again.

"I mean, Jesus Christ, it's your birthday, you're in some motel room a thousand miles away babbling about things that happened ten–twenty years ago, and you sound so small. You sound so *small*, Mattie."

There is a sliver of window visible between the drawn curtains and just enough light in the room that I can see half my face reflected there. "Laura. This is less pathetic than it looks. Really."

"You mean it feels less pathetic than it is?" my wife answers, and when I laugh, she does too. The laugh doesn't last; it feels good, but not good enough.

"Last question, Mattie." She has not softened. "Are you telling me this—me, specifically—or would anyone do?"

"I don't know," I say, wanting to get it right, to be truthful. I owe her that. "I think it's you. I want it to be you."

"You'd better find out." I hear her shift on the bed and realize she's about to drop the receiver into the cradle.

"Don't hang up like this," I say in a rush, and when she doesn't, I hold the phone tight. "Do you want to come here? Experience first-hand Mattie's Quest for Peace?"

"You've made it pretty clear this is a solo thing."

"When? I don't remember being clear about any of this."

"Hmmm," Laura says. My invitation apparently surprised her less than it did me, but it also seems to have soothed her a little. She's strumming her banjo again. I can hear it this time. "I wouldn't want to interfere with your focus or anything. Hell, you've already given me the real explanation for the corpse hand we've had hanging on the wall all these years."

"It's not a corpse hand."

"That's what you told me: *They're images of people that have become ghosts.* Remember? I do."

At least her hostility is aimed at my drawings now instead of me.

"I never knew you didn't like those drawings."

When she speaks again, her voice has become gentler. There is love for me in it, or at least the affectionate disregard that both of us have perfected and that has, until the last year or so, made most of our nights together impervious to the pain we're quietly causing each other.

"What's to like, Mattie?"

She strums her banjo. I sag back onto the bed and listen as the strumming subsides. Our familiar, comfortably constricting silence settles around us once more.

"Good night, Laura," I say. When she doesn't hang up, I say it again, even more softly.

She hangs up.

A few minutes later, the wind is flinging chunks of snow at the window. I stay under the covers, rooting around for a memory powerful enough to transport me somewhere else for a while.

Louisville, Kentucky, Saturday, May 6, 1989. The year of my one and only gallery show, before I started designing subdivisions for money. Days before, Laura, at age twenty-three, just eight months younger than I, had abandoned her home and her parents' memory of her brother for a studio efficiency. To celebrate, she took me to the Derby at Churchill Downs.

She'd had a cold and her voice, for the first time in the four months since I'd known her, was not her voice but a variation of it, and its scratchy familiarity seemed the most intimate thing we'd so far shared. Already, she had touched off a physical desire in me more profound than any I'd yet experienced. She represented my first sustained emotional contact. I was drawn to the artist in her, the way she bent over her banjo like a welder, molding notes to notes, building marvelously complex musical models from scores dug out of folklore libraries and shared among friends. The intensity in her craft both calmed and aroused me.

That day, though, it was the light as much as Laura. Thunderclouds were rising in waves beyond the stables, and lightning bolts flickered within and between them like streaking schools of fish. The track was raked flat, the infield a ferocious blue-green. Laura stood next to me in a sun hat and a long gauzy dress.

It happened when she leapt out of her seat at the start of the first race, and again when she folded back. Halfway between sitting and standing, the light and the color transfixed her in the air like a hovering butterfly, something you could almost hold. Her hair snapped free of her hat in the wind, the hem of her dress rose just above the ankle, and the skin on her back shaded itself into unpredictable patterns, as though creating camouflage for shifting shadows.

I did not touch her. We did not sneak off to make love in the car. As I remember, we went straight to the Secretariat Club, which was packed with horsey people, because Laura had a gig that night and she wanted to drink away her ten-dollar winnings before she strapped herself to her banjo again. It was the first time since the WANTED drawings that I had thought about painting. If there's a logic to longing, I sometimes think I glimpsed it there.

Later that same evening, I introduced Laura to my visiting parents . . . which reminds me now that I need to call them too. Doing my best to hold on to the sensual languor that memory has draped over me, I lift the phone once more and dial. My mother answers on the second ring. She has not been sleeping.

"Where are you?" She was always blunt, and once she gave up dyeing her hair she became blunter still.

"Louisville," I tell her. "Midnight bowling."

She has to know I'm joking. Even I don't baffle my mother anymore. But when she speaks next, her voice cradles a flicker of hope I haven't heard in years. The last time I heard it, I realize with a start, was the day we left Detroit.

"Oh, Mattie," she says. "Really?"

"I'm in Troy, Mom."

"You had to go."

"You know I did."

"I know you're a fool. Let me get your father, he'll want to hear this too. He's almost as big a fool as you. Wait till you hear what he's doing."

The line goes quiet for a few seconds. Too soon, they're back.

"Okay," says my mother.

"Hi, Dad."

"Mattie?"

"What are you doing?"

"Oh. Building a Tyco track out of a box I found in the garage. In honor of your trip, I guess. I think I might be able to get it to work."

"Jesus," I mutter, imagining him in his dungarees at his workbench, playing Prokofiev's *Romeo and Juliet*. He always plays *Romeo and Juliet* when he putters. He says it helps him think and not-think in just the right combination. So tonight he is thinking and not-thinking about my being here, while my mother probably has not stopped fretting over it since I announced I was coming last week. I wrecked this place for her, and she's convinced it wrecked me, having finally accepted, seventeen years later, that she couldn't have accomplished that all by herself.

My parents' Lexington house looks and feels pretty much the way our old Detroit house did, so much so that until I started school the fall after our expatriation, I wasn't sure we'd moved at all. Piles of gutted stereo equipment continued to coagulate in closets and corners. Books, mostly science and psychology, lined the walls in no order. My parents still have the same chairs with the same coverings coming loose at the same old dining table. In my entire life, I have seen my parents purchase only one major piece of furniture: a porch swing. They rock in it together on nights when they are peaceful, which is most nights now, as far as I can tell.

"It's Detroit, you know?" my father says. "You being there. I just wanted to see if I could make your cars work again. You don't know where your cars are, do you?"

I have no idea where the cars are, but I do know how my being here is affecting him. If he thought his wife wouldn't garrote him with speaker wire, he'd probably be here with me. Not all of my weirdness is my own. Some of it, at least, I inherited.

"Remind Mr. Morelli to pick up his cleaning," says my father.

I jerk upright in bed, almost smiling. Sometimes, very occasionally, I am startled by the connection I still have with my parents, in spite of everything.

My father used to take me to the Detroit Institute of Arts every Saturday. After my drawing class, we'd wander through the exhibitions and eat hamburgers at the café, but we always wound up by the giant Canaletto. The painting takes up a whole wall, a Sunday-morning scene with hundreds of completely individualized people racing through or gathering in a piazza in the center of an old Italian village under a sky full of rain clouds newly burned apart by the sun. Each week we'd pick out a different group from the perpetually milling crowd and study their faces, trying to imagine where each figure was going, what he did for a living, whether he'd race slot cars or build stereos from scratch if he lived in Detroit.

The one we'd named Mr. Morelli resides in the right-hand corner of the piazza. He has a dog tugging him one way, a small child another. He looks harassed and happy. His house, my father and I always believed, would be a total mess. I don't know why we liked him best.

"What's it look like?" my mother asks. She doesn't sound accusatory or even worried about me, just sad, and the sadness may be as much for herself as anything else. For all her misgivings, she is not immune to nostalgia.

"Looks like Detroit," I tell her gently, feeling suddenly fond of both my parents. "Dark and snowy and industrial and ruined."

"Birmingham looks ruined?"

"I haven't seen Birmingham. It was dark when I got here."

"Will you eat an Olga's?" my father asks.

"Oh," says my mother.

"Of course," I tell them both.

"Will you go to Mini-Mike's?"

"It's gone, you idiot," my mother snaps.

"Oh, right," says my father.

Tonight will not be one of their peaceful nights, I'm thinking.

"Will you please call your brother?" my mother asks me.

"Oh, Mom, what for?"

"You ripped him out of there too, you know."

I wince. My mother almost never says things like that. She almost never blames me, not to my face anyway. "He doesn't like talking to me, Mother."

"He loved you, there. He loves you still."

This is the one and only fantasy my mother perpetuates. She understands as much about me as anyone does, but she doesn't understand this—or won't. She needs to have my brother and me settled with each other too much.

"I doubt I'll call. I might."

"Call him."

"I have to go to sleep," I say, and sigh, settling back. "I'm tired. I love you. I'll wave to Avri's for you."

"Mattie, be safe," says my father.

"And be all right," says my mother. "Call your wife."

"Oh, yeah, thanks for reminding me," I say, and she recognizes my exhausted sarcasm and laughs.

"Good night, Mattie," my mother says, and both of them hang up.

They will not call Laura. In the almost five years they have known her, they have never developed their own relationship with her, which is also probably my fault. I drop the receiver in the cradle, switch off the lights, and close my eyes. I am not comforted. I am not safe. But I'm starting to feel as if I could sleep.

When the Snowman finished with his kids, he usually dressed them in their original clothes. He tucked in their shirts and wiped their faces, like a burglar trying to put everything right. He couldn't hide the slight anal distortions on a couple of the victims, but as far as the police could tell, he did not rape them. Sometimes, he even treated superficial wounds with Bactine and Band-Aids.

I wonder if you can kill your way free of the things that haunt you. If you can, and that's why he stopped, then he's still out there somewhere, with a new car. I wonder what he did with the Gremlin.

Snatching at the light, I snap the shadows to attention and drag the county phone book onto my lap. I flip through the *D*s, pause, flip to the *F*s. I'm not ready for Theresa yet, or even for knowing I can't find her.

No Spencer Franklin in Oakland County.

I grab the book for the Detroit Metro Area and locate a page and a half of Franklins: Sol, Spanky, Stan. No Spencer, but there's an S. on Pleasant Tree in East Detroit. It's one-forty-five in the morning. I dial.

The woman who answers sounds wide awake. "Shepherd's answering service."

For several seconds, I don't speak. I have no more leads, no one else to call.

"Sir, if you need help, let Jesus—"

"I'm sorry," I say. "Wrong number. I hope I didn't wake you." I drop the phone into its cradle again and sit there. Finally, extinguishing the lights, I dive deep into the sheets in the general direction of sleep,

shunting aside for one last night the memory of the moment somewhere in that goddamn year when all the protective dikes around my
life broke apart, and my childhood sank like some mythical Atlantis,
and the waves reared up and spirited me off in a sickening decades-
long circle toward home.

1994

My plan was to get up and start dialing Franklins one by one, looking for relatives, but that alone would have taken me all day. Instead, I grab the phone book and go straight to Jon Goblin's name. Somehow, I knew it would be there. The book gives his address on Wendy Lane, which, if I remember correctly, lies directly across the creek from his parents' house. It even gives his wife's name: Corrinne.

I don't even think about it, I just call him. Corrinne answers. I ask for Jon. She says, "Sure." There's a pause with kid voices and cartoons in it, and a man gets on the phone. For a second, I feel like a doorbell ditcher who has frozen in place after pushing the button. I can't speak.

"Hello?" says the voice again.

I almost say *Hoot-hoot*, but think better of it. I wasn't a member of Jon's hooting crowd.

"Jon, it's Mattie Rhodes."

I hear silence, a breath. Then, "Mattie Roy, that slot-car boy?"

"The same."

"Jesus. Corrinne, you know who this is?"

I know her, I realize. Corrinne must be Corrinne Kelly-Dade, who wore her hair in pigtails and got up at five-thirty every morning to fig-ure skate on Cider Lake. One Christmas break, when I was maybe eight, I stepped out of our house to fish the paper out of the snow and kept walking all the way to the lake in my slippers and sweat pants and overcoat. From the top of the hill I spotted Corrinne and her coach far out past the pier. They were practicing spins over and over. I remember watching Corrinne spin and glide over ice so clear she could probably see the fish beneath her. For all sorts of reasons, I kept my distance.

"Does she still skate?" I say.

"Wow. Corrinne? It's her job, yeah. She teaches at Indolake."

When we were young, Indolake was a word of its own, a name like Baltimore or Kroger. But I realize now it's actually a slurring of *indoor lake*.

"And you?"

"Jesus, Mattie. Where are you calling from?"

"The Moto-Court near Woodward and Maple. I—"

"Roger, get down," Jon snaps, and whoever Roger is dissolves into the world he knows, and I start trembling. I feel like a voyeur, as if I've been caught in an adult bookstore and need to get away as fast as I can. This isn't my life. These people aren't my friends, and they never really were. But Jon might know where Theresa is, or at least where to look for her. His family stayed friends with hers long after we left. All I have to do is ask. Instead, I invite him to breakfast.

"Hang on," Jon says. When he returns, he suggests lunch.

"Lunch it is."

"God, Mattie, I can't wait to see what you look like after all these years. Want to come here?"

"I need an Olga's."

Jon's laugh isn't quite as infectious as it used to be, but almost. He still sounds close to gleeful. "There's like twenty of them now, you know."

"Is the original still there? The one in Birmingham?"

"Remember the Continental Market? It's gone. Olga's took over that whole space."

We agree to meet there at one. I forget to ask if he's bringing his family. I hear cars croak to life in the parking lot. Some kids are leaving their room on the floor above me, whooping their way into the cold. I wrench my jeans and heavy socks out of my suitcase and dress.

The second I open the door, the wind crawls under my coat. I clamp my arms against me and gasp. I remember this wind, this daylight so bright that it could cut you open: real winter. By the time I skid across the street, I'm laughing outright. The wind breaks in waves on the ice-crusted cars as newspapers and cup tops and bits of tree branch tumble down the sidewalk. Head down, I burrow forward six blocks into downtown Birmingham. I don't see a single store I recognize, but I feel as if I'm home anyway. The light catches and darkens under overhangs, among icicles. This day is the color of most of my memories.

In Shane Park, I look for the giant slide that dropped out of a metal flying saucer and the jungle-gym train with its red metal boxcars and black engine, but almost all the fixtures I played on are gone. In the northeast corner, half hidden in the drifts under the split-trunk birch with its right trunk jabbing off to one side, I find the stone turtle. It looks small but strong enough to carry me on its back. I sit down, rip off my gloves, feel the smoothed-flat grit of its shell. *I lived here,* I am thinking.

I lived here.

I want to call Laura from this park. I want to tell her that I really do want her to come, that I'm sitting on a stone turtle thinking about her and the not-as-gray winter sky over Kentucky. I'm more than aware that it may be too late for me to crawl completely free of this place, but that doesn't necessarily mean I can't reach her from where I am.

I'm remembering my brother Brent charging through the long summer twilight at the Birmingham Fair, which took place in this park. It couldn't have been later than 1973 or 1974, because the Brent I remember is smaller than I am, wearing blue shorts and sneakers, and still bothering to turn around to see if I'm right there. Even before, as my mother so delicately put it, I ripped him out of his life, he had stopped caring much about me. He didn't like imaginary baseball, couldn't imagine what I did with all my alone time, and thought my remoteness was either an act or a plague and undesirable either way.

I remember my father getting ill at the fair. Brent had successfully browbeaten him into taking us on the Tilt-a-Whirl. When we came off, my father was lurching like an old homeless drunk, so pale and wobbly that some woman wandered by as he was leaning over the bushes behind a bench and said, "Lord. Why don't you just hand your children a Pabst right now? You're teaching them the habit just the same."

Censorious comments—he got a lot of them, despite or perhaps because of his reserve in public—always seemed to buck him up. By the time the woman had stalked away he was standing upright, waving at her and saying, "Thanks, good idea," before sagging onto the bench.

"Ah, boys, the Midwest," he said. "No place like it."

Then he did what we'd been waiting for him to do ever since he first took us to the fair: He gave us a ticket book apiece, clutched at his stomach while stroking each of our arms, and said, "Go."

Instantaneously, Shane Park swelled into a whole wild winking world. There seemed to be no end of corners to round, cavorting teenagers to dash between, new sensations, sweet food, dark shadows. Near the Shoot-the-Stars-Out game booth, I spotted the Daughretys and dragged Brent over to them. Theresa was eating cotton candy in a red summer dress with white lilies printed on it. The Doctor said, "Hello, boys," and Theresa grinned, but instead of saying anything, she started singing. *Everybody's going/to the fair/to the fair. All your friends are there.* I sang with her, and both of us did the hip shimmy that Mrs. Jeunne, the chorus teacher at Phil Hart, would do when she made us sing this. I asked Theresa if she wanted to come on the rides with us, but she just went on singing and looked past me. She'd never been allowed on the rides. "Death traps," Dr. Daughrety said. "You boys be careful." He took his daughter's hand and steered her away.

In the end, I got Brent to go on the tower-shaped roller coaster with the track that twisted around it like an anaconda, the cage cars screeching as they plummeted earthward. My parents didn't like us going on that ride. They said kids died on it every year.

Right up to the front of the line, Brent stood beside me, not talking. When he saw the little wooden clown with the arm stuck out that showed how tall you had to be to get on, he told me, "No. Mattie, Dad said no." He was maybe a quarter of an inch taller than the outstretched limb.

"Not tonight he didn't," I reminded him.

"You just think you can scare me," he said, and he was right. I was having the same tingling sensation that would lead me, a few years later, to clap handcuffs on teachers. Do other things.

Steadying myself, I managed to smirk at my brother. "Why would I want to scare you?"

"Because you're weird," said Brent, and he sounded his age: five, maybe six. "Because you're not as scared of this stuff as me." Then he reached out and took my hand and held it all the way to the end of the ride.

I am digging at the back of the stone turtle with my fingernails, gulping frozen air until my lungs ache. I see a pay phone near the Community Center across the park. I need to call Laura. But first I need to call Brent. For once, I'm pretty sure I have something to tell him. I take one more breath and hold it until my lungs relax. Then I'm up, off the turtle's back and running.

Not until I've actually dialed the Lexington area code do I remember that I have to call information. Six weeks or so ago, Brent moved. I never saw his most recent apartment. I'm not even sure I ever called him there. I could get the number from my parents, but my mother would probably cry from gratitude, and I can't face that now. Anyway, I want to do this for him and me, not for her.

Brent doesn't answer, nor does his machine if he has one. The ringing in the receiver wriggles uncomfortably against my ear. I hang up fast.

This has been our pattern all our lives. At the rare moments when one of us actually feels a connection, the other either can't or won't respond. My relationship with Brent is one of the few I have in which the blame can probably be assigned equally. After all, he was making fun of me and my Mind Wars and my make-believe home runs long before we left Detroit. If I was an awfully strange older brother, he was an awfully cruel younger one.

But I can feel his ghost hand in mine today, and I can see him running alongside me through this park, and I wish he had been home. I wish that this morning we could at least have failed to connect in person.

1976

I t was the first school day of fall, nearly forty-five minutes past start time, and the entire population of Phil Hart Elementary had gone snow-day giddy. Kids hung in the branches of trees, throwing pieces of carefully packed lunches at each other, peeling the birch trees down to their soft insides and watching them weep. Jamie Kerflack came over to me, stuck out his hand to shake, and asked for a Four-Square rematch. We played two points and then he drilled me in the face with the ball.

The vandals had apparently struck the night before. Inside, teachers were scrubbing graffiti off the walls and picking bumper stickers off our lockers with nail files and X-acto blades. The stickers, black-lettered on white backgrounds, read ARNOLD GROSS IS A CHILD

MOLESTER. In assembly later that morning, I asked a new teacher monitoring our row who Arnold Gross was. The teacher shrugged and said she had no idea; she had just moved here from Sandusky and was already sorry she came.

"Dead judge," said Theresa, from the row in front of me. I drew my arms to my sides, not liking that she knew. As usual, I wasn't quite sure what she meant, and she wasn't explaining.

"Sandusky?" Jon Goblin asked the new teacher. "Have you been to Cedar Point?"

Our whole row laughed, and Jon and Jamie Kerflack launched into the story of our classmate Garrett Serpien throwing up on the Cedar Point Mine Ride during a Y-Camp field trip two years earlier. They'd had to shut down the coaster for half an hour to hose his vomit off the track.

I leaned forward, spotted Garrett at the end of my row, and waited for him to see me. I was the only one from school who'd been with him on that trip. We'd made up the bits about the track shutdown and hosing off his vomit on the bus ride home. Garrett noticed me and smiled, quick and easy. He seemed to be enjoying this as much as everyone else. Maybe he'd gone back and conquered the Mine Ride, I thought. Or maybe he didn't care. I was thinking about all those Koogle and paper sandwiches he had eaten over the years and the way he walked home cheerfully by himself, swinging his soft-plastic lunch box by its strap; I found myself admiring him, and my admiration stunned me.

Twenty minutes later, Mrs. Jupp apologized for the delay and said she'd be sending a note home to our parents about an emergency PTA meeting the next night. Then we broke into class groups, and I followed mine to the end of the L-Wing into Ms. Eyre's room.

A giant construction-paper tree hung over the doorway. Papier-mâché birds' nests adorned the EXIT signs. Every inch of every wall sported posters about fire prevention and multicolored INTELLIGENT STUDENTS ALWAYS . . . lists. On the back wall, by the clock, was a blown-up picture of a bald eagle with the inscription I'VE GOT MY EYE ON YOU emblazoned below it. Two canaries swung and tweeted in a leaf-strewn cage hung near the window overlooking the blacktop.

"Hoot-hoot," Jon Goblin said when he walked in.

"Caw-caw," said Jamie Kerflack, right behind him, and all his cronies laughed.

Theresa selected a desk in front, sat down, and bowed her head, saying nothing to anyone. When Spencer Franklin, the new kid, sat down next to her, she looked up, and I saw her say, "Oh." When Spencer smiled, she did too, a little awkwardly. Two of Jamie Kerflack's friends filed past them. One looked at Spencer, then at the floor, and said, "Hey."

"Hey back," said the new kid. He was wearing bright red sneakers.

"What's *he* doing here?" I heard Jamie mutter behind me. Instead of turning around, I let him slip past me and sat down next to Spencer. I watched him speak to Theresa again, briefly, though I couldn't hear what he said.

We'd heard rumors about Ms. Eyre's car accident. It had made the papers; she'd spent most of the summer threatening to sue the school board for libel, because they kept forcing her to provide document after document at public hearings to prove she hadn't been drinking. But none of our parents had talked about it much, so we all went silent when she walked through the door.

In the back, very quietly, Jamie Kerflack muttered, "Holy crap."

"Get over it," Ms. Eyre said, and dumped her books on her desk.

She was wearing a wire cage cast. Most of the damage had been done to her jaw, my mother told me later. It had to be rebroken, and would have to be rebroken again. Her nose cartilage was so crushed that the doctors had to tape it in place. But the worst, for us, was her eyes. Ringed with black around the sockets, her silver-blue irises resembled nails driven way too deep into rotting wood.

"Hot lunch?" she said, and began counting. I raised my hand and saw the new kid raise his.

"Brought lunch?" she said. I raised my hand again, holding in my smile so Ms. Eyre wouldn't notice my little subversion. The new kid, I noticed, did the same thing.

"Who's Arnold Gross?" Garrett Serpien asked.

I glanced at Theresa, but she didn't react. Ms. Eyre grimaced and tilted her head back on her neck. We didn't usually see expressions on our teachers' faces like the one she was wearing right now until after Christmas break, when they realized they still had six months to go.

"I'll tell you who he was," she said, staring down each of us in turn. "He was a Michigan state judge who decided it wasn't quite fair that the school districts out here got all the money while the districts in Detroit got leftovers." She did the tilting-head thing again, this time rubbing her eyes as though trying to scrape away some of the blackness. "A couple of years ago, he essentially ruled that some poor kids"—she said *poor*, not *black*—"would get bused to the suburbs and some wealthier kids would get bused to the city. Then he died. And our compassionate and forward-thinking suburban lawmakers and lawyers have been trying to get the ruling overturned ever since."

"Bused to Detroit?" blurted Garrett.

Ms. Eyre slumped into her chair, but I was almost sure she had a smile on her face. The crook from her broken jaw made it look surprisingly friendly.

"But that never happened, did it?" Theresa asked. "No one ever got bused out of this school, did they?"

"Nope," said the new kid, who swung around and faced everybody. "They only bus out of the city, not in."

"Bus who?" Theresa said, turning to look at him. I felt a prickle of jealousy.

"*Special* kids," he answered, and his grin was the one he'd aimed at me during lunch count. "Operation Salvage."

Ms. Eyre stared at him and leaned forward on her desk. "*Operation Salvage*? Is *that* what they're telling you it's called?"

The new kid nodded.

"Those sons of—"

"*Ms. Eyre!*," came a command from the doorway, and in marched Mrs. Jupp.

Her hair had finished graying over the summer, and the bun she'd yanked into place looked more like a punishment than a style. She wore the same overabundance of peach-colored lipstick, the same excess of rouge on her cheeks, but her skin seemed to have stretched and thinned beneath it. One smile, I thought, would split her wide open.

"Welcome back, everyone," Mrs. Jupp said, and smiled, and didn't split open. I was watching her, and the new kid, and the way Ms. Eyre was crouching in her chair with the same enthusiasm that Jamie Kerflack generally exuded during class.

"Can't wait to get started," Mrs. Jupp continued. "We have an exciting year ahead. I'm sure you've all met our new students, but let me introduce them to you."

She started in the back with someone named Marybeth, who'd moved here from Toronto, then Thomas, who'd transferred from a private school because his family had heard such wonderful things about the public schools here, and finally, widening her smile still more, she gestured toward the kid beside Theresa. "Last and nowhere near least, this is Spencer. He's from Ferndale, and he's very talented indeed."

"We know you'll make him more comfortable than your parents would," said Ms. Eyre.

We all just sat there. She sounded so mad, and her anger seemed aimed at Mrs. Jupp. We'd never met anyone who didn't like Mrs. Jupp.

"Ms. Eyre," said our principal, in her businesslike voice, "could you step into the hall with me for a moment?"

"Pencils," Ms. Eyre said to us as she followed Mrs. Jupp out the door. "Paper. We're taking the math placement test as soon as I get back."

No one took out a pencil or even moved. We wanted to hear what they said, which didn't turn out to be a problem. Mrs. Jupp did not lower her voice, and Ms. Eyre was very nearly yelling.

"I would think, Ms. Eyre, that Operation Salvage would be a program you'd endorse and support."

"Of course you would," Ms. Eyre snapped.

"Your tone, Ms. Eyre."

"*Operation Salvage*? We'll *save* you from your home and your parents, take you out where the white—excuse me, bright and ethical—people live, and—"

"Your tone, Ms. Eyre. Whom do you think you're talking to?"

In the front row, Garrett Serpien gaped. The rest of us stole glances at one another and looked away fast. Only Spencer Franklin stared openly at the hallway.

"This happen here much?" I heard him ask Theresa.

She answered, but I didn't hear her, because Ms. Eyre said, "Let's see, whom do I think I'm talking to? The We-know-you-were-drinking-even-though-your-blood-tests-and-the-police-say-otherwise Review Board?"

Mrs. Jupp's sighs were as loud and efficient as her speaking voice. This one blew through the room, ruffled the paper leaves on the paper tree, and settled us all down. "I knew you weren't drinking, Molly."

"I don't remember seeing you at the two hearings they held to interrogate me."

"I don't remember your asking me to come."

"A note might have been nice. A phone call?"

"I sent a note while you were in the hospital, remember? And as for the rest, well, I knew you could handle yourself." For a brief while there was silence. Then Mrs. Jupp said, "Don't take it out on the children, please. Enjoy being back. It's what you've been fighting for, isn't it? Besides, just think how much fun you'll have at this year's parent-teacher conferences."

Ms. Eyre moaned. Seconds later, we heard Mrs. Jupp march down the hall, leaving Ms. Eyre to lean against the doorway with her back to us. When she turned to come in, she was not smiling.

During the math placement test, she excused Theresa and Spencer and me because we'd already qualified for the new super-advanced math program, so the three of us stood at the back, rolling the first dry rubber cement of the year between our fingers. The clouds that had been gathering all morning began sifting precipitation over the asphalt. This wasn't snow—not yet—but a fine silvery rain, obscuring the paths that led through the trees and setting leaves vibrating as though something among them were stirring.

"From my house," Spencer whispered, "you can hear lions at night. I live by the zoo." He was shorter than Theresa, almost as short as I was. His red rugby shirt and red canvas sneakers and the sheer novelty of having him here made it seem as if he'd just stepped out of one of our wall-collage travel projects in Mrs. Van-Ellis's class. He wasn't the only black kid at school—there'd been at least one in my class every year—but he was the only one bused here, and the only one wearing red sneakers and not taking the math placement test.

"Do they sleep? The lions?" Theresa asked.

Spencer shrugged. "They don't roar much, if that's what you mean. But you can hear them prowling around. They're on the other side of the wall in our backyard. They make little shuffly sounds like this." He made little shuffly sounds with his sneakers.

"My all-time record for sprinting to the lunch line is forty-six seconds," I offered. "Round trip."

"What's the two-people record?" he said. We looked at each other, and then instantly, wordlessly, took to inventing a harness out of duct tape. Theresa came up with a name for the sport, though she'd never sprinted for the lunch line in her life and spent most of the time we were constructing the harness staring into the sink. She called it side-carring.

After the test, Ms. Eyre waved Theresa and Spencer and me back to our desks in the front. We would stay there the rest of the year.

Ms. Eyre asked everyone to stand up. "Now look," she said. "Look right at my face." The invitation was too tempting to resist, so we all did it. "I'm a stranger," Ms. Eyre said. "I've just driven up to you in my car."

"What's left of it," I said, tingling, which triggered an eruption of laughter while I stood with my head down, blushing. When I glanced up, Theresa was eyeing me, her little bow mouth bent in surprise. Ms. Eyre stared at me, and after a few seconds she pointed.

"They warned me about you," she said.

No one, to my knowledge, had ever been warned about me. The very idea drove my fingernails into my palms, my chin into my chest.

The tremoring in my throat could have been confusion or fear or even pride. When I straightened again, I managed to keep my eyes level with hers.

"I've driven up to you," Ms. Eyre began again, when we were quiet. Her eyes shone in their black sockets like bat eyes in a cave. We grew quieter still. "Hey, little girl," she said softly. "Want a piece of candy?"

The only response was rain pattering on the roof, searching for a point of entry. Then Theresa gestured to the window next to Ms. Eyre's desk, which had a hand outlined in red tape in the lower-left corner. "Run for the house with one of those hands," she said.

"Eagle-eye Daughrety does it again," said Ms. Eyre, and then blinked, releasing us. "Divide into writing groups. No more than five per group. You can choose your own for now; I'll choose for you later. Spencer, Theresa, and Mattie, I want you in your own group, please."

Two minutes before lunch, Ms. Eyre was called to the office over the PA system, which gave Spencer and me plenty of time to slip into our harness. Our classmates looked up from their writing pads and snickered. The bell rang. Side by side, Spencer Franklin and I shot out of the doorway, aided by Jon Goblin's shove from behind, and lunged past chattering students and teachers demanding that we stop, down the hall, and through the library toward the lunch line. Twice, the harness tangled and we had to slow up. Once, Spencer got a half-step ahead of me and almost yanked me into the trophy case, where I noticed a photo of me standing beside the painting of my dad fixing his speakers that had won first prize at the YoungArt Fair last year. But by the time we reached the corridor outside Mrs. Jupp's office, our movements had synchronized, and we were flying.

1976

I t was the cold, they said, that drove the yellow jackets into the grass. Within a week of Labor Day, frost crept through the trees, plucking the still-green leaves from their stems and driving startled robins and blue jays south in waves. By midmonth, when Indian summer hit, all the maples and oaks were bare, and Mark the Bird Fidrych was faltering in his quest to win twenty games in his rookie season. (He didn't make it.) Ms. Eyre orchestrated a field trip to the Channel 7 Weather Bureau so we could explain to our parents what had happened to the traditionally glorious Michigan fall.

Despite his size, Spencer had signed up for after-school flag football, and he'd convinced me to do it too, for the first time ever. He even convinced Theresa Daughrety to come watch the first game. There were girls—quite a few—who came out to watch those games, and one or two who played, but Theresa had never been one of them.

Mr. Lang ran the league, so of course he put Spencer and Garrett Serpien and me on the same team. He named us Mathilda's Minions and pitted us against the Goblin Squad for opening day. The game took place on a cloudless Tuesday, on the second soccer field, under the bare trees.

Jon Goblin kicked off, way over our heads, and jogged beside his teammates down the field. When Spencer blew by his two pals with the ball, they started screaming, as did everyone watching, but Jon just snapped taut like a sail in the wind and surged across the field, freeing Spencer's flag from his pocket and dropping it on the grass.

"You're fast, man," he said to Spencer, as he coasted to a stop and clapped him on the back.

"You're faster," said Spencer, smiling as if he couldn't have cared less, so it surprised me when he clapped Jon on the back too and told him, "Won't help you, though."

During this exchange, I stood with Garrett in a half huddle. I was watching Spencer and Jon but also glancing at Theresa, who was studying the sky and roping the black ribbon around in her hair. She looked at Spencer and Jon, and she smiled too, sort of. At least, I think it was a smile.

"What'd you say that for? You're just going to make him mad," I snapped at Spencer when he rejoined the huddle.

"What's the matter with you?"

I thought about that and shrugged. "Nothing," I said, but I'd already figured it out, and it actually felt pretty good. I'd never had enough friends at the same time to feel jealous of anyone.

"Bomb to Spencer," Garrett said. "Mattie, you decoy."

"No one does it better," I said, and Garrett looked at Spencer and nodded.

"He speaks the truth."

"You see him run?" I heard Mr. Lang say to somebody on the sidelines. "Legs look tacked to him, don't they?" I knew he didn't mean

Jon, although I wasn't sure exactly what he did mean. I just knew it made me nervous.

"On four," said Garrett.

At the snap of the ball, I grabbed my leg. The kid opposite me froze. I yelled "Aaah!"—which froze Jon Goblin for a split second. Then I darted past my opponent and ran about five yards from the line of scrimmage, yelling, "Here, here!" while my defender chased after me, calling me *dickwad*.

Spencer, meanwhile, was gone, five steps ahead of Jon and streaking for the end zone.

Garrett Serpien actually could throw the ball. His problem was staying upright long enough. When the count hit three-mississippi and the rusher came after him, Garrett would usually stagger and fall. He was staggering as he threw this one, which is the only reason that Jon Goblin caught up to it.

I sometimes think he would have caught up to it anyway. He was the fastest human being I ever saw (or at least ever knew), and the most graceful, and when he leapt up to intercept the pass, I knew Spencer's bravado of a few moments ago was just so much talk. Jon had power here, not just to run or jump but to bend things to his will. That day, the ball seemed to hang in the air for him, like the last apple suspended from a ghost tree. He picked it one-handed, took two steps the other way, and then the yellow jackets boiled over him.

They did not come in a cloud. Somehow, I could see every one of them as they rose in dozens, engulfing Jon's calves and arms and throat. He crumpled. Being Jon, he held on to the ball.

After a few paralyzed seconds, Mr. Lang ran toward him, waving his arms and screaming. The wasps paid him no mind, which made me think about the way injuries always seemed to stalk Jon. In second grade, he'd suffered a compound fracture climbing a chicken-wire fence. Last year, he'd had appendicitis. Now he'd been swarmed.

The paramedics carried him off on a stretcher. That night, Mr. Arias, the janitor, took a fine wire screen and dropped it over the hole in the field where the yellow jackets had nested. He poured gasoline through the screen, lit a match, dropped it, and flames leapt to life with a soft *boom*, like an echo of thunder. The lawn whispered as it burned. I didn't actually see this or get to hear those sounds until our neighbors also found nests in their yards and set them alight.

As the last of the spectators strayed from the soccer field, I stirred from my mesmerized stupor and spotted Theresa still sitting in the bleachers, twisting her hair ribbon between her fingers. I started toward her and, then saw Spencer climb into the bleachers beside her. They both turned and looked toward me. Part of me wanted to run away, not because I was mad or jealous or anything but because the day had resurrected all my old social anxieties, and the sight of the two of them sitting there, smart and shaken and waiting for me, proved more disturbing than the sight of Jamie Kerflack and all his asshole lackeys pointing at me and laughing. I wasn't used to having people look at me and wait. I wasn't sure how to respond. Eventually, I just walked over and sat on the bleacher beneath them.

"Wow," said Spencer.

As soon as I was settled, Theresa got up and walked away. Spencer and I just watched her go. When we realized she wasn't coming back, we got up too and walked the two blocks to Stroh's Ice Cream, saying nothing until we were crossing the minimall parking lot.

"She's kind of out there, you know?" Spencer said.

"Yep." In fact, she struck me as considerably more *out there* than I was, which was saying something.

After we'd eaten our cones, Spencer called his mom to pick him up and told me to go home. I said I'd wait, but he insisted. He said his mother wasn't someone you could just casually meet. So I left.

The next day, Jon was absent, but Spencer and Theresa took their usual seats, and the three of us went on bantering and competing and sidecarring with increasing familiarity.

That weekend, my mother came streaking into the house from mowing the lawn with yellow jackets on her legs. She was swearing and laughing, and she wound up lying on the couch while Brent and I brought her RC Colas and my father tended to the stings, spread salve, and spoke to her in exactly the same tones he used with his stereo wires. I spent the rest of the morning sitting on the stoop, listening to the yellow jackets hiss around the hole in our front lawn.

I was still out there when the Foxes, Mr. and Barbara, walked up our driveway. Mr. Fox was wearing jeans and a dress shirt tucked in tight at the waist. Barbara lagged behind in shorts. Her tan had faded, but not much, and the memory of her leg over mine nudged my thoughts away from my father and the ways I might be like him.

"Morning, Mattie," said Mr. Fox. He sounded different. I couldn't tell how.

Barbara peered over his shoulder. Then, slowly, she smiled.

"Watch out for the hive," I told them, pointing.

My father opened the screen door. Behind him I could see my mother up on her elbows, staring.

Mr. Fox had combed his hair. Even the hair on his body looked contained. His eyes were red, but a pinker red than usual, the color of new skin around a scab. In a few months, I thought, Ms. Eyre's eyes might look like that.

"I've been going to Meetings," he said to my father. "I have a Sponsor and everything."

"Good for you, Phil," said my father, sounding welcoming and relieved.

Sighing, Mr. Fox dropped his hand on my head and started into the house. Without turning around, he said, "Coming, Barbara?"

"No," she said, and sat down next to me. She muttered something else I couldn't quite hear. It sounded like "Go bathe in it."

As they went in, Mr. Fox asked my father if he could keep the screen door open. Barbara moaned and dropped her head on my shoulder. Her black hair spilled down my chest.

"Is it hard to be home?" I asked, feeling her hair and her cheek against my skin, and she sat up fast.

"Now I remember why I liked you," she said, and stroked my back. Then she muttered, "Hard to be in *his* home. I don't know why I'm even here. It's why I left, you know? I have to coax him out of bed, tell him it's all right, that it'll keep being all right, stand in the goddamn bathroom doorway and make little comforting sounds so he can go to the. . . ."

Her voice trailed off. I held my breath, as if I were overhearing adult information I wasn't sure I wanted to know.

Inside, I could hear Mr. Fox talking. Mostly, he rambled, sounding too much like someone at school doing a book report, and an unexpected sadness crept over me. I watched the wasps and the noon light in the trees and on the rooftops, and I saw how people roll around the world—to Vietnam and Africa and Ferndale—and then roll home again like marbles in a maze, and sometimes the world tips over and someone slips through an old slot into a new one, which can lead back to the beginning or on to the end, but never out. There is no out.

"Sing for me," I said.

And Barbara, who I suddenly understood would never notice my leg against hers—I'd always known that, but until that moment I'd been kid enough to dream—said, "Okay. But you have to do the response. It's all call and response. Like this." She sang a pattern. "Ya-ya, yah-ah-ah-ah-ahhh."

She did some throat-clearing and rolled her head around on her neck. "This is about returning to the village from a good hunt." She smiled, but the smile looked as if it hurt her. She began to sing.

The first few times, she had to nudge me when my part flew by, but I caught on soon enough. Bit by bit, we fell into a rhythm, Barbara stringing up patterns of words to snap in the wind like sheets on a line, and me following, pinning the melody in place with my refrain. The patterns never changed, but they worked their way into me, and into her, too. We were swaying there on the stoop, still singing, when Dr. Daughrety pulled his Jeep into the driveway.

Most of the time, Dr. Daughrety would keep his car running when he brought Theresa over. But today, he turned it off and hopped out with her and Spencer. I'd forgotten they were coming. We were going to the hospital to visit Jon, and then to Mini-Mike's so I could trounce everybody with my Mustang.

"I want you to meet my friend Spencer," I told Barbara, gesturing toward the Jeep, feeling proud that she could see me having a black friend and also embarrassed for feeling that way.

"Is he the one whose dad writes for *Creem*?" she asked.

"How do you know that?" I said, startled, but Barbara didn't answer.

The Doctor strode straight for us, but halfway up the drive, Theresa broke off from Spencer and walked out onto the grass to crouch on her too-white legs and stare at the yellow jackets.

"Hey," I heard her father call after her. An expression flickered across his face, surprise or fear or something, and then slid away, quick as a shadow.

Still crouching, ignoring him, Theresa looked up and smirked at me. The smirk was about her father, I thought. I began to reconsider my lifelong impression of the United Daughrety Front.

Beside me, Barbara stopped singing momentarily and mumbled something. But I heard her this time. "It's the little loon," she whispered. Then she went on singing. Without my refrain, her melody tumbled away on the air, catching on the pines before disappearing altogether. Behind us, Mr. Fox had returned to the doorway, still rambling. My mother was off the couch and limping behind him, saying, "We're so glad to see you like this, Phil. Come on Tuesday. Bring a salad."

"Thanks, Joe, thanks," Mr. Fox repeated to my dad, and he came out with his head bobbing and his throat twitching above the hair on his neck, as though he couldn't quite get something swallowed.

"Well, hello, Phil," Dr. Daughrety said to Mr. Fox as he stood on the porch. He said "Matt" to me, and nothing to Barbara. He smiled at Barbara.

Barbara kept on singing.

Mr. Fox patted my head. His hands were shaking. I watched him draw his shoulders straight and look at the Doctor, and I suddenly thought he might throw a punch. Instead, he said, "Daughrety." His watery eyes stayed riveted on Theresa's dad.

"Is she casting spells?" Spencer asked, as he flopped down on the other side of me and crossed his red-sneakered feet.

"She's singing griot," I said.

Barbara stopped. She didn't finish, just stopped. I wondered if these songs *had* a finish. "*Gree-oh*. Silent *t*, remember? And a griot's a person, Mattie. A storyteller."

"Are you one?" Spencer asked.

Once more Barbara's smile looked painful. She was watching the tops of the trees. I wondered if she could see the way out, after all. She stood up and took her father's hand.

"See ya," she said, mostly to me.

Dr. Daughrety nodded to them as they walked slowly away. He turned just in time to see Theresa stretching one slow tentative finger toward the hole in the lawn. "Thrr-girl, get away from there."

Theresa withdrew her finger, but she didn't get up or look our way. So often, when I think of Theresa, I think of her like this: crouched, with her back turned, watching something I had already seen but seeing something else entirely.

To my surprise, Dr. Daughrety accepted my parents' invitation to come in for lemonade. I don't think he'd ever been in our house before. He'd been invited, but he'd never come. Through the window, I watched my father show off his stumpy speakers on their stumpy stands. They didn't look like things that would one day erupt into glorious sound. Unlike the Doctor's masks, they served no mythic function. Dr. Daughrety nodded distractedly.

Minutes later, they were back at the front door. Theresa was still watching the nest, and Spencer had wandered down to the drainage ditch. Something heavy in the air cast a pall over everything. None of us felt very talkative. Not that Theresa was ever talkative.

"The father makes me a little nervous," I heard Dr. Daughrety say. "Bit of a wild man, apparently. What does he do, write for *Creem?* But she says he's never around anyway, right?" He glanced down at me, out into the yard, and I had the surprising impression that they'd been talking about Spencer, which made me uncomfortable and a little angry.

Then my mother said, "Phil's so afraid of everything," and scratched cautiously at her leg. My father took her hand to keep her from doing it.

"Barbara's scared too," my father said. I didn't like him talking about Barbara either, especially to the Doctor. It felt wrong, like a betrayal.

"I'm afraid that's normal in families of alcoholics," Dr. Daughrety said.

"I think he's leaning on her awfully hard," my father said. Dr. Daughrety nodded and said nothing, for once, and my mother sighed and held my father's hand. It was strange to see him participating in this kind of discussion. He didn't gossip or go bowling; he rarely called friends on the phone, barely seemed to acknowledge anyone outside the house. But sometimes he said surprising things. This time, he said, "She's letting him. She hates it, and she stays anyway, and he won't stop."

"She needs to stop it herself," said the Doctor quietly. "For her own sake. And soon."

Remarkably, all of them glanced at me as well as each other when they spoke. I felt powerful, privileged. I wasn't anywhere near perceptive enough to recognize or comprehend the guilty bittersweet pleasure of discussing a friend who is falling apart while the friend isn't there. But I felt it.

Sometime that fall, I had a dream—daydream, maybe—about honey soaked in gasoline and set alight, turning black as it burned. I dreamed about something giant and invisible flitting among us. The Snowman had taken two children the past winter, a boy and a girl. He hadn't been christened but he was there, hovering, wasp-like, in the restless, hungry air.

1994

The message on our machine is banjo no longer, and it greets no one but me. It says, "Northwest, Flight 252, Mattie, nine-twenty-five tomorrow morning. I'll be there or I won't."

I should probably process this now, I decide, because I sure as hell need to know what I think before she gets here. But I'm late for lunch, and freezing, and I still have to find Olga's. Last time I was here, Olga's was a stand with benches, which Spencer and I rearranged into hurdles as part of our first sidecarring decathlon. Hurdling with our legs tied together involved a sort of kick-hop onto the bench seat and then over the back that we never quite mastered. Spencer blamed me for never getting my leg high enough, and he was probably right.

I can see the trademark Olga's pennant snapping in the wind. It's
going to taste like an ordinary souvlaki, I find myself thinking, like
something I could get in a mall. I almost wish I'd suggested someplace
else. At my feet, little sparkles of sunlight shoot around in the ice like
tadpoles. Calliope music floats over the trees from the new carousel
in the park with its stable of snow-white horses. I am trying to picture
my wife here, trying to feel her hand in mine as I show her the stone
turtle, my old house, the Daughrety place. But at the moment, Laura
seems as imaginary as the people I have come here to find. From the
freshly painted green bus-stop bench in front of Olga's, Jon Goblin
stands to greet me with the help of a cane. I make a sound like a whimper, but I don't stop; I even manage to avoid slowing visibly as I lift my
hand in greeting. His hair has darkened to tan, but it still curls over
his cowlick in the same tumbling wave. He's still lanky, not so much
muscled as honed, a steel spring in a work vest. The vest says JON over
the pocket and has screwdrivers in it.

"My God, Mattie, you've hardly changed," he says, extending
the hand that isn't holding the cane. Then he makes the sound.
"Hoot-hoot."

I laugh in spite of the compression in my chest, relieved to find that
Jon's teasing goodwill still overwhelms all resistance. "Sorry I'm late."

"You're not late. I came early. I was kind of excited." He ushers me
into the restaurant.

"Anywhere!" shouts a stout Greek man from the waiter station, his
voice loud and confident as a square-dance caller's. Spotting an open
table by the fireplace in the back, Jon points us forward with his
cane. He doesn't so much limp as lean, and I suspect he has had
the cane for some time, because it glides with his steps like an extra
limb. We're halfway across the room when the doors to the kitchen
flip open and the smell of lamb and cucumbers and newly baked
pita floods my senses, and I remember what I've been missing all
these Olga-less years. There really is a difference. There's a sweetness
in this bread.

The stout man arrives at our table, his black hair matted, his skin
sweaty, as if he's been carving the lamb from the giant skewers him-

self between orders. "You need menus?" he asks, as if he can't imagine we would, then calls "Anywhere!" once again to a new family coming through the door.

"Souvlakis," I say. "Lemonade. Right?"

"You're asking me?" says the waiter. When we offer no protest, he disappears into the kitchen. Our lemonades arrive moments later.

"Mattie Rhodes," says Jon.

I smile, slurp my lemonade, then gesture at the cane.

Jon shrugs. "Fell out of a tree."

"Bull," I say, but I think again of wasp swarms and ruptured appendixes and the way Jon used to explode out of his legs like a rocket jettisoning spent sections. I watch him grin, and a new sadness slides through me like an ice floe. It could sweep me out of Detroit if I let it. "You were never lucky about things like that."

"I guess not. I did it at U of M the day before the first round of the Soccer Regionals. I was chasing Corrinne's roommate—Lindy Ames, you remember her?—she stole my shin guards, ran all the way across campus, and eventually threw them up in an oak tree in the quad. I broke my leg four different ways when I fell."

He doesn't say this as though it was the critical juncture of his life.

"Sounds like something Garrett Serpien would have done," I say.

"Garrett's managing editor of *Car and Driver* now." Suddenly, Jon smiles.

"No shit," I say, but I'm not really surprised. I knew Garrett would find his way.

Jon is still smiling. "Mattie Rhodes, the Criminal Mastermind. Right here in front of me."

I wince. I don't want to talk about that now, Jon wasn't part of it. But I realize I probably should have prepared an explanation for my presence and for my phone call to him.

The food arrives on plain white plates. Lifting my souvlaki, I can see little white lily blooms of *tzatziki* sauce in the pita's crenellations, slices of white onion nestled among the strips of lamb, a wheel of tomato atop it all like a bow. I take a bite, and my father materializes in front of me, lips dripping sauce, eyes shining.

"I think, if I lived here, I would eat this every day," I say, around a mouthful of food.

"That's because you don't live here," Jon answers.

In between and during bites, Jon tells me about dropping out of school a year after his injury and becoming an electrician. Mr. Alight, he calls himself, plucking at his vest. The Man with Magic Hands. He says he wished he had finished college, but he can't complain. He likes his job.

I tell him about designing shopping malls and subdivisions. Mr. Atrium, I pronounce myself. At one point, we look up at exactly the same second, catch the expression on each other's faces, and start to laugh. What we're seeing, I suppose, is mostly bewilderment. We were trained early on by virtually everyone we encountered to expect more from each other's lives than there appears to be.

Meanwhile, I have begun to notice the similarities in our mannerisms: the way we both make jokes, cocking our heads and pressing our lips together at punch lines to keep from laughing; the way we watch the room more than we watch each other, cataloging faces in that gently judgmental suburban-Michigan way. Seventeen years have gone by, and yet in some ways I have more in common with this man, who wasn't ever quite my friend, than I've had with anyone I've known since, including my wife. Maybe the ability to fully engage with other people begins to fade after the age of ten. Maybe that's why everyone I know who has moved away from their hometown fills up with longing, sooner or later.

I mop my plate with the last of the sweet pita and feel it float in my mouth like lightly crisped air. Jon talks about his wife, the house he just bought, and his six-year-old son, Roger.

"You have a six-year-old son," I say, and Jon blushes.

"Seeing you makes everything seem unreal, you know?"

"Everything now, or everything then?"

"Well, I haven't hooted since the eighth grade, but I keep wanting to answer you with it. So is that now or then?"

We both sort of shrug.

"You're not teaching Roger to hoot, are you?" I ask.

I should let this lunch end right here, leave this man to his world and whatever sense he's made of it, and try some other way to locate whatever it is that has always seemed lost to me. I know that. But I can't do it. I've come too far. And Jon might actually have some answers. "Whatever happened to Joe Whitney?" I ask. I can barely picture Joe's face, don't have any significant memory of him. But he's an easy place to start.

Jon nods as though he's been expecting this part of the conversation all along. "Would you believe Harvard Law? Hard to get ahold of, these days. Busy dude."

"Marybeth Royal?" I'm stalling. I never even got to know her. She was only there for my last year.

"God, you should've seen her in college," he says. "She was Homecoming Queen three years in a row. First time that's ever happened. You know, I was her first kiss. You were there for it."

I blink. "When?"

"Remember the last Mind War? Remember the island in the middle of the lake where we went skating afterward? Where Theresa always used to disappear? Perfect spot, man."

This first hint of Theresa shoots off little firecrackers behind my eyes. But I'm still not ready to ask about her yet.

"Marybeth's a school shrink now, at Orchard Lake Elementary," Jon continues, as though nothing has happened. And of course, nothing has, except that I've stopped breathing properly. "I saw her once at the circus or Pine Knob or somewhere. Her kid's right around Roger's age. She married Wally Beck."

I start to nod, stop. "I don't know who that is."

"He came later, I forgot. Cool guy; you'd like him."

I'm finding, to my surprise, that I'm awfully comfortable with Jon. I envy him less than I used to, but I like him more. There is less malice in him than almost anyone I've ever known.

"Mattie, what are you doing here?" he says, his eyes grabbing mine.

I don't know what to say, and finally murmur, "I wanted to come home."

"Home? After all these years?"

Jon stares at me awhile longer. When I don't respond, he nods, then goes down the list of people he thinks I knew. I remember most of the names, a few of the faces. He tells me about two of our classmates who were jailed for tax fraud, and then about Jamie Kerflack, who got drunk after his suspension in tenth grade and drove his parents' Camaro through the high school's front window.

"He got shot to death in Southfield last year, being carjacked," Jon tells me. "I went to the funeral. Hardly anyone we knew was there. His wife was tiny, maybe five-foot-one. She sat there the whole time crying into her hands. I never even saw her face."

It's hard to imagine that anyone I knew then—other than the Snowman's victims—could be dead, Jamie Kerflack especially. He was such a stubborn, vicious little bastard.

Behind me, the door to the restaurant opens, and I feel freezing air on the back of my neck. The Snowman's breath.

"Tell me about your wife," Jon says.

The words fall from my mouth; they don't feel like my own. I don't seem to be thinking them first. "I'm not sure how happy we are," I say.

Looking down at his plate, which has been mopped as clean as my own, Jon nods, clearly not knowing what to say. Why should he? I sure as hell don't. I don't even know what I'm feeling. It could be love or loss. I can't tell the difference anymore.

"What about Spencer Franklin?" I ask steadily.

"Strange dude," Jon says quickly. I'm thinking he will say the same about me if anyone ever asks. "He lives in East Detroit somewhere. I saw him on TV not too long ago. He's some kind of preacher."

I stopped listening the moment he said East Detroit, because East Detroit is where I called last night.

"He's a what?"

"He was on *Detroit Beat*, rapping about the Lord. Larry Loreno wanted to set up a contest, Spencer versus Hyper Horst, the stereo guy, to see who could rap the fastest. Spencer laughed when Larry suggested it. Said he'd give him ten pounds of salvation if he couldn't beat Hyper Horst's best spiel. Larry thought that was hilarious."

"Larry Loreno," I say. He was the host of *Eyeing Detroit,* the show that signaled the end of after-school cartoons on Channel 50. He wore brown leather jackets with fur collars and sunglasses in the middle of winter. I remember him looking about twenty years old, standing in the snow flurries on some gray, empty downtown street corner, rambling on about a new night spot or "the incredibly vital revitalization of this incredible city."

"Didn't Larry Loreno ever make it to news anchor?"

"Oh, yeah," Jon says. "But his son died two years ago of leukemia. He took a long time off, and he hasn't been the same since."

Right before we pay the bill, Jon drops his smile, and I get my first real glimpse of the adult that grew behind the face. I'm afraid of what he's going to say next.

"Are you all right, Mattie?"

I feel myself relax. "It's not really that weird, is it?" I say. "My showing up like this?"

Jon shrugs. "I don't know. Sort of. What made you call me?"

"There are maybe five people I remember well from when I lived here. You're one of them."

He nods, and a smile flickers over his face. "Guess we both grew up somehow, huh? Made it through." He reaches out uncertainly and touches my shoulder.

Even today, I realize, I have underestimated Jon Goblin. He understands the oddly impersonal nature of the affection we both appear to be feeling. In the end, the inevitable question slips off my tongue with such ease that I barely notice saying it. "How about the Daughretys?"

"The Doctor died, you know."

My tongue locks. I hold my breath and stare.

"I guess not," Jon says, and I realize he's trying to sound comforting, though he clearly has no idea why I'm reacting like this. "Lost control of his car and drove it into Cider Lake. Knocked himself unconscious or something and drowned in five feet of water."

"When?"

"Nineteen ninety-two, maybe? Nineteen ninety-one. Not long ago. Nobody'd seen them for quite a while."

"What do you mean? Why not?"

"Well, after everything . . . they just got weird, Mattie."

"They were always weird."

"You don't understand," he says, shaking his head. "Theresa went away for a while. A long time. I heard they moved to Cleveland or somewhere eventually. The Doctor had family there, I think. He came back every other week to look after the immunization clinic he set up downtown. The family didn't want a funeral, but the mayor's office organized this tribute day in Phil Hart Plaza. We all went. It was weird, like the fourth of July. He was a big deal because he did all this charity work in the city, so they had posters of him in a lab coat pasted all over the place. Kind of freaked me out."

"Were. . ." I'm, having trouble with the words. "Did you see the rest of the family there?"

"I think Barbara was already gone. Or she didn't come back for the tribute or something. Anyway, I didn't see her."

"Theresa?" I say, fast.

Jon looks right at me and shakes his head again, then lifts himself over the cane to his feet. He has remembered, I suspect, why this answer might be so important to me. "Mattie, I don't know. No one does."

1976

I n Detroit, Halloween is an anticlimax. The real danger comes the
night before, on Devil's Night, when all the city's children slip out
of their homes with a decades-old mandate to vandalize.

The first real snow of 1976 fell on Devil's Night afternoon. From
our front window, Brent and I could see it slanting with the wind, a
spectral web across the oncoming dark. Occasionally, we saw the clustered shadows of teenagers moving through the strands of snow.

Arson had not yet become the Devil's Night activity of choice, especially in suburban Detroit, but the mayhem was getting nastier every
year, and the adults reacted accordingly. Mr. Fox turned his drainage
ditch into a foxhole and sat there with a pump gun until well after midnight. Kevin Dent's father booby-trapped trees by sawing the lowest

branches almost all the way through, so that the slightest pressure—
from a roll of toilet paper, say—would bring them crashing down on
the perpetrators below.

Meanwhile, entire crates of eggs evaporated from local markets.
Soap bars and shaving-cream cans were spirited out of bathrooms, and
fist-sized rocks collected in school lockers. Editorials condemning the
holiday and bemoaning the deterioration of civic responsibility in our
city's youth ran on the front pages of the *News* and the *Free Press*. By
evening, everyone not out to wreak havoc had secreted themselves in
their houses, and the entire city seemed submerged.

At our house, Devil's Night was spent on alert. My father would
deploy my mother by the back bedroom window and Brent and me
by the big one in the living room. At the first sign of movement, we
were instructed to wave a flashlight at my father's spot behind the front
door or, in my mother's case, to just yell, and he would go bursting into
the night whooping and bellowing like a Scooby Doo demon. Invari-
ably, he'd be laughing when he returned. Devil's Night seemed to trigger my father's most singular skill as a parent: the ability to animate
dead time.

Later on, he'd take us into the garage and help me finish constructing the costumes that Brent and I would be wearing to school
the next day. By now, I was designing the costumes for both me and
my brother while my father mostly sat on the washing machine and
made suggestions. My mother baked brownies and brought them out
to us and then stood in the doorway and watched me take care of the
final details. That year, after Mr. Fox finally left his drainage ditch and
went to bed, his house was paint-bombed, and all the cars in the
neighborhood got draped with frozen strung-together animal dung.

The next afternoon, Mrs. Jupp had organized a Halloween costume
contest in the gym. My brother Brent wound up winning, which was
fine with me. I'd spent more time on his costume than I had on my
own, because I liked his more. I came as the Bird, along with half the
other boys in the school and more than a few of the girls, although my
hair design was more realistic: a perfect tease-woven mass of spaghetti
string and gold glitter to give it the winking effect that Mark Fidrych's

hair always had during night games. More spaghetti string was used for my brother's costume. I stuck it to a giant papier-mâché plate that I had hooped around his collar, then spray-painted parts of it red, stretched a red shower cap over his head, dripped ketchup streaks down his face, and voilà! my brother, the walking meatball dinner.

Most of the reason Brent won, I think, was because his costume made Mrs. Jupp laugh. She wasn't laughing at many of the costumes that year. Particularly in my grade, there was a marked increase in the number of shock outfits. Today, of course, no one would blink at the stuff we wore, but then, the scariest outfit we'd seen belonged to Tripp Gardiner, a fifth-grader who always went trick-or-treating with a hollowed-out pumpkin on his head. Every year, the face gouged into the pumpkin got a little less human.

This time, Tripp came to the gym with a hatchet wedged into the top of his pumpkin head. Mrs. Van-Ellis wrenched it out the moment she saw him, but he wasn't the worst, not by a long shot. Jon Goblin— way out of character—came as a crone, with pink slime dribbling down his rubberized lips. And a Chippewa third-grader I barely knew named James Sea came as a wolverine, his body swathed in fur complete with scrapes and bite marks and a mouth full of teeth that may well have been dulled knife blades. Mrs. Jupp actually shuddered when she saw him, reached out to touch the fur, then shook her head and walked away.

She was everywhere that day, directing us, commanding us, attending to us in her Mrs. Jupp way. She almost seemed to know what was coming, as though she could feel it drifting down from the Upper Peninsula. After the costume contest came the habitual warnings. We'd had them before in regular assemblies, but Mrs. Jupp went through her entire list again. Once more, Officer Drum was sent by the Troy Police Department because someone thought his sheer bulk, combined with the scraggle of hair that hung between his massive shoulder blades, might help bad kids identify with him. As always, he warned us to check the packaging on our candy carefully.

"Sealed or no deal," he chanted, and he made us chant it with him a few times.

No one was paying much attention, even when we were chanting, until he stopped suddenly and stood there, staring up and down the rows of children as if he were identifying bodies.

"He's awfully good," Spencer said to Theresa and me, and grinned.

Mrs. Jupp spoke for another fifteen minutes about not taking apples because they might have razor blades in them, but this was unnecessary. Adam Stork, the third-grader who'd been cut by one last year, had peeled back his bandages and shown everybody his tongue.

Theresa was sitting between Spencer and me, but her lone acknowledgment of the holiday was a black and orange hair ribbon instead of her plain black one. She'd said next to nothing the entire morning. Once, while Officer Drum was ranting, I glanced over and saw her sitting up straight on the bleachers, her mouth slightly open, and I started to laugh. I had never in my life seen anyone look so vacant.

"You look like a parking meter," I told her, but she didn't react.

As Mrs. Jupp issued her final instructions, I leaned behind Theresa and asked Spencer, "What are we doing tonight?" I was surprised when he'd invited me over to trick-or-treat. We'd done all of our outside-of-school playing at my house; and among the kids I knew, only Theresa said less about her parents than he did. He talked about his neighborhood all the time, calling it *real Detroit*, whatever that meant, but he never mentioned his parents.

"Air hockey, for one thing," he said.

"Sidecar air hockey?"

He smiled.

"Your mom's not going to try and go trick-or-treating with us, is she?"

Spencer stopped smiling. "She might."

"My mom hasn't gone trick-or-treating with us since I was eight."

"Yeah, well, bully for your mom. Shut up."

"Is your neighborhood dangerous?"

"My neighborhood kicks the crap out of this one."

I was about to ask him if his mother would make us go to bed early when Theresa blinked, tipped back so she was perched between us, and dropped her bombshell.

"I think I'll come," she said.

Neither Spencer nor I understood her at first. We weren't even sure she was talking to us.

"If there's trick-or-treating, I'm coming." This time she smiled and inclined her head a little toward each of us.

Spencer leaned forward abruptly and stuck his face into hers to do what he always did, whenever he had an excuse.

"*Duh*," he said.

No saying or gesture I brought home from school ever annoyed my mother more. I loved it. But one look at Theresa convinced me that it was time to get Spencer's face out of hers, for his own safety. I shoved my hand against his forehead and pushed him back into his own space.

Theresa didn't get annoyed. She blushed. I couldn't remember ever seeing her blush. But she did that day, then narrowed her eyes. I'd never seen her do that before, either.

"I'm sleeping over too. My dad saw your mom driving out—"

"My mom?" said Spencer, skipping past by far the most interesting part of this conversation. I was pretty sure Theresa said she'd be sleeping in the same place that I was tonight. I started to sweat. She was wearing a friendship bracelet on her right wrist; the dark colors in the band emphasized the paleness of her skin.

Theresa was glaring at Spencer. "Your mother's nice," she said.

I still couldn't get past the sleeping arrangements.

We were quiet for a while. Mrs. Jupp was talking about the safe-house hands again. "If anyone, *anyone*, ANYONE comes for you, just run, kids. *Run.*"

"We can play Murder in the Dark," Spencer whispered.

"In the *real* dark," I said.

Theresa had already gone back to staring at something neither one of us could see. But she was smiling faintly, like someone at the rail of a boat drifting toward the open ocean.

At dusk that evening, I knocked on the Daughretys' door. No one answered, so I stood on the stoop in the swirling snow and wondered if Spencer's mother would even let us go outside because of the cold. On the street, little kids were already out in their Spider-Man and

Glinda the Good Witch and Mark Fidrych costumes, with their parents or older brothers trailing behind them. I was still watching them when the door opened behind me.

I turned and stuttered, "Oh, my God," then staggered off the edge of the porch into the pricker bushes.

She was draped in lakeweed, her cheeks whited out with makeup, her lips painted purple. I couldn't decide if it was her costume or her relentless, targetless stare that made her look so convincingly dead. My Mark Fidrych hair had caught on the pricker branches, and some of it came out when I yanked myself free.

"What the hell are you?" I finally managed to say, when I had climbed back onto the porch.

"Drowned girl."

"Why didn't you wear that to school?"

"I wanted to see you fall off the porch."

Behind her, the Doctor appeared, beaming, the way he had after the last Mind War. "Got ya, didn't she?" he said, mussing his daughter's hair, but delicately, like a lady-in-waiting brushing a princess. Somehow, that gesture always felt very different when he did it to me. But Theresa just made a face and became even ghastlier.

Five minutes later, he loaded us into his Jeep, and we sped toward Ferndale with the canvas sides open. I said almost nothing because, without explanation, Theresa had climbed into the backseat and was riding beside me.

One block after we turned off Woodward, the shops and streetlights shed their Corridor sameness and became an actual neighborhood. We passed a record store with a giant black catfish painted on its green awning, and lots of shop windows with the words PAWN, GUNS printed on the glass. The houses looked older than the ones in our suburbs, though not necessarily rattier. Some had uneven porches or yards without grass, but not most. The streets had fewer lights, but the darkness didn't frighten me. From the first frost until April, Detroit was always dark, no matter where you lived.

While Dr. Daughrety slowed to study street signs, I leaned over to Theresa and said, "Tell me about Spencer's mom." I got closer to her than I meant to, almost nudged her ear with my mouth, and a stray hair that had slipped from her black ribbon tickled my cheek. Her only answer was a smile stretching her purple lips.

Dr. Daughrety pulled up in front of a two-story wood-and-brick house with plowed dirt for a yard. The banister railing that ringed the upstairs veranda had warped outward, so the deck resembled a cupped palm. In the yard, strategically placed between mounds of dirt and snow, little Tonka dumpsters and bulldozers sat on their wheels and rusted. They looked hilarious crouching there, as though the enormity of their task had shrunk them. I pointed and laughed. Theresa laughed too. Even Dr. Daughrety smiled, although I wasn't sure he understood what we were laughing about.

Spencer emerged from the house in his Fat Albert costume and red sneakers. His mother was right behind him, and for the second time that evening, speech and breath knotted in my throat and stuck there. She was a tall red-haired woman, too thin. A tall *white* red-haired woman, wearing a strange gold overcoat that flashed like metal.

"Should I get you a coat like that, Thrr-girl?" Dr. Daughrety murmured, more to himself than to his daughter, but he answered Mrs. Franklin's wave with his own.

Theresa was already out of the car, and somehow I'd scrambled out too, although I couldn't remember doing it, sunk as I was in the onrush of my own thoughts. Was Spencer adopted? She looked like him, a lot like him: same smile, same cheekbones, so high they created cavities under her eyes.

The Doctor stopped halfway up the walk to pat Spencer on the shoulder and nod at Mrs. Franklin. "Thanks for having my daughter," he said, sounding like the herald in a King Arthur movie, announcing the arrival of the Queen.

"Thanks for bringing them both," said Mrs. Franklin.

Dr. Daughrety nodded and sketched a wave, then turned to me, and for a single moment I thought he was about to apologize, though I had no idea why. Theresa moved past her father, but the Doctor grabbed her, spun her around, kissed her on the forehead, and touched her paint-swollen lips.

"Be safe, you," he said.

She wriggled free of his hands and marched up the walk into Spencer's house while he stood and watched.

Spencer was a few steps away from me and closing in when I shook myself out of my stupor. I didn't want him to get close enough to do the *duh* thing again, which he was clearly preparing to do.

"I'd have to hit you," I said as he swooped toward my face and stopped. His smile was tentative, not his usual smile at all.

"You coming in?"

"I kind of want to play with those trucks," I said, and he went blank for a second, then remembered the Tonkas and laughed.

"You would."

"Where's your dad?" I asked Spencer, but it was Mrs. Franklin who answered.

"Mattie, I've heard so much about you. Mr. Franklin travels. He won't be here this time, I'm afraid. Come on inside, kids."

Behind us, I heard Dr. Daughrety's Jeep start, and I glanced back and saw him drive off.

"You have a white mom," I whispered.

"And a working fireplace and an air hockey table."

"And a white mom."

"So do you."

For half an hour or so, until it got nighttime-dark, we all played air hockey in Spencer's basement while Mrs. Franklin set up cots and sleeping bags, two at one end of the room, one at the other, and whistled songs I didn't know to herself. She didn't speak to Spencer. He didn't look at her. The air-hockey table made a soothing, breathy sound under the clack of paddles and puck.

Mrs. Franklin disappeared upstairs for a few minutes and came back down wearing the gold overcoat again, plus matching metallic-gold boots and a bright white scarf. Spencer glanced up from the air-hockey game he was losing to Theresa, saw his mother, and groaned.

"At least no one'll notice you, Ma."

I would have laughed if Spencer did, but he wasn't joking. He was angry.

"Just consider it my costume," Mrs. Franklin said, lifting one boot and waving an arm in the air like one of the prize girls on *The Price Is Right*.

"What about the other three hundred and sixty-four days of the year?" Spencer snapped.

"Just imagine how embarrassed you'll be if your weird-dressing mom takes your friends out trick-or-treating and leaves you alone in your room," she said mildly. "I'll be waiting upstairs."

Theresa had plopped herself down on one of the cots, her morbid face blank, even closer to dead under the white makeup.

"Why are you so mean to your mom?" I asked Spencer.

"She bugs me," said Spencer. "Let's go."

We collected paper bags from the kitchen and met Mrs. Franklin by the front door. She didn't speak to us until we'd passed the Tonka trucks and were standing on the sidewalk. Then she touched Spencer's arm and said, "Longview and Pine. Fifteen minutes. Got it?"

"Got it," he said, and raced away down the block.

Theresa and I just stood there, unsure what to do. Mrs. Franklin was gazing into the branches of the frozen oak trees, humming. It seemed to take her a while to notice us. Then she said, "Go on, kids. Just make sure you meet me where I told him."

We'd almost caught up with Spencer when two high school kids in leather jackets and rubber zombie masks jumped out from behind a pine tree and screamed. The effect might have been tremendous, except that one of them got a good look at Theresa as he lunged our way and said, "Jesus Christ, what the fuck is that?"

Spencer had come back for us, and he clapped one of the high school kids on the back. "Hey, Murder," he said.

"Spence," said the zombie, still staring at Theresa. "You got scary-ass friends."

"Don't I know it," he said, preening and jiggling his fake fat around. "We can't stand here talking. We got food to get."

We left the zombies by the pine tree and started down the block. There were fewer red-tape palm prints in the windows here, and fewer trees or expanses of unbroken snow, which meant less whiteness

reflecting the moon. Spencer seemed to know each gaggle of little kids
and every meandering high schooler who passed. Once or twice, he
introduced Theresa and me, but mostly he just tugged us along behind
him. Always, he kept moving. I felt like I was being taken on a hayride
through some haunted country that had proven to be farther from my
own than I'd expected.

At the first house, a scarecrow man sat on the porch under a red
lamp with a candy bowl in his lap. I wasn't sure he was fake until we'd
all cajoled each other close enough to jab our hands into the bowl and
grab a fistful of Three Musketeers, then scramble backward.

We were one minute late getting to the corner of Longview and
Pine, and Spencer's mother was seething. "Corner of Lake and Dry-
den," she said to Spencer. "Fifteen minutes. If you're late, I call the
cops. Got it?"

"That'd embarrass you more than it would me," Spencer said.

"I am no longer capable of being embarrassed," Mrs. Franklin said.

We went on. I had the hum from the air-hockey table in my ears,
the crunch of my boots in the snow, and it felt strange, lonely-strange,
to settle into this new but comfortable rhythm. I was part of a whole
world I knew nothing about, but at least it didn't make me nervous anymore to have more than one friend walking beside me. It was the first
time I had ever wanted to leave home and live somewhere else and
the beginning, I think, of my restlessness. Not the beginning of my
trouble, and certainly not the end, but a resting place, perhaps, a
haven where I felt grounded and safe for a while.

We checked in with Mrs. Franklin two more times. The last place
we stopped was a house without shutters, where cheerful paper skeletons dangled from the porch beams and jerked in the wind, more like
tap dancers than hanged men despite the wire nooses suspending
them. On a rocking chair with one runner sat a pumpkin with a wig
of gray hair and cardboard glasses. Beside it lay an old leather book,
and on its spine was a word I did not know: GRIMOIRE.

Spencer didn't yell trick—or treat—or even ring the doorbell. He just
reached forward, unlatched the door, and yelled "Hey!" into the house.

"Nice," I said.

"Shut up," said Spencer.

I heard footsteps behind us and turned to see Mrs. Franklin step up to the bottom of the porch stairs and wait.

"Hellooo?" Spencer chanted into the open doorway. "Hellaaay?" He was finally acting like the Spencer I knew at school, making exaggerated Fat Albert noises, his laughter radiating all over everything like a searchlight.

The two residents of the house came to the door huddled so close together that they looked attached. They were old, black, wrinkled, without much hair. The hair they had was white.

"Well," the woman said, beaming at Spencer. She picked up something we couldn't see behind the door and held it out in front of her. It was a plate of homemade brownies, still steaming. I smiled, nodded, thought of Adam Stork, took one step backward, brushed one of the paper skeletons, and set it dancing.

"Don't be a baby," said Theresa. She hadn't said a word since we had left Spencer's house, but now she shrugged past me and grabbed a brownie off the plate.

Then Spencer did something I had never in my life felt comfortable doing, even to people related to me. He reached out and stroked Theresa Daughrety on the arm, while she bit into the brownie.

"You'll be eating these," Spencer said to me over his shoulder.

I took one, after tugging off my glove first. The brownie felt like someone's hand, warm and dense and soft when you pressed it.

"Get up here," the woman said. It took me a few seconds to realize that she was talking to Spencer's mother.

"I'm fine, thanks," Mrs. Franklin said behind us.

"She didn't ask how you were," said the man. His voice was mostly a whisper, but it crackled and popped like something wet on fire. "She told you to get up here."

"We'll sic Monster on you," the old woman said. Spencer laughed, and Mrs. Franklin swore. Then she climbed the steps anyway, slid past us, and took a brownie.

"If Monster were home, you wouldn't have said a word to me," she said.

No one spoke for a while. Spencer, Theresa, and I retreated to a dark corner of the porch to watch the street, the snow, and one another.

"Grandparents?" Theresa asked, around a mouthful of brownie.

"Sort of," said Spencer. "They're my father's stepbrother's parents."

I had no idea why, but the peace I'd been feeling all night left me then, as quickly and lightly as a bird lifting off a telephone wire.

"Monster?" I said.

Spencer grinned. "My uncle. My dad's stepbrother. He doesn't like my mom being white. He doesn't like anything. He's pretty cool."

By this time, Mrs. Franklin was talking quietly to the old woman, and her shoulders had slipped down to a more relaxed position under her gold coat.

"Boy," the old woman said suddenly, and Spencer immediately returned to the doorway. I watched the old woman's lips draw all the way flat as she leaned forward to kiss him. Her husband bent in unison, so that both of them were kissing his cheeks simultaneously. "Take the rest of these home," she said, handing him the plate. "And be nice to your mother."

Mrs. Franklin made a snorting sound and started down the steps, shaking snow from her red hair. She reminded me of Ms. Eyre, defiant and sad.

"Maybe next time Monster goes on vacation you can invite us all over for dinner," she said.

"You know that's not fair," the old woman said softly. "Good night, Susan."

"Good night. Come on, kids."

We'd gone maybe five steps when cop cars leapt from the shadows at the end of the street and came squealing toward us. Red and blue flashes of light filled the air like thousands of discolored fireflies. The cars skidded to a stop and then cops were everywhere, yelling at everyone.

"Everybody go home," they shouted, waving nightsticks. "Stay away from the bushes and trees and get inside. Please go home, right away!"

Mrs. Franklin stopped dead and waited for us, then put an arm around Spencer's shoulders.

"Ma'am, get these kids home *now*," said one of the cops. He looked like the Skipper from *Gilligan's Island*, overweight and white and puffy, with red cheeks.

"Why? What's going on?"

"Lions," he said, and ran off.

"I knew it," Mrs. Franklin snapped. "I knew this would happen sooner or later. Goddamn it."

At the Franklin house, we sprawled on the green shag carpet and watched the TV news together in Spencer's living room. On the screen, everyone was hunting for lions. Somehow, three of them had escaped over the Detroit Zoo wall near Spencer's house. The cops had caught one of them right away, but the other two were still out there, slinking through backyards full of swing sets and clotheslines, which must have seemed much more like a jungle than the jungle-style environment the zoo had created for them.

"Oh, my God, that's right outside," Spencer said, and we rushed to the windows to watch the passing camera crews. One cameraman was creeping between the Tonka trucks in Spencer's yard, glancing from his camera to the hedges and the snow-streaked grass. He looked terrified.

Later, when Spencer's mother had gone into the kitchen to get us milk, all three of us snuck to the front door, cracked it open, and, after counting to three, stepped out onto the porch.

"Listen," said Theresa, but all I could hear were power lines humming through the bare trees.

"Get the hell in here," said Mrs. Franklin behind us, and we scurried back inside.

Eventually, we went downstairs and played air hockey and Murder in the Dark. It was well after 1 A.M. when Mrs. Franklin came down with a half-eaten brownie in her hand, wearing a nightdress that flashed like her overcoat, and ordered us to bed. But it was 2:30, according to the flashing digital clock mounted to the wall, before we stopped whispering about the wild beasts lurking in the bushes, sniffing us out. And it was very nearly light when we growled ourselves to sleep in our sleeping bags, listening for the snapping of twigs, the low and feral sounds of a whole city tilting dangerously toward dread.

1994

Three hours have passed since Jon Goblin went home, and I am standing in Shane Park's grove of evergreens where the flying-saucer slide used to be. My fingers have frozen in my pockets, my knees have locked, and my lips have crusted over. If I stay here much longer, some kid will mistake me for a jungle gym and climb me.

It's the kids I've been watching. They race over the snow through the tree shadows, their footprints charting their movements in a frenetic cursive all their own. On benches or beside swing sets, in tiny groups or alone, adults slump in varying attitudes of exhaustion or amusement or, most often, both. Today, at least, in the winter sun, it seems as though Detroit has not carried its Snowman with it, or the failed renaissances, or the plant closings and downsizings, or even the riots. And I am as invisible to the citizens of this place as I am to the gatherers in Mr. Morelli's plaza in the Canaletto painting. But none of that makes what happened here any less disturbing.

Eighteen years ago tomorrow, twelve-year-old Courtney Grieve had a fight with her mother, stalked out the front door, and disappeared into a snowstorm. She was gone for fifteen days, the next to last of which was Christmas. She came back dead, her head laid carefully atop a pillow, her body lying alongside the John Lodge Freeway. So much time was spent discussing the significance of the pillow that no one connected her murder to the disappearances of James Rowan and Jane-Anne Gish the previous winter. Three victims into his spree, the Snowman remained a shadow figure, unrecognized and unnamed.

There would be more victims, at least nine children in all who would have become adults I'd never meet but now feel like my own children instead. They followed me to art school and then to Lexington. They have prowled the periphery of my marriage with their mouths open, as if they're preparing to speak. I am sick of them.

With a grunt I force myself into motion, striding across the square and out of the park toward the Moto-Court. My nose and cheeks are so numb I can barely feel the wind against them. In my coat pockets, my hands lie like dead pigeons against my ribs. It takes me several tries to fumble my key into the lock and open the door to my room. My skin begins stinging as soon as I'm inside, and finally the stinging becomes so fierce that my eyes well up. I don't want to look in the mirror. But when I do, my face is red, not frostbitten, and blinking back at me through a haze of tears.

I sit on the bed and drag the phone book across my lap, flip it open, and scan the page and a half of Daughretys. There are no Theresas listed, but there is one T. The number is in Orchard Lake. I remember going to Orchard Lake once very late on a school night. "Skate-driving, Mattie, watch," my father had said, and spun the steering wheel to the left and then to the right, and the car slid softly from lane to lane. Our destination had been a bookstore called Iris, with giant pupils wearing spectacles painted on the door.

"Ruth?" says a male voice on the other end of the phone, as if it's a password, not a name.

"Hello?"

"Who is this?"

"No one you know, I'm fairly certain," I say. "But maybe you can help. I'm looking for another Daughrety. You are a Daughrety?"

The man doesn't respond, but he doesn't hang up either.

"The Daughretys I need lived near Cider Lake in 1977. A doctor and his daughter."

"Which lake?" says the voice.

My breath stops, starts again. "Cider Lake."

"Sorry," says the man. "I knew a motorcycle mechanic and his two daughters over on Crandall Lake. Big Lions fans."

"Okay," I say, "thanks," and hang up. Part of me feels relieved, which makes me angry.

Just to try it, I dial Theresa's number that I dug out of my mother's old red address book the last time I was at the house. *The number you have reached*, says the icy prerecorded voice of dead ends nationwide, and I put the phone down.

The problem, I have decided, and one of the primary reasons for coming back here, is that none of my stories have endings. Spencer, Theresa, Scuzzie, Laura, the Snowman: all of them just go on wandering through my head, their paths crossing and recrossing; none of them ever lies down to rest.

I remember the day in May 1987, three and a half weeks before graduation, when Scuzzie Li packed up his colors and his box of Daily Racing Forms and left Parsons for good. The furor over my WANTED drawings had long since died down by then, and Scuzzie had returned to his position of prominence, winning the Spring Prize for the third time in our senior year. I, meanwhile, had returned to near anonymity, although everyone treated me differently after my lone artistic awakening. They seemed suspicious, almost, and at first I thought they wondered if I'd stolen my only original idea. But Scuzzie corrected me while writhing on his bed early one morning, in the middle of a free fall from a crystal-meth high.

"They think you're an idea bomb," he muttered. "Tick-tick-tick, go-off, *boom.*"

I didn't see Scuzzie much during those last two years. He continued to eat with me, and he'd drag me off to Aqueduct every now and then. Once, he took me to a café called the O-Mei on Mulberry Street for dim sum, and I learned something about where he got his work habits. The food arrived on carts that never stopped circling the room, piloted by white-robed waitresses whose tiny hands dealt plates of dumplings in a whirl of skin and silk and steam.

But the smile he turned on me when I arrived in his doorway on his last day at school hit me like a blast from a fire hose, obliterating all doubts about his decision to forgo graduation. In all the time we'd spent together, I'd never seen him look so close to happy.

I sat on his bunk and watched him arrange paint tubes in pyramids in a deep square tin box. I'd come to tell him to stay and also, I think, for reassurance that I hadn't let him down. He'd never told me I had, but every time he came to my door, he'd sneak a look over my shoulder to see if the idea bomb had gone off again.

"Final project," he said, wiping his hands on his leather pants. "Don't even know which tube is which." He wasn't quite focusing on me. Whatever he'd shot into his body this time had burned his pupils red.

All the tops had been twisted off the color tubes inside the box. The tubes were pointing in every possible direction like a gnarl of veins in an arthritic hand. The colors inside weren't what the labels said they were anymore. They'd been mixed into Scuzzie's trademark spooky, glowing shades and somehow sucked back into the tubes. Affixed to the lid was a square steel plunger. When the lid shut, I realized, the plunger would crush the tubes.

"The final insult," Scuzzie said.

I sat, trying to make sense of it. "Is that the title?"

"Oh, no, no. I call it, Organ Donor Box. Dedicated to you." He bowed.

I lifted my foot and very nearly kicked it over. I wanted to strap him to his bed and keep him there until he slept. What stopped me was knowing Scuzzie's dreams. He'd been having failure dreams. In one, his father floated over the ocean from China to stare at his paintings and floated away again. He'd been dreaming that, he said, since before he could speak, back when he had nothing but colors sloshing around in his brain. I knew what it was costing him, every day, to stay here. He knew he would never be a significant painter. And I loved him a lot.

I smiled at my friend, then shoved my palm down into the tubes. Paint shot everywhere. I have no idea what he'd done to those tubes, but they exploded, splattering colors all over the box, onto the carpet, into my hair. When I lifted my hand, I saw no palm print, just pieces of fingers and half-joints floating in the glowing muck. Scuzzie hadn't moved to stop me, and he didn't laugh. But he lurched forward when I was finished so we could peer together into the tin.

"Our first collaboration," Scuzzie said, turning his head this way and that before shuffling off in his platform shoes.

When he'd finished packing, locked his room, and gone, I sat on my own bed for hours, watching the water tower on the roof of the building across the street glow red in the sunset. I wasn't thinking about anything except Scuzzie's colors, so I have no idea what drove me to pick up the phone and call the Daughretys' number.

I was hoping to get the Doctor or, better still, a college number for Theresa. I was hoping she had made it to college somehow.

"Hello," said the Doctor, his voice more brittle than I remembered and no friendlier.

"Hello, may I speak to Theresa?" I waited, and when nothing seemed to be happening, I said, "It's Mattie Rhodes."

He said, "I thought it might be," smugly, as if he'd been expecting my call. Never mind that it had been a decade since we'd last spoken.

I was still reeling when he said, "Hold on, Mattie, might as well try it."

He put down the receiver, and I heard nothing else. No background sounds or music or talking or television. I thought of the teeth mask, the Mind Wars, and I very nearly hung up.

"Hello?" said Theresa. Her voice had dropped too, but I would have known it anywhere.

"Did you get my letter?" I said.

"Letter?"

"I sent a letter, maybe two years ago."

"No," she said.

She apparently felt no more surprise at hearing from me than her father had. She wasn't nervous or irritated or anything but blank. She sounded the same way she had on the day she told me about becoming the lake, only even more absent.

"I've been thinking about Murder in the Dark," I told her. I started to say something else, but she stopped me.

"Hey," she said, then sighed. I remember it as mournful, lost, but that could very well have been me.

Without warning, she was gone, and her father got back on. "Not working, is it? Well, it was worth a shot. Thanks for calling, Matt, let us know how you're getting on in the big bright world." The line went dead.

I don't know what it is about that moment that always makes me screw my eyes shut and suck in my cheeks to control my frustration, but I'm doing it again as I suddenly remember what Jon Goblin said about Spencer preaching on Larry Loreno's show. It's time to call East Detroit again.

"Shepherd's answering service," says the woman from last night.

"I'm trying to reach Spencer Franklin."

"The Lord and his Shepherds are always available to those who need them, sir." She sounds calm, patient, like a counselor on a crisis line. I suspect she has been trained.

Swallowing, I say, "That would be me," I tell her.

"You'll find Shepherd Franklin at the church."

"Shepherd Spencer Franklin."

"At the church. I just told you."

"Which church?" And I close my eyes as she directs me south, back down the Woodward Corridor, past Ferndale, toward Highland Park and the First United Church of Flaming Salvation.

1994

Nothing happens when you cross the line. No splatter of graffiti or instantaneous deterioration of buildings alerts you to the fact that, as soon as you cross Eight Mile, you've left the suburbs for the city. But soon afterward, the barbed-wire fencing lining the pedestrian bridges, the flat gray color of the freeway's barrier walls, and the pale winter light combine to make the place feel like a prison, or worse. I turn off Woodward, following directions to the First United Church of Flaming Salvation. More than anything else, at the moment, I feel like a fake: fake friend, fake artist, fake husband, fake human being.

Listening to my tires rolling through the slush, I turn down a street of ruined row houses and then the church blazes out of the night, white and spired and smooth as ice, crowned with orange spotlights, palatial on its manicured lawn. The snow is falling in hard gray flakes. I pull into a parking space under a darkened streetlight between a Cadillac with no wheels and a Mercury with no windshield or seats or anything else.

When I step out of the car, I hear nothing at all. I start forward and slide on the ice. The front steps of the church have been recently salted, and my insufficient walking shoes make crunching sounds. The glass front door glides open, admitting me to a foyer redolent of newly cut wood and central heating. The place smells like a sauna. The door glides shut.

"Now this is what I call Lost," says a voice behind me, and I wheel around, lose my footing, and fall on my ass, and two huge black arms sheathed in tuxedo sleeves jerk me to my feet. My eyes slide up the arms and along the enormous shoulders to my rescuer's face. He has a beard and black eyebrows bent toward each other as if they're conferring.

"Hi," I say, when my lungs have sucked down some room-temperature air.

Past the man who caught me, through two giant oak doors, I see more men in tuxedos, accompanied by women in evening gowns and little kids in dress shirts and tennis shoes. They're milling around a banquet room of circular tables with lacy tablecloths and centerpiece crosses made of red roses twisted together. I am badly underdressed, and there are no white people anywhere.

"Wedding?" I ask.

"You need something?"

"What?"

"You need to tell me what you're doing here," says the man. He's not being hostile, particularly. But he's not kidding either. "Otherwise, I'll boot you back out in the snow. Okay?"

For the first time, I'm beginning to feel the enormity of the task I have undertaken. In addition to wearing the wrong clothes and the wrong skin, I am a thousand miles and two decades and at least one lifetime removed from my current home. I have never had a religion to lose or to find.

"I'm here to see the Shepherd," I say.

The man's arms slip to his sides. "Well, now. Why didn't you say so? Which Shepherd do you mean?"

"Shepherd Franklin."

"Well, now. For Shepherd Franklin, you may have to wait awhile. He's a busy man. But we'll see what we can do."

He guides me to a table in back of the banquet room. The only other person seated there is at least eighty years old and leans crazily out of his wheelchair like a potted plant. He's sound asleep. I can't help it, I'm reminded of the freshman fraternity-rush scene in *Animal House* where Flounder gets dumped in the corner with all the other hopeless cases, and it's all I can do to keep from patting my guide's stomach and beating him to the part where he tells me, "Don't be shy about helping yourself to"—wink-wink—"punch and cookies." Church has never been good for me.

"Just listen awhile," the guide says. "Sometimes, all you need to do is listen."

Soon after he leaves, the music begins, a low rumble that quickly gets louder. Eight black baby grand pianos ring the room, their tops thrown open, the strings inside revving like race-car engines. Two just-out-of-college-aged men are standing before each one—no benches in sight—and pumping the low-octave keys with the reverence of altar boys. Playing the centermost piano are two older women—they must be sisters; they have the same white halo of hair and frowning red-black mouths—in long low-cut, royal-blue gowns.

On some unseen cue, the performers start to sidle, side by side, toward the center of their instruments, climbing the keys toward audible registers. People around me leap up and begin stomping. The grandmothers are first to their feet, the grandkids second, and by the time all eight pianos have burst into a ripping blues-gospel stroll, almost everyone in the room is slamming their shoes into the hardwood, throwing their heads back and clapping their hands.

I, meanwhile, am beset by the old tingling sensation. Some sick part of me longs to start a bunny-hop chain or try to pull out the tablecloth in front of me without upsetting the dishes. I'm not making fun. In fact, I'm more than slightly awed by how blissful most of these people seem. It's just that now I feel even more pathetically lost than I did fifteen minutes ago.

The music goes on, unbroken, for almost an hour, while the heat breaks in waves across the room. The pianos pound, the floor shudders as though everyone is intent on pummeling their way to glory, and right when the music has reached a roiling boil and some of the kids start to droop into their seats—not the grandmothers, not a single one—Spencer Franklin appears in front of the two white-haired sisters, kisses each one on the back of the neck, slams the lid of the centermost baby grand shut, and hops atop it.

The floor shivers beneath me like the deck of a ship about to break apart. "Hello, Spencer," I whisper, to no one at all. None of the people near me hears or looks my way.

He looks thin. Other than that, his face hasn't changed, and the way he bounds around reminds me of his red sneakers, his lightning grin. But his body has grown out of proportion. His shoulders stick out past the ends of his spindly arms, and the legs of his glossy tuxedo pants ripple as he moves, revealing no hint of leg underneath, as though hanging empty on a line. Even from the back of the room, I can see the shine in his eyes. Either he's wearing reflective contact lenses, or he's crying, or he's found something inside him that has lit him on fire.

"I've had a *hard* week!" he roars, in a trained version of his old voice, and the pianos rumble. "*Hard!*" Feet stomp around me so fiercely that the guy in the wheelchair wakes up and sighs before keeling over again. "But I am in church now," Spencer whispers, into no microphone, and somehow it's instantly quiet enough to hear him. "And I feel . . . better."

His lecture feels less like a sermon than a litany, except that he does not mention God. He talks about the day the head Shepherd of this church found him in an alley with a heroin needle halfway through his arm. He talks about sick people who aren't in this room, grieving people who have come for solace, and the heavenly music that can wring all ills from you. I cling to my chair, mesmerized by what he is clearly doing for everyone around me. I don't feel converted. I don't feel welcome. God knows I don't feel saved. But for once I'm increasingly sure that I'm where I need to be at this moment.

For nearly three hours, I sit on my folding chair at the back of the banquet hall of the First United Church of Flaming Salvation. The leaning man next to me awakens only once in all that time, during the most shattering of the twelve-piano interludes, and says "Lord," followed by "Pass the shrimp-a-licks," before he's spirited back to his dreams.

Between long musical intervals, in voices that exert at least as much pull and twice the dynamic range as the clamoring keyboards, various Shepherds rain litanies onto the congregants, who respond by flinging back their chairs, throwing up their hands, and standing, eyes closed, mouths open, as though hoping to catch the holy name on their tongues.

Near the end, a woman, maybe twenty-five, climbs onstage. She is wearing a spangled gown with a plunging neckline. The graying Shepherd who has been testifying for a full twenty minutes stops in mid-metaphor, bows his head, and takes a step backward. The woman approaches the microphone and says, "You know, I was found in a campus dorm room—University of D—and you know that don't mean I was studying there. I was there to sell my body—and not just my body, understand? But when I got into that room, I found *this* man, and don't think I've forgotten, Shepherd Griffith-Rice. Don't think I'll ever forget." Behind her, the Shepherd doesn't raise his head, but he smiles. The woman glances back and grins. "He was wearing full clerical dress, people. I mean, *robes*. And I took one look at him and said, *Oh, no. I don't do no weird virgin shit.*"

People laugh, but not hard. They're too busy yelling encouragement. They aren't tired or bored or even sure of the outcome, but I can tell they've heard this story a thousand times before. They just smile and snack on shrimp-a-licks, as patient and delighted and distracted and peaceful as relatives at a baby-naming.

Four more penitents come to the stage and tell similar tales. Some crack jokes, but most don't. At the part when they "finally felt it," or "touched the Livewire," or, in one case, "realized I had to get up in His great lap and give Jesus Lord a snuggle," the crowd erupts into applause and shouts of *Yes!* and *I know, sweetie,* and the pianos rumble in their low, reckless key.

As the service—or banquet, or party, or whatever this is—reaches its close, everyone stands. The leaning man awakens, shoots his hand across the table, and grips mine as I struggle out of my seat. He grins in his wheelchair, breath reeking of sleep, and when I try to tug my hand free, I feel the straining tendons in his arm, the twist of will and muscle around my wrist like a shackle.

Everyone is holding hands. The pianos are rumbling low and loud; the Shepherds are swaying on the lip of the stage. Spencer is still there, as he has been since the beginning, conducting the pianos louder, then softer, touching the shoulders of congregants, his spiky hair framing his radiant face like rays in a little kid's drawing of the sun. I can't get used to his thinness. He looks like a cartoon image of himself after being squashed by a steamroller.

Still smiling, he moves in front of the centermost piano, where the white-haired women are playing with their heads bent, their skin shimmering with sweat. Closing his eyes, he starts to murmur, and instantly the furor in the room evaporates into silence, and Spencer's voice becomes audible once more. The other Shepherds join him, not singing exactly, but their voices fold over his in complex harmonies, creating a sound as rich and melodious as a tonic chord in a requiem mass. After a long while, in harmony slightly more ragged though no less beautiful, the crowd calls its response.

"Who will it be?" Spencer says, and the Shepherds murmur with him.

The crowd says, "Lord, let it be me."

"Who out there is going to open their hearts to receive their Gift?"

"Lord, let it be me," say the congregants.

"Come out," Spencer says, nowhere near the microphone, but his words fill the room. The Shepherds are still murmuring, but only as accompaniment, like members of a doo-wop group.

"Come home, little darling, come home," Spencer continues.

I don't remember his having a voice like that when we were children. I don't remember knowing anyone with a voice like that, ever.

It swells around its own overtones like a French horn. It doesn't call to me, maybe because I was his friend before any of this and I am still hearing him at eleven, angry and playful and lonely. But it calls to everyone around me, and I am overwhelmed by a sudden need to escape the room, for Spencer's sake as well as my own. I'd do it if it weren't for the leaning man holding my wrist. His arm jerks taut like a guide rope whenever I move, as if he's the only thing anchoring me to the earth.

Ten–fifteen minutes later, the panic subsides, and I very nearly drop to my knees. I'm not sensing the proximity of the Lord. I am just so tired. If I volunteered to receive my Gift, I think blearily, it might get me out of here.

Then I see the woman in the front right corner being led to the stage by a friend. She has tears in her eyes, and the whole crowd is humming its support. Onstage, she stands among the Shepherds, sobbing quietly as they surround her, whispering and touching her gently on the shoulders. She nods and looks comforted and goes on weeping, then leans into the nearest Shepherd, who folds his arms around her. With no more fanfare, everyone drops hands, picks up their coats, gathers their loved ones, and begins to leave.

The piano players stop, stand up, then sag to sitting positions on the stage or climb down to join their families. There is no climactic chord, but one of the white-haired sisters breaks into a few bars of boogie-woogie stomp before letting go of the keys and wiping her sweat-soaked forehead.

The Shepherds come off the stage next, hands extended, and the crowd closes around them. Spencer is the last to step down, and, curiously, almost no one gathers to meet him. They all touch his arm or shake his hand as he strolls by, head lowered. Quite a few say his name. I hear, "Thank you, Shepherd Franklin," and "The Lord loves you so, he loves us for bringing you here," and one fellow Shepherd says, "You fed us our eggs and Jesus tonight, Shep." Then Spencer is level with me, fifteen feet away, heading straight out the door.

Everything in me says to let him go. My leg muscles quiver, my eyes ache, my throat constricts like a wrung sponge. Mostly, I think, I just wanted to see him. I wanted to know he got through, found something. It seems to me that he has. And then, out of nowhere, I see Dr. Daughrety trapped in his car, drifting in the weeds the last seconds of his life, inhaling the lake. And I am staring at Spencer Franklin in the doorway, one long stride from escaping me for good, when he stops abruptly and lifts his head. It's as if he can smell me.

"Go," I try to say, but my voice doesn't sound.

He turns his head and we are face-to-face. Surprise registers, but not enough, and I realize he hasn't recognized me yet. It's just the presence of a white person here, or maybe anyone he doesn't know. He starts toward me. I watch his face reassuming its comforting Shepherd expression. His hand reaches for mine, and then he knows.

"*Fuck* me," he says, and his knees collapse as though the bones have been yanked out of them and he's on the floor, punching the ground once, twice, as dozens of people rush to his aid. "I'm all right," I hear him snapping from the center of the crowd. "I'm okay. Excuse me. I'm fine." He has regained control, and he has scrambled to his feet again, dazed and staring at me through the crowd. No one leaves his side. "Ladies and gentlemen," he says, closing his eyes. He wipes his brow and opens his eyes again. A fair approximation of his radiant smile returns to his face. "I want you all to meet the Devil."

No one even looks at me. Every eye in the place is trained on Spencer, and there is nothing in anyone's expression but concern. I find myself wanting to laugh, although I'm not at all sure that he's joking. Spencer sways from side to side, his skin so slicked with sweat that he looks like an ice sculpture melting in his own light.

"I had to come," I say, and he shakes his head, waves a finger.

"Devil, know your place. Not here. Do you understand? Not here." He's still swaying, but he's also nodding at the people around him, touching their shoulders. "It's okay. He's an old friend. I'll see you all tomorrow, yes?" Meeting each worried glance with a smile and a squeeze of his hand, Spencer steers his parishioners out the oak doors into the night.

The last to go is the man who'd rescued the former prostitute in his clerical robes. He is easily the oldest of the Shepherds, sixty at least, and his jowls lie in uneven folds like sheets on an unmade bed.

"Are you going to be up later?" I hear Spencer ask.

"All night, brother," he says. I keep expecting him to turn on me and stare me down, but he looks only at Spencer. "All night."

Then Spencer and I are alone in the great room. For a while, we just look at each other. He says nothing. I wait, letting him dictate the tone for whatever's to come. After all, I've spent years making the decision to come back here. He deserves at least a few minutes to adjust.

Finally, he reaches out and plucks at my crumpled sleet-streaked overcoat, stares at my jeans. "You are one lost puppy."

I grin. It's him, all right. My Spencer. "Always was."

"Always was," Spencer murmurs, but instead of answering my grin, he squeezes his eyes shut one more time and shudders. Then he waves me out the door.

Rattling home three dead bolts with a long gold key, he directs me toward his waiting Caddy, one of those hideous early eighties Sevilles with the bulge in the trunk. As I climb into the passenger seat, his eyes slide away from mine, and he slips into the driver's side without a word.

We don't speak. Spencer stares out the windshield; then he starts the car and heads down the street, which is already deserted. "Moon," he says, and I remember how surprising it was to see the moon in the middle of winter here. Most nights, the cloud cover locks down like the top of a coffin, and the only light comes from the streetlights reflecting off the snow.

We slip through silent side streets, and gradually the ragged bushes knit themselves into neatly trimmed hedges that line recently shoveled footpaths and driveways. The zoo water tower glows gray-white like a monument to the moon, and I know we're back in Ferndale, not far from Spencer's old house. I recognize the PAWN, GUNS signs in the shop windows and the oak and pine trees on one of the corners where Mrs. Franklin made us meet her on the night of the lions.

"Ah, home," Spencer mutters, and we pull up in front of a low cement building on the corner of a residential street with a lit-up Pabst display in the window. A red neon sign across the entrance identifies it as the Spindle. Red Rolling Stones–style lips pout over the double doors. There is one other car, an anonymous late-seventies Pontiac, in the tiny parking lot.

Inside, oak tables and benches are nailed into the red carpeting like furniture on a ship. A jukebox is playing a Stevie Wonder song to an empty room. Behind the bar, the bartender appears to float on his own rolls of fat like a frog on a lily pad. He nods at Spencer and pours him a plain tonic water, saying, "Evening, Shep." Out of Laura-inspired habit, I order a Rolling Rock, and when the bartender stares at me blankly, I ask for whatever's on tap. He draws a draft and then floats down the bar again.

All the booths along the wall have curtain rods hung above them with red beaded curtains dangling down. Along with our drinks, the bartender hands Spencer a bowl of steaming somethings that look like coals but turn out to be walnuts, grilled almost to ash. I trail him to a table in the back, where he waits for me to sit, then draws the curtains shut around us.

To my astonishment I discover that I'm in tears. There is no particular feeling attached to them, they're just there. "I don't know what this is," I say.

"That's how it hits you sometimes," says Spencer. His fingers dig around in the dark nuts and draw two from the bowl. Shells fall away like snakeskin, and just as I'm about to speak he gets up, throws the curtains to the side, and walks to the jukebox. He drops in some coins, punches a number without consulting the play list, and by the time he returns and draws the curtains once more, The Nightspots' "Down in Downtown" has kicked in. All my life, I have loved the sweet, strutting Motown stomp of that song, and it seems both comforting and strange to be sitting here with Spencer and listening to it now.

A slow smile spreads over my face, and I begin to sing. "'Got those gravy-good women there. Think I'll . . . get me one.'"

"*Crazy*," says Spencer, shelling more walnuts and dropping them in the bowl or on the table without eating them. "*Crazy*-good women. Not *gravy*. Jesus dog."

"Not in my house. That's how my brother Brent used to sing it, so we all sang it that way."

"Your brother Brent," says Spencer. Then, for the first time, he looks right at me, takes in my adult face. Even in this dead light, with no piano rumble beneath him, his eyes flare like raked embers. "Jesus dog. I always knew you'd come."

"You could sound happier about it."

"If I did, I'd be lying."

My stomach twists in its cavity as though it's trying to find its proper place. I am queasy and achy and sad, and sick of being all three.

"I thought it'd be sooner," he says. "For a while, every time I opened the mailbox I expected to see a letter or a postcard. Right until the end of high school, every time the phone rang, I kept thinking it might be you."

"You could have called me, you know."

"Yep." His chin drops to his chest. "There's lots of things either one of us could have done. Look, Mattie—" Then he stops, shakes his head, and smiles for the first time. "Mattie Rhodes. Jesus dog."

"Hi, Spencer."

His smile disappears. "It's not you, understand? The way I'm acting. I don't mean to be nasty. We were what, eleven years old? It's not personal."

I stare at him while he sips his tonic water. He's sweating, seemingly from the effort necessary to stay in this booth with me. There are tears in my eyes again, but this time, they're mostly from frustration.

"Spencer. How the hell could it be anything but personal?"

"You don't know everything," he says. "You don't know anything. You just left."

"I was eleven. I didn't leave. I was taken away."

"Let's talk about something else."

"Like what?" When he doesn't answer, just sits there and shakes, I have to clench my fists in my coat pockets to keep from grabbing one of his wrists; I want to yank him out of wherever he is so we can talk— just talk. But all I can think of to say is "How?"

For a few minutes, we don't talk, just ride the rhythm of another Stevie Wonder song. I sip my beer and think of Louisville and Laura. Both seem like utterly insubstantial fragments of someone else's life.

"When did you start believing?" I ask. "In God, I mean?"

Surprisingly, Spencer is still looking at me. He's still sweating too, but he's not squirming quite so much. "I always did a little, I think. And I'm not sure if what I feel now is belief or gratitude or relief or joy or something else I don't even have a name for. But it is powerful, and it is real, and whatever it is, it gets in my bloodstream like oxygen, and I breathe it, Mattie. I breathe it."

He takes a breath now. Then he continues.

"They found me in an alley, you understand? I had a syringe hanging out of my arm, because I thought maybe a few more drops would dribble out of it eventually. My veins were popping out all over, and my memory was gone. Gone. Nothing."

"Nothing?"

His expression darkens toward outright hostility. "For a brief blissful time, pretty much nothing at all."

"How's your mom?" I ask quickly, hoping to find common ground, the familiarity that came so easily with Jon.

Nothing moves on Spencer's face. He stares at me until I look away, then picks up his paper napkin, unfolds it carefully, and presses it hard over his eyes like a compress. "She has more up days lately," he says, "now that she's back on medication. I have to take her word for it, of course. She doesn't like to see me."

I can feel my cheeks redden, as if I'm facing into a wind. I have spent the better part of my life imagining myself as a sort of Gatsby in reverse. Instead of a mansion and a future, I have clung to a ruin and a past. But it has been my choice, all along. I had the opportunity to leave it all behind, whereas no one who stayed here ever did. Maybe that's why I can't leave this booth. With Spencer here, tabletops and peanut shells and plain everyday survival have a tangible quality all their own. I don't want him more than five feet away from me any time soon.

"I dreamed you, Mattie," Spencer says. "In a heroin dream. You and the Cory twins switched heads a few times, then looked at me and said *Boo* while I just lay against the fender of an abandoned Olds and laughed and laughed."

"I think of them every day," I say. "Courtney Grieve. Peter Slotkin."

"Mattie, for God's sake. Was it necessary, really, to hunt me down and tell me that? You haven't changed at all."

"What do you think I'm doing here, Spencer?"

"That's wha—"

"Do you think I imagined you'd be happy to see me?"

His mouth hangs open, but he doesn't say anything.

"Well, I did," I say suddenly.

He grabs for his tonic water, knocks it over, and spills it across the table. I look at this man who was my first real friend, nervously sopping up water with a napkin. "Spencer. I have a plan."

"Devil," Spencer murmurs. "I need to make a phone call." He gets up and throws open the curtains. He is gone for almost twenty minutes. When he comes back, he slumps into his side of the booth and looks at me for another little while. I wait, patient and determined as a fisherman casting a lure.

"You know what I can't forgive you for?" he says.

Only now do I realize that I'm sweating profusely too. We've been here at least half an hour, and I've yet to shed my coat.

"Go ahead," I say.

"Spoons."

"Spoons?"

"How you can't see yourself reflected right side up in a spoon, no matter which way you turn it. That gave me nightmares for years. I'm not kidding."

I watch his hands rise toward his face, watch him force them back down. I don't remember telling him anything about spoons, but I probably did. So many things I learned when I was a kid stuck in me like shrapnel.

"Spencer, I want to find Theresa. I need your help."

One of his arms flies off the table and stays poised in midair between us, as if he's trying some sort of judo blocking move. After a few seconds, he draws the arm to his chest and says nothing.

"I can't believe I found you. I can't believe you're here. I've missed you."

"Please," says Spencer. His hair has lost its early-evening spike and is beginning to droop. "Please." His eyes flash. The ache inside him is even older than mine, I think. I watch as his shoulders slump and his hands twitch.

"Look," I say. "I don't know about your life, but Theresa is pretty much an adjunct member of my marriage. When Laura and I start to talk about having kids, I see Theresa lying on her back in a snowdrift, staring at nothing. You remember how long she could lie there, as if she didn't even feel the cold? Like she was already frozen?"

"Mattie."

"Or we're eating dinner, having a perfectly normal conversation, and there's Theresa at the end of the table, scrawling answers in the middle of a Mind War. She never looks at me. She never talks to me. But she followed me to college, and she follows me to work and sucks whole hours out of my life, and I don't even feel them go. I tell Laura the story over and over and she just plays her banjo and listens, sort of, but she's heard it before, and she doesn't understand—how could she?—and sometimes she'll ask why I spend so much more time day-dreaming ghosts than talking to her, and I have no answer. I don't want to lose my wife, Spencer. I'm tired of losing people."

"Wife," says Spencer. "Someone actually married you?"

I smile a little. "Yep."

"What does she do?"

"She's a bluegrass musician, if you can believe it. How about you?"

Spencer rolls walnut skins in his fingers, looks at the table. "No," he says.

"Girlfriend? I guess I figured that's who you called before."

"I called Shepherd Griffith-Rice. The guy I was talking to right before we left the church."

"The one who rescued the prostitute?" I ask, and he winces.

"Rescued the woman from prostitution. Better, no?" He glares at me for a second, then drops his eyes. "He's been my mentor for years. He taught me how to get over people like you. Days like this. You don't go back, Mattie. You don't relive. You say your apologies and mean them. You let your regrets hammer at you until they've exhausted themselves. And then you fill up your days with activities that help people. And after a long time, you don't mind the dead moments so much."

The jukebox has gone silent. No glasses clink, and no one speaks. I watch Spencer stare at the booth cushion behind me, and his eyes well up.

"You said you don't mind the dead moments," I say, trying to communicate my affection without launching him out of the booth. "That means you still have them."

"Everyone has dead moments."

"I don't think everyone sinks into them the way we do. At least, not without waving their arms and calling for help and getting pissed off about it."

"Mattie, we can't go find her."

"Why not? Maybe then you could sleep."

"We can't, Mattie," he whispers. "I can't. You don't want to see her, even if you could. Trust me. Please. I am praying here. I'm praying to God, and I'm praying to you, if that works. Leave it be."

I can feel him giving way in our unspoken tug-of-war. One more good pull might just do it. "Did you know the Doctor died? Drove himself into Cider Lake, and drowned."

At first, Spencer continues to stare at the cushion behind me. Soon, though, his head starts to swing back and forth, and his eyes close. "I did not know that," he says. For a second, I think he's lying, but I dismiss the idea. Why would he bother?

"Jon Goblin told me this morning."

"Jon Goblin," he says, as if he has swallowed a stone. "You rousted him too?"

"He didn't seem to mind. In fact, he seemed perfectly happy to see me."

"How lovely for you both."

"He's a sweet guy. He walks with a cane now. He broke his leg falling out of a tree. He married Corrinne Kelly-Dade—the ice-skater, remember? They have a six-year-old son. He became an electrician and refers to himself as Mr. Alight. How Jon is that?" Spencer nods dully, makes a sort of groaning sound. "Spencer, let's say we find Theresa. What's the worst thing you could imagine? If she's in trouble or she's still screwed up, maybe we can help her. Maybe we're the only ones who can."

Spencer's eyes grab mine. Both of his hands drop flat on the tabletop and twitch. He really is terribly thin; his cheekbones protrude like the tops of cliffs.

"You've got guts, Mattie," he whispers. "You always did." He picks up a spoon and stares into it. "You want to know what you've done? You want to *know* it rather than just daydream it? Well, sir." He pauses a moment. Mock-dramatic effect. "This is your life. Not mine anymore, just yours. I know more than I ever wanted to know already." He makes that sound again, like a fluorescent light buzzing, and something in his eyes goes blank before flickering back to life. "I saw her once."

His voice is almost a growl, and he bursts into a cough. A premonition trickles down the back of my throat, a physical thing, icy cold.

"Should I be lying down for this?" I ask.

"I don't know." Spencer shakes his head. "I've never told anyone about this. Of course, there wasn't any goddamn reason to tell anyone before. You're the only one still stupid or lost enough to ask. So just sit there and listen. I am the Ghost of Christmas Fucked, and what I'm going to tell you will hurt, and there's not a thing in this world that can change it. Try to understand. You might save yourself and, more importantly, the people you say you care so much about, some very real pain and truly horrendous dreams."

I can almost hear pianos rumbling beneath him.

"I want you to picture my house, Mattie. My mom's house, I mean. See it? The little Tonka trucks in the yard? They're still there. Those old yellow curtains with the cigarette burns from whoever owned the house before us? They're still there too. My mother is at work. My father is long, long gone. He abandoned us right about the time you did."

I let that go. I'm too busy seeing Spencer's house. I can smell it, too—a faint but permanent burnt-popcorn smell. Not quite enough light ever came through those curtains.

"I was eighteen, maybe. Nineteen? The beginning of the real bad time." He's clenching shells in his hand, breathing hard. "That's a lie. I was well into the bad time by then. I'd already discovered needles. I'd already stolen every last dime of my mother's emergency money out of the sock hamper in the attic, though she didn't know it was gone, at this point. On the afternoon you've come all this way to hear about, I had a needle in my arm. I was pushing the junk in real slow. You do it right, you can actually feel it bloom in your vein. I was staring through the yellow curtains at the snow. It was midday, middle of the week, and magnificently silent. Not a soul moving out there. Then I heard a knock on the door. Not hard."

He taps the table with his fist and goes silent again. But with the rap of his hand, every bone in my body freezes, as if I've been dropped in dry ice. Tiny fissures open at the joints and trace down muscles and arteries. If Spencer tapped on me now, he could shatter me like glass.

I know that knock. But I never told him about it. I never told my wife, or my parents, or the police, or anyone else. In fact, I had blocked it out of my conscious life until now. Spencer drops his fist on the table again, just as lightly, and I rattle in my seat.

"That tap came six, seven, fifty times, how would I know? I was just sitting there, feeding the need, sucking in the silence. Finally, slowly, because that's how everything happens when the H is in you, I become aware that I'm annoyed. Another six, seven, fifty knocks and I realize why. I ease the needle out of my arm, so I can see the skin and vein pucker. That pucker's as pleasurable as breaking the skin on new peanut butter, man; I almost suggest you try it sometime. So I float to the door. I find the doorknob and it feels wrong, too small. I can't get a grip, and I almost fall over when I turn it. But I do. And the door opens. I see my yard and the new snow. And there she is."

He goes quiet, and it seems like the silence of his house has slipped out of the story and into this room.

"She looks . . . a little different." The words come out in clumps, as though Spencer is having trouble getting them through his teeth. "She's wearing a shiny skirt. Satin, something, like she's been to a ball, except she's also wearing a T-shirt that says REST AND YOU SHALL RECEIVE. She has on sneakers with no socks, and that's it. No jacket, no gloves, nothing. It's pouring down snow, and she is completely oblivious. Her hair is long and straight, and there's a lot of it. *Tonic!*" he shouts abruptly. "And put some damn gin in it. Matter of fact, hold the tonic."

Startled, I watch Spencer stare at the table, his shoulders shaking, his skin soaked. After a long time, so long that I start to wonder if the world might be gone out there, the curtains ripple, then part, and the face of the enormous bartender floats through the opening.

"You say something, Shep?" he says.

With an effort, Spencer shakes his head. "Just talking to the Big Bartender in the sky." After five or six long breaths, he musters a smile.

"He's got what you need," says the frog-shaped man, nodding.

"Yeah, but He's stingy with it sometimes. Go on, now."

The curtains ripple again as the bartender leaves. For a while, Spencer and I look at each other. What I'm seeing, mostly, is Theresa at his front door, her long hair shrouding her face like fronds from a weeping willow. I see her in her drowned-girl costume. Eventually, I ask, "You don't drink?"

Spencer sighs. "I'm not allowed to have any addictions whatsoever. I won't allow it. And you're not allowed to talk again until I'm done. No matter what I say, don't say a word. I'm only doing this once. And it's the last time, ever, until the Accounting."

"The Ac—"

"Judgment Day. Shut up."

Without warning, his whole body jerks, as if he has just been defibrillated. But his face stays expressionless, and his eyes stay on me.

"*It'll be all right*," he says, and I can't tell if he's talking to me or himself or just repeating a mantra he has used before.

"That's what I've been trying to—"

"Not you. It will never be all right for you, not in the way you want. *It'll be all right* is what Theresa said when she walked through the door. And I told you not to talk, by the way."

I don't talk. I barely even breathe.

"She brushed so close that in the state I was in, I half thought she'd walked through me. One of us, I remember thinking, is a ghost, and I was standing there in the open doorway trying to figure out which one when I noticed her hand grabbing mine around the fingers and pinching like a crab claw.

"By that time, I was pretty sure she was the ghost, because she was so cold she might as well have walked to my house from Troy. Only it wasn't a house anymore, it was a cave I'd crawled into to hibernate, and now I was being disturbed. I had this single moment of panic, and I think I even managed to stiffen at least one of my legs and slow our progress away from the open door, but the H won, and I got passive. The H told me this was a vision, maybe even an interesting one. That was comfort enough for me."

For the first time, self-reproach has crept into Spencer's speech cadence. I recognize it instantly—it's an old friend—but where mine is a steady throb, his comes in quick vicious strokes, leaving bloody welts in his sentences and making him gasp.

"'I'm cold,' she tells me. 'Can you make tea?'"

"I stand next to her and think about that awhile, and then I say, 'I can make water hot.' I remember this so clearly, Mattie. Because I was watching it, see? Like a movie. It wasn't me in it.

"We go in the kitchen, me and Theresa Fucking Daughrety, and I'm concentrating on my task, and she's floating around to the table and the windows, rubbing her arms, looking at the snow. 'Lions,' she says, and I nod at her, and she goes on anyway. 'I remember standing next to you and looking out this window for lions, just like this.' Then she nods and sits down in one of our kitchen chairs. White plastic, red vinyl seat cushions, a little ripped and moldy. I give her a cup of hot water and she wraps her hands around it, puts her face over it, and I sit down next to her and watch her cheeks turn red. Then the whole kitchen goes a little red, to me, as if I'm looking through a filter, or bloody water, but it's not scary, just red. And sad.

"'I've been gone,' she says, looking at me through the steam.

"'Welcome home,' I say, fascinated by her face and not thinking anything.

"'I can't . . .' She's clasping the cup like it's one of those heart pillows people pass around in high school psych classes that give them permission to talk. The effect is intensified by the fact that she has started crying. 'I can't get used . . . to rooms. Spencer.'

"The sound of my name is like a punch in the chest. It doesn't wake me or pull me out of my stupor, it just makes everything ripple. It wrecks the high. The smooth. Whatever you want to call it. The question I should be asking does occur to me—I remember thinking about asking it—but it's easier to let her lead. If she leaves my name alone, I can just float in her wake.

"For a while she doesn't say anything, just sits there red and crying, and now the silence is starting to bug me, because she's in it, like a faucet-drip. So I ask, 'That water warm enough?'

"Theresa looks at me, and then she starts murmuring, real fast, and that's better, kind of soothing. 'Sea of Vapors,' she says. 'Sea of Serenity. Sea of Cold. Sea of Rains.' Lots of other seas.

"It occurs to me, after a while, to interrupt. 'They don't have rooms, where you've been?' And that shuts her up for a while. The water, I think, is not going to warm her hands, and she's not drinking it, so it's not going to warm her mouth or heart or stomach. I think she should make better use of it.

"'They had . . . beds. They had areas. With TVs in them. And Yahtzee. I'm good at Yahtzee.'

"'What does that mean?'

"'Choosing well,' Theresa says. 'It's about choices.' And then she just up and tells me about the years since I've seen her. Just lays them in front of me, like a fabric salesman. Cool as you please. For the first few months, I guess, afterward—after you were gone—her father wouldn't let her go anywhere. She doesn't remember this, understand; she remembers getting lost in windows and rug patterns, and then becoming aware that she was screaming. She remembers Barbara Fox making her apple tea. She remembers running all the way to Cider Lake one late-summer night and swimming out to the raft in her pajamas and standing there rocking and waving her arms in the air and seeing a catfish in the water. Then she went to the place with no rooms, and she stayed there seven years. Then she came home. Then she came to my house."

In the dim bar light, with the curtains drawn, I can't tell if Spencer's face is soaked in sweat or tears or both. I only know his hands root furiously in the bowl of walnuts but find only shed skin, and he can't seem to get his mouth around the air anymore; I can almost see it whistling past him, through him, as though he were a cave. I also know my own hands are clenched so hard under my knees that my elbows and shoulders ache, the way they do after a tetanus shot.

"What was the Seas thing?" I finally ask, when the silence has gone on too long.

Spencer snatches a breath, closes his mouth and his eyes, and for a second he looks almost grateful, or at least relieved. "She told me that," he says. "Can't tell you when. Sometime that afternoon. It's a technique they gave her: listing things. She said it works like an anchor. You drop a chain of things you know, related things, and it helps keep you where you are."

"Spencer, please. I don't understand. Was she all right? Was she . . . herself?" Even as I ask that, I decide it's a stupid question. How would either of us know?

His eyes open, and I can't help it: I jam myself back against the padded wall of the booth. The panic and remorse I see there are no longer familiar, no longer like mine. They drill straight down into him, all the way through him, cold and blue and permanent like a millwell on a glacier. "At some point," he says, "somehow, don't ask me how, we wound up in the basement."

His voice goes quiet, and there are definitely tears in his eyes now, and he's bobbing up and down on his seat as if he can't get warm.

"What I remember is her sitting on the air-hockey table. At some point one of us must have switched it on, because I could feel the fan underneath us. I imagined it lifting us like a magic carpet. *Table*, I remember thinking, *take us elsewhere*. But it stayed in the room. Names of things were spooling out of Theresa: kings of England, tropical fruits. She just kept tossing them overboard, but I don't think they were catching on anything, because I could feel her going rigid beside me, arms gripping the table, voice turning all breathy. Then she went completely quiet for a while.

"That quiet, Mattie. Of course, in my then-current state, all I could think was, 'Thank God. Just stop babbling.' And for a long time—so long I think I forgot she was there—she did. We just floated, aimless as the snowflakes outside. Nowhere to go but to ground. Nothing to do but land and melt. It was perfect peace, brother. As in perfect emptiness. Then she grabbed me."

One more time, Spencer goes quiet, but I don't interrupt him now. When he starts speaking again, it's as if he's talking through a phone with a faulty connection, though I can't tell if the problem is with his voice or my hearing.

"'The problem is,' she says, 'I can't make it stop.' She's holding me tight around the elbow, staring into my ear like it's a crystal ball or something, and I can't seem to get my head turned to look at her. But right then—for the first time—the smooth cracks. Like a shell, understand? No choice now but to poke my head out. Because it's Theresa Daughrety next to me, and I can feel her all over my skin, like frozen sunlight. I know you know what being near her feels like. 'I can't,' she says. 'It won't. *It'll be all right*, but it won't. Do you see?'

"I don't, obviously. But I tell her I do. That turns out to be a bad move. She starts talking faster, chanting it like a mantra, but even iced up as I am, I know this is no tool they've given her in the place without rooms. This is the real bad shit. 'It doesn't stop. They say he will, they say he does, they say it's me, but it can't stop, it won't, it can't, it won't, it can't,' and she goes on like that for God knows how long. Ten minutes? Twenty? Two hours? I can't feel time, just the heaviness in my veins and Theresa's hands around my arm and the fan underneath us that won't lift us up, and finally—"

Suddenly, surprisingly, Spencer 's eyes drop directly onto mine, and I see the panic still raging in them, and something new too.

"Mattie," he says. "maybe you *are* the person to tell about this. Maybe you're the only one who could possibly understand. Because you know what it's like to want to help that person that badly. Remember?"

The ferocity of his stare is searing; I can't quite hold it. But for the first time all night, Spencer is talking to me as if we were friends. As if we still might be, someday. I don't know whether to be terrified of what's coming—what's past—or grateful for what is.

"What do you think I'm doing here?" I say.

For a few seconds longer, Spencer holds my gaze. Then he drops his head back against the booth padding, takes a last long breath. "All I was thinking," he says, "all I could think of to do, was make the chanting stop. Push whatever it was that had surfaced back down where it could be managed or ignored. And I'd found such a grand, gorgeously effective way to do that. Do you understand?"

"Uh-oh," I say.

"We were practically sitting on top of it: my stuff. It was like fate. 'Just wait there,' I told her, while she went on chanting about stopping, not stopping, he does, he can't, it won't. I dropped under the table, unfixed the fan cover, dragged out my little bag of junk, my spoons and lighter and my nice sort-of-sterile needles I'd gotten from my source—my uncle Monster, my dad's brother, you ever meet him?—and went to work. Got everything ready. When I was done, I got out my black rubber tubing, and then I stood up, right in front of her, and I grabbed her hands, and she said, 'It won't stop,' one last time and went quiet. I looked into her eyes, and it was the old awful feeling, Mattie. That sixth-grade feeling. Because I couldn't tell if she was even in there.

"'It might not,' I told her, 'but it might sleep.' And then—I have never done anything, kissed a cross, cuddled a puppy, anything, as gently as I did this—I slid the tubing around Theresa's arm. It was so pale, Mattie. So thin. Jesus dog. Like a cricket wing. She was weeping. Her veins came right up. 'There you are,' I said. 'Hello, Theresa. I've missed you.'

"I was even gentler with the needle. I swear to God, I don't think either one of us even felt it go in. I saw her eyes widen as the H bloomed. Then I was so tired I just sat down on the floor.

"That blissful silence. . . . It lasted I don't know how long. Awhile. I was floating along the walls, man, out into the snow, back again. But when I drifted down into myself, plugged in my ears like headphones, I finally began to realize just how wrong I'd been."

On the table between us, Spencer's hands fall open, and his head tilts to the side, as though there's a weight attached to it. "Oh, Mattie. That sound. Like a kitten, mewling. Like something run over. There weren't any words in it for a while, or maybe I was too bleary to make them out. Then there were words. *It'll be all right.* Over and over, like someone dying, just easing themselves right out of the world. I staggered upright, and the heroin dropped out of me. I felt so naked and cold and terrified. Theresa was bolt upright on the table with her legs kicked straight in front of her, and she just kept saying that. *'It'll be all right. It'll be all right.'* And then . . . and then, and then, and then. . . .

"The first seizure hit her like a wave in the air, just slammed into her, and she lifted up on her hands and twisted and her hair flew out, all wild, and then she folded down and started shaking. 'Jesus Christ, Theresa,' I said, and I flew up the stairs for blankets and came back down, and she wasn't speaking anymore, just mewling, and after a while she wasn't doing that either. She'd go still for a few seconds, as much as a minute, before the next seizure hit her. Her lips kept flapping as if something was strumming them, and her eyes went crazy, spinning all around; it was like a cartoon. I didn't know what to do, and I couldn't get it to stop, and this went on forever.

"It was so bad, Mattie, so terrifying, that I swear to you I don't even remember my mom coming home. I just noticed, after a while, that she was beside me, crushing Theresa against her and rubbing her up and down and telling me to get hot water and not looking at me. Upstairs, waiting for our dented metal kettle to boil again, I noticed it had gone dark outside. You remembered wrong, Theresa, I was thinking. *This* is when we looked for lions. In the dark. When they were really there and we couldn't see them.

"Then we were at the front door. My mother with that stupid gold coat, not even shiny anymore, wrapped around Theresa, who wasn't really walking. 'You understand, Spencer,' my mother told me, 'you may wind up in jail. He'll press charges.'

"I just stared at her. I wasn't high anymore. I wasn't anything. 'The Doctor?' I finally said. 'You don't have to tell him.'

"My mother stared back, and her mouth opened, and for the first time she was crying. At least, I noticed it for the first time. 'Yes, I do,' she said. 'I can't stand this right now. Don't be here when I get home.'

"They were halfway to her car when it occurred to me to lean out the door and ask, 'Do you mean ever?'

"And my mother turned around. The color in her hair was too cranberry once she started dyeing it. She never could get it right. She was shivering in her too-thin sweater as she held Theresa. 'I don't know, Spencer. I don't know.' And that was the last I saw of her, or anyone else I knew, for roughly six years."

With a slap of the tabletop, Spencer flees the booth, and I hear him banging between tables through the bar. I don't chase him. The blood, it seems, has frozen in my chest. I can see them, Mrs. Franklin and Theresa, pulling out of that yard, through the whistling snow. The black ribbon in Theresa's hair shakes when she does. I can see Spencer in his socks on his porch, screen door pushed open, freezing air swirling around his feet. It's like the film's stuck. That scene just keeps repeating. Spencer and me in doorways, Theresa wrecked and hurtling away.

A long time goes by, enough for me to wonder if Spencer has left me here, with no way back to my car, no clear idea of where I am. I haven't heard any noise beyond the curtain in quite some time, so maybe the bartender has gone too. If I'm alone, I am thinking, I might just lie down on this bench booth and spend the night here. The effort of throwing that curtain back, finding a phone, dialing information, calling a cab, describing where my car might be, retreating to the hotel, all the simple actions of coordinate location and signal emission that those of us who don't rely on banks of memorized names of things use to maintain the illusion of a place in the world, seems too much to manage.

I am picturing both my friends lifted off the ground by the swirling snow, gently shaken apart by the relentless wind, and scattered amid the Tonka trucks and frozen dirt of Spencer's parents' front yard. I hate that it happened, and I hate that I wasn't there for it, wasn't a part of it, which just makes me feel sicker, even more screwed up than I generally do.

The curtain slides back, and Spencer slips into his seat across from me. His eyes are dry, flat, his skin wiped clean of tears. He has left the curtain open, and I can see the red room, the stools stacked upside down on top of tables, the jukebox dark.

"Now, of course, you see, right, Devil?" Spencer says.

I look at him and say nothing.

"You see why we can't go after her. Why we need to leave her be."

"I don't understand this, Spencer," I tell him. I don't want to fight or rouse his anger. But his attitude baffles and infuriates me. "Your story only makes me want to find her more. And it doesn't explain why you don't."

"That's because you're one dense narcissistic pup."

"What if she needs us? What if she needs to find us too, but she's not capable of it? She doesn't even have the Doctor anymore, and God knows what family she had in Cleveland, or where Barbara Fox went. Jon Goblin said Barbara hasn't been seen by anyone he knows since the Doctor's memorial service. He thinks she may have gone back to Africa or something. And that means we could be the last two people in this world who actually know her."

"Ah. So you feel we know her, Mattie. That all the positive effects we have had on her life give us some sort of propriety, or at least unique insight."

"We know what happened to her."

"We do?"

I feel myself flush. Pretty soon, I'm going to start screaming. "We know she was gone. We know she came back. We know that while she was away, she must have . . ."

"Right," Spencer says, letting the long silence linger.

My hands clench on the table. "Come on. She had to have been there, right? Probably, she had to have been. You've thought about it, don't tell me you haven't. She had to have seen. And even if she wasn't actually with him, didn't see anything, whatever she went through changed her forever, and it—"

"How do you know?" says Spencer, his voice low, determined, like a motor left running so it won't freeze. "You haven't seen her since the day she came back. Am I wrong?"

"I—"

"Am I wrong?" He doesn't wait for my answer. "You don't know what happened, because no one does. You don't know she's different, because you don't even know where she is. And if you remember, neither of us exactly understood what was going on with her even before it happened. Not for lack of trying, I'll grant you. But we didn't, Mattie. And it's too late now."

"What if she needs us?" I find myself saying again, because I can't think of anything else, and because I want to stop talking about where Theresa went before she returned, because I'm not ready to face it again. Not while I'm awake. I face it too damn much in my sleep as it is.

"You're not here for her," says Spencer. "You're not doing this for her."

I put my hand up, nod my acceptance, and then stop with my mouth halfway around the words. I think about it, then say, "I'm here for me. Of course I am. Is that what you're waiting for me to say? You're the public servant now, but I'm the same old selfish bastard? Okay. But I'm also here for my wife, my parents, maybe my brother, and the Foxes, Theresa, for sure. You, for sure. Plus Amy Ardell, the Cory twins, and James Sea."

"Don't you say that name. I don't want to hear it from you. As a matter of fact, get up; I want to take you home now."

Before I can argue, he's out of the booth, dropping a twenty on the table. The bartender, I sense, has gone. The Marlboro clock above the bar reads two-twenty.

In Spencer's car, with the heater gushing and the headlights drilling into a city dark more total than any rural emptiness I've found in Kentucky, Spencer's story wriggles around like some hideous new fish in my internal aquarium of horrors. I let it settle, circulate. Spencer says nothing, just shivers a lot, and because he's so gaunt, I keep expecting him to rattle like a maraca. But he also looks young, despite the thinness and the obvious wear in his face, the surprising gray along his temples.

To my amazement, I realize that not everything I'm feeling at the moment is bad. In my own only slightly mythologized nightmare, it has always been the events of that one Detroit winter that cast me adrift, left me frozen and bewildered in a relentless private snow. But now, I'm not so sure. Maybe the Snowman isn't what blocked me from life; in a way, he is the force that sucked me into it. He was, along with everything else, the first experience I was ever sure I shared. I shared it with this man, who won't look at me and who may never want to see me again. We share him still.

"Spencer—" I find myself saying as we turn by the church, and then I stop because I'm not sure what he's willing to hear. I point to my car, and he brakes beside it but leaves the engine running. We sit, and I stare at the dark houses and make myself wait. The house nearest the car has no windows, just cardboard and black tape in the empty spaces.

"You're easy to be friends with, Mattie," Spencer says, and his majestic voice softens. "You're smart. You're relatively insightful. You mean well, genuinely seem to mean well, and that turns out to be a rare and extremely seductive quality."

"Does that mean you'll come with me tomorrow?"

"It means get out of my car." He punches a button, and the locks spring open. "Get out, and don't ever come back. For your own sake, and if that's not enough inducement, then for mine. I want my life the way it is. I want the people in it, and the community I've joined. I want the little bit of God I can taste, because sometimes, Mattie, I really can taste Him. And if that's still not enough, how about for her sake?"

"What do you mean?" I say steadily. When he doesn't respond, I feel a rising desperation that should, it seems to me, have more anger in it than it does. "You can't disconnect from me that easily. And neither one of us is ever going to disconnect from her, and you know it. Maybe, if we help her, you'll even feel like you deserve what you have. You don't seem to feel that way now."

"Get out," Spencer whispers, and then sits with his mouth gulping at nothing. I don't move. After a long while, the gulping slows, and his shoulders sag. The tears are back in his eyes, but there's also a bent little smile on his face. It's very nearly the sidecarring smile. We really were, for that one year, tremendously good friends. "Mattie. You idiot. You poor misguided soul. Don't you see? There are two possibilities. Either she's safe somewhere, and better; her dad and Barbara dried her out, and she spent a few more years listing phyla of extinct fish and candy bars that start with *c*, and then she got free one day and she's somewhere else now—Boston, maybe—watching the snow out her window and thinking about cleaning she needs to pick up and living a real live life. Or"—he looks at me, and I can't bear it, the tears in there, the still-flickering fire of the boy I knew, for not even one year— "or she's somewhere with no rooms. Either way, Mattie. Either way. Think of what both of us must represent to her."

Through my own tears, I see him lean his face into the nearest vent, bathing in the dusty horrible heat. I resist the impulse to touch his shoulder or do the same thing, out of solidarity, contrition, something. "The thing is, Spencer," I say, "I don't know what I represent to her. I never knew. I admit it. You might be right, completely; we could be the monsters in her memory. But we could also be the only people left on this earth who are still out hunting for her, calling her name."

"We were never that, Mattie. Don't you see? We thought we were. We told ourselves we were. That's how it happened. I will never let it happen again. Never. So the answer is no, my old friend. My most dangerous companion. I will not help you. I will not come with you. I will not even wish you well."

"Great to see you too," I say, and kick the passenger door open. The cold is a fanged thing and rips at my face.

"I didn't say it was bad to see you," I hear Spencer murmur, and when I turn around, he's looking at me, mouth pursed, eyes still wet. "Not all bad. God, Mattie, I can see him. I see him floating in his car in that goddamn lake—with his eyes open. . . ."

"Me too," I say, as gently as I can. "And I imagine Theresa sitting at some window—"

"Stop, okay? Just stop. Please. Let it go." He squeezes his eyes closed, drawing more tears. When he opens them again, he is looking straight through the windshield.

"You're sure?"

He shakes his head, holds his breath, and lets it out slow and even. "I'm sure of nothing, Mattie. Except that I'm still here. That some days I do some good for some real live people. As for Theresa Daughrety . . . I just can't afford the risk. Neither of us can."

1977

He came to us through the air vents in my parents' home. Between bursts of heat, we could hear my father and mother talking, the TV turned low, the wind whistling through the icicles. All of them were saying his name. At Stroh's Ice Cream one Saturday night, Brent and my mother and I sat silently over hot-fudge sundaes and listened to two bald men in matching M GO BLUE! jackets arguing.

"He takes them downtown," the one closer to us said, and sucked up a mouthful of chocolate malt with an audible slurp. "Bet you. There's so many abandoned buildings down there, he could have his pick. He keeps them there until he's bored, and then that's it. He kills them."

"But what does he do with them for two weeks?" said the other. "Challenge them at checkers? Take them for riverfront strolls?"

They went on like that awhile, but I stopped listening. By now, speculation about the Snowman seemed routine, as familiar a thread in the conversations around me as cursing the Lions or Jimmy Carter peanut jokes.

Amy Ardell, the Snowman's fourth victim, was found on Cavanaugh Lane near the Oakland Park Cider Mill, ten minutes from where we lived. He'd laid her in the snow on a city councilman's lawn with her clothes freshly washed and her coat zipped. I used to lie in bed wondering why he took such care and somehow came to the conclusion that he was protecting whatever remained in her body after it died. Keeping it warm.

This was mid-January. The weekend afterward, Spencer came to my house to sleep over. Theresa came too, and she was supposed to stay late, but right after dinner Dr. Daughrety called and demanded that she come home.

"Of course," my mother kept saying into the phone, her hands in her yellow rubber dishwashing gloves, her hair creeping toward gray as the latest dye treatment faded. Her cocked hip brushed against my father's where he stood, utterly still, his eyes on his reflection in the window or the dark beyond, one hand wrapping and unwrapping a dish towel around a fistful of forks. By the time my mother hung up, Theresa had already gone into the laundry room for her jacket. She had the back door open before my mother bolted to stop her.

"You can't walk home alone," she said sharply. Then she held Theresa tight while my father dressed. Spencer and I dressed too.

"Take the car," my mother said.

"What'd he say?" my father asked as he pulled on his gloves and the pom-pommed Red Wings hat that made him look like such a dork.

My mother shrugged. "I wouldn't want my daughter anywhere but home right now, either. Don't let her wander off, okay? Joe?"

My father was wearing his dazed expression again.

"Joe? Take the car."

Instead, we walked down the driveway, out of range of our front-porch light into the night. My father and Theresa took the lead while Spencer and I lingered a few steps behind. At the bottom of the drive, Spencer darted into a ditch for a snowball, and my father snapped, "Hey. Get back here." The snap, coming from him, yanked Spencer right back into line beside me. We did not look at each other. We watched the dark places in the empty yards and listened. Pine trees bobbed on their own shadows like buoys. Snow wraiths rose from the drifts, herding us along the frozen center of the street. The houses seemed oddly unmoored and uninhabited, drifting with their windows lit but no one visible inside.

In the Fox house, a television was playing to an empty room, and the loneliness there started to crawl up my back. I almost yelled for Barbara, but my father glanced hard at me and I stayed quiet.

"Leave them alone," he said.

"I can go from here," Theresa announced when we reached the shortcut through her neighbor's yard.

"Nope," my father said.

"Dad?" I said. "What, exactly, would you do if the Snowman jumped out at us? Run at him and whoop?"

"Die, probably," he said. Then he looked at me. Suddenly, there were tears in my eyes, which made me more irritated still. He touched my shoulder with his glove, and I shrugged him off. "Sorry, Mattie."

Theresa had stepped off the road into the yard, and Spencer had followed. "Hey," I said, and hurried after them.

"Goddammit," my father murmured behind me, and trudged after us. Spencer and Theresa were walking side by side, partially hooded in blackness. I stepped up my pace and drew level with them. At the edge of Theresa's yard, we stopped. Not too far away, someone was calling a cat. I could tell it was a cat by the way the voice trailed off at the end. No answer was expected.

"I don't want to go in my house," Theresa said, out of nowhere.

"Let's go find *him* instead," Spencer whispered. He was grinning.

We didn't ask which *him* he meant. I felt my knees clench. I'd known, of course, that we were all exactly the same age as Amy Ardell, but I hadn't really thought about it until then.

"Let's be her," said Theresa, and she flopped down on her back in the snow.

The thing hurtled across her so fast that she never even saw it, just sucked in her breath and shot upright while my father said, "Jesus!" and stumbled to his knees. I leapt backward and so did Spencer.

"Cat," Spencer said. "Little gray cat."

"I hate cats," said my father, standing up.

But Theresa had laid herself back down, and now she spread her arms, making a snow angel. "See?" she said. I had no idea what she meant. She lay there a little while longer, until my father extended his hand and helped her up.

The Doctor was waiting at the sliding glass door in a red sweater, arms folded.

"Thanks for bringing her, Joe," he said to my father, but his eyes never left his daughter.

"Not a problem," my father answered. We were all watching Theresa. After a while, he said, "She all right?"

"I don't know," the Doctor said, which scared me badly. Never in my life had I heard him admit confusion about anything, least of all his daughter.

"Jesus Christ, I'm fine," Theresa whispered, and stomped into the house.

"She's okay," I announced.

The dark seemed to thicken around us like stirred paint. Finally, the Doctor retreated inside and we all started back down to the street.

"She's been weird," Spencer muttered to me.

I nodded.

"I mean weirder."

It was true. The week before winter break, she'd announced that Spencer and I were distracting her and demanded that Ms. Eyre give her the Solitude Desk in the front left corner of the room, which was normally reserved for punishments. Spencer and I had been sent there several times already for sidecarring. And at recess, she had taken to whistling for us, then ducking out of sight into the woods. Sometimes she stayed in there until seconds before the final bell. Then we'd see her emerge from the trees to slide across the empty blacktop, head down, white hat bobbing.

My mother was sitting in the dark in the living room when we got home. We didn't even know she was there until she switched on the table lamp next to the couch. "Thanks for taking the car like I asked," she said, her voice icy flat; she seemed to be talking to all three of us, not just my father. Then she stalked past us into her bedroom.

My father sighed, sounding exhausted. "Try not to make too much noise. Tough night for your mother, Mattie. For me too, actually."

We went to my room, but we didn't play much. For a while, we rolled a couple of Hot Wheels cars back and forth across a game box; then I took out my baseball cards and we read the backs of those. It was well past my usual bedtime, almost midnight, when my mother appeared in the doorway to turn out the light.

"Are you scared?" she asked as we climbed into our bunks.

"No," I said, meaning that I wasn't *only* scared. I was also enjoying the tense evening walks, the strange school assemblies, and my friends.

Spencer said, "Yes," and my mother came all the way into the room, kissed him on the forehead, and told him that he should be. Then she closed the door most of the way but left the bathroom light on without asking.

We couldn't sleep, though. We got up and took turns racing my new slot car around on the Tyco track's single working lane. The track was a figure eight with a jump that was never set up because the inside lane had shorted out the same day we fitted all the pieces together. The controllers were plastic, poorly made, but you could feel the power in them when you squeezed the trigger, which transformed your slot car into a living thing.

I forget where Brent had been all night, probably sleeping over someplace. We hadn't shared a room since I was seven. But I remember feeling a little sad. It had been a long time since I'd played in the dark with my brother.

Eventually, we climbed back into our bunks and I lay still, trying to generate sleepy thoughts. None came.

"Mattie?" Spencer said, and I bent over the edge of my bunk and looked down at him. He was propped on his elbow and seemed to be made more of shadow than skin. He kept patting the sheets with his free hand. "What do you think happens when he's got you?"

"Maybe he ties you up," I said. I leaned back and closed my eyes.

Brent is curled up—in a basement somewhere—on a concrete floor, against an old furnace that makes occasional kicking sounds way down inside, as if there were something alive in there, about to be born. There's a window high on the wall with a white shade drawn, an overhead light spotted with bug wings, exposed pipes. The Snowman appears as a shadow, and Brent screams, "Fuck off!" at him, but his voice comes out croaky, and his lips are sucked in tight, the way they get on fast fairground rides.

"Does he feed you?" Spencer asked, half dazed, as though he'd been dreaming, too.

"Chef Boyardee," I said. "He wants you to like it."

"Do you get dessert?"

"Ho-Hos."

"Gross," said Spencer. "My mom says the stuff in Ho-Hos causes cancer."

"I heard some guy got cancer from a Whopper."

"What the hell are you talking about?"

"There was a tumor in the meat. A guy bit into it, and it squirted all over his face, and then he got cancer."

"You're sick, Mattie."

"I'm just telling you what I heard."

It was a delicious night.

The next afternoon, Spencer and I walked to the Burger King for lunch. A new snow had fallen overnight. The world looked familiar again, except for the little hands outlined in red in every other window we passed.

We hadn't even cut past Cider Lake when we spotted our first policeman. He was leaning against a lamppost, snapping gum in his mouth. When he saw us, he smiled, then swore and fished a Chap-stick out of his uniform's shirt pocket. As soon as we'd rounded the bend, Spencer grabbed a handful of snow and pitched it at the near-est house. It hit the cedar siding next to the front door and popped like a big wet bug. At the next house Spencer did it again, except this time he hit a window, and we took off down the block.

"What are you doing?" I asked after we'd slowed.

"Marking territory," he said. "A little game we play with the cops in our neighborhood. Especially white cops."

I thought the words sounded weird in his mouth. "You don't like white cops?"

Spencer shrugged. "It's just a game."

Dropping a few steps behind my friend, I scraped some ice-crusted snow off the hood of a station wagon and pegged him in the back of the neck. Laughing and screaming, we scrambled up the hill behind the Marathon station and hit Telegraph Road, red-faced and sopping. The cuffs of our jeans hung heavy over our boots and dripped snow into our socks. Our soaked scarves cleaved to our necks so we couldn't get our gloves underneath to peel them back and ease the itching. Together, we stomped into the Burger King parking lot.

Always on Saturdays, this was one of the places where kids in my neighborhood went, but more kids were there today than I had ever seen before. Dozens of my schoolmates were seated around tables in the same configurations that they usually formed during recess or outside lunch. Older teenagers were milling around the parked cars, kicking through snowdrifts in the center of the lot and throwing ice balls at the NO PARKING signs on the curb. First- and second-graders were crawling all over Burger King's pathetic plastic swing set and tent full of red plastic balls. I had never seen anyone using that equipment before. The ordering line stretched out the door, and by the time we got to the counter, they'd run out of french fries. Spencer got the last hamburger patty. Everyone who came after us got fish.

Quite a few parents had come with their kids, most of them stand-ing sheepishly in the back like chaperons on a field trip. Every now and then one of them would say something and the others would frown and shake their heads and search the crowd for their children, who ignored them.

For a while, Spencer and I lurked near the counter, listening to three girls we didn't know tell maybe ten other girls that they took intermediate ballet class with Amy Ardell on Saturday mornings. She wore green leotards, they said, and got the teacher mad because she wouldn't put her hair in a ponytail.

I spotted my brother crouched at a cluster of tables among most of the other nine-year-olds he knew. I couldn't help but wonder how he did it. Friends flocked to him.

"Isn't that your brother?" Spencer said over my shoulder, and started in his direction. I wished he hadn't, because I knew Brent would rather I left him alone.

"Hey, Brent," said Spencer cheerfully, and snaked two french fries from my brother's tray. "Thanks, man. Bite of my Whopper?"

Brent looked at where the two missing french fries had been. He had his hood up and his red ski jacket wrapped around his shoulders. He wanted me gone so much that his hands, palm up, kept twitching on the table like rolled-over spiders. It wasn't that he hated me. He just never knew what I was going to do. I'd seen him have the same reaction to my father once or twice. I'd had that reaction to my father too.

Without acknowledging us, Brent slid over one chair. I sat down next to him and nodded, but he wasn't looking at me. I wanted to say something older-brother-like and smart and not embarrassing. But I couldn't think of anything.

Spencer took another fry.

"Don't," I said, and then—because it was the only thing that came to mind—I started to sing, "*I am Leonardo, I am a retardo, I live on the ninety-ninth floor.*"

It was, at least, a brother memory, a stupid song from a long time ago that we'd learned somewhere and sung endlessly in the backseat during car vacations. It did nothing to make Brent happy I was there. I kept singing anyway, and eventually he said, "Shut up, weirdo," but he sounded less harsh than either of us might have expected.

Spencer took a fry from the kid next to him. His name was Randall, I think, a tiny sometime-friend of Brent's whose top lip turned out slightly and looked perpetually fat. I don't think Brent liked him much. Randall shrank back against his chair.

"Jesus Christ, kid, don't be scared of me," Spencer said.

For a second, Randall didn't move. Then, with no warning whatsoever, he jammed his little elbow into Spencer's ribs, ripped his tray out of reach, and announced, "I ain't scared of you, butt-wad." He stuffed a fistful of fries into his mouth while Brent bounced up and down with glee.

I thought Spencer might actually be hurt, from the way he clutched his side. Then he smiled. "Hey, Mattie," he said, in his most resonant voice, the one that would become his Shepherd voice. "Think we should tell them what we saw last night, over in that basement near the lake?"

Everyone at the table went quiet. Several tables of kids around us went quiet too. My little brother stared straight at me for the first time all day, his face scrunched into a question mark.

I shrugged.

Only Randall kept eating, folding fries into every corner of his mouth like tabs of X-ray film from the dentist. He chewed awhile, glared at Spencer, and finally, with his mouth full, he said, "What's grosser than a dead eleven-year-old in a garbage can?" A good thirty seconds passed before he swallowed his fries and continued. "A dead eleven-year-old in ten garbage cans."

All of us burst out laughing, although we already knew the punch line. It had been a dead-baby joke, but it was a Snowman joke now, which made it ours.

1977

ever in my life had I come up with so many excuses to go outside as I did in the weeks following Amy Ardell's death. When the Snowman kidnapped and then killed Edward Falk and Peter Slotkin one weekend apart after two major snowfalls, I offered to walk the neighbors' dogs, left my lunch box—on purpose—at the new bus stop at the end of our street (Mrs. Jupp insisted we all take the bus, no matter how close we lived to school; no more walking), and did anything else I could think of to get out, especially right before dinner when the dark pooled under the maple trees. The whole neighborhood became a sort of haunted-house ride, complete with winter light, drifting snow ghosts, and at least one monster. Sometimes Brent would come with me. Often I spotted other kids who'd gotten out also, and we'd chuck ice balls at each other, shoot glances at the twitching shadows, giggle uncomfortably, and finally race back inside.

Evenings, I did my homework early so I could watch the nine o'clock Special Update with my parents. Assorted news reports detailed the progress of the investigation. One revelation involved the discovery of a mild sedative in the blood of each victim, leading police to draw conclusions, at last, about the Snowman's method of murder: "He drugs them just enough to put them to sleep," a police department spokesman said. "Then—very gently, wearing gloves, so that he leaves no marks of any kind in the skin—he just closes up the victim's nose and mouth. Like this." The spokesman made a delicate pinching motion in the air, as though picking a bug off a plant.

Most nights, though, there were no revelations, just footage of kids crossing streets among a phalanx of cops or cars churning through slush in a shopping-mall parking lot. The reporters informed us that all we could do was *wonder where, when, and how this inhuman monster will strike next.* Every night, my father would ask my mother why we had to subject ourselves to this horror while she would sit on the couch under her half-knitted quilt, hypnotized. Later, she'd creep up to the doorway of my room, not knowing I was awake, and lean into the hall light so that her silhouette stretched across the floor like the shadow of an evergreen.

School got stranger with each new kidnapping. Within five minutes of the first bell, a messenger from Mrs. Jupp's office would appear at the door of our classroom and wait as Ms. Eyre took attendance. When she said the name of a kid who was missing, the rest of us would swivel toward the empty seat and then one another until someone said, "Oh, yeah, I talked to him yesterday. He's sick." If no one said anything, the whispering would start, and it would continue all day long.

Ms. Eyre had had more surgery on her shattered cheekbones over winter break, and her face looked less ghoulish now. She'd grown paler, though. All those surgeries and treatments required that she shield herself from even the wintertime sun. She looked frail, like a china plate someone had broken and glued back together, minus one or two tiny all but unnoticeable chips.

At recess, an all-new team of elderly volunteer security guards would station themselves at twenty-yard intervals along the perimeter of the woods. They'd face the playground, not the world outside, so they could keep us in sight. Sometimes, when the industrial-colored Detroit snow clouds closed over the school, I imagined an army of Snowmen emerging from the woods and mowing down the helpless guards in rows.

In the classroom, Theresa dominated as never before. At the end of January, we had Gunning for Gum Balls Day. Any right answer earned a pull on Ms. Eyre's candy dispenser. Theresa earned her first pull five minutes after class began by reeling off sixteen consecutive world capitals. The last of them was Reykjavík, which she also spelled. The machine yielded three gum balls to her tug. When Theresa put gum balls in her mouth, it meant she was satisfied or bored and would let someone else win for a while. This time she put them in her pocket, and on her way back to her seat she delivered invitations to her birthday party and the 1977 Mind War. She invited Spencer and me, Jon Goblin, and Marybeth Royal, the new girl from Toronto who always wore button-up skirts with the bottom button left undone so you could see her knees. Whole days, I remember, my eyes would drift toward that bottom button, the open clasp.

"Shit," Spencer murmured as Theresa returned to the Solitude Desk. "She's in no-mercy mode."

By lunchtime, she had earned fourteen pulls on the gum-ball machine, and Ms. Eyre had ruled her ineligible for the afternoon session. Spencer and I had earned the only other pulls, a couple a piece, mostly while Theresa was in the bathroom. I beat her on Current Events, which had pretty much become Snowman Trivia. That day's question involved a psychological profile from the morning paper. I still remember the article, which was printed alongside a sketch drawn from the police psychologist's best guess.

At recess, I gave all my gum balls to Garrett Serpien. The insides of those balls had no flavor whatsoever. It was all on the coating, a strawberry spray. Once that wore off, it was like chewing your tongue. Meanwhile, Theresa spent the entire lunch period wandering between the guards near the perimeter of the schoolyard. It was Spencer who noticed her dropping gum balls in the snow, one by one.

"I don't really know how to talk to her," he said to me and Jon and Garrett and Marybeth. "It's like talking to a goldfish. A goldfish that can spell Reykjavík."

Everyone nodded, me included. I felt guilty, standing there, not because of anything I'd done but because it all felt new and thrilling to me: being just another neighborhood kid, having at least one shared demon, not understanding Theresa because I was more like everyone else—except that I would rather have been with her. I wanted to fire an ice ball at her like a harpoon so I could drag her back to us.

In February, Detroit experienced a dry spell. The temperature rose above freezing, and hysteria over the Snowman hit a peak and then dulled just a little. Cops still closed around us at intersections and escorted us through crosswalks. Parents still left work by three so they could be at the bus stop ahead of their children. But at least they were allowing us to play outside on the 40-degree days, after issuing the usual precautions. The nine o'clock Special Update was cut from thirty minutes to fifteen. Psychiatric profiles and columns about possible leads sank below the fold of both newspapers into a semipermanent home at the bottom right corner of the front page, outlined in blue. No one believed he was gone; we could still feel him, like the weight in the weather before a storm. We were just sick of talking about him.

My parents had their usual argument on the morning of Theresa's birthday about whether the Mind War was healthy for me. This year, however, I went into the kitchen and announced, "Someone really needs to destroy her. For her own good." Then I smiled.

They both looked at me, my baffled father and my lonely mother. I don't know what had made me realize she was lonely.

"You do that," my father said. "Bring us home an Honor Feather."

My mother put down the baking pan she'd been drying on the counter and said, "If someone doesn't get her out of that house, there's going to be trouble. Huge trouble."

My father jerked as if she'd stuck him with a safety pin. "Jesus Christ, Alina. What kind of trouble, exactly?"

"Sorry," she said, and dropped her head on his shoulder. I thought she was about to cry. I had no idea what was going on.

"What about some sympathy for *him*?" said my father. I thought he meant the Snowman for a second. Then I had no idea what he meant.

My mother made a sound that could have been a laugh or a sob or neither, but my father seemed to understand it, because he stopped talking and touched her hand with his.

Moments later, Mrs. Franklin honked out front and I grabbed my coat from the hall closet. My mother followed me to the front door, stuck out her head, and waved. Mrs. Franklin didn't turn off the car or roll down her window to the cold, but she waved back with one gold-mittened hand as I piled into the front seat of her rust-wracked Impala next to Spencer.

We slid down the street, and the bright morning light flashed and faded through the bare trees as the sun slipped from cloud to cloud. Neither Spencer nor his mother said anything. When we pulled up in front of the Daughrety house, I got out of the car, let Spencer slip wordlessly past me, then turned back and said, "'Bye, Mrs. Franklin. Thanks."

She said something I didn't hear because Spencer pegged me in the ear with a snowball, and I swung around and raced after him. We threw each other to the ground in the Daughretys' front yard and rolled around a little; then Spencer got to his feet, spun on his heel like an army sergeant, and tromped onto the Daughrety porch as his mother drove away. He jabbed a finger in the doorbell and yelled, "Hellooo? It's wet out here."

I swear to God, I remember my next breath, a sweet stinging thing, opening like the petals of a frozen flower and sticking in my lungs. There are days, long strings of days, when I believe I've never dislodged it since.

Barbara Fox opened the door in her stocking feet. She acted as if she'd always been there. She had been, it turned out, for months, just not when anyone else was around. She was wearing a kilt, knee length, with her hair in a black bow not all that different from Theresa's. Thinking this gave me all sorts of queasy sensations I tried to ignore. She took Spencer's scarf, his coat, and my coat, and as our hands brushed she squeezed her fingers around mine.

"Are you baby-sitting?" I said, almost naturally, knowing it wasn't true. The queasiness inside me got worse.

"I'm here to watch you rout the Queen of Silence," she whispered in my ear. Then she squeezed my hand again, lined up my butt with her foot, and nudged me forward into the hallway. She'd lost her African tan; she was pale, wan, a Detroiter again.

During the next hour, I hardly saw her at all, mostly because I avoided her. Theresa had burned the popcorn balls, but her father took a tray of them around anyway. They tasted like raspberry sauce over crunchy ashes.

"Looks like brains," Spencer said, but he ate one anyway.

I sat with Jon and Spencer. Marybeth Royal came with the girls from Theresa's church, though she sat closer to Theresa than anyone else. A few times, Theresa whispered something in Marybeth's ear, and both of them giggled. It was a strange sight, Theresa giggling with a girl. When I leaned over to say something to Jon, I found him watching Marybeth. Every time she smiled, he did too.

Theresa's presents seemed lifted from some generic birthday-party catalog. The best were a bright red backpack and a hand-carved doll that had probably come from one of the booths at the Ethnic Festival downtown. Spencer and I bought her a miniature gum-ball machine. *You'll need this when we start beating you in class*, we'd written on the card. She smiled when she read it and said "Thanks," but she didn't look up. Then she said something else to Marybeth, who giggled again.

Instead of birthday cake, the Doctor and Barbara brought out black cupcakes with steeples of white icing that everyone licked like ice-cream cones. I saw Barbara say "Happy birthday" when she gave Theresa hers, with a lit candle in it. "Make a wish," she said.

"Can I wish you'd go away?" Theresa said, and my mouth fell open.

"You don't even have to wish. Just ask," Barbara said, and she retreated across the room.

"*Happy birthday to you*," the Doctor abruptly started singing, and everyone else joined in. I did too, eventually.

When everyone was finished eating their cupcakes, Dr. Daughrety directed us to the dining room table, adorned with yellow pads and

sharpened pencils. He pulled out his black notebook full of questions—all the questions from the last five years as well as this one.
Spencer sat down, licked the last of the icing from his lips, and pushed
my chair away from him.

"What are you doing?" I asked.

"You're blocking my view of Dr. Strange and Strange Daughter."

I looked at Theresa, found her staring back, and something shot
through me that I had never felt before, not on Gunning for Gum Ball
Days or in math class or even at previous Mind Wars. I was going to
win today, or Spencer was. And Theresa seemed oddly resigned to it.
An adrenaline ball the size of a fist engulfed my heart. I shuddered in
my chair, feeling the hard wood grind against my shoulder blades.
Theresa, I suspected, probably felt like this every schoolday of her life.

Barbara Fox sat at the Doctor's elbow. She put her hand on his knee
and drilled her eyes straight into mine until I looked away.

For ten questions, one entire round, Spencer and I ran the table.
He'd answer, I'd answer, and all the while Theresa sat in her chair and
chewed her pencil. Occasionally, she'd look up from the paper at us,
or at least in our direction, which was the most you could expect from
her at any given time, but especially in the middle of a Mind War. I
imagined her father slipping toward the edge of his chair with every
right answer his daughter didn't give. Spencer and I were like batter-
ing rams storming the gates of his cathedral.

Even during the second round, we controlled the action, although
the monster in Theresa was clearly awake by then. The game got
faster, the answers quicker. So quickly did the three of us fling
responses and reload, in fact, that we got a lot of answers wrong, which
kept our scores lower than they'd been in years.

The speed round jerked past like pages in a flip book: Dr. Daughrety checked his watch and raced through questions; Barbara Fox
kissed his earlobe while he shooed her away. Jon Goblin whispered
something to Marybeth Royal, and she blushed; Theresa gnawed
through the base of her pencil eraser and flecked her lips with yellow
paint. Finally, the Doctor dumped his black book on the floor,
grabbed the score pad out of Barbara's hands, and stared at it.

We waited. At the other end of the table from me, Marybeth poked Jon in the arm.

"Some birthday," Spencer murmured.

"This can't be right," the Doctor snarled.

Spencer glanced my way. I was watching Theresa. She had her hands over her eyes but her fingers were spread as if she was playing peek-a-boo, and she was smiling. I couldn't see her mouth, but I knew she was smiling and I'm fairly certain she was smiling at me.

"Wow," said Dr. Daughrety, "it is right. Okay, folks. We have an overtime round. Spencer and Theresa are tied at the top, Mattie's three points off the lead. Everyone still plays. Ten questions, fifteen points each. Ready?"

He picked up his black book and opened it to the page where he'd left off. Then he stopped, looked at all of us, and grinned. I'd seen other grown-ups do that, my parents and grandparents and one or two teachers, absorbing us through their skin like sunlight. But I'd never seen Dr. Daughrety do it.

The first question he asked was about Commodore Perry opening up the Orient. Jon Goblin had just done his Nineteenth-Century Heroes report on him, so he got that one. Then Jon answered a sports question about the Red Wings. Out of the remaining eight questions, Jon answered five, either because Dr. Daughrety happened to hit on his areas of expertise, or maybe because those two right answers had triggered Jon's own adrenaline burst, the one that fueled him on the soccer field, which was at least as powerful as Theresa's. A couple of panicky wrong answers from Theresa, one each from Spencer and me, and it was over. Jon wound up winning by over fifty points.

From the pocket of his white cardigan, Dr. Daughrety lifted the Honor Feather and sat there a moment like a cat, staring in bewilderment at the remains of something he'd devoured.

"Jon Goblin," he said, "your parents will never believe it."

He reached across the table and dropped the feather over Jon's pad of paper. We watched it drift down. Marybeth Royal actually kissed him on the cheek when it landed.

Barbara took us skating on the lake afterward. The Doctor stayed home. Theresa got so far out in front of us that she disappeared into the little outcropping of half-submerged trees and swamp grass we all called the Island in the dead center of Cider Lake. Jon Goblin and Marybeth Royal skated out there too, and they didn't come back for a while. Theresa didn't reappear until we'd stopped calling her name and yelled that we were going home. I was the one who caught sight of her gliding out of the tall reeds.

Back in the Daughretys' living room, the heat seeped into our cheeks as we unlaced our skates and mercifully released our ankles. Theresa congratulated Jon Goblin but still avoided talking to Spencer or me. She almost sliced Barbara with her skate blade when Barbara tried to help her untie her laces. Barbara just straightened and shrugged and said, "You get the other one."

Later, after my mother had driven Spencer home to Ferndale, I told her about seeing Barbara kiss Dr. Daughrcty. She just nodded when I said it and then sat for a few moments, staring out the windshield while the wipers cut the blooms off the ice flowers forming there. When she looked at me again, she was close to tears.

"He's a goddamn son-of-a-bitch," she said.

1977

ven before the woman realized what she'd seen, thrown up her dinner, and called the police, the Cory twins' abduction was different. All of us had felt it coming, first of all. There was something about this particular snow—a gray vapor that lingered for days and stank like floodwater—that seemed unusually filthy even for Detroit.

That night, the nine o'clock Special Update returned to all three networks. It stayed on for hours, tracking the progress of house-to-house searches on a map, as though they were part of a storm front closing over the region. The woman who'd seen it happen told her story to the police, then to the networks, then to some private detectives who never revealed who had hired them but otherwise talked freely to the press, and then to a shadowy group of men who showed up at her door in the middle of the night in black turtlenecks and demanded that she tell them everything she knew for the good of us all.

What she knew was that the Cory twins, age eleven, had been standing in a parking lot outside a comic book shop in downtown Birmingham, talking to a long-haired man. The shop was less than a hundred yards from their house, and they walked there every day. She had seen the two boys climb—willingly, as far as she could tell—into the long-haired man's car. One kid had held up the seat so that his twin brother could climb in the back, while the long-haired man stood on the other side of the car and grinned. The car itself was rusted almost all the way through along the molding. The police gave her photos of various models, and she identified one instantly: a blue Gremlin.

On the second night of the Cory twins' disappearance, I had my first Snowman nightmare.

I slip on the ice, land next to a basement window. Peering through it is like looking in the lake. I don't want to, and do. Through the snow-light glare, I see a long-haired man in a red down ski jacket and a baby propped in a high chair, gagged and stuffed like a doll. Only it isn't a doll. The long-haired man keeps leaning over the baby and whispering, and every time he stands, the baby looks shinier, less human. Right at the end, the long-haired man turns to me. His face is red and flat, like a STOP sign.

The next day, I saw the Snowman's real face for the first time. It appeared on telephone poles, at the post office, in the newspapers, in people's windows. The woman who'd seen him hadn't been able to provide much description aside from the long hair, but the police artist had already come up with a face based on psychological profiles that bore a striking resemblance to her description: blurred charcoal eyes and a smeared indeterminate mouth. The face looked almost fetal, as if it were only now taking shape.

Mrs. Cory made a single public appearance, on the Saturday after the kidnapping. She had weird gouge marks in both cheeks, as though she'd been fitted for a bit. Her hair fell in a dark sweeping wave off one side of her face and was tucked in tight against the other. I don't know whether it was sympathy or admiration that caused it, but within a week, dozens of women were wearing their hair that way.

Mrs. Cory did not cry. She stared at the camera from her own living room, ignoring Larry Loreno. Larry was on his first hard-news assignment, dressed in a dark blue suit instead of the jeans and Tigers cap he usually wore for his *Eyeing Detroit* feature. He kept shifting in his chair, as if he wasn't sure where to place his hands. For what seemed like forever, Mrs. Cory said nothing at all.

"Ladies and gentlemen," said Larry nervously, but the camera never left Mrs. Cory's face. "We'd like to bring you this exclusive plea. Mrs. Cory?"

"What the hell's an exclusive plea?" my father barked.

Mrs. Cory opened her mouth, closed her mouth. Finally—still without tears, her voice breaking—she cleared her throat, blinked, and said softly, "Goodbye, boys." Then she stood up and wandered out of the room.

"Mattie, get to bed," my father said, and my mother began to cry.

Until then the adults had seemed mostly scared, crouched in their houses or behind their work desks, clutching us to them at every opportunity. But now they were angry.

I remember one night, the Special Update crew suddenly cut away from their map of the suburbs to a live shot at the corner of Telegraph and Long Lake, where a circle of coatless women had erupted from their houses and ambushed a blue Gremlin at a stoplight. They'd yanked a college kid out of the driver's seat, grabbed chunks of ice and gravel off the shoulder of the road, and begun stoning the car. This went on for forty-five minutes—with a few passersby pulling off the road and hopping out to join them—until someone stopped at Kroger and called the cops, who came blazing onto the scene and dispersed the women by waving nightsticks. Then they grabbed the college kid, who was protesting wildly, bent him over his blasted hood, threw on handcuffs, and broke into the trunk of his ruined car with a crowbar.

"You know what?" one of the women told a reporter. She was wearing no makeup, no shoes, just a bathrobe, and looked as if she had sleep-walked onto her driveway. "I didn't even notice the kid. I wanted to kill the car."

On the way home from school the next day, we all sat in silence on the bus and listened to a guy tell a talk-show host on WJR how he'd been stopped twelve times in sixteen hours the day before and ordered out of his Gremlin, which wasn't even blue. And this morning the police hadn't even waited for him to leave the house; they just showed up at 5 A.M. with a warrant to search his garage.

"Get new wheels, asshole," the talk-show host said and cut him off.

The twilight forays into our front yards got shorter. Brent and I slipped out once, when we were supposed to be setting the table, and pelted each other with ice balls while the sun sank behind the pines and split them with white-red light. Cold air crawled along the mouths of our gloves and clutched our wrists. My brother generally demolished me in snowball fights, but that night I scraped up two fistfuls of snow and sprinted at him. By the time he recovered from the shock, I was in his face, driving ice into his neck. He crumpled to the lawn and gave. Then we snuck out of the yard and down the block, past the Foxes' house, which was empty and lightless, and wound up hunched in the drainage ditch at the new bus stop on Cider Lake Road. We hadn't seen much of either Fox for a while. I thought of Barbara in the Daughrety house and missed her.

"What would you do if it came?" Brent whispered.

A van churned past, followed by an old Camaro, deep blue and rusted, with a shadow driver behind the tinted windshield. From far behind us, startlingly clear, came our mother's call. "Boys?" The call got clearer still, and louder. "*Boys?*"

Both of us heard the tone in her voice, the way the end of the question tailed upward in panic. Brent stood immediately. When I didn't, he kicked me in the ribs.

I didn't really want the Snowman to come. But I could imagine myself gone, could almost hear everyone at school, everyone I knew, talking. I wanted to hear what the Snowman said to get you to come with him. More, I wanted to hear his voice. I could almost hear it already, summoning me through the blowing snow: the Pied Piper, with charcoal for eyes.

Brent kicked me again, and I got up and kicked him back. Then we raced down the middle of the street, yelling and waving to our mother where she stood at the end of our driveway, ankle-deep in the drifts in her stocking feet.

1977

I t was that next weekend, just before they found the Cory twins, their bodies freshly laid and unmarked, on the putting green at the Maple Hills Country Club, that Spencer and I entered Theresa Daughrety's house together for the last time. We came at six o'clock, and Barbara fed us macaroni and cheese at the kitchen table, under the twin dogface masks with the bared black fangs. Her hair swung in rings around her shoulders; random curls hung near her ears like seahorses. All through dinner, she smiled at me the way she always did, for no apparent reason. It was a tired smile, more eyes than mouth, but it made me happy to see it. Except for one moment, when she put her hand on my arm as she handed me my plate and asked what I'd been drawing lately, she didn't speak to me specifically. She didn't speak to

Spencer either. Instead, to my utter astonishment, she spent most of the meal talking to Theresa. Last time I'd seen them, they'd been kicking skate blades at each other. And no one I knew had managed even a one-way conversation with Theresa in recent weeks. Even so, they weren't saying anything much, as far as I could tell. Barbara talked about skating, a half-painted wall in the guest bedroom, Dr. Daughrety's Jeep, an African book that she had given Theresa called *Things Fall Apart*.

"Hard man," Theresa said through a mouthful of macaroni. I guessed she meant someone in the book.

Barbara responded with a nod and folded her arms across her chest. "Hard," she concurred. Then she glanced my way and smiled.

The tingling sensation stole over me as I stood to clear my plate. I don't know what it was—something about the way Barbara was smiling at me while conducting easy conversation with Theresa, or the memory of Barbara singing next to me on our front stoop, or maybe just the fact that she was making us dinner in that house—but suddenly I found myself saying, "He isn't good for you."

The statement did what I wanted, I suppose. It jarred her, got her looking straight at me. But her smile evaporated. "Which *him* do you mean?" she said. "Who the hell do you think you are?"

I started shaking, trying to figure out what I'd just done and how to take it back. Theresa and Spencer sat, their faces as frozen as the masks on the walls. The phone rang. No one moved.

On the fourth ring, I said, "Should I get that? Barbara?" I was fighting back tears.

When she still didn't respond, I stood and pulled the receiver to my ear. "Daughrety house," I said, sounding tired and sad like our school secretary.

"Mattie, is Barbara there?" my mother said. I blinked in surprise. "Mom?"

"Mattie, put Barbara on the phone. Right now."

I stretched the phone toward Barbara. From the look on her face, I thought she might swat the receiver from my hands.

"I'm sorry," I murmured, my voice still shaking a little. "It's my mom."

Barbara took the phone, and just a little rigidity drained from her body. "Hello?" she said, in a deeper voice than usual.

For a long time, she stood, saying nothing, staring at the wall. Then she said, "Fuck him." I gaped at Spencer. He was gaping too. Even Theresa flinched. "*Fuck him!*" Barbara yelled. Then she said, "Okay, okay, I'll be right there." She slammed down the phone and fled the room.

We could hear her rummaging through the living room closet. I wanted to go in there, but I was caught in another one of those chasms between my life and the lives of adults, and there was no one to yell to for help.

"They let *her* baby-sit you?" Spencer broke into my thoughts.

"Shut up," I snapped.

"Well, what the hell?"

"I don't know."

As if someone had pressed on the back of her chair and ejected her, Theresa stood up, blew a breath, and walked out of the kitchen. I followed her with Spencer close behind. She stopped right behind Barbara and stared at her back. She didn't speak. Barbara was putting on her coat and drawing the hood over her hair. Her face was red, her eyes wet.

"I have to go out," she said to Theresa.

I couldn't believe it. She was about to leave us alone. No one else said anything. "Where are you going?" I blurted.

Tears slipped from her eyes. "My dad, Mattie. My goddamn dad. He shot the windows out of our house. Now he's wandering around the neighborhood with a gun, and I have to find him before he starts shooting someone else's house, or the police decide he's threatening someone and try to stop him. If they yell at him to put the gun down, I'm not even sure he'd do it. That's how crazy he is. Can you guys take care of yourselves for a little while? The Doctor should be home any minute." By now, Barbara had the front door open, and she was no longer looking at us. "Be good, kids. Please." Then she was on the porch, pulling the door closed.

I didn't want her to go, and I didn't know what to say. Every day, the world kept tilting farther out of balance, and now people I'd known all my life were starting to slip off the edge. "Let us come," I said.

The door stopped closing, and Barbara's face hung in profile, wreathed in her breath as if the winter air were molding a Barbara mask. Once that mask was fitted, I thought, she'd never get it off.

"Stay here, Mattie," she said. "Take care of Spencer and Theresa. I'm counting on you. When the Doctor gets home, tell him what's happened. Tell him to call your mother."

"Maybe we should all go over there."

"Just stay put." Her voice hardened. "She wouldn't want you outdoors with all this going on. Neither do I."

I wanted to hold her there a few seconds longer, but she was out the door, sliding the lock home with her key.

Instantly, the smothering silence of the Daughrety house stole over us. Spencer and Theresa were kneeling on the couch by the living room window, and I joined them there. Together, we watched Barbara skid out of the driveway in her Pinto and disappear down the street. In the glow of the porch light, ice buds quivered in the trees as if they were about to bloom.

At first, we were so baffled and unsettled by what had happened that we actually did the dishes. Theresa cleared and stacked in her usual daze. I washed. Spencer dried. In the window above the sink, our reflections hovered in the dark, suspended on strings of snow like shadow marionettes.

"Could Mr. Fox really hurt anyone?" Spencer asked both of us.

I shook my head. "No one but himself. That's what my mom says." But I wasn't so sure.

Theresa just shrugged and went on drying. It was almost twenty minutes later, as we put away the last of the pots, that it dawned on us we had the house to ourselves. I'd been left alone with Brent a few times, and once or twice with Jon Goblin and Joe Whitney. But not with a girl, and not in this house, and not since the Snowman had been spotted and named.

"We have to take advantage of this," I said abruptly, and from that point on everything happened very quickly.

"Let's bike to Stroh's," said Spencer. It would have been a decent idea, but we didn't have any money, and none of us really wanted to go outside.

"Mind War," said Theresa, visibly stirring. "I know where my dad keeps the notebook." This was good too—a direct defiance of the Doctor, and more daring still.

"Murder in the Dark," I said, and both of them stared at me.

Spencer said, "Fuck no. Not tonight."

"Yes. Oh, yes," Theresa said, and raced out of the room in search of a flashlight. I could hear her giggling as she went down the back hallway.

To this day, I can't remember all the rules for Murder in the Dark, but rules weren't the point. The game was just an excuse to go down in the basement, turn out the lights, and imagine yourself in terrible danger. We used playing cards to determine our roles. One of us was the killer—the Snowman, naturally. One of us was the victim. And one of us played the policeperson and carried the flashlight. The flashlight was supposed to be a gun, and the policeperson got to use two blasts of it. If the killer got caught in one of them, the policeperson won unless the victim was already dead. I have no memory of the rules for murder. And it's funny, because I remember getting the Snowman card that night, which should have meant that I was the one doing the killing. But that can't be right.

The light switch for Theresa's basement was at the top of the stairs, so we had to descend in the dark. I'd been down there once before— also to play this game—but I can't picture a thing about what the basement actually looked like. I do remember the smell, a combination of dampness and dirt and just-mixed house paint, and there was a sound, too, a rasp of hot air gasping through cold ducts.

I went down first, drawing that damp dark around me as I eased my way into the room in search of a hiding place. I edged between wicker chairs, suitcases, and an enormous piece of fiberglass that might have been part of a sailboat hull and felt colder to the touch than the air around it. I hit a wall, stood flat against it, and realized to my horror that there were masks hanging there too. I would never have looked at them with the lights on, but that night, I crouched beneath one and stretched out my fingers. It had a horned forehead and empty spaces where the nose and eyes should have been, and when I drew back my hand, it seemed to vibrate, as though something had strummed it.

I heard Spencer come clomping down, followed a minute or so later by Theresa, who came one step at a time, as if she were marching to a metronome. By then, my eyes had adjusted to the dark, and I could just make out her shape, thanks to the line of light under the door at the top of the stairs. Then she dissolved in the blackness, and I heard and saw nothing for a long time.

The silence lasted so long, in fact, that I began to get nervous. I was kneeling near a La-Z-Boy with a hole in the seat cushion, toying with the fabric, listening hard. The lone window over my head shed no light except a faint glow, like asphalt in moonlight. No flashlight shot had been fired. Nothing moved. Fear swelled inside me, the kind I thought I'd left behind years ago when I first went to sleep without the hall light on. My breath fluttered and my skin tingled, charged by the current in the air and the heat in the ducts, which seemed to hum in my head, saying, You're here now; you're going to die someday.

You're going to die someday.

It wasn't just fear, I realized, or I wouldn't have remained kneeling. It was exhilaration too. My eyes kept leaping from dark place to dark place, and my ears were straining. I wanted to scream out, impale myself on the policeperson's flashlight beam, and let the electricity blaze through me. I opened my mouth to release the pressure in my throat, and Theresa clapped her pale hand over my lips. I couldn't see the paleness, but I could feel it, a cold more profound than the ice outside. Her fingers splayed across my face, and I could feel her pulse on my skin. Her hair tickled my neck. Her breath whistled in time with the gasps from the pipes. Against my ear, I felt her laugh, soft and wet as snowfall. Even her breath was cold. I could feel my own body swelling, changing, because of her but also because of fear, snow, moonlight, silence. For one suspended moment, we floated together under the masks in the murmuring dark.

Then she jerked. She made no sound at all but went completely stiff. Her fingers dug into my cheek, and I said, "Ow." Spencer speared us with his flashlight beam.

"Ha," he said, and I blinked and saw him prancing toward us. Then he said "*Shit*" and dropped the flashlight. Theresa let go of me and backed away.

"Hey," I said. My first thought was that something had happened to my face, that it had blurred, become alien somehow. But that couldn't be it, because neither Theresa nor Spencer were looking at me. They were looking over my head. Images of masks floating off the walls flooded my brain. Then the window rattled in its frame and a voice shot through with wind whistled, "Let me in . . ."

"Mattie, get away from the window," Spencer snapped, and I whirled around.

The moon lit the wild white hair. The eyes glowed orange like a jack-o'-lantern's, and the mouth worked in spasms.

"It's Mr. Fox," I breathed. "Hey, Mr. Fox."

"Let me in," I saw him mouth. The twitch in his lips seemed to streak up his cheeks. "Let me." Then he rocked back on his knees and drove his face through the window.

"What the *fuck*?" Spencer howled, and I saw him leap for the stairs, stop, spin around. "Where's Theresa? Mattie, grab her, *run.*"

But I was stuck where I stood. A torrent of frigid air had erupted into the room, and I was standing in the blast of it. Mr. Fox's face hung in the window frame, a Daughrety mask made flesh. Red rivers raged down both cheeks and into his coat collar. Shards of glass sparkled on his eyelids, and he screamed when he blinked. He pulled his head back through the window frame and dislodged the last fragments of glass from the pane, which raked his scalp. He struggled to his feet and was gone. I saw snow, part of a tree, black sky, white moon.

Light bloomed around me. Shivering, I turned around and saw Spencer scurrying back downstairs after flicking on the light switch.

Theresa was crouched against the far wall, her arms flung out to the sides as if she were trying to levitate. Her eyes were shut, and she let out a grunting sob that shook her body so badly she almost tipped over. Spencer and I converged around her, held her up, helped her upstairs.

We stayed in the front hallway, away from the dining room's giant windows. Spencer brought us water and a box of Saltines. Theresa's body hadn't unlocked, but she ate a cracker when Spencer gave it to her. We leaned together in the foyer and listened.

"What the hell?" Spencer whispered.

"I don't know," I said. "Barbara doesn't live with Mr. Fox anymore, she lives here. He drinks."

"My dad drinks. He doesn't put his face through windows."

"My dad doesn't drink," said Theresa, startling us. She stuck out her hand for another cracker. Her weeping was so silent, so subtle, that neither of us noticed it right away. Teardrops hung in her lashes. Like glass, I thought. Finally, keys scratched in the front-door lock, the door swung open, and Dr. Daughrety strode in. His scalp glinted with windblown ice crystals, and his cheeks were red. I knew he'd been driving with the Jeep's side flaps open again.

"Well, hey there," he started, his coat half off his shoulders, and then he looked at Theresa. "Theresa? What? Mattie, what's wrong here?"

"Mr. Fox," I said. "He put his face through your basement window."

"He put—" Dr. Daughrety stared at me. "What?"

"Barbara says you should call my mom. Mr. Fox shot the windows out of his house, and no one could find him, and then he came here. He wanted to come in, and then he—"

Dr. Daughrety shoved me out of the way and grabbed Theresa. "Are you all right, baby?" he murmured, his hands against her neck, her back, as though checking for wounds. Theresa stood statue-still in his arms. "He didn't touch her, did he? He didn't touch any of you?"

"He didn't come in."

"Just his face," Spencer muttered.

Dr. Daughrety stood up, his hand still buried in his daughter's hair. "Where's Barbara?"

"She went to find him. Before he came here, I mean. She said you should—"

"She left you here?"

I looked at Spencer, and we both nodded.

"I want you to stay where you are," Dr. Daughrety said, his voice level. He let go of Theresa's hair. "Don't move. Don't talk. Don't make a sound. Watch the windows. Listen. You see or hear anything— a dog bark, anything—you yell for me. I'm going to make sure he isn't downstairs."

He slammed the dead bolt home on the front door and brushed past us down the basement steps. He didn't pick up a shovel or a baseball bat or even a flashlight. But for Mr. Fox's sake, I found myself praying that the Doctor didn't find him. We stood and watched and listened.

"Next time, how 'bout we have our sleepover in my neighborhood?" Spencer whispered.

"Sssh," I said. Then, surprising myself, I reached out and touched Theresa on her neck, right where the Doctor's hand had been. I felt a single pulse beat and yanked my hand back. Theresa sat like a television set that had been switched off.

"*Phil!*" we heard the Doctor bellow, just once. There was no reply. A few seconds later, the Doctor reappeared in the front hall, rebuttoning his coat. "Anything?"

Spencer and I shook our heads.

"He can't have gone far. There's a lot of blood down there. I'm checking the yard."

He opened the front door, and I could see the night rippling like dark water. I could feel its pull, sense the monsters in its depths. "Stay here. I'm right outside." Bending low, he held his lips to Theresa's forehead, and then we all heard it, the squeal-skid of a car rocketing way too fast toward us on the iced-over road.

Dr. Daughrety flew out the door, hands waving, yelling "Barbara!" He didn't make it off the front porch before we heard the crunch, like a frozen log dropped on a fire. A second thump followed, then one more skidding screech of tires and dead silence.

"Tell me that was the mailbox," Spencer hissed in my ear. None of us moved, although Spencer and Theresa were closer together now, touching at the shoulders.

Barbara's scream began low, sliding up and up until it pealed through the night like a siren. Lights burst from the surrounding houses, and smaller lights bobbed across the dark. Gradually, I became aware of the frigid air filling the house. Spencer looked at me, at Theresa, and then darted out the front door. I was right behind him.

Barbara was still behind the wheel of her Pinto, which sat steaming, half sideways in the center of the road. I could see most of her face in the cone of streetlight. She made no move to get out. Spencer and I stumbled side by side through the drifts, scraping our shins on the crusted snow, until we reached the curb. The Doctor was crouched over a sprawled pair of legs. We watched him stand, stare a little longer at the body, then jerk open the passenger door and drag out Barbara. She didn't move at first, and then she started beating on him, yelling, not saying any words, just yelling, breathing in heaves. The yells flew up in pitch, then down, almost as if she were singing. If only she'd taught me the response for this, I thought, and I stepped into the street. I didn't know where I was going. But the sight of Barbara balled against the Doctor, her head tucked tight against his neck, made me angry. And the way he was holding her, I knew he wasn't going to let her go, which made him just like her father, it seemed to me. The cold cut through my lungs like the blade of a circular saw.

All around us, voices began to buzz. I was ten feet away, trying to decide what to do, when I saw the Doctor drop his arms and then stagger in place as though he'd been punched. Barbara slipped to her knees in the snow. At first I thought she might be praying, and then she turned her face into the light. It was red and ravaged, the eyes staring at nothing as she started to sob. Only gradually did I become aware that all the humming voices had choked to a stop.

I saw the Doctor say "No" and stagger again. A woman screamed. Slowly, helplessly, I felt myself turn around.

I saw Spencer first, standing in the path of Barbara's headlights, his legs twitching, his arms flapping about him as if most of the tendons

that held him in place had been severed. I started to say something—
and then I looked where he was looking.

Mr. Fox lay where he'd fallen, his arms flung over his head, his head
cocked sideways, with the cuts from the window glass etched in his
skin like hieroglyphs. His legs were still partially attached to his waist,
but they hung at an absurd angle, and there was almost no torso at all,
just a spatter of frozen blood and crushed bone in the snow.

And that was where Theresa Daughrety knelt, right where Mr. Fox's
belly used to be, the dead center of him, her skirt spreading in the gore,
hands near her heart and her mouth wide open.

1994

From two blocks away I can see the glow, whitish orange, as if someone lit a fire in the heart of a snowdrift. I never did learn the story of why the East Birmingham Community Library opens at first light on Sunday mornings. I know there was a Polish man named Mr. Borowski who ran the place when I was a kid and had a raspy East European accent that crushed vowels between hard consonants. He'd lost both his feet in an assembly line accident. I remember the stumps that stuck out of his pant legs, sockless and pink in the antiseptic library light, and the shriek of his electric wheelchair as it grooved dark furrows into the slush-gray carpet. How he got from the assembly line to the library, and from his very Polish working-class Hamtramck neighborhood near downtown Detroit to the WASP world I grew up in, I had no idea. But two Polish bakeries had followed him here, one on either side of the library, and they opened before dawn on Sundays too.

Three or four times a year, my dad would wake my brother and me, trundle us into our coats, and drive us down these dark blocks of houses, past looming hedges and wide front porches haunted by cats with slitted eyes. There was something magical about going to the library at five in the morning. My father would station himself at the record bins, and I would wander down the rows of books with my fingers brushing the spines, confronting my reflection in each passing bay window as it dissolved into the oncoming day. Always, on those mornings, I made sure to claim one of the yellow beanbag chairs in the center of the reading room. That way, the Daughretys couldn't possibly miss me. They came here every Sunday without fail. Mr. Borowski once told my father that all three of them—Doctor, mother, and infant daughter—had been waiting outside at five-fifteen in the morning on the Sunday after Theresa was born.

The library now has sleek new glass doors and a whole windowed wing I have never seen before that stretches from the left-hand side of the original building into the lot where one of the Polish bakeries used to be. The other bakery is still here, although it appears to be closed.

I did try to sleep. I got in bed at two-thirty and stayed there until close to four, but I never actually dozed off. I kept seeing Theresa step out of the shadows to wrap me in an icy embrace. Spencer's story played over and over in my mind, his gaunt, glowing face floating above me and mouthing the words. Every now and then, Jon Goblin limped into the room and waved his cane. I flicked on the light. The whole experience of locating Spencer, hearing him tell his terrible tale in his powerful voice, and seeing him all but safe in a community of people who clearly valued him had left me far too anxious to sleep. I got up, reached into my duffel bag, and drew out the blue spiral notebook that Theresa had given me one of the last times I saw her. The top coil had come out of its holes long ago. The cover is scratched, streaked with black slashes of ink. I once believed the key to everything could be found in this notebook. I think I still believe it. But I've never been able to translate the scrawls covering every page. Theresa had written up and down the margins and into the pockets, where she had crammed marked-up maps of Oakland County, Macomb County, and downtown Detroit. Her father couldn't make any sense of it, and neither could the police. Sometimes I open it and chant some of the clusters of words I can actually decipher as if they are spells.

This time, I just thumbed through the pages for the thousandth time. I saw the place where my name first appears, underlined in red, in the midst of what looks like a street-by-street inventory of every business within a three-mile radius of where we lived. Burger King was there, and Kroger, and Stroh's, and Mini-Mike's, and Avri's. I was listed under Avri's, though I never went there with her. Next to the name of each business—but not next to my name—Theresa had drawn a tiny face with dot eyes and a jagged jack-o'-lantern mouth in red Magic Marker. Down the right-hand margin of the page is a sketch of what could be a stalactite or a spear dangling upside down, and beside that, written vertically like the solution to a section of an invisible crossword puzzle, are the words *missed* and *home*.

I turned more pages and stopped at the one where Theresa had meticulously whited out each of the college-rule lines, creating a sort of relief map of blankness. In the middle of all that nothing, Barbara Fox's name floats in black-ink block letters. It occurs to me now— and not for the first time—that my one celebrated artistic idea wasn't even my own. I pretty much got it from this notebook, although God knows what Theresa was trying to communicate. By quarter to five I was still awake, and I couldn't sit still. I got up, layered every T-shirt I'd brought with me under my sweater and coat, slipped Theresa's notebook into my backpack, and stepped out into the cauterizing cold. The morning was weirdly bright because of all the snow illuminated by the suburban streetlights. I drove past Phil Hart Elementary and saw that the school looked exactly the same: red brick, long asphalt blacktop, twin soccer fields, century-old maple trees. I sat in the long circular driveway where the buses lined up every afternoon to take the students home and recalled Mrs. Jupp sounding pinched and trapped in the PA system speakers. From there, I circled Shane Park a few times before remembering the library.

For one moment, as I pull open the library's glass door and the heat spills out, a premonition whistles through me. Theresa could be here. In a way, it's more likely that I'd find her here than anywhere else, curled up on a beanbag with her legs underneath her, reading a fat hardback nineteenth-century novel. In the early days of 1977, mostly to annoy her father, she read *The Shining*, which I remember because of the featureless little kid's face imprinted on the book's embossed silver cover—a blank white blot with hair on top. I remember starting toward her and then shying away because I didn't want to go near that face. It looked porous, like a sponge, capable of absorbing me completely. But one look around the library's original room, and I know my premonition is wrong. At the study tables by the window, three white-haired red-eyed men look up in unison with outrage on their faces, and I almost start to laugh. They look like the neglected husbands of Macbeth's three hags, deposited next to their Sunday papers so the wives can conjure on the blasted heath. After a few seconds, one of them snaps, "Shut the goddamn door," and I do, shielding my eyes against the bright fluorescent light.

All my life, even in Louisville, I have loved libraries, though not for the books exactly, and not for the mythical library smell that my father used to rhapsodize about. I prowl libraries the way divers search sunken ships, looking for nothing in particular, something old and algae-covered and meaningful in ways I haven't yet learned. None of the books I see here have that sort of allure. I suspect they don't even have the little checkout cards that provided clues about whose lives they had touched last.

The new wing turns out to be a long row of computer work stations with no books in it at all. The drawers of catalog cards that once partitioned off the entranceway and made it a separate space are gone. The slush-gray carpet has been replaced by red shag. Flyers for community theater productions and local right-to-life and AA meetings fill slots in a hanging bin beside the coat rack. Best-sellers fan out on the nearest table under the two-week rental sign. This is nowhere I know.

"Heathcliff?" says a silky voice straight out of *Masterpiece Theatre*, and I glance toward the circulation desk. Behind it, a thirtyish dark-haired woman with perfect posture stands next to a computer terminal, sipping from a black mug that says GRRR in orange letters on the side. She's a little taller than I am, and her very slightly red mouth curls upward at the edges like an ember crisped by fire. Her white sweater is loose and soft-looking. Her hair tumbles over itself to her shoulders.

"I'm sorry," I say, shaking my head. "What?"

"You've come from the moors, yes? To sweep me away?" Her smile is quick, friendly, private.

"For your sake, I hope not," I mumble. The fact that I am immediately attracted to this woman at this particular moment in my life is the most ridiculous thing yet about this weekend.

The woman claps her palms gently. "Oh, good. I do like a doomed man." It's her glasses, I think, that make her eyes flash in this lifeless light. "Elizabeth Findlay, senior librarian, and yes, I chose this shift. You may call me Eliza."

Sensation returns to my numbed limbs, and my lungs adjust to the book-heavy weight of the library air. This woman seems even more exotic and more out of place here than Mr. Borowski did.

"You're awfully cheerful for East Birmingham, Michigan, at dawn on a Sunday morning," I say.

"In the middle of a miserable winter," adds Eliza, "with the coffee machine broken." She taps once at the computer screen and looks at me with a disconcertingly familiar expression, something related to hunger and hope and hurt but not quite any of those things. I can feel the trademark Mattie Rhodes awkwardness seep into the room. I open my mouth before I know what to say, and she speaks first.

"So just who is it, Eliza wonders, that has wandered into her world, looking as though he's just returned from an alien abduction?"

I'm trying to remember the last time I flirted with anyone. If I could only slip free of my perpetual mindset, I half believe I could charm this person. I've been charming before, once or twice. But what would be the point?

"Can I help?" she says, a little less warmly. It's apparent that I've been standing here too long, saying nothing.

"Not without years of training," I say, and she smiles again. "I'm looking for someone."

"Aren't we all?"

"A dead someone. Do you have the *Free Press* obituaries on microfilm?"

"On disc. By date. Which year did you want?"

"Oh," I say, just to slow this down a little, then feel a swell of nausea and lean against the desk.

"Do you want some tea or water?" Eliza asks. "You look awfully pale, my new doomed friend."

"Nineteen ninety-one," I say tentatively. "Maybe nineteen ninety-two. I think 'ninety-one." She retrieves a disc from the file behind her in a matter of seconds.

"This is the whole Metro section of the paper from that year. Do you need help searching it?"

My gaze hovers around her deep brown eyes, her curled mouth. "No, thanks. I can figure it out."

Eliza shrugs, and her voice turns professional again. She seems a little disappointed, which amazes me. "Why don't you tell me who you're looking for? There may be other sources."

"I don't want to bother you."

"Do I look busy?"

"Colin Daughrety," I tell her, breaking eye contact. "He died in a car accident."

"*Dr.* Colin Daughrety?"

I take one breath to keep my heart from kicking a hole in my chest. "You knew him?" I say.

"Did you?" says Eliza, her expression surprised, curious. "We all knew him here. He was our Sunday morning regular. We even held a memorial service for him in the new tech wing over there."

"Did he . . ." I start, but the words spill out so fast that I feel as if I'm spitting. "Did he bring his daughter with him?"

"Theresa?"

My knees give way and I sit down on the red carpet.

"Oh," Eliza says. "Sir, are you drunk? You have to leave if you're drunk."

"You know Theresa Daughrety?" I say from the floor.

Eliza studies me. I wait for her to call the police, or security, or the three old guys at the newspaper table. Instead, she comes around from behind the circulation desk and kneels next to me. Her black skirt rises just above her knees. For all kinds of reasons—this place, the Doctor, my wife, and now this woman—my chest begins to ache.

"I never saw her," says Eliza. "The Doctor used to check out books for her." She eyes me warily. Then she says, "You know, I think it might be time to try standing up." She stands first, her skirt falling into place as she offers me her hand. "You grew up here, then?"

Eliza's hand slides into mine and pulls me to my feet. When I'm up, she lets go but doesn't turn away.

I nod. "In Troy. My name is Mattie Rhodes."

To my astonishment, she gasps. Her eyes are bright, and her mouth has slid open. "You're that kid. Oh, my God, I know you!"

The heater breathes and hums around us. The old men at the newspaper table shift, rustling their papers.

"Apparently, you grew up here, too," I murmur.

"Sweet Jesus, in West Bloomfield," she said. "I was twelve years old then. I knew all about you."

"Don't say that," I say, feeling the muscles in my legs start to quiver.

Eliza watches me a few seconds longer and then says, "I think I may be able to help."

Still shaken, I follow her as she glides down a long row of clear plastic library spines. At the end of the aisle, through a tall narrow window, the rising sun colors the pine trees and snowdrifts red. I look up when she stops. And there it is, staring straight at me with its horrible hollow eyes. Then I'm tipping again, very nearly toppling into a bookcase. I swear I can hear my sense of balance grinding like the gears of a grandfather clock. *Tic-toc.* Doesn't life ever, for one second, stop?

Either Dr. Daughrety hung this here himself or he provided instructions, because the teeth mask tilts to the left at exactly the same angle I remember, its ivory fangs flashing, its black throat swallowing the light. I wobble backward a step and remember to close my own mouth. Then, all at once, the old fear recedes, leaving behind a taste like unsweetened cocoa, mostly bitter but tinged with the promise—or memory—of sweetness. This thing hung in Theresa's house as a guardian, but it protected neither the Doctor nor his daughter from anything, as far as I can tell. And, like me, it has wound up in exile.

"Hello, old friend," I say. My eyes tear up, and I feel ridiculous.

Eliza is watching me with her head cocked at nearly the same angle as the mask. Her gaze is solicitous, still curious. Laura used to look at me that way, before she got frustrated with waiting for me. "Are you all right?" she asks.

With an effort I muster a smile. "Childhood monster," I say, nodding toward the mask. "I used to have nightmares about that thing. It once hung in the Daughrety living room."

Beneath the teeth mask in a gold frame is a plaque that reads, *For you, fellow hunters of the Sunday dawn, to keep you safe and well.* A photograph of Dr. Daughrety hangs next to it, outlined in black. He's still bald, and his eyes look just the way I remember them, hard and unforgiving. I almost mistake the dates in the frame for Dewey Decimal: *1942–1990.*

In another frame just below it is the obituary I came here to find, dated November 11, 1990. It calls the Doctor a "leading philanthropist," recalling his establishment of two scholarship funds for inner-city students.

Every weekend for the last eighteen years of his life, he donated fifteen hours of service to a free clinic that he helped to establish in one of the most troubled areas of downtown. Dr. Daughrety is survived by his loving wife Barbara and daughter, Theresa.

"Do you know what caused the accident?" I ask after a while.

"Drinking, I heard," says Eliza.

"No. I knew him. I can't picture him drinking."

"Really? No one here was surprised."

That is not what I want to hear. The idea that the Doctor was a closet alcoholic is even more upsetting, somehow, than his being dead. I stay where I am just a moment longer, feeling like a mourner in a funeral-parlor viewing room, except that no matter how sorry I am,

I know I could never quite grieve for this man, although hating him no longer makes any sense.

"How was Barbara through all this?"

Eliza blinks. "Who?"

"Oh. The Doctor's wife. Theresa's . . ." Step-mom, I guess, but I can't bring myself to say it.

"Never met her. Never heard him mention her."

I close my eyes and allow myself the hope that Barbara, at least, is safely away, outside a hut in the sun somewhere, working and singing.

"Is this what you needed, then?" Eliza asks.

I open my eyes. "What I need may not exist in this world."

Eliza lifts her eyebrows and smiles, carefully, just in case I wasn't kidding. There is a part of me, abruptly, that wants to go right out back and build an igloo, and ask this woman to bring me coffee and books from time to time.

"Actually," I say, "what I'm looking for is Theresa."

"Mmm," says Eliza, not moving, which unsettles me.

"What does that mean?"

"Just . . . remembering what I know of your story, that's all."

I blush, murmur, "So no igloo for me," and Eliza stares.

"What?"

"Nothing. I'm sorry." I start back down the aisle. But as I reach the best-seller table, Eliza calls after me in a stage whisper, and I turn to find her returning to the circulation desk but watching me.

"Mr. Rhodes. You wish to find her, yes?"

I nod.

"I'll be here a few hours yet. Check back, will you? I'll do a bit of rooting around. I may have something for you."

"You sure?"

She grins. "You were easily one of the most memorable stories of the memorable winter of 1977. I always wondered how it turned out."

"Me too," I say, and before she can see that I can't grin back, I turn and push back out the door into the snow.

On Woodward, the International House of Pancakes is open, and cars are slushing through the parking lot. If I can't have sleep, at least

I can have coffee, maybe even a little food. I park my car in the back corner of the I-HOP lot and wade through puddles before pushing open the double glass doors and sliding into an orange plastic booth. Within seconds, a face pops up in my line of vision. It is apple-shaped and apple-colored. The mouth forms an oval, open slightly. I remember this sort of slack face on so many high school girls. It always made me sad.

"Take your order?" she says.

"Apple pancakes, sausage, as much coffee as you can bring me."

"You look like you haven't slept in a month," she says, snatching the menu out of my hands. "Maybe you should lay off the coffee."

"I don't need sleep," I announce. "I'm above sleep."

"Okeydokey," she says, and pads away.

I'm thinking of the Doctor drinking silently in his car on the way to a death he never would have dreamed for himself. I imagine Theresa floating beside him, discovering a second dead parent, and I'm more desperate to find her than ever. My pancakes come and I close my eyes. Then the waitress is back, shaking me against the booth.

"Sir?" she says, and I open my eyes and squint. The white winter sun is flashing off car hoods and icy streets. "Sir, I'm sorry, but you can't sleep here. We need the tables. There's a line."

"I fell asleep." My words feel coated in fuzz.

The waitress rolls her eyes. "Sir, really, we —"

"What time is it?" I snap.

"Ten after nine."

"Jesus Christ," I say, stripping bills from my wallet and hurtling out of the booth.

"I didn't mean you couldn't eat your breakfast," she calls after me.

It's not really possible to get from Birmingham to Metro Airport in fifteen minutes, but I come close, strewing red lights behind me. I have time to think of nothing but the consequences of not being there when Laura gets off the plane. I have my windows open, and the freezing air slides down my cheeks like the edge of a razor, shaving away the exhaustion.

At the airport, I skid into a parking space, race into the terminal, and arrive at the gate in time to see the plane crawl over the tarmac and shut itself down with a sigh. The last time Laura was up at 6:48 A.M. was probably during high school, so I'm not optimistic about her mood. I imagine my weary solitary wife walking down the jetway.

A middle-aged businessman wanders out first, his gray hair mashed flat from being pressed against a window, his tie loosened but still tucked inside his collar. He's followed by a glassy-eyed father and son wearing matching Louisville Cardinal basketball sweatshirts. A woman with a ski mask balanced on her forehead steps forward to hug them. Eventually, the flight attendants walk off, clustered around a chirping five-year-old boy in a wheelchair. Apparently, the Sunday morning flight to Detroit isn't a very popular one. Then it's just me, leaning against a pillar, my heart racing. Ten minutes go by before I accept that she's not coming.

I have no idea what to feel about this, even though I should have predicted it. I go to the nearest bank of pay phones and punch in calling-card numbers, but my fingers won't work properly. It takes me six tries. In my house, the phone rings and rings and rings. Laura doesn't answer and neither does our machine. Thirty rings later, I hang up and stand there. I feel like an arctic explorer at the moment his supply ship disappears over the horizon.

"All right. Okay," I say to myself.

In the car on the way back to the motel, the numbness starts to wear off, and tiny needles of terror begin to pulse through my skin. "Okay," I mutter again. She'll be at Casey's, I decide. Casey is a fortyish overweight mandolin player in Laura's band who wears her hair in a long black braid and sings cheating songs as if they're hymns. Of all Laura's friends, Casey likes me the least. A month or so ago, after the last show of Laura's I attended, Casey and I sat at the velvet-lined bar in the back of the Secretariat Club and watched Laura drink herself down from her performance high. When she stood unsteadily to go to the bathroom, we watched her weave between the tables as if she were staggering down the deck of a rolling ship, her hands grabbing chair backs and random shoulders to make sure she didn't tumble overboard.

That's when Casey turned to me and snapped, "You're more like her neighbor than her husband."

I almost dropped my beer. I considered stalking out. Instead, I asked, "Is that what Laura thinks?"

"Laura wouldn't know the difference, Mattie," Casey said, sounding surprisingly civil.

My marriage is ending. I should hop the next plane and be at my house by noon — before she and Casey have a chance to load Laura's stuff into Casey's pickup. I'll drag Laura to the couch, sit beside her, and say . . . what, exactly? That I found an old best friend who wants me around even less than you do? That I dug up my childhood and discovered it was frozen and gray and full of echoes?

I've been sitting in the Moto-Court parking lot for at least five minutes before it occurs to me to shut off the motor. And it's another two before I open the door and realize that the battered blue Buick next to me has been honking nonstop, and Spencer Franklin is at the wheel.

1977

After Mr. Fox's death, Theresa disappeared altogether. My parents said that the Doctor and Barbara came together to Mr. Fox's funeral, but Theresa wasn't with them. Mrs. Fox came too and tried to talk to Barbara before the graveside service, but Barbara just leaned into the Doctor and cried quietly and stared at the bare maple trees. Her mother wound up standing by my mother, and they held hands all through the ceremony.

"Cynthia looks the same," my mother said, that night over dinner.

"It's only been three years," said my father.

"Almost four," said my mother.

I couldn't really remember much about Mrs. Fox except that she made giant macramé baskets for hanging plants and had red hair that plunged down her back in multiple directions like seaweed in a rip-tide. I knew she had been gone for a long time and that she'd given up on trying to get Mr. Fox to quit drinking. Barbara was already in college by then, but she said her mother had abandoned her family all the same.

Every day from then on, I would stand at the bus stop and watch the spot between the maple trees where Theresa would appear if she was coming to school. But she never did.

Twice during that time, Spencer and I tried to see her. One Saturday afternoon, we made my father stop at her house on the way to Mini-Mike's. We rang the bell, got no answer, and walked around back. The basement window had been replaced. All the curtains were drawn, and the whole place felt like a churchyard cemetery. Spencer had started for the car when I hopped up on the front porch and rang the bell one more time. I almost flew backward when the door swung open. The Doctor was standing before me in a checkered bathrobe. He had stubble on his chin and a coffee cup in his hand, and he looked as if he hadn't slept in ages.

"She's not ready to see you," he said, without even a hello.

"You could try asking her," Spencer said, coming up fast behind me. I tensed. I didn't think he meant to sound so nasty.

But the Doctor just gave us his arctic smile and said, "No."

On impulse, as the door swung shut, I stuck out my arm and pushed it open again. Then I stared at my hand, not believing what I'd done. But the action had triggered a strangely comforting suction, as if I'd drawn something poisonous to the surface.

The Doctor's face reappeared.

"Can I say hello to Barbara?" I asked.

Sighing, Dr. Daughrety leaned into the living room and called, "Say hello to Mattie, Barb."

"Hello, Mattie," said Barbara's voice. She didn't come to the door. The Doctor nodded, raised a hand to us—or maybe to my father, who was still watching us from the car—and shut us out.

The second time, we came alone, at night, and we were not going to leave without getting inside. Spencer was sleeping over, and we'd been in my room, taking turns shooting a slot car around my Tyco track's one working lane. Since Theresa's absence, Spencer and I had spent more and more time together, but we'd spoken less and less. At recess, we just stood side by side in the patches of filthy snow clinging to the edges of the blacktop, slowly twisting together like the trunks of two birch trees stretching for the same dead light.

That night was the first of four in a row that Spencer was to spend at my house. When his mother dropped him off, she told my mother she was going on a "save the marriage" retreat with her husband. My mother made the sort of practiced but genuine sympathetic murmur she'd long since mastered, but she looked uncomfortable. I glanced at Spencer, and he shrugged.

"They go to Lake St. Claire and go dancing. Sometimes they have fun."

After a couple of hours passing the slot-car controller back and forth, I got up to go to the bathroom and stopped in the hall. I could hear my parents talking low in the living room. They only did that when there was something they didn't want me to know, so I crept to the hallway door to listen. Spencer peered out of my room, then tip-toed up beside me.

"Did Cynthia actually see any of this?" my father asked.

My mother sighed. "No. Colin won't let anyone into the house. Barbara had to meet her at Avri's Deli."

"At least they finally talked."

"Kind of," said my mother, and I heard her breathe once, long and hard, and I knew she was crying. "Oh, Joe. Cynthia said Barbara just sat there and wept the whole meal. And smoked. When did you ever see fresh-air-queen Barbara Fox smoke?"

The muscles around my ribs slithered to life and began to squeeze. Spencer sat down next to me on the hallway carpet and leaned against the wall. Lately, waiting around had become our primary shared activity.

"When did it happen?" said my father.

"Two or three days ago, I guess. Theresa just woke up, got out of bed, and slashed every curtain in the house to ribbons with an X-acto blade. She draped strips of fabric everywhere as if they were animal skins or something. Barbara says Theresa has been lying under a quilt with her face mashed against her window ever since. She has crying fits in the middle of the night."

"Jesus," said my father.

"Colin makes her get up once a day and take a bath. Barbara says she spends the whole time singing."

"Singing what?"

"Hell, Joe, I don't know. Just singing. Staring at the walls. Barbara has to bathe her; she won't do it herself."

"Should we go over there? Maybe there's something we can do."

"Even if we could do something, he wouldn't let us," my mother said.

My head started shaking wildly back and forth. I looked at Spencer. His red sneakers were tucked so tight against his drawn-in legs that they looked manacled to his body. I knew what he was thinking. We were used to Theresa's monumental silences. But the thought of her slashing curtains or having crying fits caused an all-new sort of anxiety. My parents stopped speaking, and after a while I gestured to Spencer and we slipped back into my room. For a long time, we lay under the covers in our bunks, fully clothed.

"We have to do something right now," Spencer said from the lower bunk. I knew he was right. I had ideas, too, but they all seemed babyish, and I didn't think they would do anything to make Theresa feel better.

"Her dad can't help her," I said.

"If we don't do something now, we might never get another chance," said Spencer. "She'll just be gone."

I ignored him, continuing my thought. "He doesn't know how."

"She hates Barbara," Spencer said.

"Not anymore," I said. "But Barbara just ran over her father, so she's no use."

"Point," said Spencer.

"So what do we do when we get there?"

If not for the rustling of the sheets, I might have thought Spencer had fallen asleep, because he took such a long time answering. Then he said, "Don't your parents ever go to bed?"

My dad was especially restless, roaming back and forth from the hallway to the living room. Twice, he stopped outside my door, but he didn't come in. Once he went into his bedroom where my mother was, but he came right back out again. The glowing green rocket hands on the solar-system clock on my desk read two in the morning before I heard the familiar sag-and-creak of my parents' bed and knew he was down at last. Wordlessly, Spencer and I slipped into our jackets and crept straight out the front door, heading for Theresa's.

The street was full of mud from a week of rain. In school, we'd been learning about ankle-deep oceans flooding the land during the Cretaceous period and giant creatures splashing through the too-warm world, beginning to die. So for our walk, Spencer and I became brontosaurs, gnawing on last year's leaves as we puddle-stomped our way to extinction under the stone-gray moon.

At the bottom of the hill that led to the Daughrety house, Spencer slipped and bellyflopped and came up covered in muck. "I hate the suburbs," he snapped, scooping palmfuls of mud from his sweatshirt and jeans. He was still doing that when we reached the edge of the Daughrety patio.

I pointed through the maples to Theresa's porthole window. "Okay, city boy," I said, and my fingers began to tingle, but not from the cold. "Let's wake her up."

Spencer stared at me, one hand dripping mud, his face settling into the same determined expression I'd seen the morning I first met him, during our premiere sidecarring run. But it had looked playful then, not sad. He cocked his arm in football-throwing position, and mud traced down the inside of his wrist like iodine revealing a vein. "Ready?" he said.

I nodded. He threw.

The mud gob burst on the glass of the porthole window, and we both dropped to our stomachs. I think I actually flung my arms over my head the way we were told to do during tornado drills. I held my breath. But when I looked up, there was neither movement nor light in the house.

Collecting my own missile, I shoved to my feet. The mud felt slick and weighty in my hands, like a pig heart in formaldehyde. I reared back and threw it as hard as I could. The mud ball smacked into the cedar shingles, and something rustled in the bushes behind us. We whirled together, but no one was there. We turned to the house again, expecting lights, sound, something, but we saw nothing. Theresa was gone, or at least she wasn't showing herself. Suddenly, I was furious. I was thinking of Mr. Fox's bleeding face. I wanted to kick through the porthole window, howling, *By the hair of my chinny-chin-chin, let me in, let me in!*

"We could light the place on fire," Spencer said.

"Got a match?" He'd been kidding, sort of. I was too. Sort of. But I wanted into that house. I had to see Theresa, and the pressure was swelling inside me like helium in a balloon. "Maybe they're in the basement," I said. "I bet he's keeping them all hidden."

Spencer studied me, as though he could see the shift in my mood rising off me like steam. "Mattie, I think the Doctor's as much of a spaz as you do, but he's not the Snowman. He's not keeping Barbara and Theresa locked up in the basement. It's cold down there. Come on, let's go."

"Shut up," I said, and he stared at me some more.

Gradually, silence settled over us. That made me madder still. We'd snuck out of my house, stormed the gates of the Daughrety fortress, and we hadn't even triggered the Doctor's defenses. It's like we're dead, I thought. The Snowman has killed us without our knowing it, and now we're floating around inside his invisible world, unable to affect it in any way. I missed Theresa. I could hardly remember what it was like to speak to her, or even catch her glance across the room. I'd liked catching her glance. And I think maybe I loved her, without any idea of what that meant except it was different from anything I'd felt for my mother, or Barbara, or anyone else,, and it made me unhappy.

"Okay, let's go for now," I said to Spencer. "We'll have to come up with something else." He nodded, and we retreated down the hill.

The next day was chaos. For the third time in two weeks, Ms. Eyre didn't show up. This time, she hadn't even let the school know until seconds before the bell sounded, and Mrs. Jupp had to phone for an emergency sub and then sit with us until the sub arrived.

"Is Ms. Eyre sick?" I asked Mrs. Jupp. "Did she hurt her jaw again?"

Behind her perpetual mask of peach makeup, Mrs. Jupp looked as exhausted as every other adult I knew. "I really don't know, Mattie. I don't know what's happening to her, except that this has been an extraordinary year. Extraordinary. We all need some time away."

The sub turned out to be a grandmother in her late fifties who spent the first half hour confiscating paper airplanes and the rest of the day dodging them. During English hour, Jamie Kerflack, in perhaps the most inspired act of his vicious elementary-school career, wrote his entire set of homework sentences backward on the board. When the sub balled him out, he announced that he was dyslexic and started to cry while the rest of us roared with laughter. At lunch, Spencer and I slipped on wet linoleum in the middle of what would have been a record-setting sidecarring run down the hallway and slid feet first into Mrs. Jupp's office door. Furious, she dragged us inside without even letting us untangle the harness.

"There's not enough going on in this place? I don't have enough to do with your suddenly unreliable teacher and child-killers and God knows what else? Now I have to put up with your nonsense too?"

"Mrs. Jupp, where's Theresa Daughrety? Why isn't she coming to school?" I asked abruptly. Mrs. Jupp gurgled to silence as if I'd grabbed her around the throat. Her lips tightened. "Mattie, let's just see what happens, all right? It has been a monstrous year."

"But where is she?" I was very nearly yelling.

Beside me, Spencer said, "Whoa."

"Don't you use that tone with me, Mattie Rhodes."

I lowered my eyes, not from acquiescence or regret but as a ploy. Mrs. Jupp had information, and I wanted it. I was becoming a master of such manipulations.

"She's home, Mattie," Mrs. Jupp said. "At least, that's what her father tells me. I don't know when she'll be back. What I do know is that she's just too bright a penny to be lost forever. I know you're worried about her. I know you're trying to be her friend. But she really will be all right. Now, back to your classroom. Don't make me have to ask you again."

When I left Mrs. Jupp's office, what I felt, more than anything else, was rage. It had mostly to do with Theresa's absence, but I also had the sense that time was running out on a game I hadn't even known I was playing. Back in class, Spencer and I avoided talking about Ms. Eyre or Mrs. Jupp or the empty desk between us. Instead, we talked about slot cars and Mark the Bird Fidyrich, who had ripped up his knee during spring training in Florida. The last paper airplane I built that day was a masterpiece, with landing gear and a paper-clip propeller. Finally, as our classmates began to wind down, Spencer looked out the window and noticed the snow.

"Snowman weather," he said.

It came down singing, the way it always did in Detroit at the end of March. The wind whined and the first returning jays took turns protesting from atop the power lines as the road ice slid down the asphalt into the ditches and the muddy ground succumbed almost gladly to one last whitewash.

Mrs. Jupp announced over the PA system that the storm was expected to be severe, so the buses would be arriving soon to take us home early. We all cheered, more from habit than enthusiasm.

"Your parents have been called," Mrs. Jupp droned on, "and all of them are making arrangements for you to be met at your bus stops."

"You're sleeping at my house, right?" I said to Spencer as we packed our bags and stepped through the crumpled paper airplanes littering the floor and crunching like dead locusts under our feet.

Spencer peered into his backpack. "Got toothbrush. Got undies. Looks like it."

We filed onto the bus. After the near riot in our classroom, the ride home was strangely silent. I sat next to Spencer and turned in my seat a few times, half expecting Theresa to materialize behind me. Cars passed with their headlights floating in the gloom like giant winter fireflies gorging on snowflakes. By the time Spencer and I jumped off, there was an inch and a half of new snow on the ground, and heavy clouds were ushering in the dark.

"Your mom isn't here," Spencer said.

"She's working in Romeo this month," I said. "It'll take her a while to get home."

Davy McLean, Brent's best friend from two blocks away, started a halfhearted snowball fight while the shadows of the evergreens rolled toward us like an incoming tide. More quickly than usual, everyone dispersed. Brent went home without acknowledging my presence. That left Spencer and me alone on the street. For a while, we didn't talk, just drifted along the snow-blurred edges of lawns. I opened my mouth and imagined myself preying on all this snowflake plankton. I didn't want to go inside until my mother came home, because she'd probably keep us there.

"Let's go to the Daughretys'," I said.

"What for?" said Spencer, sweeping caked snow from any tree branch he could reach.

"Maybe he'll let us in today."

We went, but the house looked derelict, its windows blank. We were about to give up when I saw Theresa's face floating in the blackness of the porthole window like a jack-in-the-box underwater, and I grabbed Spencer's arm.

"She's there." But when I looked again, she was gone.

Spencer studied the lightless house. "You're seeing things, Mattie."

"I don't think so," I said. But I wasn't completely sure. I listened to the snow and the barely there wind through the leafless trees and peopleless yards. And suddenly I knew—just knew—that if I didn't do something today, it would be too late. Spencer turned back toward the street, but I grabbed his arm again, only harder. "Wait," I said.

"Mattie, what do you want to do, put your face through the window, Mr. Fox–style?"

I shrugged. If I'd thought it would do any good, I would have gone to the front door and banged until my hands bled. I would have pitched a screaming fit on the Doctor's front porch until he had no choice but to let me into his sanctuary of masks. It terrified me and made no sense, how much I missed his bow-mouthed girl.

Finally, I let Spencer lead me straight down the center of my street. The mud-soaked ground under the snow sucked at our shoes. I thought about mud running down Theresa's leg into Cider Lake like the hair dye on my mother's cheek. I thought about skating during her last birthday party, when she disappeared among the reeds. I thought about her face floating in the porthole window, and Mrs. Cory with her arm raised, saying, "Goodbye, boys," and about how dearly I'd loved this year, in spite of everything. Or maybe because of everything.

All at once, as though every one of my cells had been asleep for months and now awoke simultaneously, the tingling feeling exploded all over my skin. I was crying a little and stomping my feet. I think Spencer thought the tears were from the wind. Two houses from mine, I stopped dead.

Spencer stopped with me and sighed. "Mattie, I'm cold. And your mom's going to murder us if she comes home and we're not there."

"My mom isn't home yet. I have an idea," I said, and pointed to the Fox house.

Spencer looked at the long red-brick ranch-style house. All the rain and snow had caused the gutters under the roof to sag. There were no lights on, of course, no cars in the mud and drift-caked driveway.

"Who lives there?"

"No one. It's empty."

"So why are we going in?"

"Practice," I said, feeling a brighter, wilder version of my sidecarring smile spread over my face.

"Practice for what?" Spencer said, but his voice had changed, and he wasn't hopping up and down anymore.

"Operation Theresa."

"Which is what, exactly?"

"Just come with me," I said, and stepped off into the Foxes' yard.

"What the fuck," I heard Spencer mumble, but his boots came stomping behind me. I couldn't stop tingling, and I couldn't stand still, and I didn't know quite what I was doing except that Mr. Fox was dead, and this house was yet another place I used to go that was now forbidden to me.

I stalked around back and found the key to the back-porch door taped under the picnic-table bench, right where it had been all my life. I pulled it loose and held it up to Spencer.

"How'd you know that was there?"

"This is Barbara's house. I used to come here all the time when she baby-sat me."

"Mattie, your mom's gotta be home by now."

"She's not. Stop being a baby."

The lock was old and half frozen, and it took several tries before the key turned. Then the door swung open, and Spencer and I stepped out of the twilight into a thicker, mustier air. When I shut the door I saw the nearest curtain ripple, but nothing else moved. Even the shadows seemed still. I was tingling so hard I had to sway back and forth to keep from crying out.

"Creepy," said Spencer. "We could play Murder in the Dark, if Theresa was here." The spirit of the moment had caught him a little. He edged toward the kitchen.

I stayed by the door. I wasn't afraid, but I couldn't catch my breath. I was thinking of Barbara laughing at me in the grass, Ms. Eyre's bruised eye sockets and caged jaw, blue Gremlins prowling through the snow like escaped lions, having a best friend for the first time in my life. Then I was thinking of Theresa's hair ribbon, and her open mouth as she knelt over Mr. Fox's crushed body, and everything else disintegrated.

Theresa needed my help. Her father was too proud; Barbara was too angry, Ms. Eyre was too bitter, and Mrs. Jupp too blinded by Theresa's brain to even see the cliff edge she had wandered toward, let alone yank her back.

"Spencer," I called, feeling almost deliriously calm, "what if a blue Gremlin pulled up in this driveway right now?"

I wasn't even looking as I strode past the yellow couch, the glass coffee table that reflected nothing but accumulated dust. I stopped briefly

by a picture of Barbara and me on the wall, part of a framed collage
of childhood photographs. She looked gawky and gangly, a teenager,
and I looked like Brent had looked when he was five, only smaller. We
were both in bathing suits on the shore of Cider Lake on a gray day.
Barbara was watching the water. I was watching Barbara. Neither of
us was smiling.

"Why do you say things like that?" Spencer said, and flopped into
a nearby brown vinyl recliner. Dust puffed out like smoke and
obscured him. I was grinning again, tingling madly.

"What if the Snowman got you?"

He wasn't paying attention. He drummed his hands on the arms of
the recliner, and more dust billowed into the air. "Poof," he said.

"I mean, what if you were gone? What if I went home right now and
told my mother the Snowman got you?"

Spencer kept beating the arms of the chair. He waited for the dust
to settle. Then he looked at me and said, "Mattie, what the hell are
you talking about?"

"She's your friend too, you know."

"She? What she?"

"Theresa. Listen. What if I told my mother we were having a snowball fight by the bus stop, and you ran into the Daughretys' yard, and
when I looked up I saw Theresa waving in the window but I couldn't
see you, and there was only this rusty blue car pulling away down
Cider Lake Road. And you were gone."

Spencer stared, opened his mouth. "Are you cra—"

"Someone would have to talk to Theresa. She would have seen
something, and I could say I thought she'd talk to me, maybe. They'd
have to let me in then, see? They'd have no choice. The Doctor
couldn't stop them."

"Let me think about this for a sec." Spencer closed his eyes, opened
them. "Okay. Done. I'm hungry. Let's go."

He stood up and started for the front door. I grabbed him hard
around the arm and pulled him back.

"Ow," said Spencer, jerking his arm away. "Stop doing that."

It was already happening, though. I'd lost control of everything in my world. Very possibly, I'd never had it. But I knew I could make this happen. I could get to Theresa by using the Snowman.

"We have to help her. She's in huge trouble, Spencer."

"So you figure we can help her by getting into even bigger trouble ourselves."

"You saw her kneeling by Mr. Fox. *In* Mr. Fox. I'm telling you, Theresa's really screwed up. Something's really wrong."

"I know that, Mattie. Everyone knows that."

"You've seen her dad. You've seen how much he wants her to win everything. You see how she is at school. Everyone else in our class treats her like a freak."

"She is a freak."

I shook Spencer's arm, thinking it through, tingling. "Just tonight. After I get in to see Theresa, I'll come and get you. A couple of hours, Spencer. Overnight, tops."

"What about my mother?"

"Your mother doesn't come back until Sunday."

With a grunt, Spencer wrenched his arm out of my grasp and stepped back, and we both looked out the window. Through the snow, the houses and trees of my neighborhood were dissolving into dots of color. No dream I'd ever had felt any less real than my current waking world, with its dead neighbors and singing snow and monsters and lost girls.

"How about we both stay," said Spencer, and I realized with a shiver, part pleasure and part knee-buckling excitement, that he was starting to give in. I wanted this to happen more than anything I'd ever wanted before. I knew it was going to get me in big trouble. But it also might get me in to see Theresa. It had to.

"When it's over, I'll explain to my parents. They'll understand. They're afraid for her too." We stood awhile longer, feeling the undertow of our intentions sucking us into an all-new and much larger netherworld. Finally, I grinned. "Maybe I can even bring Theresa here. Then we can really play Murder in the Dark."

The thought made me tremble. I could already see Theresa and me in the snow, on the run, racing to where Spencer would be waiting for us. It could happen. I could make it happen. It would be the first brave thing I'd ever done. "Come on, Spencer."

"I'll do it if the TV works," he said.

It did.

I left him sitting cross-legged in front of a *Brady Bunch* rerun. We'd found canned food in the kitchen and the stove worked too, so he was having cream of mushroom soup and corn for dinner. In the backyard, I taped the key back under the picnic bench and saw Spencer's shadow rise up in the glass. I thought he was going to chase after me, yell for me to stop, but he just waved.

That was almost enough to send me racing back inside. I didn't want to leave Spencer there. But I wanted Theresa beside me in the snow. I wanted her sitting next to me in school at her regular desk. I wanted to wipe that blank expression from her face like condensation from window glass, so I could see what was underneath it at last.

I looked at Spencer, felt sick, waved back. Then I made myself walk around to the front yard. When I was out of sight of the Foxes' front window, I grabbed a handful of snow from a bush and drove it into my face. That's when I started laughing uncontrollably. I couldn't help it, and I couldn't stop. I was laughing so hard it felt like crying. I *was* crying, in fact, which is probably why it worked.

My mother was already on the driveway, of course, shivering in the dark and snow. When she saw me coming, she closed her eyes and yelled, "Goddammit, Mattie, do you think you can just disappear whenever you want?"

But I still couldn't control my laughter, and the street seemed to be sliding beneath me like a roller coaster track, propelling me toward the inevitable drop. Through the tears in my eyes, I saw my mother's face freeze.

"Mattie?" She grabbed me around the shoulders as soon as I was close enough, but I just laughed harder. "Mattie, what? Jesus, what? Where's Spencer? Mattie, where is he?"

Down the street, I tried to say. At the Foxes'. But I couldn't get my mouth to work. I couldn't get the air down my lungs. And in the end, all I got out—so quietly that I couldn't even hear it myself—was "Blue Gremlin."

But my mother heard me. And before I could stop her, she was screaming into the house, dragging me behind her as she lunged for the phone.

1994

Spencer doesn't lay off the horn as I approach the car, though he
appears to be looking right at me. He's wearing his black Detroit
Tigers baseball hat pulled down over his forehead. I bang on the
hood of the Buick, and the horn goes silent.

"You trying to get someone to call the police?" I say.

Spencer rolls down the window and tilts his face up to me. The sunlight illuminates him. He looks exhausted. "Morning, Devil," he says.
"Just wanted to make sure I got your attention."

"Surprised to see you, Shep."

"Not as surprised as I am."

The driver's-side door has hollows and welts all over it, as if it were
left out during a meteor shower.

"Weren't you in a Caddy last night?" I say.

"Church car," says Spencer. "And we are not in church now, brother. Get in."

Spencer twists the ignition key twice. On the third try, black exhaust billows from the back, filling the parking lot with fumes. I drop my knapsack on the floor and lean back in the seat as Spencer pulls out of the lot.

"Sometime around dawn," Spencer says, "for absolutely no reason, I got sort of excited about you being here."

"I'm glad," I tell him. "Going through this without you doesn't make a hell of a lot of sense."

"As opposed to going through it with me. Which makes all kinds of sense."

"What do you think we should do?" I say.

"I have no thoughts, Mattie. I am a walking iceball of sleep deprivation and temporarily repressed panic."

"Then let's go to the Daughrety house."

"The Daughrety house," says Spencer, too brightly, as if I've suggested Boblo Island Amusement Park. "Righty-o."

He slides the car backward, and in seconds we're shooting up Maple toward the outskirts of Birmingham, where the trees get older and the houses larger and the lakes lonelier and deeper. We pass Shane Park and that second smaller park I never knew the name of, with the creek and the little waterfall in the middle, then the shopping courts of low wooden buildings where there used to be a take-out place called Jiggly's, the only place in town that sold red packets of Pizza Dust, which jumped on your tongue like pop rocks but tasted sort of like pizza. I don't think I ever went there with Spencer, and I didn't like Pizza Dust much. But I remember it. Jiggly's is long gone, of course, a casualty of the Domino's–Little Caesar's firefight for pizza supremacy in the Motor City.

"You sleep?" Spencer asks.

"A little, in an I-HOP this morning." I'm thinking how relieved I am that Laura isn't here and how terrified that she may be gone for good.

"I didn't. Not one wink. I sat up talking to myself all night. Turn here?"

He's already turning, though. He knows exactly where he's going. Nothing in this part of town has changed. We pass the golf course under the arch of old pines and come to the signpost for my street, which is still crooked at the top like a beckoning finger. Two more turns, a scramble of tires on iced gravel, and we're there.

The house sits in the back center of its cul-de-sac, almost entirely obscured by the overgrown pricker branches climbing the dark front windows. Needle-shaped shoots of frozen grass poke through the frost, rising to shin height, so that the yard resembles an enormous loom. One of the side gutters on the roof has split in half and dangles from a splint of old rope.

"Does that place look inhabited to you?" I ask.

Spencer shakes his head. "Not by anyone we want to know, cousin." The giddiness is gone from him now.

"Bet the neighbors have filed complaints."

Spencer glares at the neatly painted Christmas-light-strewn suburban homes around us, seated on their perfect snowy lawns like figurines atop a birthday cake.

A white-haired woman in a blue bathrobe and long overcoat has appeared on the driveway next door. She begins inching toward us. When she's most of the way to the street, she picks up her newspaper, shivers in her slippers, and shuffles a little closer to my side of the car. After a few seconds of studying us, she motions for me to roll down my window.

"Please tell me that you're thinking to buy," she says. Her voice reminds me of a grade-school teacher's.

"Are they selling?" I ask.

"They are if we can help it."

"We?"

"Everyone on the block." The woman takes a step closer. "You gay?"

Spencer bursts out laughing, and the woman waves her arm. "Just wanted to let you know, we don't mind. We welcome anyone with a lawn mower."

I almost smile at that, but the woman isn't smiling, and it isn't funny, and I miss my wife.

"And curtains. We prefer curtains to soap."

I glance back at the Daughretys' front windows. The house is dark, I realize, because the windows are caked with layers of streaky gray-black frozen soap, as though a thousand Devil's Nighters have had a field day.

"Who owns this place?" Spencer asks, his voice low and unsteady.

"A doctor's family owns it, but they don't live here. They don't even live in the state."

"Family?" I snap, my eyes locking on the woman's, and she takes a step back.

"The Doctor's family."

"You know them?"

The woman cringes, but she doesn't retreat any farther. "No. I've only lived here three years. I hear he was a wonderful man, though. Sad. When he died, his wife deeded this place to relatives. They're all in Cleveland and Milwaukee. But for some reason, they won't sell. Won't rent, either. When we tried to get them to rent it, we received all these ridiculous affidavits from a lawyer proclaiming that the house 'was not meant for investment purposes' and 'has intrinsic value to the family and will not be occupied until the family sees fit.' God, I can still quote those things, they were so insane. So there it sits, rotting, full of rats and spiders. Stray cats, too; you can hear them fighting some-times." The woman shudders, tightens her coat around her, and shuf-fles up her driveway without looking back.

Around us, icicles ring in the trees like wind chimes. If this is the end, the last trace I will find of Theresa Daughrety, at least it's a quiet one. I could almost resign myself to it, I think, watching the sunlight, listening to the ice. Then I look at Spencer. His eyes are red, his mouth twisted.

"What?"

Spencer shakes his head but refuses to look at me. "Nothing," he says, and starts the car.

The day has blossomed into one of those rare Michigan midwinter days, hard and icy and brilliant with sunlight.

Spencer asks, "Where to?" His face still hasn't relaxed.

"My place. My old house, I mean."

He seems relieved, almost pleased, as he spins us back up Theresa's street and around to my own.

We pass the Fox house, bright red in the sun, sprouting twin miniature satellite dishes on the roof like little cat ears. The street seems only a little smaller than I remember. The lawns still stretch from house to house, and the birch trees still have most of their bark picked from them. Spencer coasts to a stop at the foot of my yard, and I feel a momentary flicker of deliciously uncomplicated nostalgia as I stare across the drainage ditch we once used as a moat, mock grave, end zone, and hiding place.

But the house is not my house anymore. It has a second story over my room, for one thing, a cedar-shingle addition that pokes through the pines like a treehouse. The living room window has been blocked off by a white wooden carriage swing. The swing is far too big for our little front stoop, which these people apparently consider a porch. A row of Christmas lights festoons the freshly painted gutters, and a reindeer sleigh rides the slope of the roof. I have one flicker of memory, my mother at the back kitchen window with the phone tucked into her newly dyed hair, chattering away to Mrs. McLean, her best friend. I have not seen my mother chatter like that even once, to anyone, since we moved.

"We could ring the bell," Spencer says. "See your old room."

"What time is it?" I ask. "Do you have a clock in this thing?"

"Caveman car," Spencer mutters.

"It's like ten, isn't it?"

Spencer's eyes slide from the road to me. "Mattie, it was after ten when we started."

"Shit. We need to go back to the motel," I say.

"What for?"

"I have a source."

Wiping a hand across his mouth, Spencer makes a little humming sound, way back in his throat. "You're a drug dealer now? What does that mean?"

"The librarian at the Birmingham Library. She was going to do a search for me. She said to check back."

"This is ridiculous, Mattie," he suddenly snaps. "I'm going home."

I just stare at him. His shifts in attitude are making me dizzy. After a while, I say, "Fine. Drop me off."

Spencer says nothing. He drives.

The way to the library looks less magical by daylight. All the porch cats have disappeared. There are kids playing football across two of the yards.

Spencer pulls into the library lot, and I pop open the door. But as I start to climb out, his gloved hand grips my arm and drags me back against the seat.

"Just tell me this. Are we trying to find Theresa? Or are we trying to piece together what happened since we saw her last?"

For a few seconds, this seems like an important question, and I wrestle with it. Then it melts away like a snowball held too long. "Is there a difference?"

"Answer the question," says Spencer.

I watch his face twitch. I have no idea what he's getting at. I haven't, in fact, for most of the morning.

"Park the car," I tell him. "Come with me."

Spencer opens his mouth, but he seems closer to vomiting than speaking. He's so thin, like a paper skeleton folded into the seat.

"Are you all right?"

"Are you joking?" His lips twist downward violently, the way they did when he was young and angry, and I almost laugh. I can't help it.

"It's good that you came," I say, and get out, and he slides the car into the nearest space.

I'm worried that Eliza will have gone, but as soon as I enter the library, I see her hunched over the newspaper table. Piled before her are three massive manila folders stuffed with printouts and clippings. She glances up, sees me, and grins again. "I — um, had a bit of luck," she says. Clippings flutter off the table to her feet. She bends down to retrieve them, and I reach her just as she's collecting the last page. It's a facsimile of an old *Free Press* headline, in triple-size black letters, that reads FACE OF A DEMON?"

I know that headline. I could probably reconstruct the story that goes with it word for word, complete with every print blotch and picture caption. Certainly I could draw the police artist's sketch of the Demon's face.

"Son-of-a-bitch," Spencer mutters behind me.

I try to remove the folder from Eliza's hands, but she folds her arms on top of it.

"You got me curious," she says, looking over my shoulder at Spencer. "Shepherd Franklin, isn't it?" she says, and Spencer blinks in surprise. "That is the proper appellation?"

"Shepherd," Spencer confirms, and he and Eliza eye each other in a way that makes me uncomfortable. It's as though I've stepped all the way into Wonderland now, and everyone has stopped behaving properly.

Eliza's smile widens. "Eliza Findlay," she says to Spencer. "Librarian. You've done some remarkable things." She touches the sleeve of my coat with her hand. "If you've found Shepherd Franklin, there's probably not much here you don't know, Mr. Rhodes."

"Mattie."

"Mattie," she says, and we sit down opposite each other at the table.

"We better go," says Spencer, and both Eliza and I look up at him. "You don't have long, Mattie, you're going back today, right? And she says she didn't find anything."

"Mmm," says Eliza, smile fading, curious expression trained on Spencer now. "I don't think I quite said that."

Spencer plunks down on my right. He's mumbling to himself under his breath. Except for the new librarian behind the library desk—a bespectacled, fortyish man with black and gray curls of hair dangling down his cheeks like dreadlocks that have come uncoiled—we appear to be the only people in the room. Eliza props the top manila folder in her lap and opens it.

"Look," says Spencer, his voice unreadable, strange. "Anything in there about neighborhood lawsuits? Or lawyers? We're trying to track down the current owners of the Daughrety house."

Why he's speaking this way, I have no idea. Eliza just eyes him. His mouth seems to have come unhinged, because he can't quite keep it shut. Eventually, Eliza looks down, thumbs pages, then tosses me a small sheaf from the stack in her lap. The first piece is a feature from the Metro section about a threatened community lawsuit concerning the condition of the home of *one of the city's most prominent physicians and social activists, who died tragically two years ago. Speaking for the estate, Mrs. Rosa Daughrety Mills of Shaker Heights, Ohio, would say only, 'We understand the concerns about the upkeep of the house, and we are doing all we can afford. But my brother left instructions in his will that the house is to be kept for his daughter, should she ever want or be able to use it, and we plan to honor his wishes.*

"Nothing about what's happened in the suit since then?" I ask, looking up to find Eliza still watching Spencer, who may or may not have been mouthing something at her.

"I don't think it's been resolved," Eliza says. "I think that would have turned up in my search." The light in here skims the surface of her brown-black eyes but illuminates little underneath.

"Do you have a pay phone?" I say.

"Over there." She gestures behind her.

I start to stand, then reach across the table and grab her hand. The gesture isn't so much surprising, I think, as clumsy. "Thank you," I say.

"A pleasure, Mattie Rhodes," she says, with no pleasure in her voice.

The operator on the Cleveland end produces the number for Rosa Daughrety Mills of Shaker Heights, Ohio, and with a single click another phone in a whole new Daughrety house begins to ring. I turn around to signal Spencer and find him leaning toward Eliza, whispering.

"Yep?" says a cheerful male voice on the other end of the line.

"May I speak to Rosa Daughrety Mills, please?"

"Telemarketer?"

"What?"

"Do you always ask for people by three names?"

"Is she there?" I say. "Can I speak to her? I'm a friend of Theresa's."

"Of Ther—" The line goes silent, and for a moment I think I've been cut off. Then I hear him exhale, and when he speaks again, the cheerfulness is gone. "Hold on." Back at the table, Eliza's face has reddened under her tan.

"Who the hell is this?" says a voice in my ear, and my tongue cleaves to the roof of my mouth. "Well?"

"Ms. Mills, my name is Mattie Rhodes."

"So what? Why are you calling me?"

"I'm a friend of Theresa's. I'm calling from Detroit."

"What does that mean, *'friend of Theresa's'*? Friend from when?"

"Years ago."

"Be more specific, please."

"Look, Ms. Mills, I'm sorry if I'm bothering you. I knew Theresa in grade school. I'm . . . I'm here trying to find some old friends who meant a great deal to me. Theresa is one of them. Do you have any idea where she is?"

When I called Jon Goblin, there was a constant hum of activity in the background—dog, child, vacuum cleaner. But Rosa Daughrety Mills's house is as silent as the Daughrety house I once knew.

"I don't think I can help you," she says. "Theresa never mentioned you."

"Ms. Mills, please. She really might want to hear from me."

"Mr. . . . Rhodes, is it? I seriously doubt that Theresa could give you whatever it is you're looking for, and if you ever really knew her, you know she doesn't respond very well to surprises."

"Wait!" I practically shout into the phone, closing my eyes in anticipation of the severed connection. When it doesn't come, I open my eyes again. "Can you tell me how I can get in touch with Barbara Fox?"

"Is that some other *friend* of Theresa's?"

"Oh. Sorry. I mean Barbara Daughrety. Your brother's second wife."

"If you find her," Ms. Mills says, "you can tell that gold-digging, self-centered, self-righteous little bitch never to get within a hundred miles of Cleveland, or she will have me to deal with. Got it?"

The line goes dead. I stare at the wall while aftershocks vibrate all over my body. A long time passes before I turn around.

Spencer and Eliza are no longer talking. Only Eliza is looking at me. Her cheeks are red, her eyes narrowed. She looks determined, or flustered, or furious. Spencer is staring at his knees.

"Success?" he says, without lifting his head.

"Weren't you listening?" I mutter, and drop into the seat next to him.

"I think you should tell him," Eliza says. Several seconds go by before I realize she's talking to Spencer. Snow ghosts sail past the window on the rushing breeze.

"Tell me what?"

"This is public information, Shepherd Franklin. He'll find it anyway, if he wants it."

But Spencer is still speaking to Eliza. "You don't know what you're doing," he says. "You're messing with things you don't understand. And you're going to hurt somebody. Or you're going to help him hurt somebody. Again."

Coolly, Eliza flips open the massive folder in her lap and begins lifting pages out of it. Her eyes stay fixed on Spencer's. "Mattie, I was hunting through the archives this morning and I came across something strange, right about the time of the Doctor's death. I don't know what connection it has to whatever you're looking for or how your friend here got involved, but I suspect it might explain a lot. I suspect Shepherd Franklin thinks so too, though I admit I'm baffled as to why he would—"

Spencer flies to his feet and rips the pages out of her hand. I jerk backward, stunned. Eliza barely flinches. "I'm sorry," she says. "Really, Shepherd Franklin, I am. But I don't see that you have a choice. And I don't see why you'd want one."

"Tell me what?" I say again.

"Fuck you," says Spencer.

"Tell him."

"I'm trying to protect her, goddamm it."

He drops the pages on the table, face down. When he looks at me, his eyes are blazing in their sockets like black suns going nova. His body doesn't shake so much as rock on its heels, too far back and then too far forward.

"Spencer. Where is Theresa?"

He collapses into a chair, as if I've let out all the air that held him upright, and his arms drop limply to his sides.

He knows. He's known all along.

1977

My father yanked me inside, grabbed me around the shoulders, and crushed me against him while my mother screamed into the phone for the police. I tried to free my mouth from his sweater, spoke fast.

"Dad, I think if I could just talk to Theresa—"

"Sssh," my father said.

"Dad, really. I think she saw something. Maybe it's not what—"

Our yard exploded into light. The first three police cars and the famous red-and-white Special Update Action Van arrived simultaneously, horns and sirens screaming. All four vehicles careened to a stop in front of the drainage ditch at the bottom of our lawn. Twitching red lights from the squad cars and one blazing white beam from the

Action Van's floodlight raked the neighborhood. The van's side door slid open, and Coral Clark, the Special Update on-the-spot reporter, spilled onto our driveway, her hair teased into its Farrah Fawcett wave, the snow-white jacket she always wore snapped tight up to her neck.

Coral Clark and her two-man camera crew reached the doorway first. My dad had fallen back somehow, and I found myself drifting outside. I was mesmerized by the lights and the cameras and Coral Clark cooing at me. Shapes detached themselves from the shadows of trees along our driveway and slithered toward me. Neighbors, I told myself, but I couldn't see their faces, and they moved spastically in the whirl of light. A microphone appeared in midair and hovered near my mouth like a fat black wasp.

"What?" I asked Coral Clark, realizing she'd asked me a question.

"Don't talk to them," said the first police officer to break through the circle of television people. I didn't see his face, but his badge winked in the glare, as if he were some cartoon crusader coming to my rescue. The badge bore his name: SGT. ROSS. He put one enormous hand on my shoulder and said, "Come inside, son." His voice came out slow and thick, like syrup.

With no warning, I burst into tears, and the cameras zoomed in. They were panic tears, as far as I could tell. I didn't know what to do or say. But I had to tell someone the truth right now. I didn't want to tell it on TV or to a policeman. I was thinking I'd go to jail, that Ms. Eyre and Mrs. Jupp would hate me. But mostly I thought I'd never be allowed to see Theresa again.

"Did you see his face?" Coral Clark asked me again.

Still hypnotized by Sgt. Ross's winking badge and the snow tinted red by the lights, I shook my head.

"Did you see anything?"

"His car," I mumbled, as freezing breath burst in my chest. In my mind, a blue Gremlin was pasted onto Cider Lake Road like a Colorform. It was disappearing down the block toward the lake, brake lights flashing. "It was rusty," I said. "Blue."

"And your friend—Spencer, right?"

"He waved to me," I said. I thought of the Cory twins at the moment of their abduction, walking and laughing with the long-haired man. Then I thought of nothing at all. Dazed, I raised my hand and waved to Detroit.

One of the cameramen yelled, "*Great!*"

The other said, "Shut up, man," and Coral Clark patted me on the head. She wore bright red gloves that still smelled like leather. The neighbors' faces had been seared free of features by the lights. Sergeant Ross dropped his hand on my back and practically lifted me through the crowd toward my house.

When I came through the door, my parents engulfed me in their arms and began to sob. I became aware of their smell, the way they clutched me and each other. It was like being present at my own conception, suspended there between them, already myself at the moment they made me. Slowly, I emerged from my protective stupor and tried to talk. My whisper must have been audible; I could hear myself so clearly.

"It's a lie," I said, while my skin tingled and stung. I tried to repeat it, louder this time. But the louder I got, the tighter the words knotted in my throat, until they became indistinguishable. "*It's a lie it's a lie it's a lie.*"

Sergeant Ross's hand fell on my shoulder again like a lump of snow off a roof, and he steered me toward the living room couch. Alarmed, I dug my heels into the carpet, to no effect. He let me sit down on my own and then sat beside me, his bulk pinning me against the armrest. My brain buzzed as thoughts sizzled through it. I couldn't take my eyes off that ridiculous winking badge. Stiff strips of black licorice had been arranged in the pocket of his uniform like pens. When he saw me staring, he offered me one. I took it, but I had no desire to eat. He must be the department's Kiddie Cop, I decided.

"I think Theresa saw something," I said, and then bit the insides of both cheeks. "She was at the window."

Sergeant Ross didn't move or drop his gaze or change his tone. "Who is Theresa?"

"She's my friend. She lives up the block. Spencer and I were playing in her backyard. We should go talk to her. We have to hurry. We—"

"Mattie," Sergeant Ross said, his voice like a snake charmer's flute. "Why don't we start at the beginning?"

I looked at the letters of his name. He had a thick chest. He was young.

"Mattie, what were you and Spencer doing this afternoon?"

I shrugged. "Playing."

"Playing what?"

"I don't know. Playing in the snow." I flushed as I said that, and my voice broke.

"Mattie, did you notice anyone following you?"

I shook my head. "We came on the bus. There could have been someone following the bus, I don't know."

"But as far you remember, the street was empty."

"Please, if we could go to Ther—"

"Let me ask you this. If Spencer managed to escape, where would he go?"

"I don't know," I said. "My house, I think, if he got away fast enough."

After that, Sergeant Ross was silent for a while. Then he asked, "Is Spencer happy at home?"

I thought of Mrs. Franklin in her flashing gold coat, and a new but fainter sadness slashed through me like distant lightning. "I don't think his mom is happy."

Once more, Sergeant Ross went quiet, but I could feel his eyes. When I finally glanced in his direction, he said, "You're an interesting boy, Mattie."

I wondered how interesting he'd find me when he learned I was lying, and I bit the inside of my cheek so hard this time that I drew blood.

Sergeant Ross leaned forward again. "Now. I want you to think hard. Forget this room. Think about the street. Think about this afternoon." He said this as if it were much longer than half an hour ago. "I want you to tell me about the very last moment that you were sure Spencer Franklin was with you."

"In the Daughretys' backyard," I said immediately, relieved to have the conversation steer back toward Theresa. "I threw a snowball at him, and he ran, and then I saw Theresa at the window. We have to go there. Let's go."

"We'll send someone, Mattie. Try to relax."

"What about me?" I jerked up my head as though I'd been challenged to a fight, then made myself drop it again. I didn't like the way this sergeant kept watching me. "It has to be me." Tears swept down my face.

"Mattie," Sergeant Ross said in his slow-syrup voice, "help me understand what you mean."

I took a deep breath, then another, and wiped tears from my face, but more appeared. It was like staring through a windshield in a relentless misting rain.

"Theresa," I said, as calmly as I could. "She's . . . sad right now. She sits at the Solitude Desk. She saw Mr. Fox get run over and sat in his blood."

For the first time, Sergeant Ross blinked in surprise. "She what?"

"She's been out of school for a long time. She won't talk to almost anyone. She doesn't even talk to her dad anymore."

Sergeant Ross leaned against the couch. "She doesn't talk to anyone," he said. "But you think she'll talk to you."

"I *know* she'll talk to me," I said, trying to control myself. "She has to. There's no one else."

Sergeant Ross made a clicking sound with his tongue. Then he sat forward, pinning me against the armrest. "I want you to think about this very carefully. I want you to think about it, and I want you to answer, do you hear?"

I didn't move.

"What is it, son, that you haven't told me?"

Right then, I almost told him all of it. I wanted to, but the words wouldn't come. And so all I did was look at my hands, cry some more, and say, "We have to go there. Please. Or it'll be too late."

"Bert," Sergeant Ross said, in a much louder voice, and a second cop detached himself from his post by the door. He was huge too, with blond hair and a too-small head cocked sideways on his lumpy shoulders like seed spilling out of a feed bag. He limped and chewed green gum with a smack.

"Bert, let's send detectives to the Daughrety house. Mattie, do you know the address?"

"You have to take me. It won't work without me. She won't talk to you."

This time, Sergeant Ross sounded more like my uncle than a policeman. "We'll send two detectives first. They're very, very good at their job. Don't worry, Mattie."

Frustration sizzled under my skin like an electrical current. "I have to see her," I blurted.

"What's he babbling about?" said Bert, not unkindly.

The coolness in Sergeant Ross's voice was confusing. "He thinks the Daughrety daughter may have seen something. He also thinks she'll only talk to him."

Bert started to laugh. Again, the laugh was gentle, but I didn't like it. And I didn't know how much more of this I could stand. "If we sit around talking much longer," I snapped, "Spencer's going to be dead." Bert stopped laughing, and Sergeant Ross stared at me.

Then he stood up. "Stay here, Mattie." He stepped through the kitchen doorway, and I saw him talking quietly to my mother and father. Finally, he came back out and told Bert, "We're going to take Mattie and his father to the Daughretys."

My father bundled me into my jacket. The last thing I saw as we left the house was my mom kneeling against the kitchen door frame with her head in her hands. Guilt began massing in my chest as my father shepherded me out the door, through the throng of television reporters, to a waiting squad car. The policemen sat up front and directed us into the back behind the grate that protected them from prisoners.

"At least tell us where you're taking him, officers," said Coral Clark, hustling around the hood of the car with her white jacket open at the throat, her red nails curled around the microphone. Bert answered by gunning the engine, and the car lurched backward down the driveway, skidding halfway into the drainage ditch across the street before its spinning wheels grabbed the icy dirt and we shot down the block. Behind us, reporters scurried over our lawn and climbed into their vans to follow us.

The Daughrety house hunkered at the back of its cul-de-sac like a stockade. Opaque white drapes had replaced the ones Theresa had slashed to shreds. The driveway had not been plowed, and small drifts dotted it like the dens of snow animals.

"Are they even home?" Bert said.

"They never leave," I answered, and my father looked bewildered.

Reflected red light from all the police cars in the neighborhood floated in the topmost branches of the maple trees. The houses nearby nestled in the dark like porcelain toys wrapped in black crepe. At the door, Sergeant Ross rapped the brass handle while we stood behind him. There was no response. The drapes didn't even rustle. He knocked again. This time we heard the Doctor say, "Don't answer it."

"Don't answer it?" said Bert. He withdrew his nightstick and began to whack rhythmically on the door until chips of white painted wood splintered and flew off. Sergeant Ross winced, let the swinging go on a while longer, and then grabbed Bert's arm and stopped him.

"Police," Sergeant Ross called. "Open up, please, sir. Right now."

The door remained closed.

"Okay," said Bert.

He retreated down the driveway to the squad car. Moments later, siren scream pierced the silence. Doors flew open all around us. People peered out, saw the police car, froze. Then the front door of the Daughrety house swung open and Barbara Fox stood facing us.

"Better," said Bert, and shut down the siren.

She was wearing a thick navy-blue sweater that was coming unraveled at the wrists. Her hair hung in a braid down her back and looked uncharacteristically heavy. She blinked against the strobing red light, looked at Sergeant Ross, and saw me peeking from behind him. Behind her, I could see the hall of masks. The tiled entryway sparkled, weirdly sludgeless. No tiles in Detroit houses sparkled that way at the end of March.

"Ms. Daughrety?" said Sergeant Ross.

"No," said Barbara. "What do you need?"

"M'am, we have a situation here. Can we come in?"

Barbara's mouth puckered, as though she'd just bitten into a crab apple. Her eyes watered too, though I couldn't tell if she was crying or responding to the freezing air.

My father stepped forward, reached out to touch her arm, and then lowered it again. "It'll just take a second, Barb," he said uselessly, though I knew he was trying to calm her.

Finally, she slid backward in her stocking feet to allow us entry. In the hallway and the living room, the lights were on but dimmed. We wiped our boots on the mats just inside the door, and Dr. Daughrety emerged from the back hall. He had on exactly the same robe that Spencer and I had seen him wearing the last time we'd barged in on him. There were black circles under his eyes, and the skin around them was pale and puffy. It seemed to take him a moment to make sense of our being there.

"Joe," he said, with no trace of curiosity in his voice.

"Colin," said my father. "Sorry to intrude, but—"

The Doctor trained his gaze on me, as unforgiving as ever. "Mattie?"

"Dr. Daughrety?" said Sergeant Ross.

The Doctor continued to stare at me, ignoring the policemen. Then he inclined his head slightly.

"Dr. Daughrety," Sergeant Ross said, "we need to speak to you and your . . ." He glanced at Barbara.

"Fiancée," Dr. Daughrety said, his shoulders squaring out of their unaccustomed slump. He was beginning to look more like himself.

"And your daughter."

Dr. Daughrety looked at Sergeant Ross. I thought he was going to laugh.

"No," he said, and turned toward the living room.

"I'm not actually asking," said Sergeant Ross.

Dr. Daughrety stopped, but he didn't turn around right away. When he did, he had his head up, his mouth set. "All right," he said, and proceeded into the living room.

"Jesus," I heard my father mutter, and then, with no warning, Theresa glided into the room. She was listing to the left, her long skirt brushing her bare feet. She moved across the hallway, looking neither up nor away but straight ahead, volitionless, like a toy boat dropped into a river. It was Barbara who grabbed her, pulled her tight against her stomach.

"Gentlemen," Barbara said, gesturing in the direction the Doctor had wandered.

Maybe the spell that had transformed Theresa into a sleepwalker was contagious at close range. No one seemed able to speak. We watched her blank stare, her pale neck fading into her pale white sweater.

Sergeant Ross leaned over and touched my arm. "See what you can do," he said, with a surprising hint of camaraderie. My knees locked, my teeth clamped together, and I thought I was going to faint.

The adults filed past Theresa into the living room. Barbara was still holding on to Theresa and watching me. To my astonishment, I saw Barbara's bottom lip quiver, which made her look like a little girl.

"Mattie, what the hell is happening?" she said.

"The Snowman," I said. "Spencer." Tears burst out on my cheeks again. I didn't want to lie to Barbara.

"Oh, my God," she whimpered, and bent to grab me. She held both Theresa and me against her. She still smelled of Africa, or at least the way I'd come to imagine Africa smelling from being around her. Theresa smelled like candle wax and soap. I twisted my head and stared straight into her muddy brown eyes.

"Hi," Theresa said, and Barbara's arms slipped apart. I teetered backward as Theresa glided toward her room.

"She hasn't said a single word in a week and a half," Barbara said.

My heart thundered against my chest, and the reverberations rattled my rib cage. This was going to work after all. It was going to be worth it. Even my parents and Barbara and Ms. Eyre and Mrs. Jupp might think so. I glanced once more at Barbara and then followed Theresa down the hallway and entered her bedroom for the first and only time. The rest of the world and everyone in it evaporated.

Theresa wasn't waiting for me, exactly. She was leaning against the drapes that shrouded her porthole window, humming to herself and staring through the slit in the curtains. The Daughretys' furnace muttered in the vents.

She had a canopy bed, all white, with a sort of gray mosquito netting wrapped around the wooden posts. On the plain white nightstand stood two pictures in matching wooden frames, one of the Doctor with one arm holding a plaque and the other around his daughter. I could tell the photo had been taken in the Phil Hart Elementary gym. The other picture had been taken in the Daughretys' backyard. A blond-headed woman in a blue winter coat was sitting on a sled, cradling an unpeeled orange in her mittens. I'd only seen Theresa's mother a few times. After the very first Mind War, she'd served us black-bottomed cupcakes. She used to hum under her breath too, I thought, and shuddered. At least she'd been humming that day.

The rest of the room was lined with books. Two white freestanding bookcases stood on either side of the bed. Another set of shelves hung on the opposite wall, and a long shelf of unpainted wood stretched across the top of the walk-in closet. Almost all the books in the room were hardbacks, their dust jackets wrinkled or ripped, their spines cracked and drooping, which told me that nearly all of them had been read. I watched her profile, her pale skin against the pale curtains, her mouth moving slightly like a dreaming baby's.

"Where have you been?" I said.

Theresa turned from the window, studied me a few seconds, then sat on the floor. I couldn't tell if she recognized me or not. I'd never seen anyone look that blank.

"We miss you. Everybody's talking about you." That wasn't exactly true. Given the rest of the year's events, Theresa's strangeness and her absence barely qualified as noteworthy for most of the people in my universe.

"He moves in circles," she said, and pursed her mouth.

"What?"

"Oak Street, Wrigley's, the mall."

I didn't understand. I recognized the words, but none of them communicated anything to me. As usual when I talked to Theresa, I found myself feeling small, somehow.

"Oak Park, Pleasant Fields, Covington Junior High, Wrigley's, the mall," said Theresa. "Concentric circles." From under her pillow, she withdrew a blue spiral notebook and thrust it at me.

"Here," she said happily, and pushed it against my chest.

I took it, felt my hand touch hers. I was expecting her skin to be freezing, corpselike. But it was warm. Just plain skin.

In the other room, voices got louder, and I heard people moving. They'd be coming for me soon, and I wouldn't get another chance. I tucked the notebook under my jacket, against my sweater. I didn't want the Doctor to see it and take it from me.

"Theresa, listen, please," I said. "Please, are you listening?"

She didn't answer, but at least she looked in my direction.

"It's a lie," I said, and realized she didn't know what I was talking about. "Spencer and I planned it so I could get past your dad and talk to you. It's okay, all right? Nothing happened. Spencer's fine. Please come back. You have to come back. Please come to school on Monday."

"I wouldn't count on it," Dr. Daughrety said from the doorway, and strode straight past me. He sat next to his daughter, drawing her head to his shoulder. Then he looked at me. For a wild moment, I thought maybe he had heard me say that Spencer and I were faking. I wanted to scream for him to get out. I needed more time, although I didn't really think that more time would make a difference. I watched Theresa touch her hair with a finger, drop the finger to her lap, and stare at the curtains again.

"Mattie," said the Doctor, "I'm so sorry. I don't know what to say. I can't believe it. We're all very fond of Spencer."

Tears slid from my eyes. Dr. Daughrety wouldn't just be disappointed when he found out the truth, I thought. Dr. Daughrety was going to hate me.

My father came in and began tugging at my arm. I wanted to throw myself through the porthole window. I'd failed. And I was in huge trouble. I wanted to go where the Snowman was, because right at that moment, disappearing seemed safer. Better.

"Jesus, Joe," Dr. Daughrety said. "Tell Alina I'll come by. I'll call

Susan Franklin, too." One of his arms had completely encircled his daughter, and he was rocking her back and forth.

"Susan isn't in town," my father said. "Alina's still trying to reach her."

Sergeant Ross appeared in the doorway and trained a slow, steady gaze on me. "Mattie, Dr. Daughrety says Theresa could not possibly have seen anything. She had . . . a rough night last night, he says. She was sleeping on the living room couch almost all day."

"She woke up about five minutes before you came," said the Doctor.

Theresa's didn't say anything. Her smile looked carved into her face like a jack-o-lantern's.

"Mattie, come on. Let's go," my father said, and he guided me past Sergeant Ross, who still hadn't taken his eyes off me.

Minutes later, Bert was hustling us through the reporters buzzing in the Daughretys' yard. As soon as we were in the squad car and moving again, they all shot for their vans. We flew back down my street, past policemen and more reporters huddling under every streetlamp. Once more, the snow had begun falling.

I'd failed. I'd made it to Theresa's room, but I hadn't reached her. Loneliness more profound than any I had known or dreamed crushed down on me like an avalanche, and I was buried beneath it. I couldn't even imagine how to dig myself out. And I knew no one would ever find me.

Sergeant Ross ushered me and my father into our house again and talked quietly to my mother, who hadn't moved from the kitchen doorway. On his way out, he stopped in front of me and said, "We'll be in touch, Mattie. If you think of anything that might help us, anything at all, I want you to call me. Your parents know how to reach me. Okay?"

I nodded and felt my heart beat against Theresa's notebook, which I'd all but forgotten I had clutched to my chest.

Angie McLean, my mother's best friend, was hovering above her, trying to give her a glass of water, but my mother kept pushing it away. Mrs. McLean was wearing a somber gray dress I'd never seen before, with a dark gray ribbon pinned to the collar. Every year, she won first prize in the *Detroit News* Unique Homemade Ice Cream Contest. The prize came with seventy-five dollars and a silk ribbon dyed to suggest the winning flavor. Every year, she took the cash and bought a new dress to match the ribbon, and at every formal occasion for the next twelve months, she would wear that year's dress and ribbon. She'd won for her Cream Peach, Rose-hip Mint, and Chocolate Baked Apple, and I wondered dully what flavor this year's dress commemorated. Asphalt Ice? Michigan Yard in Winter?

The film of tears in my eyes caused everything and everyone to blur, as though I was looking up from under the frozen surface of a lake. I slipped Theresa's notebook out of my jacket and laid it on my lap, but I couldn't bring myself to open it. I kept thinking of her mother in the photograph, the unpeeled orange in her hands. I thought about the way Theresa's eyes had looked, so dark and lifeless, almost plastic. Mr. Potato Head eyes. We were too late. We'd lost her. In a way, the Snowman had come for us after all, or he may as well have.

I saw Brent emerge from the back hallway with his head down, taking little baby steps. I'd heard my father say that Brent was going to the McLeans' for the night, but when he glanced up and saw me, he stopped dead and then ran straight at me with tears in his eyes. Horrified, I threw up my hands to ward him off. I'd forgotten, somehow, that Brent would think this was real, too, and would soon know that it wasn't. He crashed into me, shoved his head into my chest, and hugged me. Stunned stupid, petrified, I hugged him back while he cried. That got my mother distracted, at least. She got up and stood before us, cheeks swollen, irises shot through with little red lines, like the shells of bloody eggs.

"He loves you," she said, and touched me on the cheek. She was choking back sobs. It was the first time she'd touched me since I came home. I clung to my brother. The weight of what I'd done almost drove me through the floor.

Say it now, I thought. Right now.

But at that moment, Mrs. McLean stuck her head out of the kitchen and said, "Susan Franklin's on the phone," and my mother gave a little cry, drove her face into her palms, and I shut down completely. I couldn't face this. In my mind, Mrs. Franklin was calling from a pay phone somewhere, her red hair and shiny gold coat billowing around her.

I heard my mother say, "Oh, Jesus, Susan" as she grabbed the phone, and then she wept for a while and leaned into the kitchen door with her head down. Mrs. McLean rubbed her back and shook her head over and over.

"I was on my way home. The school sent the kids home early because of the snow. They were right down the street. In full view. I don't know. We'll find him, Susan. We'll—"

She stopped talking but didn't move otherwise, and I knew Mrs. Franklin was gone.

In the living room, my father had switched on the television. I turned to the window and watched the snow float down like a net in water and listened to my city go wild. The black-turtleneck men had returned to the streets. Mayor Young and Detective Frederic Verani, head of the Snowman Task Force, had held a phone conference to discuss possible tactics, and, according to Larry Loreno, both men had broken down crying. On Gratiot Avenue, a used car dealer had lined up three blue Gremlins in front of his lot, doused them with gasoline, and lit them on fire.

I felt like I was living in my own dream cocoon, engulfed in a slow-building silence. I believed that silence had come to insulate me, to help me detach from everything around me so I could do what needed to be done. I didn't know it could get inside you. So I gave in to it, and fatigue seized me like a fever. After a while, my mother drew me up by the arm and led me to bed. Spencer was probably asleep, I decided. Theresa was doomed, or at least gone from me. I would be despised no matter what I did. For one more night, at least, a few final hours, I wanted my mother to love me.

My mother eased Theresa's notebook from between my locked fingers and laid it on my desk. Then she undressed me, kissed my forehead, and stayed while I struggled to get under the blankets. She stared at me awhile, new tears squeezing out from her swollen eyes, blew me one last kiss, and closed the door.

To this day, I don't understand how the night lasted as long as it did. There should not have been enough time. The morning should have come. But the world had spun to a stop, and the night lay like a tarp

over Detroit and smothered it. It was already well after midnight when
my mother settled me down. After she'd gone, I lay for what felt like
hours, willing my skin to stop itching. Everywhere I touched the sheet,
I felt prickly. I scratched the inside of one knee so hard that I bled into
the mattress. I thought about the black-turtleneck men lurking by the
evergreens, and the Snowman with his long hair blowing in the wind
and his head tossed back, his mouth open to catch the snow. I thought
about my brother weeping against me. I was face down in my pillow,
itching, clicking my back teeth together, when the first tap rattled my
window. The sound shot straight down my spine. I couldn't move.
Tree branch, I told myself. With a twist of the blinds lever, I would
know for sure. I'd see the birch branch, laden with new snow, and
maybe there'd be pink streaks in the sky like scratches down a cheek,
and I'd know I'd made it to morning.

Then came the second tap.

The third tap was more of a punch, and the pane rattled in its
frame. The next one, I thought, would smash the window. Scrambling
to my knees, I opened the blinds and saw Theresa Daughrety pressed
up against the glass. I gagged back a scream.

She was wearing her white hat with the pom-pom. Her cheeks and
mouth glowed red, and in her eyes was the same blankness I had seen
earlier that night, like the charcoal Snowman sketches in the newspaper. It seemed impossible that those eyes could blink or see or weep.
I pressed my face right up to hers, almost touching it. My face, glass,
her face. One mittened hand, clutched into a fist, uncurled at the sight
of me and flattened against the pane. Several seconds passed before I
realized she was waving.

"Hi," I said.

"Come on," said Theresa, in her best Murder-in-the-Dark whisper.
"Hurry." She took a single step back from the window, and snowflakes
obscured her face until she seemed utterly insubstantial, no skin, no
bone, just whiteness and night.

I had done it, after all. I very nearly whooped. Theresa had come
for me. She had chosen this impossible hour to appear at my window
and invite me back into her life. It had all been worth it. Tomorrow I

would present a talking, smiling, alert Theresa to her father and Barbara and my parents, and maybe they'd be furious, but they would understand. I grabbed my sweatshirt and jeans out of my half-closed dresser drawer and pulled on yesterday's socks. I paused long enough to listen for sounds from the hallway. There was a rustling in my parents' room, but no talking or footsteps. Edging down the hall, I waited a few seconds by the front door before opening it. My house groaned and creaked like a houseboat rocking in the dark, the way it always did when I got up in the middle of the night. In the living room, everything was out of place. The chairs and lamps were crooked, the throw rug bunched up. Three red plastic cups lay on their sides on the floor, and one of my father's speakers teetered on the edge of its stand. The room looked like a shoebox diorama of our living room that someone had given a single sharp shake. Blinking against the cold, I stepped out.

The wind whistled relentlessly, with occasional crescendos as if airplanes were taking off over our heads. Theresa was standing by the tall pine in the front yard. In her white hat, with her pale skin, she was all but invisible in the blowing snow. Pulling the front door closed, I walked to her with my head down, watching my feet bite marks in the new soft ice. The trees I knew so well seemed pressed flat at this hour. Suddenly, Theresa spun on her heels and headed for Cider Lake Road. I rushed to catch her. My half-buckled boot tops flapped against my legs.

"Hey," I said when I caught up to her. I had to grab her by both arms to stop her from moving, but once she stopped, she stayed rooted, utterly still. All I could think was, Here we are at last. Theresa Daughrety and me, alone in the world. It was what I had always wanted.

"How'd you get out?" I said.

Vaguely but unmistakably, she smiled. Then she stopped smiling. I watched breath stream from her mouth. Then words spurted from me like blood from an opened artery.

"We kept trying to see you. Your dad wouldn't let us in. School's weird. It seems empty, even when we're there. It's like we're all gone. Ms. Eyre doesn't even come half the time. *Where have you been?*"

I glanced toward the Fox house, which was dark and silent. Theresa was here. Spencer was here. For the first time in my life, I felt powerful. I had applied pressure to the world, and the world had responded.

Theresa continued staring past me.

"Spencer's right here," I said. "He's fine. He's in the Fox house waiting for us."

Realizing that I still had hold of her arms, I let go, then watched them flutter in the air before falling to her sides. Nothing I'd said seemed to have made an impression. She looked as if she had no idea where she was.

"Theresa, we were scared." I was agitated, exhilarated, speaking way too fast. "And it kind of worked, see? You're here. Theresa? See? Oh, just come on." I took her right hand, gently this time, and led her toward the Foxes'. She did not acknowledge me, but when I pulled she slid along behind me like a wagon.

The street felt like an empty puppet stage. Another few hours of wind, I thought, and the houses would tumble away into Cider Lake. I pulled Theresa into the Foxes' yard, and she made a moaning sound but continued to follow. I scanned the windows to see if Spencer was watching but saw neither light nor movement.

No moon or stars lit the path as we made our way through the latticed shadows of hedge branches and overhanging birch trees. Down the street, a dog growled low and long, then went still. I found the key under the picnic table bench where I'd left it, unlatched the door, and pushed it open. Theresa's hand melted out of my grasp, and when I turned, I found her staring and shaking her head. And singing.

"*Frère Jacques. Frère Jacques. Dormez-vous?*"

"Come on," I said, but she didn't follow. Her voice dwindled away, but her mouth continued to trace words in the air. "Theresa, come see Spencer. He's right here. This is where Barbara used to live before she lived with you, remember?"

She didn't respond, just kept singing.

In exasperation, I grabbed her arm once more. "Let's go find Spencer." I dragged her into the house and shut the door.

"Spencer?" I called. I waited for the lights to flash on, for Spencer to jump out and yell "Surprise!" in his giddy Spencer way. Then we'd all sit down on the floor together. I wasn't sure what would happen next, only that it would be good, because something, at least, would have gotten better, and the improvement would be permanent. No one knows where we are, I thought, and I bounced up and down on the balls of my feet.

But the lights stayed off, and nothing moved. In the pit of my stomach, new fears squirmed to life. My hands twitched. Theresa drifted deeper into the house, past the wall of photographs where I'd spotted myself just a few hours earlier. He's sleeping, I thought, and my hands stopped twitching. Spencer must be sleeping.

"Stay here," I said to Theresa's back, and she stopped like a trained dog and stared at the photographs on the wall. She started singing "Frère Jacques" again, too.

"Spencer," I called, "where are you? We're here."

The door to the back bathroom was open, and a halo of weak white light glowed inside. A nightlight, I realized. I covered the hallway in three quick steps, threw open the first bedroom door, and Spencer slammed his fist into my cheekbone, which drove me to my knees.

"What—" I started, and he was on me, fists flying. I threw my hands over my head. Spencer's knees locked around my waist as he pummeled my ribs and my upper arms. The beating was bad, but the silence was worse. He didn't speak or grunt or scream, he just flailed away. The pounding lasted so long that I stopped being able to focus on it. I thought about the soft spots in the center of bruises, the way color and pain seemed to fold inward rather than radiate outward, like light from an imploding star. I wondered which photograph Theresa was staring at now, and why. Several seconds went by before I noticed that Spencer was no longer hitting me.

He hadn't loosened his legs, though. He still wasn't making any sound. I stayed in my protective curl but slowly uncrossed my wrists from in front of my face. When I breathed, my lungs grated against my swollen rib cage, and I wanted to cry out. I didn't feel any grinding, though. Nothing broken.

Cautiously, I glanced up at Spencer, recognized the look on his face, and knew the beating was over. He wasn't angry anymore. He was scared to death.

"I've been watching TV, Mattie," he said. "I've seen the mayor. I've seen—oh, a few *thousand* policemen. I've seen myself, too: our fucking class picture, right there on Channel Four. The cops were here. They banged on the door and rang the doorbell. I thought I was going to jail. Then I thought maybe I'd hitchhike to Ferndale and never come back here, ever. Mattie, you asshole, *what have you done?*" He threw a last punch at me, but he put nothing behind it, and his fist bounced off my chest, then lay against it.

"Spencer, it worked," I said, wincing, as I tried to roll away from him.

"*Your mom will never even know,*" he sneered. "Has anyone even tried to find my mom and tell her the truth, maybe, before she sees it on TV?"

"She's on her way home," I said. "She doesn't know it's a lie."

"Jesus Christ. She probably thinks I'm dead. I'm going to be, when she's through with me."

"Spencer, you're not listening."

"They're going to kill us. We deserve to be killed. I hate you. I hate you so much."

I knew it was dumb, but I felt myself getting angry.

"This is all your fault, Mattie. This whole year has been your fault. You come up with these plans, and for some stupid reason I listen to you, and we keep getting in trouble, and my mom thinks there's something wrong with me—"

"Because you yell at her all the time—"

"Did you see the guy who lit the cars on fire?"

I thought about my mother crouched and sobbing in the kitchen doorway and Spencer's mother standing alone on a street corner with her gold coat blowing. "Theresa's in the living room," I said.

Spencer's lips bubbled and he sat there and blinked. "What?"

"Get off me."

Sliding to one side, Spencer let me roll to a sitting position. As soon as I stood up, the shooting pains in my ribs subsided into small dull aches. I probed a few of them with unsteady fingers.

"She's really here?" he whispered.

As the pain receded, the tingling returned to my skin. I looked at Spencer, saw disbelief, then hope flicker across his face. I almost grabbed him and hugged him. "Spencer, we did it."

Without warning, he began to laugh. The laugh sounded horrible in that house, a desecration of the gloom. I kicked him hard.

"Shut up. You'll scare her away."

Spencer kept grinning. Suddenly, I grinned too. Everything he said was true. We were in trouble. We'd done a terrible thing, betrayed everyone we knew. It was mostly my fault. But she was here. Nothing else made any difference.

"What about the police?" he asked.

I shrugged. "They'll be back."

Spencer bounded past me out the bedroom door. I raced after him. We reached the living room in a dead heat, Spencer already sliding to his knees next to Theresa. And then I saw her face.

It was as if she had been frozen in midscream, her lips a huge red O, her skin so white I could see her veins, her eyes too wide, the lids rolled farther into her sockets than they should have been able to go. From deep in her throat came a low steady gurgle, like trickling water in the back of a cave.

"It was Mattie's idea. We were—" As if someone had sucked the words from his mouth, Spencer stopped talking. Time, speech, everything froze.

Theresa had removed a photograph from the wall, and now she laid it on the coffee table. It showed the birch trees ringing Cider Lake in autumn. Fallen red-brown leaves floated on the surface of the water like a fleet of tiny paper boats. I could almost imagine them floating out of the frame and swirling around us.

"Pretty trees," she said. "Pretty dead leaves to lie on."

Neither Spencer nor I had any reply to that, so we stood still. And there we stayed, the group of friends I'd always dreamed of having— an equilateral triangle, as Ms. Eyre had taught us—not moving, not touching, but locked together, sidecarring through the world. For long stretches of time, nothing fired in my brain. Then quick crazy thoughts lit up inside me like signal flares. I thought maybe we could all just stay here, for good. Theresa could look at photographs and read. Spencer and I would dust, make the beds, draw the curtains to shut out the light, and every day we'd bring her food and water, tend her like a plant.

"Mattie," Spencer said, his voice scratched and cracking, as if he hadn't used it for days. "Do something."

I looked out the window and saw the white dawn pouring through the trees like lava and petrifying everything. I knew, now, that we had done the worst thing, the most hurtful thing possible. If anything, we had driven Theresa deeper into the crawl space she had dug inside herself, and we couldn't reach her, and we couldn't lure her out.

"I did do something," I said, hoping that Theresa could hear me, at least, and would understand what I'd intended. "Remember?"

Slowly, like an astronaut rising off the surface of the moon, Theresa floated to her feet. Either Spencer or I could have reached out and caught her, but neither of us did. For a moment, she swayed between us, and when she looked up, something seemed to have kindled behind her eyes.

Still swaying back and forth, she drew her hands together at the waist. And then she looked at me. And it was Theresa, or a collage of Theresas, the one who grinned at me in the middle of the Mind War and the one who ignored me as she squashed me in class and the one who wasn't there and the one I kept dreaming. "Hello, my dwarves," she said. And she broke into a giggle.

I stared. "Theresa?" I said, very slowly. I wasn't sure. And I didn't want to scare her away. But it seemed, just maybe. . . .

"Dwarves?" said Spencer, and he leaned forward, all but grabbing for her hand.

"It's perfect," she said. "It's amazing. This house in the woods. All of us in hiding."

I wasn't positive, but it seemed as though Theresa was just plain speaking to us, the way she used to. Before. I didn't understand, but I felt like I should. I watched her lift her hand toward Spencer's face, and I thought I saw tears in her eyes.

"You were gone," Theresa said.

"I'm sorry," he said. "I didn't mean to scare you. I just wanted—"

"The white half for you," Theresa whispered, and smiled. A sad, scared smile. "The red half for me. To make a wish on."

"Theresa," Spencer and I blurted, almost together, and she shuddered and went still. "Theresa," I tried again, much more gently.

But Theresa stopped smiling, stopped looking at us, and started to sway again. "Courtney Grieve. Amy Ardell. Shane Park. See?"

Spencer looked at me, his eyes flooding with panic. "What's she doing?" he said. "Why is she talking about them?"

"I don't know," I said.

"The Corys. Avri's, and the quiet."

"Mattie," said Spencer. "Call her back."

A new frozen exhausted sadness washed through me. The day I now had to face loomed ahead, towering and shrouded in mist, and I couldn't even imagine the other side of it. "This isn't getting us anywhere. Let's walk her home."

"That's it?"

"Spencer," I said, feeling myself sink away, dissolve to nothing. "Look at her."

We watched Theresa sway between us. Then we watched her glide to the back door, twist the handle, drift out into the yard, and the falling snow swept her away. We followed, of course. But we stayed well behind, watching as her white pom-pom bobbed on the dark as though she were being sucked out to sea. I expected to hear police and reporters and screaming parents as soon as we hit the street, but everything was quiet and motionless, empty even of shadows in the flat, featureless light. We stopped at the bottom of her yard and watched her pass through the trees, spectral in the snow. When she reached her back door, we turned without speaking and started home.

At the Fox house, I stuck out my hand and stopped Spencer. He stood beside me, jacket open to the cold, mouth slack. And yet he looked so much more alive than Theresa did.

"Let me go first," I said.

"Oh, Mattie, what difference does it make?"

I couldn't explain. Mostly, I just wanted to tell my parents alone.

"I'll tell my parents," I said. "Then I'll come get you, and they'll help us figure out what to do."

Spencer broke down crying. I knew I should be crying too. But in the spot Theresa Daughrety had always occupied was a new and terrifying hole. No matter what I dropped in there, it would never hit bottom.

"Just let me get this over with. I got us into it. I'll get us out. I'll take all the blame."

Spencer slashed a hand across his face and yanked his jacket tight at the neck but didn't zip it. "They're going to send me back to Ferndale," he said. "Or my mother will make me go back. Operation Salvage aborted."

I stared at him. I hadn't thought of that. In one night, I'd probably lost both my best friends.

The look on my face must have satisfied Spencer for the time being, because he straightened his shoulders and nodded once. I watched him walk back toward the Fox house, hunched in his coat, head down. The snow kept falling, and light spread across the sky and hardened over it. One last time, I glanced toward the Daughrety house, eyes aimed into the wind. Under my ribs, loneliness beat inside me like some new and terrible organ.

1977

stood in the blowing snow, watching my shadow sneak from my body. If there was anywhere to go, I would have snuck away with it. Reporters were going to write about me; my parents would be furious; the police would clamp handcuffs around my wrists and haul me off to jail. Mrs. Jupp might even kick me out of school. But the worst, I thought, was over, or it was about to be. I took two steps down the street from the Foxes' driveway toward my own, and then I looked up and saw the woman on our front stoop.

She stood hunched over in her long black overcoat. Her back was to me, but I could see her head moving slightly; she was talking, I thought. The front door was open, and it occurred to me that I didn't want to be caught out here. I should be where I was supposed to be, so that when I told my parents what I had done, it would seem more like just a really bad idea than something I'd been planning all along.

I retreated behind the Foxes' hedge and scurried through the backyards to our porch. We kept our key under a rusty metal watering can that my mother used for gardening. The can was heavy, half filled with snow and hard to move. Quietly, I slid it aside, scraped the frozen key off the bottom, unlocked the porch door, and edged it open. Then I slipped inside, past the table where I played Strat-O-Matic baseball all summer long, and back into my house. Peering cautiously around the living room wall, I caught a brief glimpse of my mother, who was standing in the front doorway, twisting the tie of her faded blue bathrobe and blocking my view of the visitor. My father slouched beside her, pallid and droopy as the stained yellow cheesecloth in his workshop. I waited just a few seconds longer, then slipped behind them into the back hall and from there to my bedroom.

Shedding my coat but not bothering to hang it, I sat down on my bed to wait. The wait was not long. My cheeks were still flushed with the cold, my heart still thudding in my chest from all the sneaking around, when my father appeared in the doorway.

"Good. You're dressed," he said. Then he motioned for me to follow him.

"Dad," I said to his retreating back as I jumped off the bed. I wanted it over with. I wanted to confess right now. When he didn't turn around, I said, "Dad, wait," more loudly than I meant to. I stepped into the living room, and the woman in the overcoat turned around.

I recognized her instantly. Mrs. Cory's cheeks bore the same strange, unmistakable gouge marks that most of Detroit had seen on television the night she had said goodbye to her sons. She couldn't have been much older than my mother, but she stayed hunched over instead of standing up straight, and her claw-shaped hands never uncurled.

I very nearly fled. I could feel my skin melting off my bones. How do people know, I babbled in my head, that what they feel is an actual feeling and not something they've made up? All kinds of feelings were suggesting themselves to me right then, but I wasn't quite experiencing any of them.

Mrs. Cory moved toward me in jerks, like someone in the early stages of a muscle disease. I wondered if her sons had heard her good-bye. Maybe the Snowman had let them watch.

Faintly, I heard my father murmur, "She said she needed to come."

Mrs. Cory seized my chin in her hand. She held on to it so hard that I could feel my pulse beat against the webbing of her thumb.

"Little boy," she said, in a much more commanding voice than she had used on the Special Update.

It's a lie, I mouthed, willing her to understand what I could no longer bring myself to say. She had to have seen me do that. But she went on gripping my chin as if she were positioning me for the exe-cutioner. Then a flicker of blue and red light chased across the wall behind her, and I heard voices and the slamming of car doors outside.

"Little boy," Mrs. Cory said, through a weight I could never even dream. "Lucky little boy in this house with these people loving you." She had a German accent, and she was crying without making any sound. Her breath smelled like coffee and cinnamon gum. Mr. Fox's breath had carried the same odors. Masking smells. "My husband, silly man, he thought I should not come. He said I would only hurt myself and everyone else. Can you imagine?" She stroked my cheek, then bent forward and kissed my forehead while my stomach convulsed and I ground my teeth together to keep from throwing up. Finally, she turned and lurched away toward my parents.

I didn't just want everything to be over anymore. I wanted to be pun-ished, and worse. I wanted to be made to pay.

Outside, somebody screamed. The mumbling and scurrying inten-sified, and suddenly everything went weirdly silent, as though the sound had been switched off for the entire planet. I stared at my father's black speakers. The left one had inside wires draped across the top like a gutted fish.

"Christ, what now?" my father muttered, dragging himself to the door. Then he said, "Alina, I think you better get over here."

My mother came blinking out of the kitchen, holding the cup of coffee she'd poured for Mrs. Cory, looking as though she'd been shaken from a deep sleep. I floated behind her, and we all wound up on the front stoop. I thought of the mob scenes near the end of *Frankenstein*. Then I stopped thinking anything at all.

Susan Franklin was stalking up our driveway in her gold overcoat through a crowd of reporters who fell from her path like wheat before a thresher. When she got close, I saw the swollen black circles ringing her eyes. Her red hair lay smashed on her temples under a green wool cap. "Look what I found," she said to my mother.

"Oh, my God," my mother croaked. "Oh, Susan." Then she broke down sobbing.

Mrs. Franklin was gripping Spencer so tightly that her fingers seemed to be squeezing through his skin. But she didn't look dazed like my father or wracked like my mother or terrified like her son. Just sad and beaten and haunted. "He was just standing on that driveway over there when I drove down the street."

Spencer, I saw, had begun to panic. I could see him wriggling, tugging, trying to get free. I started toward him, but my father yanked me back. Behind the Franklins, the crowd surged closer. Cameras clicked and whirred to life. One of Spencer's wrists had come halfway free and was flailing at the air as if he were drowning.

"Let *go*!" he wailed.

"How did this happen, Alina?" Mrs. Franklin snapped, sounding as if she wanted to scream, or slap my mother, or just break down weeping. "How could you have let this happen?"

Spencer's body was shaking so badly that he seemed to dance on each breath of wind like the paper skeleton on his grandparents' porch. My father's hand had been on my back, but it slipped from me now, and I glanced up to find him staring at me, expressionless.

"Dad," I said. I wanted to explain. But his face was so blank that he seemed to be having trouble recognizing me. "We were just trying to help Theresa." Then Spencer exploded into tears.

"It was all his idea!" he yelled, but I couldn't look at him, and I didn't even want to see what my mother was doing. Sirens shrieked at the end of our street, and three police cars screeched to a halt at the base of our yard.

"They were waiting for me when I got home," Mrs. Franklin said. "They're going to be there when I go home now. We're never going to get free of this. None of us. Ever."

"Go to your room, Mattie," my father whispered.

It seemed like such a ridiculous punishment, given everything, that I almost laughed. Instead, I said, "Let me stay with Spencer." Suddenly, I was all too aware that I might not see him again for a very long time.

"Inside."

"Dad, please. You have to understand. There's a reason."

My father kept his voice low. "Spencer is going home. Now do as I say and get the hell in the house."

I fled to my room. Once there, I crouched next to my window. Cautiously, I peered over the sill. At first, I couldn't see anything but reporters and police officers clustered around our front stoop, but then the crowd parted to let Mrs. Franklin and Spencer through. Mrs. Franklin walked with her head up, her eyes boring straight into each camera lens until the cameramen fell back. One of them even lowered his camera. Spencer's head was tucked so far inside his mother's overcoat I couldn't see his face, but I could see his fists pounding against his sides as his mother half-led, half-dragged him to her car.

"Mrs. Franklin, how would you characterize your son's behavior? Especially considering the opportunities he's been given," I heard one of the reporters shout from the crowd. More questions struck her like snowballs, but she strode straight through them and never even turned her head.

"Mrs. Franklin, where is Spencer's father?"

"Do you have anything to say to the families whose children have actually been killed?"

That stopped her. She looked bewildered, as if she were staring into a blinding sunset. Around her, everyone had gone silent. Even from the house, I could hear her say, "Do you? I mean, my God. . . ."

Three policemen surrounded her and Spencer then. One of them was Sergeant Ross. He held up his hand to his fellow officers and leaned forward to talk to her quietly. Then he escorted them the rest of the way to her car. Spencer dove in the back and disappeared from sight. I saw the taillights wink on and watched them disappear down the block.

In the yard, the crowd was being herded toward the street. I spotted the president of our neighborhood association, Mr. Wetzel, standing next to the birch tree, buttoning his trench coat and staring at our house as if he'd never seen it before. He was joined by Mrs. McLean, and when they both turned in my direction, I ducked to the floor. A new voice blared out after a few minutes, and eventually I realized it belonged to Mrs. Wilkins, the woman who lived between our house and the Foxes with two sullen adult sons that no one seemed to know and three black Labradors she kept locked up in a woodchip-strewn pen beside the house. To my knowledge, Mrs. Wilkins had never been in our yard; I only knew her voice from hearing her snarl at the dogs. I peered out the window again and saw her gesturing at Mr. Wetzel and Mrs. McLean. She was wearing a black overcoat and black loafers and red socks, which made her look like the Wicked Witch of the East.

"I knew it couldn't be the same man," she said. "He's got specific tastes, our Snowman."

"Jesus Christ, Patricia," said Mrs. McLean, hunching her shoulders together as if she were trying to squeeze herself shut.

I leaned against the heating vent and crushed my hands against my temples. The hall door crashed open once, but whoever it was just went into the bathroom and left quickly. When the front door opened again, I heard aimless padding feet, and I knew that both of my parents were back indoors.

My father was speaking. He sounded calm. "Alina, it's over," he said. "The worst, anyway. We'll have to make it better from here."

"By doing what?" my mother snapped. "Do you know a cure for what's wrong with him? Do you realize how fucked up this is?"

"Alina, shhh."

"I don't care if he hears." She raised her voice. "Are you listening, Mattie?"

I didn't answer. I just tucked my chin against my chest and held my knees together.

"That's enough," my father said.

"Well, what the hell was he thinking? *Help Theresa.*" I heard her snort in derision. "What does that mean, anyway?"

"How the hell would I know?" My father was speaking so softly now that I could barely hear him.

"Oh, Joe."

After that, I heard my mother crying, and then, for a few blissful seconds, nothing at all until a new roar of activity erupted outside. I crawled back to the window and saw Dr. Daughrety scattering the neighbors like pigeons. He had frost on his eyelids and snowmelt on top of his skull. *Fe fi fo fum*, I thought. Police fell into line around him, but none of them got in his way. I heard my father swear and sprint for the front door just as the Doctor spotted me. He stuck out his index finger and held it there as if he were aiming a rifle, then marched straight up the stoop. My first thought was to dive into my closet. Then Theresa's frozen-scream face from the night before floated in front of my eyes, and suddenly I was out of my room and racing down the hall so I could stand behind my father when he opened the door.

My father grimaced when he saw me, but he didn't send me away. He put his hand on my shoulder and positioned his body so he was blocking the doorway as he stared through the screen at the Doctor.

"Colin," my father said evenly. "Can we help you?"

Dr. Daughrety's voice seemed to scrape over his bones on its way out of his body. "Move, Joe. I'm going to speak with your son."

"It's okay, Dad," I said tearfully.

My father glanced at me as Dr. Daughrety pushed past him. "Tears won't save you," he said. "If anything has happened to her, Mattie Rhodes, I swear on her mother's grave that nothing will save you. Nothing. Do you understand? Now where is she?"

I gaped at him. But before I could say anything, he dropped to his knees like a troll puppet with its strings cut, his limbs twitching chaotically. "Where is she?" he whimpered. "Did she know about this, about you and Spencer? Is she part of it?" His head tipped forward on his neck, almost as if he were praying. "What did she know?"

I saw Theresa's face at my window, saw her drifting out of the Fox house into the waiting, whirling snow.

"I have no idea," I said. "She knows Spencer's all right."

My mother leapt at me then, sprawling over the Doctor as she kneed him aside. Her hands locked around both of my arms. "Where is she, Mattie?" she screamed, the words shooting from her lips like sparks. She shook me. "*How* did she know Spencer was all right?"

I couldn't speak. My only thought was that my mother was going to have to dye her hair again soon. All at once, she stopped shaking me and allowed my arms to drop to my sides. She drilled her eyes all the way into mine until we were linked, the way she always said she had done when I was a baby to get me to stop crying.

"She came to my window," I said. "Last night, really late. We just wanted to see her, Mom. She's been gone for so long. We wanted to know she was okay. I went outside and took her to see Spencer—"

"Took her where?" she said. I'd never seen my mother look so scared.

"The Fox house. Spencer was hiding in the Fox house. I took Theresa to see him, but she hardly talked, and even that didn't make sense, so we walked her home." The terror that seized me then was brand new, a glacier that slid up my spine, through my limbs, behind my eyes until the whole world went white.

"She's gone," the Doctor mumbled flatly, as though the glacier inside me had spread through him too. He had slumped all the way into a sitting position on the slate floor.

"No. No! We left her at your back door. We walked her there."

"What time?" said Sergeant Ross, his huge frame filling our doorway. I hadn't even seen him come in.

"I don't know," I said. I was having trouble getting air through my teeth.

"Is this more of your prank?" the Doctor said.

My mother fell back. "Who the hell are you, Mattie Rhodes?"

Nothing about this made sense. "She has to be somewhere," I cried. "The woods, maybe. Or the schoolyard. She might go there, if she wanted to be alone."

"She left a note on the kitchen table," the Doctor said. "It said, *To the dwarves in the woods.* Does that mean anything to you?"

The glacier inside me slid into my lungs. "She said something like that last night. I don't know what it means. Maybe the woods behind our school?"

"It's your fault," he said, and stood. "Your fault." To my amazement, he seemed to be talking to my parents, not me. "Take a good look at your son. Ask yourself how he got that way. A little casual unchecked jealousy of other people's children, a lack of willingness to discipline, some unexamined lack of sensitivity to the rest of the world; mix them all together and you get the shining role models that you are."

My mother stayed still, but my father stepped forward and put his hand on the Doctor's chest. He looked weak, ineffective, like the crossing guards we always ignored in downtown Birmingham.

"That's more than enough," said my father. "You know we all care about Theresa, Mattie most of all. We'll do everything we can to help."

"That's just fine," the Doctor said. "Mattie's been such a big help already." His legs gave way again as he backed through the door, and my father grabbed him until he regained his balance. The Doctor glared at me one more time and then yanked the door shut behind him.

"Mattie," said Sergeant Ross, pressing me backward into a sitting position on the couch. "I think you better tell me what's going on here."

Through the living room window, I could see Dr. Daughrety sitting down in the snow. My mother covered her eyes with her hands and shooed away my father with a moan.

"We didn't plan it," I said.

"Which part?" he asked. "Is any of this real?" Without taking his eyes off me, he extracted a licorice stick from his pocket and stuck it in his mouth. "Just start at the beginning and tell me all of it. You can't make it any worse."

"It just happened," I said.

"How?"

Abruptly, I was back on my feet. "I have to go find her."

"You're not going anywhere."

"We're wasting time! We have to go."

Sergeant Ross rolled the licorice stick along his lips like the end of a pencil. He spoke very quietly. "The best thing you can do for Theresa now is to sit down and answer my questions." He leaned forward and put his huge hand on my shoulder, but he didn't grab or press or squeeze, and a little of the reassuring tone he'd used the night before crept into his voice. "I'm just trying to sort this out for myself, Mattie, so bear with me. Now tell me how it happened."

I slumped back down. "We were talking about Theresa. Or maybe we were just thinking about her. I'm not sure." I told him everything I could remember about the moment I saw the Fox house and realized we could get in there and what we could do. Then I told him about Theresa coming to my window in the middle of the night, and her silence and her humming when she was with us. At the end, I said, "It's all my fault."

"Mmmm," said Sergeant Ross. "So if I understand you correctly, you faked Spencer's kidnapping and probable death because you needed a way past Dr. Daughrety to talk to your friend."

It sounded awful, put that way. But I nodded.

"Because you were afraid that something bad had happened to her."

I nodded again.

"Mattie, what were you afraid of?"

I felt like I had thrown my arm in the air in Ms. Eyre's class in order to beat Theresa and then realized that I didn't know the answer.

"I was afraid she was disappearing," I finally said.

"She *has* disappeared," said Sergeant Ross.

Frustration knotted behind my eyelids, and I slammed my fist into the back of the couch.

"We don't have time. That's what I mean. I'm telling you, she's *disappearing*."

Sergeant Ross watched me for a while as new tears sprang to my eyes and my fists fell open at my sides. I could feel my parents watching me too, but I couldn't look at them.

"Mattie," Sergeant Ross said, "let's start again."

I wanted to scream, started to, but then my breath shut itself off before I could finish. "Wait," I said instead, and leapt from the couch. As I flew past him, I saw my mother sitting on the scratched-up slate by the hallway door with her head between her knees like a kid during a tornado drill. My father was standing beside her, silent and stiff as a palace guard. I scanned crazily around my room until I spotted Theresa's notebook, grabbed it off my desk, and raced back to the couch.

"Theresa gave this to me at her house yesterday," I said to the sergeant.

He took the notebook, turned it over twice, then peeled back the cover. The notebook's front pocket was stuffed with press clippings: Snowman Psychological Profiles from the front page of the *Free Press*, articles about the victims and their families, together with step-by-step accounts of the investigation. Inside the back flap was a map of Oakland County with printed black circles all over it.

I was so curious about the markings on the map that I didn't notice my mother right away. She had climbed to her feet, and now she was hovering over me.

"Mattie, what is this?"

I shook my head. "I don't know. It's Theresa's. She gave it to me when we went to see her last night."

"These locations," Sergeant Ross said slowly. "They're places the Snowman has been sighted, or supposedly sighted."

"Not all of them." I pointed to the winding Birmingham subdivision street where Amy Ardell's body had been found. "No one saw him there."

"No," the sergeant agreed. "We just know he was there because of Amy."

"What about there?" I said, pointing to a dark green star over Long Lake Road. I couldn't remember anything connecting the Snowman to Long Lake.

The Sergeant squinted at the map, turned it in his hands, then shook his head in frustration. "No idea. Did she know something? Do you kids—"

"Good God," my mother whispered.

"'He moves in circles,'" I heard myself say, as if Theresa's voice had slipped inside my throat.

Suddenly, my mother was grabbing me around the arm again. "What the fuck are you three playing at?"

This time, though, my father materialized beside her and touched her on the back. "Alina," he said, and she let go. She even let him ease her back a step.

I couldn't answer her anyway. Even if I could have, I didn't understand, not really, although the first chill of almost understanding had shuddered through me. As though nothing had happened, Sergeant Ross began coolly flipping the pages.

Each one was covered, front and back, with Theresa's stately, perfect penmanship. There were street names, victim's names, all sorts of random words like *Covington Junior High Swimming Pool, 5:30–9:30*, and *Farrell's Ice Cream* that meant nothing to me beyond what I already knew them to be. There were blots of ink in unrecognizable shapes that may or may not have been intentional. There were words I didn't recognize as English. The sentences didn't make sense. Barbara Fox's name stood all alone in the center of one page, first name in black ink, last name in red. Spencer Franklin's showed up several times. My own showed up more. Seeing it gave me none of the thrill I might have expected in different circumstances. It was like seeing it on a tab in a school office folder where parent-conference notes and standardized test scores were kept. If anything, it made me feel even less significant. I was an entry in this file, a name without a star, someone to be categorized.

"Son, please," said the sergeant, "you have to help me here. Do you know what any of this is supposed to mean?"

I thought I could almost smell her on the pages. A faint new-cut-grass smell. "She's dead," I said, "or she's going to be." Tears slid down my face once more, and I could feel myself bleaching away like a half-finished photograph jerked into the light.

"Jesus Christ, Mattie," my father said. "Do you think she might have figured out something about the Snowman somehow?" Swallowing, he regained control of his voice. "Something about who he is? Or where to find him?"

"Last night," I said, my voice trembling, "she said weird stuff. Avri's Deli and the names of some of the Snowman kids. I don't know. I don't know." For a lone absurd second, I felt the same way I did on gum ball days or after a Mind War: jealous, mostly, of what Theresa was capable of. Then my thoughts went screaming back toward her face as Spencer and I tumbled out of the Foxes' back hallway. I could hear her singing as I followed her into the house: *Frère Jacques. Frère Jacques. Dormez-vous?*

With Theresa's notebook clutched against him, Sergeant Ross stood up and looked at me. "Don't leave the house," he said. He sounded exhausted. "For your own protection, I mean."

"Actually, we were thinking about leaving town for a while," said my father.

"Think again," said Sergeant Ross, and he banged out the front door, leaving us alone.

Instantly, voices swelled outside as reporters rushed forward, but Sergeant Ross stalked through them down the driveway.

None of us moved from the positions the morning had washed us up in. I was sitting on the couch with my head bowed, thinking over everything I'd heard Theresa say, looking for some other clue. My mother sat back down on the floor and buried her face in her hands. My father lurked by the living room window, looking occasionally at his speakers as if expecting them to burst out in song. Finally, I heard my mother say, "Oh, Brent honey, no," and then my little brother blazed into the room, racing straight for me, fists flying.

He got in two or three decent shots to my face before my father yanked him off. The last one caught me right on the cheekbone, drove my teeth down on my tongue, and my mouth began to bleed.

I swallowed blood and did my best not to react. I considered spitting at him, at all of them, but I wasn't sure why.

"Go to your room," my mother said.

I started to rise before realizing that she meant my brother. Fists still quivering at his sides, face flushed and streaming tears, Brent stomped into the back hallway.

"Mattie," said my mother. She came over and sat beside me, and I uncurled halfway out of the ball that I'd slowly been forming.

"Honey, not now," my father said. "We're all devastated. He is too."

"Shut up." My mother gagged once. "Mattie. You little shit bastard. You don't know where she is. Do you?"

Horrified, I shook my head. "No," I said, wishing I could touch my mother, say the thing that would make everything turn better. But I couldn't imagine what that thing could be.

"What on earth were you thinking?" she said.

I couldn't help her understand, and I couldn't make her love me again, so I sat there saying nothing and a hard silence clamped down on the house. For the rest of the day and most of the evening, no one in my family said a single word, to me or to one another. Mostly, we waited for news. At some point, near dark, I moved to my room and stayed there. I heard my mother call Brent to the dinner table, but no one came to get me. After a while, I went to the bathroom to brush my teeth, leaving the door open so my family could see me. I kept brushing until my gums bled, then went back to my room and huddled in the sheets, though it wasn't even dark. I felt nothing at all except dull, throbbing fear. I left my lights off and stared at the spot where Theresa's face had been at my window. My reflection dangled there like a lure, but nothing rose to meet it. I didn't sleep, and then I did, some.

The next morning, I awoke to breakfast sounds. I hadn't dreamed, or couldn't remember any dreams. Outside, the mourning doves that lived in our birch tree opened their throats to the daylight. I didn't like the sound; it was too hollow. "Whoever they're mourning," my dad told me once, "must have died long ago." So typically strange. Scrambling down from my bunk, I wrapped my robe around me and padded toward the kitchen, rubbing my eyes with closed fists, trying to look as young and panic-wracked as I felt. My mother didn't glance up from the stove when I sat at the kitchen table.

I didn't want to ask the question, because if there was an answer, someone would have told me already. But I couldn't help it. "Did Theresa come home?"

My mother ignored that. But after a while, she set a plate of scrambled eggs in front of me.

"Can I call Spencer?" I asked when she returned to the sink. "Mom?"

"No," she said. Then she spun around, dropping her spatula on the floor, and locked eyes with me. My heart ground against my lungs. With a moan, she reached out and pulled me to her. "Mattie," she said.

My father came into the kitchen, his breath whistling through his lips the way it did when he was furious. "Want a paper?" he said to me, and dropped the Sunday *Free Press* face up on the table.

We'd made the blue section on the front page—generally reserved for psychological profiles of the Snowman—right under last year's school picture of Theresa in a white ribbon with an echo of a smile on her face. The smile made her look more like an ordinary girl, the kind who wore hair bows and always looked startled in photographs. The article reported Theresa's fondness for slot-car racing and the pickle sandwich at Avri's Deli, that she'd been slated to be our district's representative to the Outstanding Michigan Youth Summit in July. My own interest in slot-car racing was not mentioned, but the fact that I had once handcuffed a teacher was, along with sketchy details about my father's "troubled" work history and his current "exile" at the future-research lab at GM. A complete description of what Spencer and I had done was included, along with repeated mentions of the frequency with which my name appeared in Theresa's "diary." That was the word, I realized after two or three readings, that the reporter had come up with for the notebook Theresa had given me. It wasn't really a diary, I thought, though I couldn't have said what it was.

That day, the second of Theresa's disappearance, the only sound in our house, except for the mourning doves, was one fifteen-second burst of Beethoven's *Pastoral* from my father's stereo, which played actual music for the very first time. I recognized the piece right away. According to my parents, this symphony was the first music I'd ever heard. It hadn't calmed me the way my mother's staring eyes did, but they played it for me throughout my first year of life because it made me wiggle and, sometimes, laugh. Today, it just made me more afraid and even sadder, and I shut myself in my room and tried to keep my mind blank. My brother spent all day kicking his desk, as far as I could tell.

Sometime after dinner, a silver Buick Regal rolled up our street and coasted to a stop in front of our house. I returned to the living room and watched from the window as a gray-haired man in an open gray trench coat stepped into the light from our streetlamp. My father opened the door and peered quizzically into the darkness; then he murmured, "Shit." The man in the trench coat stepped closer to the house, and my father spoke a little louder, sounding nervous and a little angry. "Mr. Fenwick. So nice of you to stop by." I had never heard him use that tone before, but I recognized the name. He was my father's boss, the one who told him, "You know, your dreaming could destroy your career." My father had repeated that and shaken his head in wonder over and over to my mother last year. I had never met the man.

"Come in," my father said.

"We're on our way home," said Mr. Fenwick, his voice rumbling, gravelly, like a tire spinning on rocks. "We just wanted you to know we're all thinking of you." He made no movement toward the house, standing halfway up our drive, as if we had something contagious. The front door stayed open, and I could feel the current of cold air sweeping through the room.

"Is this the kind of thing that destroys careers?" my father said.

Mr. Fenwick stared. Eventually, he shrugged. "I don't know, Joe. I haven't had much experience with this kind of thing." He leaned back over the passenger door, and I could see the woman who had driven him here in the car's dome light. She had white hair and a mouth that was way too red and made her look friendly but also sad, like a clown.

"See you next week," Mr. Fenwick called, turning back in my father's direction again.

This time, my father sounded distracted, much more like himself. "I'll be in tomorrow," he said.

"Don't come in tomorrow," Mr. Fenwick said, too fast. "For God's sake, stay home a few days." He climbed into his car without waving, and the white-haired woman drove him away. My father stayed in the doorway for a long time. When he finally shut the door, the cold breeze flitted around the room like a moth trapped indoors.

"You think he came by just to see if we're all right?" he asked my mother.

"No," my mother said. "He came to gape. Just like everyone else we know."

As always when they talked about my father's job, my parents' lives seemed to spread out before me like one of the Great Lakes, something I could only view from the shore, impossibly big, vaguely threatening, and populated with people and events I would never know or even know about. Tonight, this sensation terrified me. I scurried back to my bedroom and shut the door. I wanted to call out, do something to shock them into remembering that I was there and that I hadn't always done the things I'd done lately.

Brent beat me to it. He put his foot through the bedroom wall. His shoe didn't get all the way into my room, but it blasted through the plaster on his side, causing tiny cracks to spiderweb from my baseboard. The first kick was enough to bring my parents running, and when he delivered a second, little flakes of white paint flew into the air. My own private snow flurry.

"You couldn't hold off for one night?" my mother screamed at him. "You just have to make things more difficult?"

"You're not doing anything!" Brent screamed back. "You're just letting him sit there. Everyone hates us. Everyone hates him. He's a freak. Get *off*, you're hurting me."

As quickly and furiously as it had begun, the screaming stopped, and in its place I heard low, intense murmuring. I crouched by the new cracks in my wall and listened, but I couldn't make out the words. Soon the relentless horror of the day had a narcotic effect, and I began yawning. I crawled into bed and lay twisting in my covers, nearly asleep, jerking in and out of anxious dreams until my mother appeared at my bedside with a pair of my jeans.

"Put these on," she said. "Come into the living room." She was wearing snow boots under her bathrobe and a scarf around her neck.

"Why?" I asked.

"Just do it, Mattie. Hurry."

She tossed the jeans on top of me, and I heard her open the door to Brent's room. The clock on my wall said 1:45.

Minutes later, my parents and my brother and I were hunched on our couch, peering through the half-closed curtains at the nine turtle-neck men standing motionless in our yard, holding lit torches over their heads. No one knew who these people were or what they intended. They may have been vigilantes, or a neighborhood watch, or nine frustrated men who felt better roaming the Snowman's night than sleeping through it. I found myself remembering the child-catcher from *Chitty Chitty Bang Bang*. All day long, I'd been remembering things that had scared me or made me feel bad, because all of them were weirdly comforting; they were so much less awful than what was happening now.

"Maybe if we gave them Mattie, they'd leave us alone," my mother said.

"Good idea," said Brent.

She might have been kidding. I glanced quickly in her direction and became aware, in a way I never was before, that my mother was a liv-ing thing, and she would not be living always. I leaned as hard as I could against her. She was wrapped in her blue blanket, and she didn't free her arms or drop a reassuring hand on me. Eventually, though, after a long, long time, I felt her return the lean. That was good enough for me. For a little while, I even stopped thinking about Theresa.

"Joe. Should we call the police?" she asked my father.

"I've never heard of these guys hurting anybody," he said.

"I'm scared, Mom," said Brent, and immediately he started to cry. It amazed me the way real emotions just seemed to surface in him, as natural as whitecaps on waves. Mine had to be called, like stray pets, and they didn't always come. Finally, at some point when none of us were looking, the turtleneck men evaporated out of our yard.

The next morning, in spite of everything, my parents decided to send me to school. They felt it was the only choice. I had to face what I'd done, they said, and get on with my life the best I could. They were trying hard to talk to me as if everything was normal. My mother, especially, was having a difficult time doing it. I didn't argue. I just got myself dressed and collected my backpack, and then Mrs. Jupp called.

I was sitting at the kitchen table, so I could hear my mother's *huh*s and *mmm*s, and I could see a new crease cut across her forehead like a fresh fault line. "I see," she said. "Why, what are they saying?" She closed her eyes. "Yeah. Yes, okay."

A few minutes later, she hung up.

"What?" I said, seeing nothing in my mind's eye but the empty Solitude Desk.

"Everyone is talking about you. Mrs. Jupp's not sure it's such a good idea for you and Brent to go to school today."

"Is Spencer coming? Are they talking about him too?"

My mother looked at the floor, and the crease in her forehead deepened. She surprised me by kneeling beside my chair. "Mattie, Spencer isn't coming back to Phil Hart. His mother and Mrs. Jupp have decided it would be best for all concerned if he went back to Ferndale. I'm sorry."

Slowly, but without thinking, I picked up my cereal bowl and threw it on the floor. Milk and Cheerios sprayed across the tiles.

"Thanks, Mattie," said my mother, and she put her face in her hands.

"This is *stupid!*" I yelled. "He didn't even do anything."

My mother's eyes hardened. "Didn't do anything? I suppose you think you didn't do anything either."

The tears flooding my eyes were equal parts fury, frustration, and loneliness. "That's stupid too."

"Don't you talk to me like that, Mattie Rhodes. Don't you dare."

"Spencer was just being my friend. We were just trying to be Theresa's friends. He tried to talk me out of it. He should come back. Everyone can't disappear." I hated the whine in my voice, but I couldn't control it.

"Mattie, I know this must be horrible for you. But maybe you should have thought about the consequences before you acted."

"I—" I started, and then I didn't know what to say. I found myself crying again. "Can I go see him? Can we please just go over there so I can tell Mrs. Franklin I'm sorry?"

"Someday, Mattie. Maybe someday. Not today."

I was crying so hard my saliva felt thick and tasted salty. "This is the worst thing I've ever done," I said.

"Oh, honey," said my mother. "Yes. Yes, it is. And it's hurt a whole lot of people. And it's going to be a long time before life goes back to normal."

"Do you think the Snowman has Theresa?"

My mother's mouth quivered, but her voice came out steady. "She's a smart girl, Mattie. She might be all right." Then she left the room.

Despite Mrs. Jupp's warning, my parents sent Brent to school anyway, because he demanded to go and kept saying he couldn't stand to be near me. I stayed in the family room all morning, watching game shows. My mother cleaned up the kitchen, and after my father went to work, she shut herself in her bedroom and got on the phone.

I stared at the TV screen through squinted eyes, praying for a Special Update break-in. "Ladies and gentlemen, this is Coral Clark, and I'm standing on the corner of Cider Lake Road near Birmingham, where a dazed but unhurt Theresa Daughrety reappeared moments ago. Indications of her whereabouts these past thirty-six hours remain vague, but she is unharmed and police are sending her home to her family. And— let's see now—it looks like Theresa has something to say. What is it, honey?" Theresa's bow-mouth twitches, and she tugs at Coral Clark and whispers in her ear. Coral Clark listens, nods, smiles at the camera. Her teeth glitter like stalactites in a cave. "Mattie Rhodes," she says, "Theresa says she misses you too."

But the break-in never came, and I gave up praying. I leaned back against the couch and let the time crawl by. Then the doorbell rang. I glanced toward my parents' room, but my mother didn't come out. On the third ring, I crouched low and edged forward so I could shut off the TV without being seen from the front stoop. I thought it might be one of the reporters or Sergeant Ross with more questions or bad news. Or maybe Theresa, I thought, and leapt to my feet.

Stamping her boots on our mat, shivering in a yellow spring rain slicker, Barbara Fox glared through the window and leaned again on the doorbell.

"Take your time, it's warm out here," she snapped as I stumbled to the door and pulled it open. She pushed past me into the living room. "The Doctor forbade me to come here," she said icily. Her voice quieted but didn't soften. "He's sitting on our living room couch like there's a lance stuck through him. He can't cry. He can't speak." She looked wildly around the room, as if Theresa might be hiding somewhere in it. Abruptly, sarcastically, she yelled, "Oh, hi, Mrs. Rhodes. Thanks but I can't stay. Troubles at home, you know. I didn't mean to come in, really. We're trying not to fall apart."

My mother sounded tired and teary when she answered from the bedroom. "Hello, Barbara, honey. I'll be right there. I'm on the phone."

"I'm taking Mattie for a walk."

I let her lead me to the coat closet. When I took too long with my boots, she bent over and yanked my jacket on tight and snapped it around me.

"Aren't you cold in that?" I asked, touching the sleeve of her rain slicker.

"It doesn't matter," she said, and tugged me out the front door behind her.

White-silver light ricocheted off the new snow and stung my eyes. Barbara's dark hair hung wet and unbrushed in rings down her back. Her fingers were twisted around my wrist, but I didn't care. It felt good to be outside with someone who'd loved me, once. Ever since I left Spencer at the Foxes', I'd felt like a fugitive, but now I had escaped, with another fugitive shackled to me.

Sighing, Barbara dragged me around to the far side of our tallest evergreen. Instead of continuing down the street, she shoved the branches aside with her free hand and pulled me into the quiet space underneath.

Brent and I had already trampled or bent most of the lower branches playing Ghost-in-the-Graveyard games under here. Many times, Barbara had been the Ghost we were hiding from. Now she sat on the needles and pulled me down beside her onto the surprisingly dry, resiny near-warmth of the ground. It was like sitting on the remnants of someone else's campfire. Barbara scooped up a palmful of needles and shook them like Pick-Up Sticks. The only thing I could think to do was put my hand on her arm, right where it stuck out of her sleeve, and I left it there.

"What have you done, Mattie?" she said.

Sergeant Ross asked me that. So had my mother. I still had no good answer.

"What were you thinking?" she asked again. "I really want to know." Each word she spoke seemed to crumple her a bit more, and she balled forward into her coat. "I want someone to explain all this to me. Right now."

She didn't sound like she was chanting, or hoping, or even asking. Her voice came out in a monotone, and her head bobbed, and she suddenly stopped seeming like the person I knew at all. *You ran over your father*, I thought, and almost said it, and then I just felt bad, and sorry, and scared.

"I was thinking I could help," I said. "I thought she needed me." I felt a single fat tear on my cheek. Barbara reached out and squashed it against my skin like a bug, but then her hand flew back to her hunched-up knees.

"Help. Need," Barbara said, as though the words were new. The smile she flashed and then swallowed was horrible.

"Barbara, are you—"

"You took them to my fucking house. What were you doing in my house?"

This time, Barbara made no move to wipe my tears. She didn't even look at me. In my stomach, the panic that had become a near-constant companion stoked itself again.

"It was a safe place to go," I told her.

"Safe?" Barbara snorted.

"It isn't even your house anymore," I blurted, and immediately regretted it.

Barbara didn't say anything for a long time. The intermittent breeze lifted wisps of snow and slid them across her face. Finally, she let out a sigh that might have been a shudder. "The Doctor . . ." she said, then let the sentence trail away with her breath. I watched her pluck a pine needle from the nearest branch and roll it against her cheek. "My dad was so sick, Mattie. And even when he wasn't sick, he was so needy all the time. I couldn't get away from him. He followed me around the house and into the yard and everywhere I went like a pull toy. I had to shower with the goddamn bathroom door open or he'd threaten to break it down."

I gaped. "He wanted to see you in the shower?"

"He didn't want to see. He just wanted to be sure I was still there. He'd sit on the hallway rug and ask me if the water was warm enough, whether we were out of shampoo, one inane question after another until the shower was over and I was out and dressed and he could watch me again. He wanted to die. If he could talk to me now, he'd probably thank me for mowing him down." She leaned her head forward and pushed her cheek against the nearest pine branch as if it were a pillow. All at once, tears detonated from her eyes, and her whole body was shaking so hard I thought she might fly apart. "Hi, Dad," I heard her say, which made no sense at all. Her throat kept making this horrible squeaking rasp, like a bicycle brake failing in the middle of a plunge downhill. The sobbing went on so long I almost ran for help. But finally the shaking subsided, and Barbara's head tilted a little toward me, and I could see her chapped lips working and then smoothing into a flat quivering line.

"That's one thing about the Daughrety house," she said. "There's plenty of space. Oh, Mattie, I know the Doctor seems cold to you. But he's different with the people he loves. He doesn't ask stupid questions. He doesn't clutter up the world with chatter, and he doesn't need much except his daughter and sometimes me around him. He said he loved me, once. Before . . . well, before." She jerked her head up and cocked it slightly. Then she said, "Something was happening with Theresa and me, too. Something nice. I can't explain it. But it's gone now, whatever it was. She showed me a picture of her mom. That was something, don't you think?" And just like that, she was weeping again. "Goddammit, Mattie, where is she?"

Right then, I was seized by a jealousy that might have been over-whelming if I could have located its source. Mostly, I think I was jeal-ous of the days going by in the Daughrety house, all those hours Barbara and Theresa had spent not talking together on the white liv-ing room couch or at the dining room table where the Mind Wars were held.

For a long time, Barbara sat with her head up, tears streaming down her face and into her coat collar. She never moved to wipe them. It looked like she was melting. My jealousy leaked away, leaving me guilty and sad. Barbara's face was so wet I couldn't even tell if she was crying anymore. But the silence was making me too anxious to sit still.

"Are you going to stay there? Are you going to marry the Doctor?"

"Mattie, I haven't had a home in a really long time. And I need one. And there are worse places, and worse people. Much worse." Her voice caught and her eyes blinked, but I was pretty sure she had stopped crying after all. Shoving to her feet, she parted the branches of the pine tree. "Get up," she said.

"Barbara, what should I do?"

"Get up, I said." She stepped out of the evergreen and waited for me to do the same. "I'll tell you what to do. Don't try anything heroic. Don't do anything else stupid. And don't break, Mattie. Your family's going to need you."

"I'm sorry about your dad," I said, and Barbara stared at me out of her wet eyes. Except for the tears, she looked as blank as Theresa, and I got scared again. She walked me to the front door and then lifted her hand to my hair and left it there, barely touching. "I have to go find

Theresa now," she whispered, with an intensity I had never heard from her. "I think maybe I can."

"Barbara," I started, trying to think of something to say that would keep her here a little longer.

But she was already halfway down the driveway, gone from me. And I knew, somehow, that she was never coming back.

I didn't go inside until Barbara was out of sight. Then I went into the family room and turned up the TV so I wouldn't have to talk to anyone, but no one came in.

Later that afternoon, I was sitting on the couch, listening to the emptiness in the world, when an ice ball burst on the window behind me. The second ice ball cracked the storm glass as I dove to the floor. Seconds later, my mother flew out the back porch door and came in dragging my brother by his ear.

"You ice-balled your own house?" I said, momentarily thrilled. My brother's temper tantrum had lasted two days. A few more actions like this one, I thought, and he just might draw a little attention away from me.

"I was ice-balling you," he said, smirking as my mother jerked him toward his room.

"Get in there," she said, shutting his door behind him. "Don't let me see or hear from you until dinner." Then she went back to her room without looking at me and closed herself in again.

My father came home early. He didn't touch his stereo, and he said he couldn't eat. He went out to his workshop for a while, but when I checked on him he was just sitting with his hand picking idly at the teeth of a circular saw, reminding me of the barber fish in *Strange True Fish Tales* that picks its food from the mouths of sharks.

For dinner, Brent and I ate hamburgers in the family room with the TV on, which we almost never did. My mother watched with us, which was even stranger, but at least we were sitting together. On *Hogan's Heroes*, Sergeant Schultz had to wear a dress. None of us laughed. No one got up to clear the dishes. At nine, we watched the Special Update. The entire show was devoted to Theresa. According to Coral Clark, Dr. Daughrety had been knocking on every door in

Troy during the past twenty-four hours, demanding access to garages and basements. He'd even gone to houses that the police had already searched and houses with hands in the windows. At last report, he was deep into Birmingham, working street by street. Police were encouraging residents to provide any assistance they could.

"A dedicated father," Coral Clark said, completing her report. "Our prayers are with him, and with you, little Theresa. Wherever you are." *In the woods. Stuffed in the bottom of a pickle barrel at Avri's Deli, hands bound, eyes blank, chanting Oak Park, Covington, Mini-Mike's, my name.*

"Jesus Christ," my mother murmured, and put her face in her hands again.

The turtleneck men came back in the middle of the night. I was up with my jeans on before my mother even called me because I'd seen torch flicker on the lawn. Through the living room window, we saw the torches planted in a row like signal flares. Their light illuminated a series of shapes in the snow.

My mouth went dry, and my tongue seemed to swell and harden against my teeth until it felt like a peach pit being stuffed down my throat. Maybe they had found Theresa's body, I thought, and brought it here. The thought rocketed me to my feet. I dashed straight past my parents and out the front door, skidding down the ice on our driveway. The turtleneck men scattered. I ignored them and ran straight to the torches and looked down. I tried to scream, but I couldn't get sound past my tongue.

Graves: deep coffin-shaped indentations in the snow, with little stick crosses planted at their heads. Each cradled an imprint of a little kid, a snow angel, its arms tucked in rather than waving, as though whatever was buried there had flown away. There were ten in all, laid out in neat plots. One each, I thought, for the eight kids already dead, plus one for Theresa. And one for me? I didn't know. I was too hypnotized by the shapes themselves, the nothingness within them.

My parents had come outside by then, their coats flapping around their bathrobes, their eyes black and hollow like real snowmen's eyes. The sight of them made me turn and run. I raced around the side of the house, bursting through the crusted snow as my jaws snapped down on the ice-laden wind. I drove straight for the towering evergreen at the back of our property, the darkest spot I knew, hurtled around it toward the place where its shadow and the shadow of the maple beside it overlapped, and slammed face first into Mrs. Cory's dangling legs. I hit them so hard I snapped them out of rigor mortis or deep freeze or whatever had locked them in place. They cracked back on their joints and kicked crazily above me where I fell in a bloodied heap in the snow.

There are crows that do not migrate away from Detroit in the winter. The strips of flesh they'd left behind on Mrs. Cory's face glistened with ice and inside color, like petals on a frozen flower. Don't break, Barbara Fox had told me, and I felt her hand through the creeping wetness in my hair. I sank back against the cold, eyes open but fixed straight up at Mrs. Cory's shredded cheeks. Suddenly, I felt nothing, the same kind of nothing I'd felt in the first few seconds after being put to sleep before my tonsillectomy. But it did seem better, somehow, to be lying in my own snow grave than the one the turtleneck men had left for me.

"I killed you," I said aloud. But I still felt nothing. I decided I should try screaming again, so I forced my mouth open, drew breath past my peach-pit tongue, but no sound came out.

A new snow began to fall. I felt my own heat melting me a resting place. Mrs. Cory seemed to be not so much dangling as hovering, a skeleton angel watching over me, made not of bone but of moonlight. My father appeared, saw Mrs. Cory, and said "Oh, no" before jerking me out of the snow to my feet. As he led me away, I wondered how on earth she had gotten herself up there.

Different police came this time. They went out back with tools and returned a half hour later with her body on a stretcher, some inanimate thing, not my angel. Most of the questions were for my parents. Brent was sent back to bed. "Murderer," he murmured at me on the way to his room. Then Sergeant Ross walked through the door. He looked the way my parents had a few hours earlier, only worse. His skin had lost its elasticity, become hardened like tire rubber. I closed my eyes and saw snow graves, dangling women, and Theresa Daughrety in rapid succession. When I opened them again, Sergeant Ross was standing in front of me.

"Why would anyone want your job?" I asked.

He just looked at me for a while—almost affectionately, I thought, though I couldn't imagine why—and then he brushed his huge hand across my shoulder. "Sit tight, Mattie," he said. "More bad news coming."

My brother was up again, and the sergeant directed everyone to the couch. My father sat like a zombie in his rumpled clothes, his eyes half closed. Behind him, my mother was almost dancing in agitation. She dropped her arm around Brent's shoulders and pulled him alongside her. When we were all in place, Sergeant Ross rubbed his bloodshot eyes and said, "James Sea."

The only reaction came from my mother, who made a heaving sound with each breath, as though she'd suddenly become asthmatic.

I didn't realize who James Sea was until the sergeant showed us his school photo. Even then, Brent recognized him first and immediately started crying. I could feel my brother's trembling all the way up my spine.

James was the Chippewa third-grader who had come to the Halloween assembly last year dressed as a wolverine. "I'm afraid he's gone," Sergeant Ross said.

"Gone," my father repeated, sounding as if he was talking in his sleep.

"He left for his bus stop yesterday, over in the Maple Lane subdivision just north of here, at his usual time," the sergeant said. "But he didn't make it there. Two other kids claim to have seen him climbing into some kind of old station wagon. Could be the Snowman, with a new car, or it could be an imitator. Either way, it's a nightmare."

"Do you believe them?" I whispered. The sergeant shrugged.

"Even more than we believed you," he said. "The story has more holes in it, but it makes more sense."

I started to fidget. Sergeant Ross was still talking, but I couldn't hear him, and I couldn't see the room anymore. Images clustered in front of my eyes. I began twisting back and forth against the back of the couch, then swung wildly around and grabbed my father's arm where it was hanging slack at his side. I could see Mrs. Cory's dancing legs, Theresa looking blank at the Solitude Desk, Barbara screaming beside her father's corpse, the Fox house floating like a ghost ship over the horizon with Spencer at the rail, and I felt as though I were locked in a little igloo in the center of a snow globe with white flakes rioting around me and giant shapeless shadows moving just beyond the boundaries of the visible world.

Even in my horrified state, I could see that this kidnapping broke at least part of the pattern. James Sea was too young. Every other victim had been eleven or twelve. He was nine, and the difference between eleven and nine was enormous. Then I thought: if James Sea was with the Snowman, where was Theresa? And that upset me so much that I staggered to my feet and stood there, swaying.

Sergeant Ross was watching me. Then he said, "I just thought you'd rather hear it from me first. It'll be all over the morning news." He glanced out the window. I'd seen the same sort of resignation in Phil Fox's face, and now Barbara's too.

The sergeant looked at his watch and said, "Fuck," very quietly. "Four forty-five. Go to bed, people. Nothing you can do. Nothing I can do either." He got up, and without another word he left the house.

After a while, I realized my father wasn't going to move. My mother was stroking Brent's hair, and he was surprisingly still, crying softly in her lap. I didn't deserve to be there with them, I thought. So I got up, hoping someone would stop me. I wanted to walk straight across the yard, over the icy surface of Cider Lake, and vanish into the Michigan mist. Instead, I shuffled off to my room, where I bolted the door and began pacing back and forth in jerking steps. At some point, I climbed under the covers and stared at the window as if I were peering into a crystal ball. "Where are you?" I whispered over and over, until I fell asleep. In my dreams, I saw her dancing along a tree branch, dropping gum balls, dressed as a wolverine. The Snowman—black and white, like the newspaper sketch—stood in the shadow of a nearby evergreen. My evergreen. When he spoke, his voice was old, like Mrs. Jupp's, and almost kind.

You'll get hurt, he said. *Careful.*

When I opened my eyes, sunlight was streaming through the window, and my father's face loomed beside my bunk.

"You were talking," he said. He was holding an unpeeled orange and an unwrapped slice of American cheese, and I thought of Theresa's mother on the sled in the Daughretys' backyard.

"Sit up, son. Eat something." He pressed the food into my hands. "Mattie, I want to talk to you about Mrs. Cory."

Her frozen legs cracked in my ears, and her ruined face floated in the branches of the birch tree outside my window.

"I just—that wasn't your fault, Mattie. I don't want you blaming yourself for what happened to her."

"She came to see me," I said. "Then she killed herself in our tree."

"She lost her children, Mattie," my father said. "Both of them. Do you understand? Of course you don't, how could you, but believe me, okay? Please. She barely even noticed you."

"Dad," I said, sounding like a four-year-old. "What about Theresa?"

"What do you mean?"

"Well, her mother died. And she's been crazy. Really crazy. Would she . . . do that? I mean, kill herself?"

"Jesus Christ, Mattie, don't ever say that. Don't even think it. Come here." He drew me into his arms, which didn't help. It just made me feel more ashamed. "Mrs. McLean's been by the school. She's bringing some homework for you. I think you should do it."

After that he just held me awhile. Then he let me go and evaporated out of the room.

I laid the cheese and the orange on my windowsill. The best thing I could do, I thought, was sleep some more, without talking or dreaming. But this time, when I closed my eyes, I felt Spencer kneeling on my chest, fists flailing against my ribs. He was my best friend, the first one I'd ever had, the brother who actually liked being around me. I imagined him prowling around his house or slouching on his uncomfortable couch or knocking the air-hockey puck into the goal over and over. And suddenly, it hit me that Spencer had been my friend from that very first sidecarring morning, and I might never see him again.

Out in the hall, I heard my father's footsteps moving toward the front of the house. "Come on," he said. "I'm going to be late for work."

"Wait!" I heard Brent snap after him.

"Just get in the car," my father said. I'd never heard him sound so impatient. A few minutes later, his Oldsmobile shuddered to life and backed out of our driveway. When he and Brent were gone, I made myself wait a little longer. There was no sound coming from my mother's bedroom. She was sleeping, I thought. Carefully, I eased the door open and edged down the hall, heading for the kitchen telephone.

I don't know why I was surprised when Mrs. Franklin answered, but I was; the sadness in her voice shocked me. I almost hung up. But the thought of that woman holding a dead phone in her hand seemed even worse, somehow, than the idea of her talking to me.

"Mrs. Franklin," I said, "it's Mattie Rhodes, please don't hang up."

There was silence. I jammed the receiver against my ear, listening for breath, crying, anything. Finally, she said, "What the hell do you want, Mattie?"

"I'm sorry, Mrs. Franklin." I felt my lungs crumple like paper bags in a fist, and I couldn't get any more air in them. Still, I managed to ask, "Is Spencer all right?"

"Why don't you ask him?"

"Can I?"

Mrs. Franklin let loose a single sob, sharp and hard as cap-gun fire. "Oh, Mattie, of course you can," she said.

Our front doorbell rang, but I didn't answer it. I was listening to Mrs. Franklin calling Spencer. They argued back and forth, and then Spencer came on the line.

"Hi," I heard my mother say. I held my breath, tucked out of sight against the kitchen cabinets, while she and whoever had just come in our front door retreated toward her bedroom.

"Hello?" Spencer said again. "Mattie?"

"Hey," I said softly.

"What do you want?"

"What do you mean, what do I want?" It felt so good to hear his voice.

"Did they find Theresa?"

"No."

"Did they find the other kid? James Sea?"

"You heard about that?"

"Why are you calling me?"

"Why do you think?"

"I'm kind of busy right now, Mattie. I have to say goodbye to my dad. He's leaving us. For good, this time."

"What?" I said. I'd meant to apologize to him, too, and to ask if he'd been to his new school yet. Or his old school, I guessed.

"I gotta go, Mattie," he said, and started crying, and before I could say anything at all, he hung up.

I stayed in the kitchen, holding the phone. There was nothing I could do. I stumbled into the living room, then back toward my room. My mother's door was open, and through it I saw her sitting on her bed, sobbing quietly on the shoulder of Angie McLean. They had been friends since before I was born. Mrs. McLean was wearing her cream-peach commemorative outfit this time. Neither of them looked up or said anything to me. After a while, they began talking in low tones, but I could hear Mrs. McLean asking my mom about Lake Cleaning Day this Saturday, and my mother sighing. "You've got to be kidding, Angie," she said.

"'Whatever you've got going don't stop the geese from shittin' on our beach,'" Mrs. McLean said. "Neighborhood motto, remember."

"They're really still doing it this weekend?"

"Got my flyer today."

"No one wants us there."

"Sweep some shit, spread some sand, and they'll be happy enough to have you. We need to be together. All of us do."

Every year, all the families around us, even the ones without children, gathered at dawn on the tiny Cider Lake beach to collect trash, sweep dung, dump new sand in the muck along the shoreline, eat hot dogs with filthy hands, and stare at the sun on the ice, which wouldn't melt completely for another month yet. I couldn't believe that Lake Cleaning Day was here already, that anyone would care, that there'd be any kids left to clean the lake for. I scrambled back to my room and resumed pacing, fast and hard.

That night, my father came home early from work and headed straight for his workshop, as he had almost every night since Spencer's mock disappearance. But this time my mother grabbed him, shoved him into a chair at the kitchen table, and held him there until dinner. She kept leaping from the stove to him, forcing him to sit back down. My brother came in from school and ignored me, but we all ate together. After dinner, my mother pulled down the Monopoly game from the closet's top shelf, and all four of us went into the family room and played for an hour or so, collecting, paying, going to jail. I looked at the clock at five minutes to nine and said, "It's time for the Special Update."

No one moved until my father reached across the board and touched both Brent and me on the top of the head. My mother leaned into him, and we held each other that way just long enough for me to glimpse our shadowy reflection on the curve of the television screen.

Eventually, everyone but me went to bed and left me alone with the game board. I stayed a long time, rolling dice, moving everyone's pieces around, paying and collecting rent while the wind swept along the windowsills and my house creaked and tilted in the dark. Eventually, I heard Brent traipse to the bathroom, then go into my parents' room. A little while later, I screwed up my courage and did the same.

No one looked up or said anything when I came in. My mother was propped on one elbow. My father and Brent were sitting up on the comforter, still as wax figures. I climbed onto the bed beside them, and the world beyond the bedroom curtains seemed to blur. It was as though our mattress had risen, *Bedknobs and Broomsticks* style, and floated out the window into the starless sky.

They found James Sea the next afternoon, nestled against the base of a basketball net on a court near his house as if he were waiting for a pickup game. He had an unlit, unsmoked cigarette tucked between his fingers like a stage prop. Like most of the Snowman's victims, he'd been dead less than twenty minutes when he was discovered. His mother told Coral Clark that he hated basketball, even though he went to the court every day, because he always got picked last. When Mrs. Sea started screaming, the cameras held her face for a second and then flashed away to a picture of her son in his wolverine costume. The picture had been taken in his living room, not at school; he hadn't put in his needle teeth yet. He was smiling.

1977

L ake Cleaning Day dawned clear and cold. I was the first one up, but not by much, and I lay in bed and listened to my neighborhood drag itself into the day. I heard my parents' alarm go off and they immediately started to argue. My father didn't want to go to the lake. He said that he'd been out there all goddamn week dealing with the fallout, engaging in a community grief that other people weren't quite sure he deserved to feel. Every time my mother tried a new tactic, my father would repeat, "All goddamn week."

Finally, my mother told him, "Until the day we no longer live here, I plan to be a part of this neighborhood. Even if I'm the scourge of it."

"No, no," said my father. "That would be your elder child."

I did not question the burst of energy that sizzled through me right then. It had been so long since I had felt any energy at all. I leapt up, pounded on Brent's door, and kept doing it until he howled, "Fuck off." I showered fast, bundled into two sweatshirts and my Red Wings windbreaker, and threw open the front door to breathe the air. Scrambling back into the kitchen, I grabbed a muffin and stuffed it in my mouth, feeling like a lion about to leap over my own retaining wall. I knew Theresa was still missing. I knew I had wrecked Spencer's life. I knew James Sea was dead. But I wanted out. My mother came into the kitchen, still in her robe. My father hadn't even made it to the shower yet. I darted back down the hall and banged on my brother's door again.

"Come *on*," I urged.

"No one wants to see you," shouted Brent as he opened the door and shoved past me into our bathroom, wearing the official Detroit Institute of Arts sweatshirt he'd been given as a prize on a field trip last year. He had never won a school prize before, and my parents kept praising him until he told them to quit it. "Mattie's won like ten thousand," he'd said.

"It's different now," I told him.

"You killed someone else?" He shut the bathroom door in my face.

I ran back to the living room closet and yanked on my coat, scarf, and boots, which I didn't bother to buckle before opening the front door again.

"Will you be warm enough?" my mother asked from the kitchen.

"I'm fine. Let's go."

She studied me. The circles under her eyes reminded me of Ms. Eyre after one of her surgeries. Eventually, she shrugged and said, "Go on ahead. We'll come soon."

"Is that safe?" I heard my father say.

My mother gestured at the windows. "The whole neighborhood's outside, or they will be momentarily."

Before she could change her mind, I was off the stoop and running all the way down the drive, though by the time I hit the street, the morning's stillness had buffeted me down to a walk. Apparently, no one but me was headed for the lake yet. So I walked straight down the center of our street between the shadows of the evergreens, feeling as if I'd just popped up from a crawl space after a tornado. Not until I reached Cider Lake Road did I realize that I hadn't heard a single human sound since leaving my house. No doors had slammed, no cars had started, no voices announced the presence of other families. I'd heard some birds, the new spring breeze teething on the tree branches, and nothing else. The feeling of freedom had deserted me. I felt like someone suckered out of bed by a doorbell ditcher.

To make sound—any sound at all, even if it was mostly an echo—I began stomping my feet on the asphalt as I moved forward again. Still, no cars passed. A crow plunged off the top of a streetlamp and skimmed my hair. Fly, little bird, I thought. Fly as fast as you can. You can't scare me, I'm the gingerbread boy, I am, I am. And I can wink you off the face of the earth. I sprinted all the way to the hill above the beach, crested it, and saw a cluster of people standing in a circle on the lake.

My first feeling was panic as my boots fought for purchase on the icy slope. I gave up struggling and let myself fall, sliding face first through the snow and skidding to a stop halfway down the hill with snow up my windbreaker, under my sweatshirts, and pressed against my chest like a cold compress. It brought tears to my eyes, but I let myself lie still, suspended, upside down, until I could identify everyone. Then the shivering started, and I couldn't imagine ever getting it to stop.

Mr. McLean was there, and Mr. and Mrs. Wetzel, and Mrs. Wilkins with two of her dogs, and others I barely knew, all arrayed in a circle on the ice to the right of the pier. Mr. McLean had one hand on his scarf, the other touching the shoulder of his son, Brent's friend Davy. Mrs. Wilkins was holding a rake against her side and had tucked one booted foot behind the other. Her head swung, too slowly, tracing the path of her third black Lab, who was loping toward the center of the lake. They looked like the people in the Canaletto painting my father always took me to see. At their feet crouched Mrs. McLean, her old gray work coat pooled around her. She was hovering over a still white form with a white pom-pom, half sunk in the ice.

I shoved myself upright, legs slipping spastically beneath me as I slid toward the shore. I could see Mrs. McLean calling Theresa's name, though I couldn't hear her; my ears seemed to have switched off completely. Then she twisted in my direction, and the look on her face was terrifying, savage, though I recognized immediately that it wasn't meant for me. Both Mr. Wetzel and Mr. McLean dropped into the same spot beside Theresa's body. They bumped each other hard, and Mr. McLean tipped over, and I heard Mr. Wetzel say, "Move over, goddammit," and then, "Go, Angie."

Mrs. McLean's head dove toward Theresa's, and her mouth opened wide, like a vampire's, I thought, and I let out a single scream. No one turned around. I watched Mrs. McLean's cheeks deflate as she pressed air into Theresa's lungs, skipping the position-the-neck step we'd learned at school. Mr. Wetzel, whom I had once seen fix a tractor lawn mower with a toothbrush, dropped his palms on the center of Theresa's chest and crushed down.

"Go," he said, but Mrs. McLean was already forward again, her hair falling over Theresa's face as her mouth clamped down. By now, I was close enough to hear her breath go down Theresa's throat. It made a sluicing sound like wind in a gutter.

I watched Theresa's chest rise and fall with each forced breath. On Mr. Wetzel's second set of crushes downward, something snapped inside Theresa like an iced-over branch breaking loose, and someone said, "Dean," and Mr. Wetzel roared, "Shut up!" as he shoved down again. I winced and jammed my fists into my ears against the grinding sound. He was right, I knew, doing exactly what Mr. Lang had told us in gym: "Can't get the heart going, they won't need the rib."

The third time Mrs. McLean dropped over Theresa, it felt almost as if I was doing it. Theresa's bow mouth was under me, her nostrils between my fingers, her oxygen-starved blood rippling and squishing against my kneading hands.

Quietly, steadily, Mr. Wetzel counted out loud as he continued pressing, one-mississippi, two-mississippi, like the rusher in a touch-football game. At five, Mrs. McLean blew into Theresa's mouth and he started again. One-mississippi. Two-mississippi.

"Checking her," said Mrs. McLean as she rocked back, jamming her hand against Theresa's throat.

"Nothing," Mr. Wetzel said as he pushed, and Mrs. McLean blew again. "Fucking goddamn."

Behind us, the roaring began, and I turned and saw Dr. Daughrety flying down the slope. Even Jon Goblin, who must have been sent to retrieve him, couldn't keep up, though he seemed to glide over the ground with his white Pumas flashing. Mr. Wetzel kept his count, and when the Doctor barreled through us and attempted to hurl him out of the way, Mr. Wetzel said, "Get off, Daughrety. You'll put your hands right through her."

I thought the Doctor might bite him, he looked so wild. Instead, he jerked backward as if he'd been punched.

"Don't you dare stop," he said.

"Four mississippi, five mississippi, never did," said Mr. Wetzel, as Angie McLean breathed into Theresa, rocked back, and all at once Theresa gagged, spat saliva, and convulsed into a wracking cough.

"Oh, my God," Jon Goblin said.

Everyone erupted into motion. The Doctor lunged at Theresa again, and this time Mr. Wetzel rolled away onto the ice and lay there.

"Oh, wow," he said. "Wow." Mrs. McLean had fallen back to avoid getting kicked by the Doctor. She was on her knees, weeping silently.

I couldn't look at Theresa. The Doctor was in the way, for one thing, surrounding her with his arms. But also, I wasn't ready to see her face. I'd gotten used to carrying her inside me like a candle, something I could set alight whenever I needed company.

A kiss landed on top of my head, and Barbara Fox stumbled by. "You're suffocating her," she murmured in the Doctor's ear. "Come on." But he wouldn't let go.

Jon Goblin grabbed me around the waist from behind and said, "Hoot-hoot."

"I can't believe it," I said, and then he was gone, off to hug someone else.

My mother came hurtling down the hill, her tan winter coat unbelted and flapping around her, mouth uttering long loud heaving sounds, eyes blinking furiously as the wind buffeted them. She looked like some insane squawking winter duck. Mrs. McLean struggled to her feet and rushed to meet her. They fell into each other's arms on the shore and collapsed together in the unspread pile of new sand that had been trucked in for the cleanup this morning.

This morning, I thought. And the connection stabbed straight through me. It couldn't be true. But it had to be. Theresa knew what day this was. Knew. Today.

James Sea is wearing his wolverine costume. He is crying, tied to a chair, the plastic kind with the half back that we have at school. There are lake-shaped stains on the cement floor where something has been dripping for years, and a scratched silver chandelier dangling from the ceiling and twitching slightly in the tricky light like a spider flipped upside down. Theresa tiptoes out of the shadows. She unwraps a ball of silver foil to reveal a pickle sandwich, its sides slick with brown mustard. She holds it to James's mouth, whispering like a friend, like a sister, the way she never did to me or anyone I knew. James continues to cry, but he also eats. Behind them, back in the shadows, the Snowman kneels, watching. Finally, he speaks. He has a next-door neighbor's voice, plain and tired. He asks James if it would be all right to leave him on the basketball court near his house. James is crying. Theresa is, too, but she has turned around to stare at the monster. She looks like a hand puppet, her eyes squares of felt. After a long time, James says, "I hate basketball," his voice slurring as the drug in his food takes effect.

Theresa rests her hand on his forehead, just at the hairline, and whispers to him as he slides into sleep. Then the Snowman steps forward and squeezes James's nostrils together as though pinching out a candle. Theresa says, "Stop," tries to scratch his arms, and the Snowman holds her back with his free hand. James doesn't struggle at all.

My eyes leapt to Theresa's face where she lay in the snow. She was coughing, jiggling in her father's arms like a rag doll, but her eyes were wide open and blank and locked on me.

I shook my head, closed my eyes, and opened them again, but Theresa's stare remained fixed, and the images of Theresa and James kept spooling through my head. All year long, she had seemed so far away. Now she didn't seem to be there at all. Mr. Wetzel had stopped too soon, I thought. There were parts of her that hadn't yet come back to life.

"Theresa," I said pathetically, "where have you been?" I don't know if she heard me, let alone understood. Nothing changed on her face. Then she gagged again, hard, and lifted one of her hands and opened it. Out fell a tiny rotted chip of wood, which disappeared into a layer of snow on the ice beside her.

All at once, as though rousted from the trees, siren wails screamed over the hill, and four paramedics and a squadron of police charged down the hill through the snow. "Nobody move," screamed the first policeman on the beach. He was young, with a black beard, and he was waving a nightstick like a drum major's baton. "The detectives need to see this place just as it is."

Policemen and paramedics swarmed the lake. Theresa disappeared among them. I was close enough to see the Doctor dragged to a safe distance by three different cops, including the drum major. Questions got fired at Theresa in choruses. "Can you breathe, can you walk, does it hurt, do you know your name, do you know where you are?" Apparently, none of them generated a response, because a second chorus followed. "Can you tell us where you've been, what he looked like, was James Sea with you, what did you see, did he hurt you?"

"Get the *fuck* away!" the Doctor yelled. "She wasn't even breathing five minutes ago. She's in shock, she needs help. She sure as hell doesn't need you."

He tried to force the cops back. But behind him, I saw the drum-major cop bending low, and then Theresa's mouth moving a little. The drum major straightened, stared at us all with his eyes wide open, and then hurtled toward the beach.

"Did she actually say something?" Mrs. McLean said as he rocketed by.

"Only his goddamn name," said the cop. He powered past my mother, grinning wildly, and ran whooping up the hill. I found myself wondering where Sergeant Ross was, wishing that he had been the one kneeling over Theresa. The news might have made him a little less sad. And he would have been gentler with my friend.

"Where's Sergeant Ross?" I asked one of the policemen standing closest to me.

"You say something, kid?" he said, in a voice I didn't like. I blushed and shook my head and edged backward.

Moments later, a phalanx of paramedics lifted Theresa onto a stretcher and carried her toward a waiting ambulance. The oldest paramedic had opened his uniform coat to the chill and held a clear IV bag above her. I saw the plastic tube attached to her arm, the liquid sliding into her skin, and wondered whether it was cold. Theresa didn't seem to notice, and she didn't even look up when her father attempted to muscle into the group and grab hold of the stretcher.

"I'm a doctor," I heard him growl.

"Dr. Daughrety, you're going to make us drop her," said the paramedic with the IV bag. Then Barbara whispered to the Doctor and eased him slowly backward. With surprising speed, the paramedics bore Theresa into the ambulance; the Doctor and Barbara jumped in behind, and it squealed away toward Maple.

For the rest of the morning, police roamed the lake in teams of two or three. They studied the ice, the new sand, the road, looking for tire tracks, traces, footprints. They didn't seem to be interested in the wood chip Theresa had dropped, so I picked it up and pocketed it.

Television vans came too, but this time the police threw up a barricade and kept reporters and cameramen away from the lake. Meanwhile, detectives questioned everyone. The Rhodes family received no special handling or attention. We were simply a part of the neighborhood once again, at least as far as the detectives were concerned, a set of potential witnesses and nothing more. By midmorning, the sun had broken completely free of the cloud cover, showering the lake with yellow light and surprising spring warmth, and everyone began shedding mittens and unzipping jackets.

A few of the neighbors wandered the lake in a silent, bewitched calm. My mother and Mrs. McLean held hands. My brother charged way out over the ice, chasing one of Mrs. Wilkins's dogs. My father never showed up. Mr. Wetzel picked up his rake, and I half expected him to tell us that the geese shit still needed to be swept away. Instead, he just leaned on it like a cane.

I crouched in the imprint of Theresa's body. She was alive. Spencer was home. James Sea was dead. I should have felt a little better, or I should have broken down. But I felt nothing. I even looked in the lake at one point, right through the surface of the ice. It was clear and empty and did not reflect me.

Finally, my mother tugged me to my feet. "Come on, Mattie," she said, and I had a brief flash, what felt like a memory, of learning to walk or maybe swim this way, straining toward her voice years before.

"Can we go see Theresa?"

"Later, Mattie. Soon. We're going home now. Brent!"

In a miniature V—my mother at the front, my brother and I on either side—we started back up the hill toward our house. The sun made the snowy rooftops wink wetly. Somewhere along Cider Lake Road, I realized my mother was singing to herself, that slow Elton John song she always liked, and I thought of Theresa's mother. Brent picked up a snowball and packed it tight, looked at me, and then pegged a snowman in the McLeans' yard.

As we turned onto our street, we saw a filthy gray Pontiac parked in the driveway.

My mother stopped singing and said, "What now?"

The driver's side door was open, and a curl of cigarette smoke drifted from it. A broad-shouldered man in a brown leather jacket and black ski boots with the buckles undone stepped into the snow. Sergeant Ross looked like a completely different human being without his uniform and his hat.

"Mind if I talk to the boy?" he asked as soon as we were near enough.

I edged closer to my mother. I wanted to be near her, even if she was nowhere near forgiving me yet. "I don't want to," I whispered.

"You don't get to choose, I'm afraid," my mother said, though not harshly. The sergeant's hand shook as he lifted the cigarette to his lips, and my mother asked, "Are you all right?"

He dropped the cigarette to the ground, stepped on it, and pressed his hand against his pants as if he were rubbing out a stain. "I don't know, actually. You?"

"Theresa's alive," she said.

"Miraculous thing," said the sergeant, and then he looked at me, and I couldn't read his expression at all. "Right, Mattie?" He motioned to me with his arm. I hesitated, watching my mother and Brent go in the house, but then I walked with him down the block, until he stopped between two birches leaning out of the snow like the masts of beached sailboats. He didn't say anything for a long time.

"She said his name," I said.

"I heard. *Richard Grace.*" He didn't sound as enthusiastic as I might have expected, nowhere near as excited as the drum-major cop. Or maybe—like me—he just couldn't believe it. "That mean anything to you?"

"What do you mean? It's his name, I guess."

"She's a pretty goddamn lucky girl."

"Sort of," I murmured, as the image I'd conjured of the dangling chandelier, the windowless room shuddered through me once more. "I never would have remembered."

Sergeant Ross looked up, and I felt him staring at me. "Remembered what?" He stepped closer, towering over me.

Same room, same light. Theresa is in the chair now, not tied, and the Snowman revolves around her, the newest strangest sun in his nightmare galaxy. Eventually, frustrated, he asks, "Where?"

And she says, "Saturday, please. At Cider Lake."

"Lake Cleaning Day," I said. "Theresa comes every year, same as the rest of us."

The sergeant's mouth opened, hung that way a few seconds, and then he said, "You think she tricked the Snowman?"

The Snowman glides behind Theresa, over the stains on the floor, hands motionless at his sides, like a dry-cleaned suit on a moving rack. Theresa just sits, stares straight ahead.

"I think she got him to leave her at the lake because she knew what day it is."

"Jesus goddamn fucking Christ."

By now I was shaking too. Saying this was even worse than thinking it, because it actually sounded possible out loud. Maybe.

"Is she that smart, Mattie?"

"Yes."

"Then it's also possible that she never saw the Snowman at all. Faked the whole thing."

"Except that she wasn't breathing," I said. And suddenly, I hated him. Him, the Snowman, the Doctor, Mrs. Jupp, Mr. Fox, my parents, every adult I knew. "This isn't a Mind War!" I blurted, unsure what I meant, wanting only to wriggle free of this whole stupid place. Spinning, I ran for my house. Sergeant Ross swore and clomped after me, caught me from behind, and held me against him. The smell of licorice and cigarettes poured over me.

"It must be horrible being a cop," I said, tears spilling down my face.

He nodded. "Sometimes it is. But sometimes you really do get to help people."

"Not this time," I said.

The sergeant waved a trembling hand across his eyes. His words came out weighted, sinking. "No. Not this time." He stepped to his car, reached through the open window, and withdrew Theresa's blue notebook. "This is gibberish, Mattie," he said, and handed it to me. "We've kept a copy, obviously, but. . . ."

The front cover had come halfway off the spiral rings. I straightened it in its place. Against my eardrums, I felt a crushing pressure, as though I were underwater in the deep end of a pool.

"We've had people looking at this thing who worked on the Enigma code during the Second World War. Do you know what that is? It was once the most complex intelligence code in human history. We've had child psychologists comb through every word. And every scribble. And the mixed-up letters we thought might be anagrams. Even the doodles. But all our experts agree that whatever this is, it's not a code because there isn't any pattern. A lot of it isn't even readable. Guessing anything from this is like telling futures in bird guts. If it means anything at all, it does so only to her." He looked down at me, and the pressure increased, as if he were lowering me away from him. Any second now he was going to cut me loose. I didn't hate him anymore. In fact, I didn't want him to leave.

"Avri's Deli," I said, fast. "The swimming pool at Covington Junior High."

"What?"

"I don't know. She was saying something about those places the last time I saw her. When we were in the Fox house."

"So—"

"Some of those places are in the notebook too, right? Maybe she worked out a formula. Places kids go. Maybe—"

"Maybe," Sergeant Ross interrupted, softly but firmly. "But whatever she worked out, it isn't in this. And she's back now. Whatever she knows, she can explain to us. So what I say is maybe, in a completely different way, this notebook will be important to you or her one day. So I suggest you take careful care of it. You're a good kid, Mattie. Sharp kid. I know you meant well, although that doesn't make you any less responsible for what you did. Keep your head down, help your family, and you just might get through this."

He clambered into his front seat and sat staring out the windshield over the trees. Finally he turned the ignition, pulled out of the driveway, and disappeared down the street.

I went back inside where my parents were waiting. I knew my mother had been crying because her face was all red. She was sitting on the couch, huddled against my father. I could hear Brent stomping around in his room.

"Mattie, get your brother and come out here," my father said, and I did as I was told. When I opened Brent's door, I found him throwing a tennis ball at his closet door. He didn't say anything to me, but when I pointed toward the living room, he followed.

My father turned from the window and directed us to sit down beside my mother. "Boys," he said, his voice even flatter than usual, "Mr. Fenwick thinks it would no longer be *productive* for me to continue at the research lab. They're sending me to another plant to supervise assembly-line design. I chose Lexington, so we could move near your cousins. We're going to start over. And we're going to do it right now."

Brent began shaking his head back and forth, as if his ears were ringing. I just looked at my father. "So you're fired?" I asked.

"Relocated."

"Because of me?"

"Oh, Mattie, come off it," he snapped. "What difference does it make? It just didn't happen for me here. I can live with it. So can you. Let's go be with our family." He started to stalk away, stopped, and let himself fall into the low green armchair.

"Okay, boys," my mother said softly, one hand on each of our shoulders. "Go pack up the things you need most."

"We're leaving all our stuff?" said Brent, his voice going screechy. He sounded maybe five.

"Our stuff will come later, honey. Just pick out what you want for the car trip."

"We're leaving *today*?"

"Oh, yes," said my mother, and she looked at my father, and for one fleeting second, I thought she almost smiled.

Brent stomped his feet on the floor. "*Fuck that!*" he screamed, and then he ran to his room and slammed the door.

I couldn't get myself to stand. Lexington, Kentucky, had about as much meaning to me as my father's work. I had been to both places a few times. I didn't exist in either. I thought about Theresa gagging to life, and Spencer sidecarring with someone else, and never seeing them again.

"We can't go," I said.

"Come on, Mattie," my mother whispered. "Hurry up."

She eased me off the couch, and I found myself walking toward my room. But instead of packing, I lay down on my bed and closed my eyes, and I must have slept, because when I opened them it was twilight and Brent was lying on the bottom bunk.

"Hey," I said.

He didn't say anything. I peered over the edge and saw him lying on his back with one palm pressed against the board above him as if he were supporting me.

"Why are they doing this?" Brent sputtered.

"Because of me," I told him.

"Mattie, I don't want to go."

I couldn't remember the last time he'd addressed me by name. In other brothers, I thought, that might have been natural. But with Brent and me, names had peeled away from neglect like wallpaper in an empty room.

"Brent," I made myself say, but I took too long.

"You wrecked my life," he said. "My whole life."

"I wrecked everyone's life," I said.

The next morning's paper trumpeted the search for Richard Grace. His name was stretched diagonally across it like a beauty-pageant sash. Beneath the sash was the familiar Snowman sketch, blown up to cover the entire front page. Snapping the newspaper shut, I hurled it across the kitchen table and went to my room.

All day, my father played his newly functional stereo and packed records in boxes. My mother stayed in her bedroom moving things around, but I never went in there. We didn't eat until after the Special Update and only then because Brent stomped into my parents' room and dragged my mother out to make us dinner. No Richard Grace had been found, but the massive manhunt continued.

I'd been waiting to be taken to see Theresa and for permission to call Spencer again, but whenever I asked, my parents refused without explanation, and late that night, I felt the reality of leaving Detroit close around me. I couldn't leave. I was tied to this place. The thought of living somewhere other than this neighborhood, away from all these people I had hurt, felt like more of a betrayal than anything I had done until now. Leaping from my bed, I ran in my underwear into my parents' room. They weren't sleeping. My mother was reading a paperback, or at least holding it to her face. My father was staring at the wall.

"We can't go," I said.

"We can," my father whispered fiercely. My mother grabbed his wrist, and they held on to each other.

"None of us want to leave, Mattie," my mother said, though I was no longer sure that was true. "But it's best. It's time. You'll like Kentucky. You'll get to be near your cousins."

"I have to call Spencer. Mom, please. Does he even know Theresa's alive?"

Against my father, her rigid body relaxed. Her head sank to his chest, but her eyes stayed on me. "Susan took him away somewhere. I don't know where or if they're even coming back. I'm sure he's heard about Theresa. It's all over the news." Her voice sounded wrung out.

My eyes filmed over. "Liar," I said.

The slap wasn't hard, but it caught me by surprise, with my mouth half open, and I felt my mother's wedding ring click against my teeth, and my cheek was stinging, and I started to scream. "Take me to see Theresa! Take me to see Theresa!"

"Oh, Lord," my father said.

Yanking me down on the bed, my mother crushed me against her and said, "Shut up, now." But she said it gently, stroking my hair, and I knew she wasn't angry anymore.

"Theresa's in intensive care. She's in some kind of waking coma. They can't get her to respond to anything."

"But she said the Snowman's name."

"I don't know why everyone assumes that's what she meant," my mother said. "All I know is that she hasn't said anything or even moved since then."

"Mom . . . can I sleep here? With you?"

"Can I, too?" said my brother, falling into the bed beside me, his elbow brushing mine.

My mother drooped against her pillow and began to cry. My father sighed. "Boys. Give your mother a rest. Give us both a little time."

"Please," said Brent.

"Tomorrow. If you still need to." He switched off his bedside lamp and turned us all into shadows. "Good night, boys," he said, and I thought of Mrs. Cory, shivered, and fled to my room.

The next morning, my mother woke us early and helped us finish packing our travel bags. In the front hall we found all four of the battered white suitcases my parents always used for car trips. On top of the suitcases, rubber-banded together, were two of my mother's Isaac Asimov novels and a stack of tapes.

Brent jammed his fists into his eyes. "We're not leaving yet, are we?" he said.

"Shhh," said my father.

"I won't," Brent said. I put my hand on his back and felt his shoulder blades squeeze like an accordion.

When my mother came out, her hair was dyed a richer, darker brown. She had deep circles under her eyes. "Say goodbye," she said.

"To you?"

Her shoulders dropped, and her lips went flat. "I do love you, Mattie Rhodes," she said, softly if not quite lovingly. "Now say goodbye to your father."

"'Bye, Dad," I said. "I'm sorry. For everything"

"I know you are. I'll come as soon as I can." He bent down and took Brent's face in his hand. "You hear that, Big B? Don't worry about a thing."

"I hate him," said Brent.

"You won't always."

"Yes, I will."

"He'll grow on you. He does that." My father looked my way, though he didn't let go of Brent.

"Why aren't you coming with us?" Brent asked.

"I have to sell the house," he said. That stung. The thought of some other family living here hurt me more than the idea of leaving it. But my father sounded surprisingly relaxed, even for him. "We've had enough of this place," he continued. "You'll see." With one hand, he reached out and touched my shoulder. He let go of Brent and held my mother with the other. Rarely had he seemed like such a strong, steady TV kind of father as he did then.

My family still loved me, I thought. But that wasn't helping. "Can I call Barbara?"

My mother looked at me, then my father. In the end, she shook her head. "You know what, Mattie? Barbara has more trouble to deal with than we do right now. I called her last night. She knows we're leaving, and she said she'd write. Let's leave her be."

"I hate you," Brent said to me.

"I don't hate you," I told him. "I never have."

Ice choked the roads, and my mother's car fishtailed a little every time she turned. Brent flopped down in the back and kicked my seat repeatedly, but I didn't respond, and after a few minutes, he stopped doing it and lay there and sniffled, and then he went silent. I asked my mother if we could listen to the radio, and when she didn't respond, I switched on WJR, just in time to hear a newscaster say, *"Doctors and police admit to being baffled today by more curious developments surrounding the disappearance and rescue of Theresa Daughrety. Medical examiners report that toxicology reports on the little girl, who just may be the only survivor of an encounter with the Snowman, reveal no trace of the sedative found in the blood of each previous victim. Police department spokesmen remain noncommittal about the significance of this discovery."*

"Shut it off," my mother commanded flatly, and I did, staring straight ahead through the windshield, bleary with half-melted ice, at the gray light leaking through the leaden trees. I didn't want to think, and couldn't help it, so I thought of Theresa's mother on the sled in the photograph, because that's what came to mind. Theresa's mother alive on her sled in the snow.

Absently, my hand slipped to my pocket, began to play with the wood chip I'd stored there—since Lake Cleaning Day, I realized, when Theresa dropped it—and finally I drew it out and looked at it. I'd forgotten I had it. The wood felt soft between my fingers, except for two little slivers poking out of one end like bee stingers. With my thumb, then each of my fingers in turn, I brushed the top of the slivers, felt their points. *No trace of the sedative.* But he brought her home. He brought her back. *No trace.* Which meant she'd let him suffocate her while she was awake—maybe staring right at him? Or she hadn't been with him after all? I touched the chip to my cheek, and the smell crept into my nose and mouth like poison gas. Sweet poison.

"What?" said my mother, still flat, glaring sidelong at me.

"Mom," I said, my voice and hands trembling, the air rotten-sweet, but I didn't lower the chip. I couldn't. I was too busy remembering. Understanding. Trying to. "Mom. Please."

"Mattie, it's icy, and I'm tired, and I'm concentrating, okay? So whatever you have to say, spit it out."

"Can we go by the mill?"

My mother didn't answer until we crawled to a stop at the Orchard Lake light, and by then the smell seemed to have seeped all the way down my skin into my boots. Why couldn't she smell it, I wondered? Why wasn't she asking what that odor was?

"The Cider Mill? They're not open in winter. What are you talking about?"

I couldn't answer. I didn't dare take the chip from in front of my mouth, for fear that the smell, and the faint imprint of Theresa's fingers I was all but certain I could feel, would fade. The last traces of Theresa I would ever hold. "Please, Mom. I just want to see it one more time."

"Me too," Brent said, without sitting up.

"You do?" my mother said, shooting a surprised look into the rearview mirror, though I don't think she could see him.

"I want to see everywhere," Brent said, and he burst out crying, and my mom's hands twitched on the wheel and her eyes squeezed shut. "I want to stay home."

"Oh, baby," she said.

"Please," I whispered. "Please, please, please, please."

Behind us, a car honked, and my mother started, jerked our car forward, and lifted one hand off the steering wheel to brush quickly at her eyes. "All right, boys," she said. "But we're not stopping again until lunch, do you hear? Not even to go to the bathroom. Not until we're long, long gone. It's time we were gone."

All the way there, I pictured Theresa, almost smiling, holding a lopsided candy apple on a stick while fat yellow jackets buzzed around the mill's dirt yard, which was never dry even in dead summer. This must have been in third or fourth grade. A school trip, right at the beginning of the year. Theresa's dress had purple polka dots on it. She was doing the Daphne voice from *Scooby Doo* for Jon Goblin and a couple of girls standing nearby. I remembered being stunned at how good she was at it, and that she even knew who Daphne was.

Turning onto the dirt road, my mother took us bumping between the trees up to the wooden gate that fronted the Cider Mill parking lot. The gate was closed.

"Can we get out?" I said. "Just for a second?"

"Me too," said Brent, and he was gone, not even shutting the door behind him as he staggered off through the drifts, around the gate into the lot.

"Five minutes," my mother said, and dropped the car into neutral. "And this is it, Mattie. Your last goodbye. I don't want to drag this out anymore, it's too hard on your brother. And you. Five minutes. Don't make me come out in the cold and get you."

I stepped out, shut Brent's and my doors, and turned to face the mill, which was mostly a giant decomposing cedar barn. The shingles had long since split and swollen. As soon as I was close enough to the building, far enough from the car, I heard the familiar high whine of the engine that runs the mill wheel. The shed that housed the wheel ballooned off the side of the main building and rose above it.

"Hear that?" Brent said.

"It's just to keep the wheel turning," I told him. "So it doesn't freeze."

"Duh."

For one moment, standing with the drifts over our ankles and the snow clouds stacking up over our heads, I thought he was going to take my hand, the way he had years ago at the Birmingham Fair. Instead, he said, "Want to go in?"

"It's closed."

Instead of answering he stomped around back, and when I followed I found him beside two shingles bent upward at the bottom, hovering off the earth like the hem of a skirt.

"Did you know those were there?" I asked.

Brent shrugged. "McLeans come here all the time to sled. We sneak in here to get warm sometimes. Used to."

He glared at me, then dropped to his stomach and wriggled under the shingles. His red down coat caught, nearly ripped, but slid free, and he was through. I could hear him tromping around on the wooden viewing bridge that stuck out from the wall in there, always slippery with water spray and apple bits. Every kid I knew spent most of their time here on that bridge, watching the paddles of the giant wooden wheel plunge down.

Kneeling, I took a deep breath, and my lungs filled with that crab-apple reek, more tangy than sweet. Every backyard in my neighborhood smelled like that, I realized. And none of them would in Kentucky. Snow and, under that, wet mud seeped through my open coat, through my sweater into my chest. I dropped my head to avoid getting splinters in my eyes, pushed myself through, and stood up.

The wheel looked like a riverboat paddle wheel, and it didn't so much spin as jerk. In the summer, with apples under it, the wheel's paddles made a squishing sound when they pressed down, like footsteps in wet leaves. The wood in the wheelhouse looked even older than the rest of the mill. Probably, I thought, because it never dried. The wheel filled its surrounding well, red-stained and cracked and knotted. When I stepped forward on the bridge, the wood sank under my feet in a familiar, almost comforting way.

Except that every previous time I'd been here, there were other kids crowded around me, elbowing each other to get close enough to see the apples loaded into the slot in the floor and smashed flat, the juice squirting everywhere. Brent had always loved this place, I realized. Much more than I had. I remembered positioning him in front of me and then plowing us forward to the rail so he could see, when he was much younger.

We had a minute, maybe less, before my mother started howling for us, but the outside world seemed a million miles away. The barn surrounded us with its scent and chill and oldness like an attic.

I watched the wheel nudge, nudge, tip forward. Behind me, Brent said, "We don't live here anymore. Thanks to you." I heard him drop down, start to slide out, but I didn't turn around. I was riveted, suddenly, to the top of the wheel.

"Oh, my God," I murmured, holding up my hand as if commanding the wheel to stop. But it didn't. It nudged forward, and the paddles swung down.

"Come *on*, Mattie!" I heard Brent snap from outside as I crumpled forward onto the banister, but all I could think was, How really fucking stupid. All those hundreds—maybe thousands—of kids who'd stood on this bridge. How was it possible that none of us had remembered?

"Shit, shit, *shit*," I said, fighting for balance as splinters shot into my palms and rusted nails scraped my flesh. I could feel blood between my fingers and tears on my cheeks. I could see Theresa's crazy stare on Cider Lake as she coughed and woke up and realized she was outside again.

I folded into a sitting position on the walkway, which seemed to swing beneath me like a rope bridge, and my brother said, "Fine, good, stay here," and tears exploded onto my face. *Hello, my dwarves.* That's what Theresa had said. *The red half for you, the white half for me.* I could still hear Miss Galerne's voice—thick and slow with her Belgian accent, as though her tongue were coated in honey--reading those words to us as we sprawled on the red throw pillows in our second-grade classroom on Fairy Tale Day. Jon. Jamie Kerflack. Garrett. Theresa. Me. Only in Theresa's Snow White, the girl goes to the witch's house, knows the apple's poisoned, knows she's going to die, and eats it anyway. The apple. Here. She figured out he'd be here. Tried to tell us. So we could follow and save her, or just so we'd know she knew? Then she came and found the Snowman and refused his drugs and stared him down while he murdered her.

Or. She came and hid here by herself, no Snowman, no James Sea—she might not even know about James Sea, I realized—and then walked all the way home to Cider Lake the night before Lake Cleaning Day, stepped out onto the ice, lay down, and let the cold take her.

Or . . .

At the top of the wheel, the slat I knew would come appeared, its front edge toothy and its bottom warped. I watched through my tears as it lurched toward me, spun slowly down, until at last I could see what I already knew was carved in the top. The crude heart. And in its center, soaked in apple guts but clearly readable, the names: Richard. Grace.

I made a sound, a sort of whimper that seemed to trickle down the paddles like rainwater and die in the floor. The last thing she saw. If she was really here. Or the last thing she remembered. Or just random bits of information among the billions scattered across her brain like stars, bright against all that emptiness inside her.

The hush of the place settled over me. Did he kill them all in here? I wondered. He could still be here. Suddenly, I couldn't turn around. In my ears, the whine of the engine began to form words, nothing I could understand, but words, and the Snowman climbed down off the wall behind me, a wet red spider. Hurling myself to my stomach, I dove straight through the opening, crying out as a sliver of wood raked my cheek, just under my eye. I jerked my feet clear and lay there weeping with my face in the snow and my heart jackhammering in my chest. Nothing, I thought. When I'd whirled around, I'd seen nothing at all.

"What the—" Brent started, and I lifted my head.

"Get Mom," I said.

"You're a freak," Brent shouted, sounding furious, terrified, and I put my hand to my cheek and felt the sloppy wetness there, snow and blood and tears.

"Get Mom."

"You're bleeding all over the—"

"Get Mom, get Mom, get Mom!"

Brent ran, while I struggled to a sitting position and kicked farther from the mill, my eyes locked on the opening, just in case anything came slithering out, even though I knew that room was empty. My heart beat so hard I could feel the throb of it in my throat and all along the roof of my mouth. What could I tell her? I suddenly wondered. What did I think I knew? Nothing, nothing, nothing. Almost nothing.

Seconds later, my mother hurtled around the side of the mill and stopped dead when she saw me. "Mattie. What did you to do to your face?"

"Richard Grace," I said, and gestured toward the wheelhouse.

"What?"

I closed my eyes. The teardrops felt freezing, little crystals of ice in my lashes, as though I was turning to snow. "Not Richard Grace. Richard *and* Grace."

Behind my mother, Brent's mouth dropped open as understanding swept over him. He stared at me, as though I really was transforming into something else, right in front of him. Then he flew straight off across the field, screaming. Leaping to my feet, I raced after him, past my astonished mother, and as I chased, Brent curled around, back toward the mill. He kept on screaming, which slowed him down, which is the only reason I was able to catch him. I dove, finally, at his knees, knocked him flat, and we skidded together into the drifts, and then I was lying on top of him, and he was punching me, trying to bite me.

"Stop it," I said, and he kept flailing, wriggling his arms free while I tried to pin them. "Brent, stop." The running around hadn't warmed me up any, just forced freezing air down my lungs. New tears slid down my cheeks, leaving fresh rivers of icy skin.

Beneath me, Brent stopped squirming, lay still. He stared up at me with his mouth still open, his eyes huge in their panic.

"Mattie," my mother snapped, stalking behind us. "Let him up. If this is another one of your goddamn jokes—"

"It isn't," Brent whispered, and I realized that he was clutching my sleeves in his hands. Staring at me, clinging to me.

Easing myself to my knees, holding on to my brother, I told my mother about the wood chip Theresa had been holding and the heart on the wheel. Afterward, we had to half drag Brent to the car. He couldn't get his legs to work, so we just laid him across the backseat. Then we were driving.

I don't know how long it was before I realized we weren't heading toward our house. As soon as we'd started moving, I felt myself shut down, empty out, and I just sat there, aware only of the sting of my cheeks and fingers and feet as they warmed and the hot, musty sighs of the car heater. Thoughts tumbled down, occasionally, like paddles on a wheel, passed behind my eyes, crushed down on nothing as they disappeared.

"Aren't we going home?" I asked.

My mother wrenched the wheel, skidding us into a strip-mall parking lot. I'd never been here before, as far as I knew, but there was an A&P and a hardware store.

"Watch your brother," my mother said, shutting off the engine and shouldering her door open.

"Where are you going?"

"To call the police. Then we're going to Kentucky. As fast as we can."

"Aren't they going to want to talk to us?"

For the first time since the Cider Mill, my mother looked at me. Her hair, wet when we left, had dried in hard, uneven clumps. Her eyelids hung heavy from lack of sleep, and her mouth was expressionless. She glanced back at Brent, still rigid on the seat.

"They're not going to know it is us, Mattie," she said. "They've talked to us enough."

She was gone a long while. I watched my brother. He just lay there, mostly, until I said his name, and then he turned his head into the vinyl seatback and wept, but without the violent, terrified heaves of before. There was something familiar, peaceful, almost soothing about watching him cry like this, like staring out my bedroom window at a spring rain.

My mother came back, started the car, and slid a Bob Dylan tape into the player.

"You told them," I said, and she nodded, and after that no one said anything until well into the afternoon.

The drive was slow and long. The sky stayed gray, the world white. My brother cried himself to sleep in the back and roused himself only to stumble into gas station bathrooms or to pick at hamburgers. I felt like I was drifting directionless in space, a little boy in a space suit with a tiny rip somewhere, so that everything inside me was leaking into the void and trailing back the way we had come.

Long past dark, my mother let me turn on the radio again. Again, the story came up immediately, reported by a female newscaster I didn't recognize. *"Acting on an anonymous tip, police today pored over every inch of the Oakland Park Cider Mill, after the latest bizarre twist in the elusive search for the child killer that has haunted suburban Detroit for more than a year. A department spokesperson would confirm only that the lead appeared legitimate, and that it changed the nature of—quote—certain aspects of the investigation."*

"Mom," I said, while she clicked off the radio, and the wheels chattered on the icy asphalt, and the full fat yellow moon glided over the southern Ohio cornfields like the eye of some monstrous nighttime bird, "will Kentucky help?"

And for some reason, that was the question that finally broke my mother down. She steered the car onto the shoulder of the road and lowered her face into her gloved hands. Her body shook in ripples like a sail whose lines have snapped. But when she lifted her head and wiped the wetness from her cheeks with the sleeve of her coat, her eyes were bright and the tightness around her mouth had loosened and she didn't look quite so old.

"Will Kentucky help?" she said. "I don't know, Mattie. But I do know one thing. And I need you to believe it. I am . . . proud of you, my strange, solitary son. I'm proud of who you are, and all the things you see, and everything you think and brood on in there. I always have been. Do you hear? That hasn't changed."

She touched my hand. I didn't know what to do. I could feel the tears massing in the corners of my eyes, but I didn't cry.

"Mattie. Do you hear me?"

Then she let go, dropped her hands back on the wheel, and without another word drove us all the way to Kentucky.

1994

"Spencer, what the fuck?"

For one second, Spencer looks as if he's going to lash out and punch Eliza. Instead, he sticks up his fist, flips her the bird, and storms out of the library. I start after him, then stop and look back.

Eliza sits with her folder open in front of her, her eyes on the door. She looks less angry than bewildered, a little sad.

"Thanks," I say. "You have no idea how much this . . .well, obviously, I'm just realizing, myself, how much . . ." The sentence dissolves in my mouth. "I have to hurry."

"Go," she says, "before he gets away. I will tell you, Mattie, his behavior makes no sense. Not based on anything I found."

I attempt a smile, but I have no idea if I intend it to be reassuring, flirtatious, grateful, or what, and it just feels wrong. Today, even more than all the other days in my life, I can't seem to deal with people from the present. Finally, I just wave and leave her at the table, staring out the window at the snow.

I find Spencer leaning on the hood of his car with his head buried in his hands. When he looks up, I catch a glimpse of the boy I'd last seen tucked inside his mother's coat as he was hustled away from me. "Just get in the car, Mattie," he says.

"You knew about the Doctor dying," I snap. "You know about everything that's happened since. You haven't told me one true thing."

"I've told you almost all true things. Just not everything. I didn't see the point."

"I assume you see it now."

"Yes, Mattie," he says. "I see it now. For everyone's sake, I have to get rid of you. That's the point. Now get in the car."

In the weak afternoon sunlight, the birch trees look like tornadoes frozen in midwhirl, their white trunks columns of whipped snow, their branches airborne detritus. Spencer drives us through Birmingham, past Shane Park, the minimall where Jiggly's was, and the turnoff to Cider Lake Road, continuing down Maple. Once we enter Bloomfield Township, the streets and sights get less familiar. Finally, not bothering to mask my exasperation, I say, "Spencer, really. I don't know why you've been lying, or what you're hiding, or what could possibly matter so much about keeping me away after all these years. Just please, *please*, tell me what's going on."

Spencer purses his lips, raises one hand and knots it into a fist, then drops the hand into his lap. We cross Telegraph into an area I never knew well. The feeling I have is completely new, a fresh and chilly combination of hope and fear and dislocation.

"Theresa Daughrety is alive and well and lives around here somewhere. Right?" Saying these words sucks all the serenity out of the landscape.

"The movie's over, Mattie. You understand that, right? You're here for the end credits, that's all. There's no one for you to save. Nothing for you to do. It's Universal Studios, man, the Tour. I'm just showing you where it all happened."

We pass an open space between subdivisions, a lake I never knew was there. It's smaller than Cider Lake, less groomed along the edges. But there are upside-down canoes humped in the snow, and I remember the day in my Lexington high school American Lit class when we read the Emily Dickinson poem about a grave being "a swelling of the ground."

"We're almost there," Spencer says.

He turns off Maple onto a street lined with older houses set on rolling, irregular lots. Oak trees and evergreens mark curving boundaries. There are no fences. Edging onto the gravel shoulder, Spencer pulls to a stop in front of a low red-shingled house nestled among several acres. Erase the suburb around us and this house could be a homesteader's cabin dug into the ground for warmth. My hands wave uselessly in the air.

"Is this it? Is Theresa here?"

Spencer eyes me. At least a little of the hostility has drained out of his face. "Mattie, I just want you to know something. The lying—it wasn't personal. I was trying to protect a whole bunch of people, including myself. Including you too, whether you believe it or not. Nothing here is likely to bring you or anyone else any closure. But your visit has already caused huge problems."

"Sorry," I murmur, though not as sarcastically as I intended.

"I've got that librarian to worry about now, for one thing."

"Spencer, what are you talking about? She couldn't even figure out why you were upset."

"Good. Let's hope she drops it." He cups his hands over his mouth and blows, and steam streams through his gloved fingers. "There is a very fragile sort of peace in what has happened, Mattie."

"Spencer, just—"

"I'm trying to tell you to be careful. I don't want her hurt again. Do you understand?"

My mouth falls open, and I can feel blood rushing to my face. "Spencer, why on earth would I hurt her any more than you would? Think what you're saying."

Spencer nods. "I guess maybe I should tell you the rest of the story first."

"Goddammit, I want to know where we are. Is this where Theresa lives?"

"I don't know if I'm going to be up to saying this later, Mattie. And I'm only saying it once. You want to hear or not?"

I feel eleven, weak and lost on the road to Kentucky. "I want to see Theresa."

"Get out, then," he says. "Go right up that drive. Holy Grail time for you. Congratulations."

Shoving open his door, Spencer twists off the ignition and gets out of the car. I snatch up my backpack and exit my own side. In the Sunday-afternoon silence, the snow on the rolling lawn seems to bubble and murmur like whitewash from some ancient tidal wave still sweeping down the continent. Halfway up the drive, I see a black mailbox and next to it, suspended from a red wooden frame, a white metal board with the words CHAPIN HOUSE painted on it in blue and yellow letters. Underneath, in smaller letters, are the words *For those in need of long-term rest.*

"Sounds like a mortuary," I mutter.

"Not quite," Spencer says.

Images of Theresa rattle through my brain like unbound discarded photographs in the back of an album. How is it, I wonder, that the person I feel most inextricably connected to in this world is someone I barely even know? Is everyone's most lasting love not the most important, necessarily, or the most lasting, but the one that frames all others? A promise of yesterday rather than a hope for tomorrow?

The house isn't low to the ground but sunk in a sort of hollow between swells of grass. A red cedar-shake roof slopes down to meet the red-shingled frame. The windows are small and tucked high under the eaves, but there are a lot of them. Frost and ice lie in thick uneven coats over the glass, so I can't even tell if the lights are on. Folded upright under the windows, a half-dozen lounge chairs have been stacked together like lifeboats. Other than its setting on the lot, the house's most striking feature is the pinewood deck sprouting ten feet from every side. On the side nearest us, I can see two sun umbrellas still open, tilting under their burdens of snow.

Spencer steps around to the back of the house and pulls off a glove with his teeth. He fishes around in his coat pocket and removes a key that he slides into the door's dead bolt. I have a sudden flash of the two of us at the back door of the Fox house, except now the roles are reversed.

"You keep her here yourself, like a prisoner?" I ask. "Sorry, I just don't get it."

"I know, brother," he says, pushing open the door.

Standing in the entryway is like looking up from the bottom of a pool; all the light collects near the beamed ceiling. A long hallway curves to the right, fronted by a trio of coat racks that cast stick-figure shadows over the hardwood floor.

Spencer locks the door behind us and removes his coat, scarf, and boots. Without looking at me, he starts down the hallway. I shed my own coat and boots and follow him along the white spotless walls, bedecked with rows of photographs. A huge percentage of them are of children, though no person or place seems to appear twice. A bearded man leans over a little boy by a fountain to feed a pigeon in a park. Twin sisters, age nine or so, slap matching yellow handbags together at the base of the Washington Monument. Squinting, I hurry by them and come into a small wood-lined den. A low fire curls and snaps around a stripped tree branch behind a grate. On the first of two plain brown-pillowed couches, situated at an angle, two women, one in her mid-fifties and the other not yet twenty, sit side by side. Between them is a toy: a row of brass balls suspended on wires. Lift the ball on one end, let it go, and watch it smack into the row and send the last ball on the other end flying. The women are taking turns, and the balls make a metallic kissing sound.

The two women with the toy do not look up or stop playing when we come in, and the metallic kissing continues, regular as a clock's ticktock. They both have their legs propped up on the coffee table, and I finally notice the circle of red plastic around each of their ankles with a blinking red light and a little electronic chip at the buckle. I have seen similar bands before in the suburbs of Louisville where Laura and I live—on the necks of dogs. Invisible Fence, the pet product is called.

"What the hell is this place?" I ask.

"A way station," says Spencer.

"On the way to where?"

"Ah," he says. "That all depends. The people here can't live at home, but their families or doctors don't want them institutionalized. It's a sort of collaborative venture. The Chapins—the owners—provide clean beds, plumbing, grounds, an alarm system, and meals. They schedule the psychiatric visits. They pay the nurses and the guards."

"Guards?"

"They only come if anyone tries to leave against the doctors' orders."

"So this *is* a prison."

"No, not really. It's voluntary, the way most private psychiatric wards are run. The patients are here because they feel safe here. And the visitation rights are unlimited."

"So Theresa volunteered to be here."

"I volunteered her," Spencer says. "But she agreed."

"Goddammit," I say softly, wanting to kick the couch and break the ball toy. "Why didn't you just tell me?" I can't get used to the way he's talking about her—as if she's real.

Spencer ignores my question. "Follow me. She's up there." He starts up the stairs, which are carpeted in thick white pile.

"Hold on," I say, grasping his arm. He turns around. "Spencer, I have to see her on my own."

"No," he says, after a brief pause.

"What do you mean, no?"

"Mattie, think. This is a fragile soul, do you understand? She always has been. She has moments where she's better, now, almost there with you sometimes. But not that many. And no one's sure what draws her out. I don't want you to drive her away."

Furious, I shove him into the wall. "I'm sorry," I say, "but that is just about e-fucking-nough."

"Keep your voice down," Spencer hisses, but even whispering, his own voice is rising. "There are sick people here, remember?"

Suddenly, everything I've felt this whole weekend, the terror and guilt and longing and loneliness, has erupted in my throat like tinder after a lightning strike, and the only way to breathe is to shout. "You still have no idea how important this is to me. I need to know if she can *see* me, Spencer. If seeing me means anything at all. The only way I'll ever know that is if I go up alone. Who the fuck do you think you are anyway?"

"I'm her Caretaker. The person who stayed," Spencer says, his voice breaking, and he's not yelling anymore, and there are tears in his eyes. He doesn't lift his hand to his face or push me away. He just stands there, crying.

"Well, I'm the one who came back," I say, and the burning in my throat subsides, leaving my tongue scorched and my mouth full of smoke. "And we both love her."

Spencer waves a hand between us. "Maybe. But I'm the one who's been acting on her behalf—Barbara and me—for a long, long time."

"Barbara? Barbara Fox? Spencer, God—"

"I told you the truth about her. She was gone. She came back. She shouldn't have, for her own sake, but she did. She comes here almost every day, even more than I do. Mattie, you can't just go up there. Please trust me on this." He sinks to a sitting position on the steps and bangs his fists on his legs. "She's . . . if she saw you . . . if you just walked in . . . anything could happen."

"Spencer," I say, and I touch him on the shoulder, very gently. "I'm glad you found her. I'm relieved that you and Barbara are here with her. But she's not *yours*. Has it occurred to you . . . I mean, isn't it possible that seeing me might help her, not hurt her?"

Spencer's expression is flat, cryptic. He says nothing.

"Look," I continue. "Clearly, none of this has been resolved for any of us. But having you stand guard over her like some kind of pit bull isn't going to settle anything."

Finally, Spencer looks up. I still can't read his expression, but his eyes and cheeks are wet. "You could be right, Mattie. You could be the Devil, or you could be right. I don't pretend to know. I didn't then, and I don't now."

"Then let me go up there. I swear I'll call you if she needs you."

"Just . . . just be careful, Mattie. Please. Be careful." Head down, he slides closer to the wall and lets me pass. "Third door on the left."

My footsteps make no sound in the deep carpet. Three steps. Five. The wooden banister feels cool under my hand. If there is a tunnel and white light when I die, my movement through it will be no more surreal than this ascent.

At the top of the staircase, another hallway curves toward the front of the house, with five tall white doors on each side. Behind one, I can hear a television playing quietly, a rerun of *Welcome Back, Kotter.* Other sounds float my way, all of them muffled. Down the hall, someone is playing Ella Fitzgerald. I don't recognize the song. The door to the room with the television on is partially open, and I can't resist a glimpse inside. The woman sitting on the railed hospital bed is in her sixties, her hair like the flying white mane of a horse. She looks up, smiles, and returns to watching television.

Three steps from Theresa's door, the seventeen-year spell that has propelled me toward this moment expires. My legs roll to a gentle stop, and all I can do is listen. The door to the room across from Theresa's is closed, but that's where Ella's voice is coming from, scatting, humming softly. From Theresa's room, there is no sound at all.

Theresa's room.

Under my feet, I can feel the floor swell, as though a wave is passing beneath it. I am lifted off the ground and falling forward through no will of my own. I have rowed myself all the way back within shouting distance of this shore, and now the world is flinging me against it.

The door is most of the way closed, and I knock on it lightly. A few seconds later, I knock again. Finally, gently, I push it open.

At first, all I can do is gape. I've seen this room before, or almost this room, or not really this room—not that bed, not this light, not the white carpeting—but the bookcases are the same. The same mismatched freestanding set has been arranged in the same order along one wall and around the one window and continuing on the other side of it. The same red writing desk sits low between them, with its red plastic chair tucked underneath. Inside the cases, the exact same books sit in their places, the long leather set of *World Classics* and the jumble of paperbacks in no obvious order except it's the one I remember. I could practically recite the titles, though I only saw them once. Seeing them here, with the pattern so systematically replicated, makes the volumes seem as incomprehensible and ancient as Stonehenge. In between the cases, the same scatter of photographs flashes the same faces: Theresa's mother on her sled; Theresa's father holding a very small Theresa's hand at the library. There are no pictures of Theresa looking older than she was when I knew her. Except for the hospital bed, the place is a dollhouse, a perfect reproduction.

But the doll that inhabits it is too big for the room. Theresa is leaning by the window with a book in her hands and her back to me. Her hair is longer, dirty blond, lying dead on her shoulders like kelp.

I want to whisper her name, sing her a song we knew, do something gentle to reintroduce myself into her life. Instead, I cry out. The sound splits the air, bites into the wall over her head like the blade of an ax. When she glances back at me, her face is a porcelain model of the one I remember, the brown eyes less symmetrical, the nose too flat. But the bow mouth is dead on.

"It'll be all right," she says, and returns her gaze to the window.

The voice is not the voice I remember, and yet it's so clearly her. That one sentence, almost devoid of inflection, has brought back every Mind War and classroom from first through sixth grades, and my whole Michigan childhood hisses around me like a cloud of wasps I have kicked from their nest in the grass.

"Theresa, it's Mattie," I say.

She swings around, and I am stunned to find her brown eyes full of tears. "I love that smell," she says. "Don't you? Ty Cobb. Wild Bill Donovan. Hooks Wiltse."

I don't smell anything and I don't care, because I'm already reaching out to touch her, hold her, I'm not sure which, when she says, "It'll be all right" again and stops me.

"Hey," I say, searching for the magic words that will release a little of the tension. When *hey* doesn't work, I try, "Theresa, please talk to me."

"Donie Bush," she says. "Wahoo Sam."

Her hair only looks that way, I realize, because it's wet. She has just had a shower or a bath. I stand still, let the waves my presence has created roll through the room, slap against the walls, and roll back over us as the hush reasserts itself. Theresa's mouth stops moving, the list of whatever it was dying on her lips. I hope it worked, I am thinking. I hope it kept her here with me. Then I do touch her, lightly, on the arm. Tears overrun her lashes and spill down her skin, and I see myself floating in her eyes, among the dead parents and lost years and ghost people. We stand together and rock in that room above the wintry world as though we're trapped together in a hot-air balloon that has just slipped its guide ropes.

"Hello there," says Theresa, and nods. "I'll be right behind you."

"It's Mattie," I say again, stupidly, while Theresa watches the doorway behind me. Does she know I'm here? Am I hurting her? Despite all the years I have spent imagining variations of this moment, I find now that I don't know what to do. So I drop to one knee before her. In another universe, in a sweeter life, I might be proposing marriage. Spencer would perform the ceremony. Instead, I unzip my backpack and take out Theresa's notebook.

She recognizes it, I'm all but certain, because, as still as she has become, she gets positively cadaverous when I put it in her hands. Her eyes lock, and she seems to stop breathing. When she starts again, the breaths come even and shallow. I stand up, close to her, and watch her peel back the torn blue cover.

"Nnnnh." She's nearly humming. "It'll be all right."

Sliding down onto her bed, she begins to flip pages with her hand, not quite looking at them. I'm watching the top of her head, thinking about the mud running down her legs on the day we became the lake.

"I'm so sorry," I whisper, and let my own tears come. "Theresa. I am so sorry. For everything."

For a while, she does nothing but turn the pages of the notebook, tipping her head to one side, the other side. She is mumbling words, maybe reading aloud, but I can't make out what she's saying. Abruptly, she stands up, too close to me. I feel her hair against my cheek, her hand, and then she kisses me.

For a few blissful seconds, I don't feel the strangeness. Her lips are touching mine without pressing, and I can taste her breath, toothpaste and apples. Through our slightly open mouths, I can feel our lives touch like the tips of our tongues, though our tongues never meet. The familiar ache in my body sharpens just under my lungs. Theresa is leaning into me the way a little kid might press her face against a car window to taste the condensation. I don't pull away until she starts screaming.

By then, she has one arm around my neck and she won't let go. Her teeth tap against mine, her whole body tenses, and she screams again, right into my mouth. I jerk backward, almost pulling her over with me, but she lets go and opens that mouth again—the black hole at the center of my world—and, to my astonishment, holds there.

"Theresa, no," I say, and she sways, mouth gaping. "Please," I say. "I'll leave. Or I'll stay. I'll sing to you. Just tell me what you need. What do you need, Theresa? What do you want? What can I do?"

"I can't," Theresa says, very quietly, and despite the fact that I see her mouth drop open again and I know what she's about to do, a horrible, tingly elation trills through me. I am all but certain, for that one moment, that she knows it's me. Then she's screaming again, and there are people pouring into the room.

I watch the notebook slip from Theresa's bed and flop face down on the floor as someone shoves me aside, grabs hold of her, and eases her back to the bed, but the screaming doesn't stop. The person holding Theresa down is enormous and wears a white doctor's coat. A second person shoves past me and stands over the bed, wearing jeans and a sweater. Curly hair. I never see his face. The third person into the room is Spencer, and he engulfs me from behind.

"You asshole," Spencer is snarling.

The man in the doctor's coat glances up sharply. "Mr. Franklin, get out. Take your friend with you and get out of here." He pins Theresa back against the bedsheets and holds her there. Spencer is grappling with me, grunting, saying nothing now, but I'm still watching Theresa, who has already gone quiet. Her arms went slack the moment everyone appeared at the door. If anything, she looks more peaceful now than when I entered the room. If the doctor let her, I half believe she would wave to me.

"It'll be all right," I say to her, almost smiling, as Spencer shoves me into the hall and stands in Theresa's doorway, panting.

I can no longer see the doctor, but I hear him say "Mr. Franklin" again. "Please. It's okay, now. Let's give her some quiet, huh?"

"Sorry," Spencer murmurs—to the doctor, Theresa, I can't tell.

"The notebook," I say suddenly.

"What?"

"Her notebook. On the floor in there. I brought the notebook back. It might not be a good idea to leave it with her."

Spencer steps back into Theresa's room, reemerges with the blue binder in his hands, staring at it.

"Jesus dog," he whispers.

"You know what that is?"

"The cop with the licorice showed it to me," Spencer says. His hands are shaking. "It scared the living shit out of me."

"That's why I thought we shouldn't leave it."

"Why'd you even bring it? What's wrong with you?"

From inside the room, the doctor snaps, "Mr. Franklin," and both of us edge toward the staircase, and I have one completely inappropriate feeling, a flash of goofy memory, Ms. Eyre whirling on Spencer and me from the blackboard and screaming at us for talking.

"Why did you bring this, Mattie?"

I have no answer, now that I think about it. What good could it possibly do her? For me, it has been a relic, a puzzle box, a treasure map. X marks the dead spot.

"It's just something I've held onto," I say, and stash it away in my backpack.

From Theresa's room, cool and steady, Theresa's voice comes floating. "One. Two. Six. Twenty-four. One hundred twenty. Seven hundred twenty."

Spencer stares at me. I stare back. For one, brief, impossible moment, it feels as if both of us are about to smile. But neither of us does.

"This was a horrible mistake," Spencer says. "Obviously. Maybe even you know that now." He starts past me down the white-carpeted stairs. I have no answer, nowhere else to go. I follow him into the sitting room, which is empty now. "Let's finish this outside," he says. "Goddammit. I should have never let you up there." He retreats toward the front hall, and we both retrieve our boots and coats and step through the door onto the deck facing the snow-laden lawn.

"Spencer," I say, "do they even know what's wrong with her?"

When he speaks again, he sounds as if he is reciting from a manual. "A patient with Depersonalization Disorder feels like an automaton. She may spend a disproportionate amount of time ruminating obsessively. The real world seems unreal, and time becomes blurred and confused. Frequently, such disorders have an undetected onset in childhood, which can make it tough to trace their evolution."

I stare at him, but he won't look at me. "We detected it," I say. "In a way."

"Yeah. Maybe. But this doctor also thinks she may be suffering from brutal and persistent Dissociative Amnesia. Which means pretty much what it says, except that it can lead to aggressive impulses."

This time, the premonition hits me like an ache in the joints, I can't get my knees straight or my wrists to bend, and I want to cry out. "Spencer," I say eventually, "please just tell me the rest. Right now."

Spencer stares out at the snow. Then he sighs. "Analissa Pettibone lived with her mother Mariannah at 119½ Decatur Street. I met her for the first time on the day I took her to the clinic over on Grand. November twelfth, 1990. She was ninety-eight days old."

Wind chases snow ghosts across the surface of the drifts, and the trees nod slightly like old people watching children race through a park. Upstairs, Theresa Daughrety may well be back at her window, watching over us, a Chagall ghost in a perpetual blue never-never.

"Shepherd Griffith-Rice had just anointed me a Caretaker."

"Which is a step below Shepherd?"

"Not below. There just aren't many Shepherds. Aren't many who are willing. It takes up your whole life. One of the clinics downtown gave free checkups when a child turned one hundred days old, including immunizations. Several of our more disadvantaged members used this particular clinic, but I'd never been there. On November twelfth, I picked up Analissa and Mariannah at their triplex downtown and drove them over. There was snow on all the buildings and ice in the streets, but the day was midsummer bright. Mariannah seemed upset, so I kept trying to calm her down. But no matter what I said, she just held her baby against her chest and nodded at me. She would've nodded if I'd said I was driving into the river to see a friend. It seems Analissa had been sick, and Mariannah hadn't told anyone, and she was afraid. Big girl, Mariannah, kind of pretty but real big. Analissa looked like a wrapped-up strawberry in her hands. One of them smelled like alcohol—the rubbing kind, not the drinking kind.

"The clinic was in one of those row houses not too far from the Arts Institute—the only house on the block that was inhabited, as far as I could tell. During the day, anyway. Plenty of parking in that neighborhood, because the only other cars I saw had no wheels and no engines. We stopped right out front, and I held Analissa while Mariannah climbed out. That baby felt like it was made of meringue, it was so light. She looked too red, feverish, but her arms were waving all around in the blankets, and she wasn't crying.

"'This girl's fine,' I told Mariannah as she took her from me. 'She's just deciding whether to dance with me or bop me one.'

"Mariannah nearly smiled. But when we got up the steps, we found a black wreath hanging on the chipped wood door. Inside, the reception area was empty except for one nurse sitting at the desk with the one receptionist. Both of them were sipping hot tea out of paper cups.

"I said, 'We have an appointment. Analissa Pettibone.'

"The nurse had little round glasses and white curly hair coming out of the sides of her cap. She kind of looked like a poodle. 'Don't you people read the papers?' she said. Then she disappeared through the clinic's inner door.

"The clinic receptionist stood up, looking apologetic. I remember her skirt because it was black and drooped all the way past her toes. She was in her forties, maybe. Blond, short, kind of stubby. She looked like a little

girl who'd been rummaging through her mother's closet. And she had
a real soft, real deep drawl; Texas, Alabama, one of those places.

"'Honey, no one phoned you?' She was talking to Mariannah, who
tensed up next to me, and I realized why. She didn't have a phone.

"'Look, we're here,' I said. 'Just tell us what's happening. You closed?
Out of business? Can we get this baby her shots or not?'

"The woman sighed and cupped her hands in front of her as if she
were about to receive communion. 'The doctor died,' she said.

"Analissa began to squeak and cough, and Mariannah sat down to
nurse her. The receptionist watched without unfolding her hands.

"'You only have one doctor?' I asked.

"The woman still didn't unfold her hands but she smiled at me, real
slow, real soft. 'Sorry,' she said. 'It's just a very sad time here. We have
three regular doctors, and they'll be back tomorrow. The lines may be
a little long, because we've been closed a few days. But if you bring
Analissa in then, we'll be sure to find time for her.'

"I thanked her, and then I waited for Mariannah to finish nursing.
We were halfway out the door—I don't even know what made me
ask—when I turned around and said, 'Which doctor died?'

"The woman's hands came unclasped. 'The founder of this place,'
she said, 'and its inspiration. Dr. Colin Daughrety.'"

I'd already guessed. I just stand beside Spencer while the wind
rises, sweeps over us, stills.

"I don't remember driving Mariannah home," Spencer says. "I
don't remember anything else about that day except I went to our
church and slept all night in a pew. I woke up the next morning with
my neck so stiff I could have chopped down a tree with it. But the
weird thing was, I felt fine. And that was such a relief, I fell down on
my knees and wept. Shepherd Griffith-Rice came in just once and
asked if I needed anything. Then he left me alone."

"Do you believe in fate, Spencer?" I ask. "I mean, it just seems like
every step we take, in any direction, leads us back to the same place.
Or back to each other."

"I believe in believing," he says. "I believe in doing. I believe that
owning up to what you've done is honesty, but that claiming owner-

ship of what happens next is hubris. I believe that there are moments in our lives when we almost get it right, and that the good we almost do is more painful to the decent-hearted than the bad we do completely."

"The good we almost do?"

He glances at me, glances away. I cling to the deck railing with my wet gloved hands.

Spencer's voice drops until he's almost whispering. "Mariannah and Analissa Pettibone returned to the clinic the next morning. I didn't go with them; I was way too shaken up about the Doctor's death—just hearing his name again, really—to Caretake. A couple of hours after they got there, they were still waiting, and Mariannah went to the bathroom. She left her child in the care of the southern receptionist. The receptionist placed the child on the chair next to her desk. The child lay there and coughed, but she didn't cry. The phone rang, and at the same time another woman who had been waiting around all morning snapped and began screaming to be let in. Meanwhile, back in the clinic, one of the doctors had somehow slipped and broken a glass beaker in his hand, and he was bleeding all over the place. People were running to help him and mop up the blood. Suddenly, everything was chaos. And when the chaos was over, the receptionist looked down at her chair and discovered that Analissa was gone."

"Gone."

"Remember, I wasn't there for this. I'm telling you what I was told. The baby just wasn't there anymore." Spencer jams his gloved hands into his coat pockets. "Mariannah dissolved, of course. There wasn't much left inside her to start with, and within two days she'd taken every pill in her medicine cabinet. She didn't die, but the pills did horrible things to her stomach and intestines, and now she eats colorless soup, because that's all her system can handle. Meanwhile, the church did what it does best—it mobilized. We sent people to every home of every person we could find who'd had an appointment at the clinic that morning. Two Shepherds went to the house of the soft-spoken receptionist. She lived in Ferndale, not far from my mother's place, with two purebred Dalmations. We even went to the police station and made a major nuisance of ourselves. We went to the mayor, and the mayor agreed to see Shepherd Griffth-Rice. They're friends from way back.

"At night, we all went to the church and prayed. Hundreds of people, night after night. I remember looking around once, when everyone was humming and the pianos were playing low down and the lights were dim and one of the Shepherds was up there swaying, maybe singing, and I remember thinking, 'God. There are so many of us.'

"I felt horrible about Mariannah. And I couldn't get the feel of that kid, that little lump in my arms, out of my mind. But I didn't feel as bad as I should have. Most days, I had somewhere to go, you know? I had comfort to offer, and sometimes it was taken, and that's a rare thing."

"I know," I say.

"I know you do."

It takes a faint wet touch on my cheek, like a kiss from a ghost, to make me realize that it's snowing. I look up, and the sky has no color, not blue or gray or white, and the flakes fall from it in silent slow motion. The wind has gone, and the snow doesn't dance on its way to the earth; it just falls.

"Two days after Mariannah's suicide attempt," says Spencer, "Shepherd Griffith-Rice called my apartment and told me the doctors said she would probably live. I knelt by my window and prayed and cried. It was sleeting outside, and my windows never sealed properly, so you could hear the cold crawling through the wood. I had nowhere left to be. Nothing left to do. I hadn't been to a movie in years, I hadn't been reading much except the Bible, I had no one waiting for me, and I was almost okay, except I kept feeling that little squirming weight in my arms every time I bent my elbows. And suddenly I knew that I wanted to see Theresa and tell her how sorry I was to hear about her dad. I didn't waste time brooding on it. I got up, left my beef stew on the table, and drove straight to Cider Lake.

"The roads were awful, sludgy. It was a Sunday night and there was no one out, I mean no one. A few of the businesses I passed on Woodward had their lights on, just to scare off burglars. I stopped at Kroger — the one by Stroh's — and bought two white lilies and wrapped them myself in clear plastic with baby's breath around them. I probably spent twenty minutes standing in that store, listening to the rain, sticking the greens on both sides of the flowers. Needless to say, I was thinking about that last horrible time I'd seen her. I wanted to get the flowers right.

"The house . . . well, it didn't look the way it does now. The Doctor had only just died, so it was still in pretty decent shape. It occurred to me that Theresa might not even live there anymore. The whole family could have moved, or Theresa might have her very own grown-up life somewhere. It seemed possible.

"I don't know why I assumed no one was home. I think it was just the stillness. I was standing there trying to figure out what to do with my lilies when the door opened and Theresa said, 'Come in.' Then she turned and walked straight into the kitchen.

"She didn't look much different from the last time I saw her. She was wearing this tannish long sweater thing that looked like a burlap bag. Maybe it was a poncho, I don't know, but it had no shape whatsoever. She was alone in the house. Barbara had been there, I found out later, until the day after the Doctor's memorial service. She took Theresa to the airport and put her on a plane to Cleveland. Her aunt was supposed to meet her at the other end. But Theresa just waited until right before takeoff and then demanded to be let off the plane. She got herself home somehow and called her aunt and said that she and Barbara had decided to stay home for a while. It wasn't until later that I found out Barbara had left the country. She went to Southeast Asia somewhere. Thailand, I think. I know she wasn't planning to come back. She told me once she was thinking she'd escape her own pattern, or at least move it somewhere warm. But she kept brooding on Theresa, and especially on Theresa with the Daughrety aunt."

"The one I talked to today?" I ask.

Spencer shrugs. "Anyway, within two weeks, Barbara was back. Too late, but back."

The aching in my joints intensifies, as though simultaneous crushing pressure is being applied to all of them. Sooner or later, it seems, we are all of us, always, too late.

"So there I was," Spencer says, "stepping into the Daughretys' hall-way for the first time in thirteen years. I closed the door, and *boom*, there was this dead, frozen silence. Every creak of floorboard was like a seagull cry over the ocean; that's how deep the silence was. Every now and then I caught a glimpse of Theresa in the kitchen, but none of her movements had any purpose that I could see. She was just pick-ing things up and putting them down. All those masks on the walls kept staring at me, and I wanted to drop my flowers on the welcome mat and go. I reached the kitchen after what felt like ten minutes of wading, and Theresa was sitting at the table, smoking. The smoke was the only thing moving for a while.

"'Theresa, how've you been?' I asked, but she didn't look at me. Behind her chair was a stack of newspapers in unopened protective bags. There were no dishes in the sink and none on the table, except for a white CORNELL MED SCHOOL mug she was using as an ashtray."

Spencer sucks in a massive breath, holds it, lets it go. I watch the snow drizzle down in skeins and knit itself together like a burial shawl.

"She didn't say anything. Well, that's not true. She said, 'It'll be all right.'"

My arms squirm against my chest. Spencer wobbles suddenly and grabs the railing to steady himself.

"Right then, Mattie—I don't know why, I think I still felt guilty about the last time I'd seen her—I got frustrated. Mad. I'd wasted so much time and thought on this person. I said something like, 'Me? I'm fine, girl, thanks for asking. The withdrawal fits? Hell, I barely even feel them these days. Can't really taste my food anymore; it seems I've done something to my tongue or my taste buds, and the world looks all washed out when there's too much sun because my retinas are all fucked up, but yeah, you're right, it'll be all right.' I don't know how much of that I said. But then I glanced toward the big bay window— she had those curtains drawn, too—and I saw the dining room table, and that shut me up. After a while, I shook my head. And then, I swear to God, I started laughing.

"In a perfect line down the center of the dining room table was a row of open jars of baby food."

"Oh, no," I whisper, and tears spring to my eyes. But the only emotion I can detect in Spencer's voice is resignation.

"Even the labels on the jars were facing the same direction," he says. "Carrots, green beans, apple-beef and macaroni, wintercorn—whatever the hell that is. Each jar had its own little spoon sticking out of it like a potted sapling. The jars were pretty near full, as far as I could tell, and that struck me as odd, but I was concentrating on the fact that the jars were there, and I said, 'Theresa Daughrety, gracious God, you're a mom. I'm so happy for you. I'm so happy for all of us.' Then I remembered why I was there, and I said, 'I'm sorry about your dad. But Jesus dog, you're a mom. Can I see the baby?'

"Then she looked at me, Mattie. And it was the same look, only worse. You saw it this morning; it hasn't changed."

"I saw it," I say, concentrating on staying standing, holding myself together.

"She gave me that look and said, 'It won't eat.' Like she was talking about a car that wouldn't start or a pen that wouldn't write. And I got so damn all-over cold that I lurched out of my chair and strode into the living room so I could get a better look at those jars. One lamp was switched on by that big white couch. Same couch, except lumpy and old. On the couch was a little bundle of blankets. And in the blankets, with her eyes wide open, was Analissa Pettibone."

Spencer looks as if he's waiting for some kind of reaction. But I can't even get air into my lungs. The worst thing about Spencer's story is its inevitable, incontrovertible logic. My eyes feel swollen and sensitive, like twin bruises.

"I made decisions," says Spencer. "Real fast. On the Last Day, I expect I'll find out if they were right." His eyes are teary now too, but his voice is steady.

"I don't know what she wanted with the child. But I don't think she meant to hurt it. This wasn't any now-I'm-the-Snowman horror movie thing. From what I saw at her house, she'd bought maybe a hundred dollars' worth of baby food and tried it all. Of course, despite all the books she's read and all that brain she's got, Theresa knows next to nothing about day-to-day living. I'm pretty sure it never occurred to her that the child wasn't eating because it couldn't eat solid food yet. It needed to nurse or it needed a bottle. After a couple of days, Analissa must have gone real quiet, and Theresa just sat at her kitchen table waiting for Christ knows what, and that went on for almost four days before I came in.

"I thought about blowing out of the house to buy infant formula. But that kid was about to die—God knows how it had survived that long. She was taking these tiny breaths, one every few seconds, like a radiator shutting down. Then she gave this little spasm and threw up, and that decided it. I don't think she had anything left in her stomach but the last of her own body fat, because the vomit was yellow-red and runny. I scooped her up and raced out of the house. Theresa didn't even get up.

"That child was light before, but now it was like holding a bubble. If I squeezed too tight, I'd pop her, and if I didn't hold her tightly enough, she'd float away. I laid her across my lap in the car and realized I had no idea where the nearest hospital was, so I drove like a maniac toward Belmont. There was probably a closer hospital, but I could already imagine the kinds of questions they'd fling at me the second I came staggering into a Birmingham hospital with a near-dead black baby that wasn't mine in my hands. And I'd just started trying to figure out what the hell I was going to say about Theresa.

"Fortunately, Belmont is near my church, near my old house, and I even knew a few of the nurses. Of course, the doctors started grilling me anyway, and then Analissa threw up some more red liquid and they whisked her away. I went straight to a bank of phones and called the police. Somehow, the media got hold of it at the same time, because the reporters showed up before the cops."

Spencer sags a bit in his coat. I just wait, because I have no choice. He's right. The movie is over. The damage is done. Around us, the snow continues to fall, and the sky dims toward twilight.

"By then, I knew what I would say to the police," Spencer says. "I told them I found Analissa bundled on my doorstep. Everyone in the church knew I'd been Caretaker for her and her mother, and I speculated that maybe whoever had taken her had known that too.

"So the next day, of course, the police came crashing down on our whole congregation, not just yours truly. They had themselves a regular Boston tea party tearing up my apartment looking for evidence that I'd done the kidnapping or masterminded it, although they never proposed any motive. Worse, the tension and suspicion caused all kinds of petty pent-up conflicts and hostilities to surface within the church, and we had a little Salem witch hunt for a while, with good prayerful people betraying their neighbors and finger-pointing at one another. By the time that died down, a lot of congregants were awfully unhappy with me, and at one point, there was a vote on a Writ of Exclusion concerning me. Many times, I've agonized over the suffering I caused the people I love and pray with and Caretake for. But giving up Theresa to the police meant sending her to a prison asylum, and I couldn't bear the thought of that. I just couldn't bear it. So I didn't do it, and I can't say I'm sorry."

For a long moment, Spencer stops, and the snow wraps around him in long white strands.

"Anyway," he says, shrugging out of his silence, "when I was done with the police, I returned to the Daughrety house and cleaned up all the baby food while Theresa watched me from the kitchen table, smoking in silence, and then she went to bed. For the next week or so, I slept on that old white couch. I went to the church when I had to, but never for more than a couple of hours. I asked Shepherd Griffith-Rice what he knew about private mental institutions. He asked no questions, just put me in touch with some people who helped me find this place. Theresa barely stirred. She would come out of her bedroom midmorning or so, take the newspaper and smooth the plastic bag it had come in until there were no wrinkles, and then lay it, unread, on the pile in the kitchen.

"One day, when I arrived at the Daughretys', I found Barbara there. She didn't recognize me until I told her who I was. Then I explained to her what had happened. She said she wondered about the diapers she'd found in Theresa's trash can. She didn't really react much, at first. At all, really. I remember being kind of worried about it, until I was leaving and came back inside because I'd left my gloves on the dining room table and found Theresa sitting with her back to us on the white couch and Barbara leaning in the kitchen doorway with both hands in her hair and silent tears streaming down her face. I didn't say anything, but after a while I put my hand against her cheek, and she leaned into my palm, and we stood there that way, not saying anything. Finally, she straightened up and looked at me. It was like signing a contract, that look. She signed it; I signed it. She nodded. I left.

"After that, Barbara and I worked together. When we had our plan completed, Barbara called Theresa's aunt. But the aunt wouldn't talk to Barbara—the family thinks she's a gold-digger—so I had to get on the line. At first she wouldn't listen to me, either, she just kept demanding that we bring Theresa to Cleveland. I tried to explain that Theresa couldn't go anywhere. Eventually, I had to hang up and get one of the doctors from Chapin House to call and explain Theresa's condition. Then I called her back. She kept saying things like 'You're betraying a great man. He would expect his wife— his pathetic wife—to take care of his daughter. Don't you think?' But she wasn't really arguing anymore, she was just angry. Sad. In the end, I think, at least she understood that we were trying to protect Theresa. I think she respected the closing of ranks. And I think the Chapin House doctor must have made it clear how overwhelming it would be for anyone to take care of Theresa alone. Also, I could be wrong, but I got the impression that she hadn't seen much of our Daughretys for some time. She didn't even come to the memorial service. She said she would come and visit Theresa, but she never did. I haven't had any additional contact with her until you rousted her this morning."

The light has gone darker still, and the snow has intensified. Spencer goes on.

"When everything was arranged, Barbara and I took Theresa out to dinner at this restaurant called the Red Fox. She spent most of the meal playing with a spoon and a Sweet 'n Low packet like a sulking six-year-old. I told her what I was going to do. I told her that going to the Chapin House would make her feel safer and better, and that neither Barbara nor I would ever leave her. She ate a whole steak and a piece of chocolate cake and didn't look at either of us once. We brought her here that very night. She's been here ever since, and now I can't imagine her anywhere else. I come at least twice a week, usually more. Barbara's here pretty much every day. She doesn't date, doesn't do anything but work and volunteer and read and come here. I worry about her, although she's strong as hell.

"The insurance policies and the money Theresa's father left are enough to pay for her upkeep for a while yet. Plus there's some grant money the Chapin House receives from the state to do research on long-term conditions like Theresa's. And there's the house, if it ever needs to be sold, although the Doctor left strict instructions that the place was to stay in the family. God knows why, it doesn't seem like there are memories worth cherishing there. So here Theresa stays. And here I am. And there you have it. That's her life. And ours."

I look at my friend. The snow seems to be chiseling tiny pieces out of him, eroding him bit by bit.

"The story made me persona non grata in my church for a long time, but it made me a kind of media hero, because Analissa survived—at least, until TB killed her a year later. I was in the papers a bit. I even got asked to be a sort of spokesperson for a couple of child protection and welfare agencies. How perverse is that?

"I've never told anybody the whole truth, not even Shepherd Griffith-Rice. Once, not long after Theresa was placed here, I went back to the clinic and described her to the blond receptionist.

"'The Doctor's daughter? Oh, sure,' she said. 'Poorsweetthing. She used to turn up here sometimes and sit in that chair.' The receptionist pointed to the one nearest her desk. 'Dr. Daughrety surely loved her. I hope she'll be okay now, with him gone.'

"One of the doctors who sees Theresa—the one who diagnosed her—thinks that what she did—the kidnapping, I mean—is the most positive sign we have that Theresa may be reachable someday. He believes she took the baby home to protect her."

"She does seem a little better," I say, not sure whether I'm telling the truth. "There was a moment there—several moments—where it felt like she was with me."

Spencer shrugs and looks away, but not fast enough. I have seen the tears. "She has those, sometimes. With Barbara especially, I think."

I close my eyes, and something locked under my ribs for years breaks free, and a gentle heat spreads through me. I'm not sure why. None of this qualifies as particularly good news. "You saved her. You realize that, right?" I say, and open my eyes. "After everyone else left or failed her, including me."

"You were eleven years old. And you saw what was happening to her first, Mattie. Give yourself some credit."

"It doesn't matter."

"It matters. It's also getting late. Maybe it's time I took you back."

Without waiting for my response, Spencer steps off the deck, and I can't think of any reason to stop him. I have spent so much of my life missing Theresa, clinging to the ghost girl I once knew. But Spencer stayed with her, working and praying and spending countless hours just sitting beside her. He has loved her in the way I have always imagined I did. He will see her tomorrow, and the next day, and the day after. I, on the other hand, may never see her again. I turn one last time to look at the red house, the snow catching the light as it falls past the high windows. A woman in a trench coat and gray wool hat is straightening the stack of chaise longues, and for a moment I imagine Barbara Fox wheeling around and waving to me. One last reunion. A happier one, because Barbara, I think, really did love me. But the woman doesn't turn, isn't Barbara, and the house stays silent. I drop my gaze and follow Spencer toward the street.

At the car, I climb into the passenger seat while Spencer fumbles with the keys. The cold billows around us. The car slides forward. I find myself unzipping my backpack and lifting out the notebook. But its essence has changed now that Theresa has held it again. Under my hands, the familiar pages fall away like dead skin. Nothing I can make from this material will ever live or breathe or laugh.

"Want to hear something horrible?" Spencer asks.

"As opposed to what?" I say, and for the first time all weekend—the first time since we were eleven years old—I hear Spencer Franklin laugh. Briefly.

"The whole Analissa tragedy feels like a turning point to me. That year probably saved Mariannah's life. She held herself together. When Analissa finally gave up fighting and died, Mariannah organized a huge wake in her honor at the church that turned into a celebration. There were pictures of Analissa all over the hall, party streamers and hats, and a two-minute video that Shepherd Griffith-Rice had had made of Analissa's christening. The next day, Mariannah went out into the world, got herself a job, and hurled herself into church work. She's unspeakably sad, and I don't think she'll ever marry or have another child, but she Caretakes like a banshee."

I look at the closed notebook in my lap while my thoughts run riot. I have carried the notebook, and everything I'd decided it symbolized, around on my back for such a long time. Adolescence, I think, isn't really about growing up. It's like ferrying across the river Lethe. If you make it, all you retain of your childhood is a taste. And it tastes like hell, or it tastes like heaven, and either way you can never wash it out.

"Will you take me back?" I say, thinking suddenly of Laura and Louisville.

"You kidding? Been waiting to hear you say that all weekend." When he sees me wince, though, Spencer shakes his head. "I think that was a joke."

"Glad you think so," I say.

For a while, we just drive, and I stare out the window at the passing subdivisions tucked in among the shadows of the oak and maple and evergreen trees. In the yards I see sleds, flying saucers. We head up Maple toward the Woodward Corridor, and I lean my head against the cold window and think about Laura's dead brother. I don't know why I'm thinking about him now, but I can see the picture of him we have framed in our hallway. He's maybe thirteen years old, wearing a polyester red-and-black marching-band uniform, holding a huge fuzzy white hat that looks like a giant Q-Tip. He's waving drumsticks in front of his face and scowling. He's her ghost, and she has never let me near him.

I've spent most of my adult years searching for the one grand gesture that mitigates catastrophic mistakes. I no longer believe such a gesture exists. Or, rather, it isn't a single act but an accumulation of actions. Maybe that's the real secret of Spencer's recovery. For me, Theresa has remained a lost thing, a crushing regret. For Spencer, she has become a person again, and he has not only maintained his devotion to her, he has acted on it, over and over. Most of the marriages I know—mine, for instance—are built on shakier foundations.

I am thinking about the Cider Mill, and the day I last left Detroit, and it occurs to me that there is a sort of triumph in what might have happened. A bitter sort. A few days after my family left, the weather warmed, for good this time. And when the snow returned in November, the monster did not return with it. By the spring of 1978, according to a letter my mother got from Angie McLean, when an entire winter had passed with no Gremlin sightings, no unexplained kidnappings or ghostly murders, people began to believe the Snowman had been caught for something else, or become aware of the noose tightening around him and fled, or killed himself.

Or, I remember thinking—lying in my old bunk bed in our new house in Lexington while my father played his fitful stereo quietly in the living room and my mother read outside on the porch swing—maybe he met Theresa Daughrety, and she changed him. Not healed him—the thought was not a comforting one—but confused him somehow. Paralyzed him. Stopped him. It seemed possible, and certainly no one—at least, no one I know—has seen him since. Back then, when imagination was still more powerful than memory, Theresa seemed capable of just about anything, to me. We all did.

Childhood becomes myth for every single person who survives it. It's not just somewhere we can't revisit. It's a fever dream, with very real monsters we can't even recall, but that settle inside us. And when the fever breaks, we're left with a handful of people whose importance in our lives is all out of proportion to our affection for them.

Bringing the car to a stop in front of the Moto-Court, Spencer shuts down the engine and turns to me. For once, he doesn't seem to know what to say.

"Take care of yourself," he finally murmurs.

"You too. Take care of our girl."

"Always," Spencer says.

"Will I hear from you?"

He watches me awhile. Then he watches the snow. "Probably. If you make me." He doesn't smile, but he watches as I climb out and stand on the curb in the falling snow and fading light. Snowflakes blot the windshield and slowly obscure his face.

I close the door, and without another word he pulls away, leaving me hovering, holding the city of my birth to my ear like a seashell. It's still snowing, and the Snowman is still gone, and the kids he took with him will never rise from their swellings in the ground. I don't relish being one of his children, but there are so many of us: James Rowan, Jane-Anne Gish, Courtney Grieve, Amy Ardell, Edward Falk, Peter Slotkin, the Cory twins, James Sea, Theresa Daughrety, Spencer Franklin, me. Some of us aren't even dead, just prowling the lakeshores and twilit backyards. We're surrounded by boundaries we create ourselves. We live in communities whose boundaries we are brought up to accept, locked into bodies whose boundaries are imposed upon us on the day we are born. Then, one day, the boundaries get breached, and there are yellow jackets burning in the grass, and we find ourselves haunted by an inexplicable buzzing in the hidden heart of the world.

ACKNOWLEDGMENTS

By intention, I used more memory than research when reconstructing and reimagining the all-too-real events that form the backdrop for *The Snowman's Children*. Nevertheless, two books provided an important factual framework. Tommy McIntyre's *Wolf in Sheep's Clothing: The Search for a Child Killer* helped me clarify, for myself, the boundaries between half-accurate childhood memories, invention, and fact concerning the Oakland County Child Killer, which I promptly blurred again wherever the story I was telling required me to do so. Ze'ev Chafets's collection of Detroit essays, *Devil's Night*, offered both historical information and insight into the sources of the communal sadness and mistrust that haunted my hometown throughout my years there.

Numerous people have made helpful suggestions or provided useful information during this book's long journey from nightmare to daydream to shared memory to novel. A few individuals, however, made substantial and consistent contributions in terms of editing and support. First among these, as with everything I write, is my wife, Kim Miller, still the most thoughtful, thorough, and constructively ruthless critic I know. Meir Ribalow has been perhaps my most attuned reader for over fifteen years. My agent, Kathy Anderson of Anderson/Grinberg Literary Management, invested herself completely in the editing and selling of this novel and has played an important role in its evolution. Emily Heckman helped solve a two-year-old problem in one two-hour phone call. Finally, Tina Pohlman at Carroll & Graf has given me both clear-eyed, perceptive editing and generous encouragement. To all of these people, I owe my profound thanks.